JIMMY MACK

Let The Good Times Roll (Side B)

John Knight

Published in 2020 by FeedARead.com Publishing

1st Edition 2019
2nd Edition 2020

Book and cover design by John Knight. Final interior by the author.

A CIP catalogue record for this title is available from the British
Library.

Dedicated to all
The young woman I knew before I was 21.

Treat life like a game, and you'll lose.
Live life, and you'll end up a winner.

CHAPTER 1

Talk Of The Grapevine – Donald Height (London HLZ 10062 - 1966)
Monday 10 April 1967

How does a real story become a legend and truth its victim? How does a legend lose what truth it possessed and become myth?

The black and tangerine Lambretta GT200 roared into the Sixth Form student's car park, it's chrome accessories gleaming in the early morning sun. James MacKinnon switched off the ignition as he brought it to a stop next to a battered Triumph Tigress. The early morning sunlight reflected off his aviator sunglasses as he dismounted. No sooner had the smell and blue smoke of the two-stroke dissipated when he noticed a small group gathering nearby. A handful of Fourth and Fifth formers stared at him in silence. Unzipping his M51 parka with lethargic slowness, he returned the stare. They shuffled closer until one finally found his voice.

"That's definitely him and no mistake." A gangly bespectacled youth announced

"See, I told you. It's definitely, definitely him. He's the one with the gorgeous birds in The News of the World photo." Confirmed another.

"My mum and dad had a shock when they saw Fiona Halloran in the newspaper. She goes to St. Jo's College. That was her in the photo with him," stated another. Mack recognised Monaghan from his church-going days at St. Patrick's.

"Which one was that?" Asked another.

"The blonde one," Monaghan replied.

"Have you done staring lads?" Mack removed his parka shell and began folding it into an Air France travel bag. "What do you want? An autograph?"

One of the other Fourth formers stepped forward. "Oh, could you? Could you get their autographs? If I bring the newspaper photo tomorrow, would they sign it?"

Mack sniggered shaking head before replying. "Gentlemen, I'll be only too delighted. But first, let me remind you good Catholic boys of lust and envy. These are two of the seven deadly sins you need to avoid. Don't forget lads. What you do under your blankets at night, you'll have to confess to the priest. And remember, it can lead to blindness too."

"Are you calling us wankers?" Monaghan demanded, miffed by his comment.

Mack was about to respond when a familiar voice interrupted.

"Is that why you're wearing sunglasses, MacKinnon? Going blind already?" Tim Smith shoved Monaghan out of the way. Someone had gifted Smith a shiner.

"What about greed? One cracking dolly bird not good enough, eh? You've got to have two. Then dammit, you get yourself splashed across the pages of the Sunday papers. Just to make it more annoying, you end up in the daily press for everyone to see."

"You know how it is, Tim. Some of us have that *je ne sais quoi,* and some of us don't. That's the way it goes. *C'est la vie* as they say. For most guys like you, it's a case of the girls you fancy *don't* fancy you. Then the girls you don't fancy they are the ones who *do* fancy you. To make matters worse, guys like me come along. We get the pick of them all just to rub you up the wrong way."

Mack adjusted the black silk hanky in the breast pocket of his immaculate three-button grey herringbone sports jacket.

"Speaking of the seven deadly sins. Where does pride come in the list?" Smith jibed.

"It's first in the queue, for Catholics like you." Mack tucked his Tootal silk scarf into his jacket like a cravat to cover the sixth-form tie. "I don't believe in any of that Catholic crap."

"You know you'll have to take the scarf off when we get to the tutor group? So why bother putting it on, what's the point?"

"The point is, until I take it off, I don't own up to belonging to this place." Mack checked his hair in one of the scooter's mirrors, before adjusting the scarf one last time. "One has to look one's best at all times."

"In case you hadn't noticed this is a boys grammar school. There are no dolly birds to impress with all this preening." Smith mocked.

Mack let out a contrived laugh. "There's always someone around to impress like the dinner ladies and the cleaners. Let's not forget the school secretary. They need someone good to look at, don't they?"

"God! You're such an arrogant poser. Are all Mods like you?"

"No." He paused unstrapping his briefcase from the rear carrier. "Every Mod is an individual. We don't want to be like everyone else."

The crowd of younger boys had continued to grow intrigued by what was going on.

Mack shouldered his travel bag. Picking up the briefcase, he and Tim pushed through the crowd walking towards the Sixth Form building. He heard one of the youths in the crowd say, "I bet he's shagging both of those birds."

Robert MacKinnon gave Effy and her two sisters a tight smile as they thanked him for the lift to school. Under normal circumstances, he would have dropped Effy and Grace near the park gates. Not today. Today he drove across Manningham Lane. Then he took the turn down Cunliffe Road to the Catholic Girl's Grammar. Jane, his wife's, had expressed concerns. There was a possibility of press photographers snooping around the school gates.

Their arrival attracted attention almost immediately on stepping out of the Ford Zephyr. The sisters formed a phalanx, with Ellen the eldest in the centre. It wasn't quite the parting of the waves, but it came close. At Grace's suggestion, they had agreed to walk past the younger pupils like true models.

The time had arrived to make use of those deportment lessons they'd attended as little girls. Heads high, backs straight, poised and in synced steps, they walked in through the gate. Radiating an almost professional confidence, they made their way through the crowded playground.

The hubbub subsided to whispered awe. Lower school pupils with backs to the trio found themselves yanked out of their way.

Without turning her head or altering her expression, Effy found the recognition astonishing. "I never imagined we'd get a reaction like this."

"Eyes forward. No talking in the ranks like we agreed," commanded Ellen, adding, "It's you they're looking at Effy."

Nearing a group of Grace's excitable waiting friends, they came to a stop. Ellen turned to Grace. "Remember what Mack's mother asked of us. From now on, it's not only Effy's reputation we're protecting. It's ours too and the MacKinnon's. Whatever we say from today onwards affects everyone. We owe Mack's family ever so much. So let's make sure nothing slips."

The words sounded unfamiliar, even peculiar, coming from Ellen. If anyone had a reputation for indiscrete comments, it was her. Since getting together with Tom, she'd changed and matured. Although younger, Effy believed she was still more mature.

Ellen continued. "After school, we meet here and wait for Mack to arrive to whisk Eff away on the scooter. Clear?"

Effy knew from fifteen-year-old Grace's tight-lipped seriousness she had absorbed Ellen's words. They watched her walk towards her classmates, maintaining her deportment. Grace acted and looked like the teen model, she would soon become known. Side by side, footsteps synced once more, Effy and Ellen joined the other sixth-formers going inside. Effy would soon find herself alone. Ellen would split off to her Upper Sixth registration group. Once inside, they removed their berets and coats. She received a surprise hug from Ellen.

"Good luck, sis. Play it cool, say nothing incriminating, and do as Jane suggested, stay dispassionate. I'll meet you at lunchtime. For once, I won't be able to blab, as I don't know what happened in London. Love you, sis."

Dispassionate. Yes, she would have to try to remain unemotional and unflappable. Left standing on her own, she wondered what to expect. It wasn't what she expected.

Angie Thornton's experience at Hardacre, Hardcastle, and Hewitt's had forewarned Mack and Effy what might await them. They could expect lots of attention and not only from the press. The infamous newspaper photograph showing them leaving London's Cromwellian Club had the nation's attention. Angie couldn't believe how the press wanted to know more and more. Silvers Fashions publicity department's response had been swift. Photos taken during the opening of Moods Mosaic had appeared in most of the Dailies during the week. Mack had also told her some of their parish hall photo shoot would feature in *Petticoat* magazine. She had to pinch herself. *Honey* already wanted to interview her about her designs. They planned to do a feature in which Effy and Angie would appear as models. Their lives were about to become a matter of considerable public interest. Mack had already received quite a few offers to use her for magazine fashion photo shoots.

So far, she'd remained elusive. The Halifax Courier had failed to find her. It guaranteed her some small measure of time to prepare. It hadn't gone down well with her parents when they'd found out. Angie knew how to brazen it out. Her explanation of events convinced her father. She'd showed him her portfolio of Mack's photographs blown up as eight by tens. He'd remained silent, appreciating how good she looked.

"You look real fetching I 'ave to admit. The lad's done good by you with his camera. Angie, I can't believe me and your mum made someone as beautiful as you."

She'd delighted in those words. He was the typical Yorkshire man not given to open emotion. Then he'd added, "I like your choice of friends. Effy's such a nice young thing and that boyfriend of hers too. You get on like an 'ouse on fire. Good friends are worth more than pounds and pence. Pity he's her boyfriend our Angie. If he were yours, I wouldn't mind him."

No longer living at home, she shared a rented house with her sister Gillian. This gave both sisters much-needed distance from their warring parents. She wanted to tell the world about her love affair with Mack, but it was not possible. The world they lived in wouldn't understand. How could you explain two young women agreeing to share their love with one young man?

It wasn't until two days after returning from London that things began to happen. The senior partner invited her into his office for a frank chat about the photograph. Mr Hardacre junior, in his most polite manner, had interviewed her about it. His secretary had brought it to his attention. Doing his best not to appear too nosey, he'd accepted her explanation of events as *larking about*. Enquiring about her prospective career as a model, she told him it was more of a hobby to help her friend the designer. Working as a receptionist and filing clerk was cushy. It was also preferable to working in the chemists and better paid. So she played the game of the prim and proper young lady. Mr Hardacre seemed embarrassed by the whole interview process. His middle-aged secretary less so given the frosty looks Angie kept receiving. Thank heavens for his final comments. "Whatever you do in your spare time is your affair. As long as it does not impinge on the good name of the firm we won't mind. Our reputation must always remain of the highest standing. We are, I must add, pleased with your work and hope the promise of fame and fortune doesn't lure you away from us."

Meeting friends in George's Square, Angie found herself even more popular. Thank heavens for Tom and Ellen's presence and long-time friends Linda and Stingray. Mack's arrival minus Effy must have started a few rumours. Like the gallant guy he was, Mack placed an arm around her shoulder, sparking a few interesting comments. Yes, they were friends and now much more, so the double bluffing began.

Root and Jenny Jackson were on at The Plebs that night. They'd gone to see them but left early as soon as the act had finished. Angie used a bad headache as an excuse to leave. Mack volunteered to take her home explaining to Tom and Ellen he had to be back in Bradford. He needed to catch up on schoolwork. The Elgins *Heaven Must Have Sent You* was playing as they climbed the steps leaving the club. He'd taken her home on his scooter.

Quivering with anticipation, she led him upstairs. There were no preliminaries this time, no words. They'd gone up in silence without disturbing her sleeping sister. An emotional mix of joy, passion, and gratitude assuaged her feelings of guilt. Angie tried not to think of Effy and the sacrifice her friend had made in allowing her to share Mack. How could she ever repay her? It was an extraordinary gift and one Angie intended to honour.

When she seduced Mack, taking his virginity, she had been the teacher. Now Mack was the teacher. No, not a teacher, Mack was more of a maestro who played her body like a musical instrument. Angie found herself moved in a series of rhapsodic climaxes.

In the morning, Angie rose while he slept. Removing last night's makeup, she freshened up before returning to bed and cuddled up to him ready for when he awoke. Angie wanted to look as good as she knew how.

It had been heaven in his arms. Mack made her feel so good she wanted to sing, to dance, to let the whole world know how much she loved him.

Mack had noticed Tony Dzerzhinsky's right hand and the fourth and fifth fingers strapped together. Before Jersey could say anything, Mack had already detected the coolness between him and Tim.

"Next time, make sure you've closed your fist before you give Tim a black eye. What did you do? Break the little finger? You should always ball a fist tight and keep the thumb outside before hitting someone."

They looked astonished as he sat down on a desktop.

Jersey couldn't believe Mack's deduction. "Who told you we had a set to?"

"Elementary, my dear Jersey." Turning to Smith. "I hope you two have made up. I can't be doing with the hassle of you two giving each other cold shoulders and evil eyes. The lass made her choice. Her privilege who to dump and who to date. So kiss and make up the pair of you."

As others arrived, they treated him to choruses of Tommy Steele, *Flash Bang Wallop.* Their bawdy dramatization of the chorus about the photograph made him grin. What a photograph, flash-bang wallop right enough.

Chloe Johnson was waiting for her outside the registration classroom. A concerned expression filled the diminutive girl's face. "How's it gone, Effy?"

"It's weird. I can't believe how they behaved when we walked through the school gate. It was like the Red Sea parting to make way for us. I don't think I've ever had so many eyes staring at me. What have the girls in our tutor group said?"

"They wouldn't speak in front of me because they know we're friends. Lots of whispering and tittering going on, I should steel your self. There could be some cattiness from the usual suspects."

"Maria Sharpe, by any chance?" Chloe confirmed with a nod. "Anyone else?"

Her friend sighed. "Katie Fox and one or two others. Brace yourself, Effy."

She gave her friend a reticent smile. "Forewarned, forearmed. I suspected I might get some comments. No problem, Chloe." Effy followed her and tried to look elegant. It was an uncomfortable experience seeing the girls' eyes studying her every move.

"I see she's covered her legs, and her hem is regulation knee length." Maria Sharpe sneered looking Effy up and down.

"Not wearing your nighty today? Not flashing your undies for all the world to see?" Katie Fox joined in with her comrade's cattiness.

Effy had planned to ignore them. Saying nothing in response was an annoying tactic.

"Gosh! Katie! That's a lovely shade of bitchiness you've got on today." Chloe's comment made her smile at her two would-be tormentors.

Today, hearing placid Chloe strike back at them on her behalf changed her mind. A polite winsome smile always seemed to work them up more. Her refusal to take the bait was a strategy that annoyed would be bullies most days. Today was different. Today she broke away from Chloe approaching them with a menacing glint in her eyes.

"My lacy undies are clean on every day and worth seeing, which is more than I could say for some."

"What a bitch!" Katie Fox started, but Effy cut her off.

"If I were a bitch, I'd make your life hell. So I'll let you two get on with the bitchiness instead. No offence intended, but you're the real experts." Her hand made an intimidating clawing action in Maria Sharpe's face, "Ciao Maria."

Effy turned to walk away. Stopping short, she turned with a bright smile. "Or should I have said *meow*, Maria? I can never remember with you."

Beyond their hearing, Chloe asked, "What was that about the underwear? Fox went bright red when you said that."

"I was reminding her of her own less than clean Aertex knickers when we were in the Third Form. She who casts the first stone and all that? Not that I enjoyed reminding her. It wasn't nice, and it was unkind of me to say it. I feel rotten, reminding her about it. The other girls used to give her a hard time. I'll find a way of saying sorry to her later."

Chloe gasped in astonishment, "Don't do that! She'll only think you're soft."

"Perhaps. If I don't, it'll be on my conscience, making her feel bad."

"He's already got a replacement," Jersey informed Mack. "He didn't waste any time? She's in the same Lit group with Chloe and Effy."

"Is that so, Tim? Nothing like bouncing back fast is there, eh? Bit like a rubber ball. I'm surprised you didn't cast your net wider. What about all those lovelies at Bradford Girls Grammar? It's getting somewhat incestuous, don't you think?"

Tim Smith ignored the comment giving Jersey an icy glare. "I don't go poaching other blokes girlfriends. Anyway, he's welcome to her. You know what they say? You should give the less fortunate your old toys when you've done playing with them."

Mack stepped between the two. Jersey gave every impression of taking another swing at Smith. "Cool it, you two. A trip to see the Monsignor for starting a brawl first thing in the morning isn't a brilliant idea."

"I bet she's already let him finger her." Smith goaded enraging Jersey. It took all Mack's considerable strength to keep the two of them from coming to blows.

"That's enough out of the pair of you. If I bang your brains together, you'll still be seeing stars at lunchtime."

In a low, less, and than friendly voice, Mack directed his attention to Tim Smith, cautioning him, "That's uncalled for, and it's unacceptable. No one with any decency would ever say anything like that about an ex. No matter how bad they felt about breaking up. You should feel ashamed. Accept it's over and move on. Try to treat the new girl something better than a rebound."

The dismay was clear on her sister's face. Gill had opened her bedroom door to rouse her for breakfast. Finding Mack asleep in bed beside her was not what she had wanted to see. Angie could see her sister's dismay turn to a despairing look. She had placed a finger to her lips, letting Gill know not to wake him. An hour later, they had come down. Her sister was still upset.

"What have you two done? How could you cheat on your best friend? And you Mack, how could you do this to poor Effy? It will break her heart."

Mack looked at Angie then at Gill. "There's something you need to know. It won't make for easy listening."

CHAPTER 2

Sharing You – Little Eva (Llllloco-Motion LP London SHU 8437 – 1962)
Friday 14 April 1967

Mack led the way as Effy followed him awash with apprehension. They had agreed to meet to talk about their threesome arrangement. Dread had filled her with panicked thoughts. In her embattled mind, she wondered if her friendship with Angie could survive. There was a silence as they exchanged uncertain looks across the living room. Then they both burst into floods of tears and rushed towards one another. Hugging and crying tears of relief, they knew their friendship was still intact.

Mack was unsure how to react to this first meeting since they'd agreed to become three. It was distressing seeing the two of them so tearful until he realized these were tears of relief. Gill appeared from the kitchen door holding a tea towel. She let out a long sigh, her face softening at the sight of the two girls. Excusing herself, she went back into the kitchen, promising to come out in a moment. The two girls looked towards him, no words passing between them.

Opening both his arms, they came over to him. Effy tucked herself under his right arm and Angie under his left. He pulled them both close together. Their arms wrapped around him and each other.

"For better or for worse," Effy whispered, "the three of us."

"The three of us," Mack and Angie echoed.

Gill returned, watching the strange threesome embrace in silence. It was touching to see him kiss each girl. She felt like a voyeur looking on. It was weird seeing them behaving like this yet somehow, though strange, it appeared so normal. Noticing her presence, the group broke up, and Effy crossed the room to hug Gill.

Angie's sister returned the hug, giving Effy a squeeze. "I hope you know what you're doing, Effy."

"Shall we?" Angie indicated to Effy the two should go up upstairs. "Gill, will you look after Mack."

"Why?" Gill was puzzled.

"We're going to sort out how our relationship is going to work," Angie replied.

"Shouldn't Mack be present?" Gill's astonishment made the girls giggle.

"He'll do as he's told." Angie put an arm around Effy. "Won't he?"

"He most certainly will," Effy confirmed, exchanging smiles with Angie.

Mack listened to their chatter as they climbed the stairs. Turning to Gill he asked, "Any chance of a cup of tea?"

Gill kept staring at him with a peculiar expression as they sat drinking tea in the kitchen. He was trying to fathom what she was thinking. She seemed unable to speak. Without warning, she asked. "How are you going to explain this relationship to everyone? Aren't you afraid how you three may find yourselves treated when it comes out?"

Mack's enigmatic smile charmed her. She could see why her sister and her friend were so in love with him.

"The one thing we've definitely decided is going to surprise you, Gill," He put his mug of tea down on the kitchen table and looked her straight in the eyes. "We've no intention of telling anyone anything. We've agreed we won't confirm or deny we have a relationship if asked."

His answer left her bewildered and open-mouthed. He continued. "You'll be the only person who knows the truth. The three of us have agreed on that already. No matter what happens, we will remain silent. It's our affair and our lives together, and it stays private and personal."

"Why me?" Gill found his words perplexing. "Why should I be the only one who knows?"

"Effy and I have agreed that as Angie's sister, you have to be there for her. You know about us already. Nobody else does. We also want you to be our go-between if we have any problems. Neither my family nor Effy's will understand or even try. We've no intention of even beginning to explain our arrangement. As far as we're concerned, you can be the only one in the know. It will be a burden for you, more so if we ever become famous. Everyone will want to know the truth about us. We're sure you won't admit anything. We certainly won't."

"How on earth are you going to carry on this *arrangement*?"

"In plain sight. As I said, we'd never admit to it nor deny it. What others choose to think would be up to them." He sounded so matter of fact as he cradled the mug of tea in his hands. "We'll let them think it's a publicity stunt."

"Pardon my lack of understanding. How are you going to carry on in full view of everyone without making the girls look foolish or silly?"

"The girls are discussing that right now. That's why we're here. We're working it out. The three of us know we can't be too blatant in public. Then again, we're not going to pretend that there's no relationship either. I'll treat Effy and Angie with equal respect at all times."

"You'll forgive me, Mack. I know you're sincere and honourable, but I cannot understand how you and they can be in love." Gill shook her head. Even though she was five years older, the family resemblance was unmistakable. "I'm sorry. I was always brought up to believe that there's one right person who you're meant to fall in love with. This is far too unconventional for me. I can't get my head around the idea, I'm sorry."

"Effy's not Angie. Angie's not Effy. They're two beautiful young women, and I'm not talking about their looks. I can't say why they love me. That's a question for them to answer. I can only tell you why I love them. I love them for themselves."

The next question was inevitable. He had half suspected she would ask. "Why do you love my sister?" Her eyes searched him, seeking the truth in his face.

After a few seconds or so of thoughtful silence he gave Gill an answer. "Why do I love her? I love her for all her qualities. It's her strength and trust. Angie is honest, loyal, and devoted. She stands by me when there's trouble. I know I can count on her. She's kind, and there's nothing she wouldn't do for me, or for Effy. What she feels for me runs deep, and I'm always aware of it. Angie keeps my feet on the ground because she's level headed. She's also funny and smart. How could I not be in love with her? She also has a unique friendship with Effy. There's a powerful bond between them. They behave like sisters. I don't understand their bond, but I know they have it. I couldn't see our relationship working without it."

Gill was weighing his answers while stirring her tea with mesmeric pointlessness.

"What about Effy?"

"We share a deep and passionate intensity. We always have ever since we met. She's strong in ways Angie isn't, but she's no less devoted, patient, and trusting. I love her for the kindness of her soul. I always think I need to protect Effy. With Angie, it's the other way around, as though she's trying to protect and safeguard me instead."

Gill stopped stirring her tea, giving thought to his words.

12

He continued, "The three of us are ambitious, and we work well as a team knowing what we want. They trust one another, and they trust me. Our relationship exists because of that trust. The most important thing for you to understand is that Angie and Effy both co-exist in me as equals."

"I'm sorry, Mack. I still can't get my head around this. If you love a person and you fall in love with another, you must have stopped loving the first one?"

"I don't believe that, neither does Effy. Yes, sharing Angie with Effy has changed things. We do still love each other and have never doubted that we still feel the same. We're still in love. Only now, Angie is a part of our relationship."

Gill let out another loud sigh, her hand reaching across to touch Mack's, "Let's hope the three of you can make this work. The thought of this relationship going wrong has me worried sick. If the whole thing should go wrong, this could end up leaving so much so hurt. If one of you found someone else, it would, and it will cause a lot of pain to the other two. You three are so young, and you can't dismiss the possibility that it won't happen."

Mack smiled. "There are no certainties in life. We're free to make our choices."

Gill withdrew her hand. Mack watched her face colour. "This relationship, you're not going to have sex together?"

Mack burst out laughing, "No. Gill. That's a definite no. The three of us look at it is as two separate lives, like compartments. I'll have time with Effy, and I'll have time with Angie. That's already decided so don't worry about anything sordid. Anyhow as a guy, I know my physical limitations."

"Well, I'm relieved to hear that. I'm beginning to understand why Effy told Angie you were seventeen going on thirty. Talking to you is like talking to a mature man. Most of the men I've met in their twenties don't even come close."

"Gill, it's my mum who keeps saying it to Effy all the time. Even my dad regards me as too mature for my age. They both think I'm a bit of a freak of nature."

"Have you thought about jealousy? How will you deal with it?"

"Gill, I won't deny it could be an issue. Effy gave me the best answer. To love someone is to trust in them. Truthfulness is the remedy for jealousy. I thought that was a brilliant answer.

An hour later, sitting down together around the kitchen table they began.

"You will respect Angie and myself as equals." Effy began. "We are your exclusive and inclusive girlfriends. No others allowed."

"Okay. That's clear."

She ticked the item on the list with her biro.

Angie took up the next point on their rough draft list. "Under no circumstances will you ever talk about our sex lives with the other. What happens in bed stays in our separate beds."

"I won't talk about it if you girls promise not to talk about it between yourselves."

"Damn!" Effy snapped her fingers, grinning at Angie.

"Didn't I tell you he'd say something like that?" Angie's smile made him want to laugh. "Looks like we won't be able to compare notes, Eff."

"We're agreed. What happens in bed stays in bed. I won't talk about it if you girls don't."

Gill blushed as she listened. It wasn't the easiest of discussions to hear no matter how the three tried to make it light-hearted.

Their future conduct in public involved a major discussion. A matter of priority was deciding how Mack and Angie behaved in public when Effy wasn't there. Also, the way the three of them would act when together in public. There would have to be some restraints. Angie insisted that Effy should still hold hands with him. Both girls agreed that they could link arms with him when they were together as a threesome.

Effy was firm. She would not snog Mack in public when Angie was present. From now on, that kind of kissing would only happen in private. Kisses in public from both girls, would be on the cheek and limited to hello and goodbye. It made sense. When not together and a slow dance number came on, both should be free to dance with him. The no kissing rule would apply. Most of it seemed like common sense. The most embarrassing item to raise its head was the possibility of pregnancy.

Angie shocked Gill with her response. "If Effy gets pregnant, they should get married, they're meant to get married. I plan on being their chief bridesmaid. I hope I don't get pregnant. If I do, all I'll want from Mack is for him to love our child and help to bring it up. I won't marry him."

"Well, it needed mentioning." Effy insisted. "These things happen, like it did to my sister Caitlin. We need to think about the possibility. Let's hope it doesn't happen to either Angie or me for a few years."

"Amen to that," Mack agreed.

"Shall I do a finished version?" Effy offered. "We can all sign and get it witnessed by Gill."

"Could I suggest something to add?" Gill interrupted. "How about what happens if one or two of you decide to end this arrangement? What then?"

CHAPTER 3

You've Been Cheating – The Impressions (HMV POP 1498 – 1965)
Saturday afternoon, 15 April 1967

"Spill the Heinz," Tom spoke in a furtive voice as Mack adjusted the tripod to set up the camera shot. They were working in Ted Bowler's studio.

"What's going on between you and Angie Thornton? Are you cheating on Effy, going behind her back with her best friend?"

"Can you bring that light unit over here?"

"Come on cuz, 'fess up, I read women like you read books." Tom could be relentless when wheedling out the truth. "Don't underestimate me. I notice more than you think I do. I know what women are like, so don't try getting clever. You ought to know me better by now, seeing as we were brought up together. I bet I know you better than your brother does. So what's the story?"

When Tom got like this, dealing with him was harder than trying to wrestle a bone from a Doberman's jaws. Tom wasn't joking. He had a genuine knack. When it came to women, Tom possessed an almost psychic talent. The time had arrived to summon help. "Tom, it's all in your imagination this time."

"You can't hide the truth from me. I've sussed it."

"Effy? Is Ellen ready? I need you here."

"What's the matter?" Effy appeared from behind the temporary curtain, separating the changing area from the rest of the studio. Ellen followed her, wearing a dressing gown.

"TC thinks I'm having it off with Angie behind your back."

"Does he now?" Effy's lack of interest made Mack smile. "Honestly Mack, didn't I warn you and Angie to be more discrete?"

Ellen's startled gasp was audible. Tom was open-mouthed. Effy placed both hands around Mack's neck and delivered a passionate kiss. Breaking free after several seconds, she turned to Tom and continued. "I just knew there was no fooling you, Tom! You're too good for us. We can't hide anything from you, can we? The trouble is Mack's too demanding. You know what I mean by *demanding*? *Physically demanding*? I couldn't cope

16

any longer. So I had to ask Angie to help me out, and now Angie's complaining she can't cope either!"

"Stop it." Mack chuckled. "Stop winding them up, Effy."

"Have you made sure there's colour film in the camera? I don't want you shooting all this catalogue underwear in black and white." Effy evaded the topic with adept diplomacy. "Nate's on a tight schedule for these. We'll need them ready and developed by tomorrow for Nate to collect and take to the printers on Monday."

"There are only three sets of bras and pants. How long do you think it will take me?"

"You've got picky and arty with your shoots of late," Effy commented. "You take ages over choosing the right angles."

"Effy, help me reposition this reflector, just move it more to the left, please." Instructed Mack.

"We can't help becoming suspicious." Ellen ignored Effy and Mack's attempts to change the conversation. Picking up Tom's dropped baton, she gave Mack an accusing look. "The three of you have been carrying on in such a weird way since London."

Effy lost patience and snapped a reprimand. "If anything is going on between the three of us, that's our business, so keep your noses out. No, Angie's not cheating on me. And if Mack wants to put his arm around Angie, or she wants to link arms with Mack, then it's okay. Angie has my full permission. Now can we get on with the shoot, please? Right sis, let's see you in all your undressed glory."

Her sister's irritated reaction shook Ellen. Numb, she began to remove the dressing gown as ordered to reveal a matching bra and brief set.

"What items are we shooting first?" Mack asked, positioning the light unit.

Effy became businesslike. "Dream Woman in satin and lace, the rose version. We need to get a suntan. Ellen looks so white, so alabaster. Can you do something, perhaps use a colour filter?"

"A filter won't do much good. Let's ask the sun to stay out for a week so we can get a tan." Mack followed this with a further instruction to Effy, "Make sure you record each pose we shoot."

"Mack, I'm not sure I can go through with this." Ellen stammered, clutching the disrobed dressing gown to her front, the nervousness unmistakable.

"Why not?"

"They'll recognise me in the catalogue! Everyone will know it's me." Came her plaintive response.

"With a figure like yours, you've got nothing to feel ashamed of, has she guys?"

Mack looked at Tom, who looked right back at him. "There's no argument there."

"Effy, I don't think I can do this."

"You should have thought about that before agreeing to take the assignment. We can't let Silvers fashions down; they need the prints by tomorrow. Nate's is coming over to collect the photos in the afternoon. You have no choice." Effy 's insistence was sharp.

"You do it then!"

"I would if the bra was my size. I'm an A cup, and you're a B, and I'd look ridiculous."

"Oh, please, Effy! You could pad them with a hanky and tissues."

"Don't be silly, Ellen! They'd show through the lacy bits."

"I'm not doing it. That's final." Ellen stamped her foot dramatically.

"Ellen Halloran, you will go through with this shoot!" Effy's uncharacteristic angry command made Ellen step back startled. "You will not let everyone down."

Mack had a sudden inspired thought. "Has Chloe left her suitcase of tricks down here?"

"Why?" Queried Effy. "Yes, it's in the corner where she left it."

"I think I may just have a way to solve this sudden attack of nerves. Tom, will you fish out my aviator sun specs from my parka?"

Chloe's jam-packed suitcase contained theatrical makeup and assorted stuff. She kept them for the amateur dramatics group. Mack recalled seeing something in the motley collection of makeup and assorted items. Rummaging through the contents, he pulled out not one, but two articles he needed. Turning to Effy, he said, "Pin her hair back tight to her scalp and put this on over the top. Let's see if we can't get away with me doing a bit of arty farty with the lens. We may need to alter her make up to match the way the skin tone is going to change."

"Damn Jimmy Mack, but you're good." Effy studied the lingerie prints. They were in the darkroom, checking the photographs as they developed. "If I didn't know this was Ellen, you would have fooled me. It was sheer genius, using those wigs Chloe had in her suitcase worked like magic. Only you could pull off something like this!"

Absorbed Mack studied the prints, paying close attention to the details. "I decided not to use a filter to make sure I captured the exact colour of the lingerie. It needs to be accurate. If I used a filter, it wouldn't look right. Glad we changed Ellen's makeup too. That made a vital change to the skin tone. I need to gen up on makeup and how lighting affects it on photographs."

"That's something Chloe could help you with, and I have a few useful articles you can read." Effy stroked her chin, studying the images. "It was a genius idea to use sunglasses. The way the lights reflect off the lenses looks brilliant. That black wig gave Ellen a chic Parisian look. Maybe we should invest in some wigs and hairpieces?"

"Not a bad idea, Eff. Let's look into buying some," he responded. Satisfied with the results, he began tidying up the darkroom. The new enlarger was expensive, but now, with the extra tank, and eye-watering expensive chemicals, even developing colour prints was possible.

"Ellen may change her mind about not doing more lingerie shoots after seeing these. It makes me tempted to have a go. Shame I haven't got a bust like hers. With shots like these, I bet you could get contracts from Berlei and Gossard for photo shoots."

"I'm not so sure about Ellen doing more after you bullied her into doing these. She wasn't too happy with you. For a few minutes, it looked as if we'd let Silvers Fashions down. Underwear is a new departure for them. I wasn't even sure I could handle developing colour prints here in the house. I was sweating, hoping I wasn't making a mistake. Just as well I'm set up, now we've new contracts coming in. I've got my hands full. Let's see what the reactions are to the *Petticoat* magazine spread first."

I don't know what my sister's complaining about. Ellen's getting paid a decent fee, and she keeps the underwear too. It's so pretty I'd love the same for myself."

"It's not cheap lingerie either," Mack gave her an unexpected kiss on the forehead. "Let's see if Grace recognises a disguised Ellen."

"We may all need to wear disguises if the reporters keep chasing us as they have done."

"So far, you've been lucky. The publicity hasn't got out of hand yet. The more exposure you'll get as a designer and model, the more the press will come after you. Let's not forget, Angie and your sisters. We're all going to become press targets."

"We'll worry about that when it happens," Effy kissed him again, her arms around Mack's neck. She was so much happier after spending time with Angie. The stress she'd felt at agreeing to their sharing arrangement had vanished. She seemed more confident and carefree once again.

Grace was sitting at the dining room table, struggling with French homework as they came in. Turning to Effy, she pleaded, "What's the French conditional for open when it's *ils*?"

"Same as the imperfect. *Ouvraient*," came Effy's almost instant answer.

Grace let out a huge sigh of relief, "God, I'm glad I got that right."

They laid the photos out in front of her.

"What do you think of these?" Effy asked.

"Wow! These are amazing." Grace looked up at Mack. "When did you start lingerie photography? And who's the model? She looks familiar. Anyone I know?"

"You may have met her," Effy teased her.

"Well, it isn't you. You haven't got a bust that size, and the hair's all wrong."

"Getting warmer," Mack dropped a clue.

The realization left Grace opened mouthed, "Oh my god! That's our Ellen? Crikey! Hasn't she's got a fabulous figure!"

CHAPTER 4

Road Runner – Junior Walker & The All Stars
(Tamla Motown TMG 559 -1965)
Tuesday 18th April 1967

Once copies of *Petticoat* hit the magazine racks, anonymity was over. It didn't take long for the press to uncover the whereabouts of Effy and her sisters. Angie remained out of the spotlight for two more days. Then reporters and photographers came stalking.

Robert MacKinnon assumed it was safe. He dropped Effy and Grace off on Oak Lane, just before Lister Park's main gates. Walking down to Keighley Road, they suspected nothing as they crossed. It was another typical grey overcast school morning. They joined a steady stream of girls walking down Cunliffe Road. Only on approaching the school entrance did they realize something wasn't right. The photographer seemed to leap out of nowhere without warning. Catching them unaware, he clicked his camera with the rapidity of a machine gun. Why Grace behaved as she did Effy couldn't understand. Standing in front of her sister, she dropped a curtsy.

The photograph would show a beaming Grace curtseying. Effy had cupped her hand to her mouth, trying to stop laughing. It would become an iconic moment remembered years later.

Worse followed. Many of Grace's classmates had brought copies of *Petticoat* with them to school. Grace had never mentioned appearing in the magazine to her friends. The news had spread among them as soon as her friend Jean knew about it from her older sister. The realities of fame caught her unawares in the next few minutes.

Ellen was more fortunate. She had made her way to school from the family home in Whites Terrace. Arriving at the last minute, she avoided the photographers. It was only during the morning break when she found out about the pouncing photographer. Not that the sisters had much time to chat. They found themselves besieged by girls. Everyone wanted to know about them modelling for the magazine.

Ellen impressed Effy with her cool response to all the questions, giving nothing away. She fended off the many questions like a professional spokesperson. Chloe engaged Effy in conversation, preventing others from joining them. Grace was less fortunate, drowning in the endless waves of questions.

For Effy, the end of the break came as a relief when she went into Maths. The tiny group comprised three other studious academic-minded girls. They had more in common with her older sister Deidre than her.

Focusing on a problem and solving the puzzle put aside her anxieties for a while. Confronted with the question beginning: A triangle had its vertices at A (4,4), B (-4,0), C (6,0.), she set about answering its component sub-questions. Her first step was to work out the equation of the circle through points A, B, C. Then she worked out the coordinates of the point where the internal bisector of the angle BAC met the x-axis. Finally, she had to find the equation of the circle passing through B and touching AC at C. There was something both satisfying and absorbing in solving the problem, to where her mind felt refreshed arriving at the solution. At least she had no time to brood.

Art was next on the timetable and always relaxing. Effy felt at home with the kindred spirits in her group. All the girls were easy-going, cheerful, and congenial, unlike the maths group. Much of the laid-back atmosphere she attributed to their male teacher. Bruce Mainwaring had to be close to retirement, she guessed. Art was unlike her A-Level English lit group. Too many of the girls were bitchy and two-faced only held in check by Miss Thorpe, who stood for no-nonsense. Most of the afternoon was a lengthy double session.

"I've decided you will study Othello as one of the required Shakespearian texts." Miss Thorpe handed out copies of the play to the group. "Envy and jealousy are central to this tragedy."

Effy opened her well-thumbed copy noting the previous users. Where were they now: Jean Dunbar, Teresa Murdoch, Sylvia Delaney, Iris Dunn, and so on as she studied the names? What had they gone to do with their lives? Her brief reverie broke.

Miss Thorpe asked Katie Fox, "Is there a difference between envy and jealousy, Katie?"

She looked flustered blushing as she found herself ambushed by the teacher. "Aren't they the same Miss?"

Effy still felt awful about her earlier comment. She and Katie Fox had more in common than the latter realized. The mousey haired girl's uniform was an ill-fitting hand-me-down like her own. The only difference, Effy had re-sewn her own to fit. Effy found herself ambushed next.

"Fiona, or would you prefer I called you Effy?" asked Miss Thorpe in an unfamiliar kind voice. "Is there a difference? Are envy and jealousy the same?"

"Either will do Miss Thorpe, I don't mind which name you use and no I don't think envy and jealousy are the same."

"Please explain Effy." That was the first time her teacher had used her favoured name instead of Fiona.

"Envy is how someone reacts to not having something someone else has. Jealousy is how you react to the loss of someone to someone else?"

"Could you clarify that with examples, Effy?" Why was she asking her when she was staring at Katie Fox?

"You might envy someone if you thought they were more attractive than you. Jealousy, I always associate with relationships. A girl might become jealous if her boyfriend became too friendly with another girl. Worse if it was her best friend."

"A good answer Effy. While they share common characteristics, they are not the same."

What took place next was extraordinary. It was not in keeping with Miss Thorpe's usual teaching style. "I will pair you girls so you can discuss the nature of envy and jealousy for five minutes. I'll give you guidelines as soon as I've paired you."

Effy looked to Chloe as her obvious partner. The shock came when Miss Thorpe paired her with Katie Fox.

What had begun as fun a few months ago was no longer funny. Not when some spotty thirteen-year-old started begging if he could get a modelling job for his older sister. Added to it all, he had received an offer a day through the post to do photo shoot assignments for magazines on the strength of his first shoot at the parish hall. Although they said nothing to him, he already knew Effy and Grace were under pressure. They had to knock out designs at short notice. The design wasn't so much the issue as the actual making of a sample. For Grace, it meant producing a working template for Silvers workshops. Thanks to Silvers Fashions, they now had access to a huge range of materials with interesting prints. The girls' attic bedroom had filled with swatches and rolls of fabric. New deliveries arrived almost daily. Grace had the floor space to layout and make the patterns from Effy's drawings. How they found the time to do their homework was a concern to his mother. Somehow they appeared to manage.

He was finding himself at the studio whenever it was free, which was most of the time. The place was turning into a real earner for old man Bowler. If he wasn't there with Effy or Grace, then it was with either Angie, or Ellen, or Alice, or any permutation of the five of them. Alice usually came over at the weekends, depending on the assignment. If Mack wasn't doing that, he was busy developing photos in his homemade darkroom for sending off to Nate and the magazines. He was constantly rushing to catch the last post. When not doing any of these things, he was cutting film into spool rolls ready for the next shoot. At the same time, he was struggling to cope with his A-Level work. Most nights he was not climbing into bed until midnight.

When the bell rang, signalling the end of the school day, Mack gave himself several minutes in the common room. He needed this brief time to sort out his priorities.

Drained after a full day's studying, he finally set off on the Lambretta down Emm Lane. It was a warm day, so for once he didn't bother wearing his crash helmet only the aviator sunglasses. Having the cool refreshing rush of air on his face was liberating. The scooter left a hazy trail of blue exhaust smoke in the afternoon sun. Riding the Lambretta, he always felt that synergy between man and machine. The scooter liberated him from the pressures and worries of the day. His driving test for a motorcar licence was looming in a few weeks.

Turning on to Keighley Road, he headed towards the city centre. Along the way, he passed Bradford Boys Grammar on his left and Lister Park on the right. Pupils were streaming in all directions. Riding down the hill on Cunliffe Road, he found Grace's friend Jean jumping out of a group of girls to flag him to a stop. Grace emerged from concealment among them as he stopped alongside the schoolgirls.

Breathless, Grace warned him, "There's a bunch of photographers waiting at the school gate for Effy to come out. She would have waited outside the gates as usual but had to dive back inside after seeing them."

"Are you okay, Grace?"

"I'm fine. Jean and my friends have sneaked me out so I could warn you. Listen, Chloe's waiting outside the school gate. She will signal Effy when you arrive. Effy will rush out to the scooter. I've got her school stuff to make a quick getaway easier. Ellen says she'll stop in the building until the reporters have cleared off."

"Will you be okay getting home?"

"I'll be okay and go with Jean on the bus."

24

Mack approached the school gates. Meandering the Lambretta at a walking pace, he sought Chloe. She noticed him before he spotted her. Removing her beret, she waved. Mack assumed this was the signal.

The photographers and reporters stood near the main gate. Two members of staff looked to have engaged them in conversation. They did a good job of drawing their attention from the school gate. Effy dashed from cover towards the scooter, impressing Mack with her sprinting. It was unfortunate that one of the photographers caught sight of her running. Leaving the others, he raised his camera. A well-aimed piece of road gravel hit the back of his head, distracting him, thanks to Chloe. She didn't wait to see the man's reaction, walking away grinning. With the practiced swiftness of a female Mod pillion, Effy was on the back of the Lambretta in a flash. Mack spun the scooter around, heading back up the road.

Two days later, both would laugh at the photo one snapper got off. It would earn iconic status among Mods up and down the country. Flicking a two-finger salute at the photographer, Mack gunned the GT200 up the road. Effy stuck her tongue out at the precise moment that Mack flicked two digits. Glancing in the rear-view mirrors, he spotted the reporters dashing for their cars. So the chase began.

At this time in the afternoon, getting back on the main road was a traffic nightmare. The lead chasing photographer was in a maroon Riley 1.5. It was closing on them. There was no choice. Mack had to accelerate hard into the traffic. This almost caused a collision and irate horn blasts. The pursuing driver tried to tail the scooter. Mack whipped the Lambretta across the oncoming traffic at the main park gates. They tore up Oak Lane full throttle. Mack glanced in the mirror, seeing the chasing Riley. If he continued straight on to Lilycroft Road, their pursuers would catch up with them. Mack whipped to the right across the traffic in an eye-watering dangerous manoeuvre. This took them into Athol Road. He took a left into Selborne Terrace, planning to lose the pursuer in the warren of streets and roads by the park.

More by accident than intention, they arrived on Victoria Road only to see the Riley. It came whizzing past the junction on Heaton Road. The screeching car brakes told Mack the pursuers had spotted them. The driver would have to reverse and turn the car around as Mack took a left. Twanging the clutch lever like a bowstring, he twisted the throttle to its full limit and accelerated hard left again. To add to the madcap excitement, an Alsatian dog chased them along the road. Barking and baring its teeth, it bounded

25

after the Lambretta coming to a stop in the road, realizing it could not catch the scooter. The chasing photographer pulled up short to avoid hitting it. Effy managed to see it over Mack's shoulder in one of the rear-view mirrors.

Crossing over Oak Lane, he went down minor back streets over cobbled surfaces to reach home. Dismounting, Effy opened the back gate to the house. Parking the scooter behind the high stonewall was something he rarely did. Leaving it out might lead the newshounds spotting where they lived. No sooner had he pulled the scooter up on its stand than he found her arms wrapped around him. Effy began kissing him with raw passion. "That was scary and thrilling," she whispered nuzzling his ear.

"My mum's looking out of the window at us right now."

Jane MacKinnon was indicating they should hurry and come inside.

"We could always nip down to Whites Terrace after tea. I feel the need to have you all over me. I can come up with an excuse."

"Let's hold that thought. It looks like my mum wants us inside."

His mother didn't look too pleased when they came in. "I've had a telephone call from Effy's school in the last few minutes from the secretary. It appears so-called press photographers were hanging about outside the College this afternoon."

Mack and Effy exchanged grins.

Jane MacKinnon continued. "They informed me that a young man on a scooter picked Effy up and while rushing off behaved in a rather impolite way. Let me quote what they told me; he made a rude two-fingered gesture. That wasn't the worst of it, was it Effy dear? Sticking your tongue out?"

"They were pestering her." Mack protested.

"One of them was there outside the school gate this morning. He snapped a photo of Grace and myself."

"Where's Grace now?" His mother demanded, expressing concern.

"We had to split up. Her classmates smuggled her out in the crowd. She's taken the bus into town with Jean. She'll be home on the Number 8 before long. Ellen said she would wait it out before going home." Effy answered.

His mum raised an eyebrow. "We need to have a talk. Now. Oh, and before I forget someone from *Rave* magazine called this afternoon. Let's sit down in the lounge. You both need a quick lesson in public relations."

26

CHAPTER 5

People Gonna Talk – Lee Dorsey (Top Rank JAR 606 – 1961 – B side)
Thursday 20 April 1967

How the press found out who he was and where he lived, he couldn't figure out. Two days after their madcap scooter ride, the photo made the pages of the red tops. A chat with the Head of the Sixth Form proved less than motivational.

A round of applause from the guys in his History group greeted him. Another rousing chorus of Tommy Steele's *Flash Bang Wallop* followed. The group gave him a theatrical rendition of the two-fingered salute as an encore. It made him chuckle and shake his head. It was Jersey's doing. He was the one who had orchestrated the welcome. By lunchtime, others would belt out the song as he passed them in the corridors. It would even spread to the lower school. The imitations of the two-finger salute would follow him the rest of the day.

'Sugar Ray' Robinson, his teacher entered scant moments later. Catching the tail end of the two-digit flicks, he cottoned on to what was happening and raised a whimsical smile. His next comment proved enlightening.

"Folklore tells us that the use of the inverted V finger gesture began at the battle of Agincourt. History tell us there is no verifiable historical evidence that this gesture was ever used at the battle."

The group went silent listening with a diligent interest. 'Sugar Ray' continued.

"According to this folk tale, the French loathed English longbow men. They feared their deadly accuracy. When the French captured any English archers, they cut off the index and middle fingers. The archers used these fingers to draw the bowstring. Agincourt saw the English longbow men decimate the French cavalry. Afterwards, the English archers waved both fingers in the defiant V gesture. The message signalled our bowstring fingers remain intact. I must stress there is no evidence to support this anecdote. Because of the circumstances, I thought this tale appropriate today."

There was a long pause as the group absorbed his words before latching on to his humorous intention. Mack groaned, understanding what his teacher intended. There was nothing boxer-like about 'Sugar Ray'. Robinson was fat, fifty, and follicly challenged with a fanatical love of history. A love he attempted to imbue in his young men with devoted passion.

"Pictorial evidence, gentlemen. What can it tell us?" He studied Mack, another smile breaking out on his face. From his inside jacket pocket, he produced a folded newspaper page. Holding it up before the group, Mack heard a concentrated burst of sniggering break out. It was the one of him making the two-finger salute with Effy sticking her tongue out.

Sugar Ray's unconventional choice of source material was a fascinating introduction to visual evidence. It created some embarrassing comments and amusement at Mack's expense. Who snapped it, when, where, and why led to some entertaining answers. As he listened, it became clear how and why a photograph was so easy to misread and misinterpret. This set him wondering what impact the photo was having on the public.

His teacher summed up by making a passing observation. "Historians don't treat image evidence with enough seriousness. We should not neglect it, gentlemen. Visual evidence is often misinterpreted or too often discounted. Our brief discussion today has, I hope, made this point. Not everything you see is as it is. Without a true context, visual evidence can lead to wild speculative interpretations. In certain instances, it's also good for spreading untrue rumours."

Effy's Head of Lower Sixth had much to hold forth about too. It was all Effy could do to prevent herself from telling her tutor to get knotted. What business was it of hers to lecture her on how to behave? Telling her to give up her silly dreams brought Effy to boiling point. It was preposterous all this modelling nonsense, the teacher continued. Her ambitions to become a fashion designer and model were giving the College a bad reputation. Effy's behaviour and the adverse publicity would do her chances of an Oxbridge place no good.

"If I want your opinion about my future, I'll ask you to fill out the relevant forms," Effy had bit back. "Then I'll file them under I couldn't care less."

The teacher's flabbergasted expression made Effy half-smile. Outraged and stuttering about how bad her manners were, the teacher challenged her. "Who do you think you are? How dare you speak like that to me?"

28

"I'm Effy Halloran, and I dare because I have a mind of my own."

The face-off lasted several more minutes. Her defiant outrage matched the teacher's. Effy's caustic responses made it clear. She would brook no interference in her life outside of school. As for Oxbridge, after today, she would reconsider her options. Even transferring to another school to do her A-Levels. If that happened, she would give the press an interview, the school would never live down. That, she said, was no idle threat but a promise. Finishing, she demanded an apology for the comments made to her about *giving up her silly dreams*. At which point, impasse reached, the trembling teacher dismissed her. Effy was shaking but only because the teacher's comment had incensed her. There was no way she would allow anyone to speak to her in that way.

Later, during the afternoon, Effy found herself withdrawn from the art lesson by Miss Thorpe. They found an empty classroom, no words passed between them until after the door closed. Her English teacher's attitude took Effy aback.

She found Miss Thorpe treated her with unexpected kindness and sympathy.

"I must apologise for the conduct of my colleague and the things she said. It was wrong of her to speak to you in such a manner. Your reaction was understandable. In your place, my reply may well have been the same… had I your courage."

Effy struggled to believe what Miss Thorpe was saying, having expected a massive reprimand. Miss Thorpe continued. "You are one of the brightest young women it has been my pleasure to teach. Yet, there is another side to you, I admire more. I heard about your recent exchange with Katie Fox. So I paired you in class to see how you would react with one another talking about envy and jealousy. It was your surprising apology to Katie I found touching. Again please excuse me for having listened in."

"Oh." Was all Effy could say by way of a response.

"You possess an obvious and exceptional talent as a fashion designer. I've followed your appearances in the newspapers with considerable interest. You are also blessed with a beauty and grace to rival the top models in fashion magazines. There can be no doubting your potential to succeed in either field."

"But…?" Effy left the question hanging. "You are a most gifted and intelligent young woman with sparkle." Pausing, uncertain how to continue, Miss Thorpe added. "Please don't abandon your studies. Don't let the lure of fame and fortune prove too great. Don't give up ideas of higher education for the present. Both of your maths teachers think the world of you. Mr Mainwaring, let me look over your portfolio of designs and other artwork. In confidence, he told me he'd never met a student with so much innate artistic ability. Yes, you do have a dazzling talent for fashion and design, but it's not all you offer the world, Effy Halloran."

CHAPTER 6

Ain't There Something That Money Can't Buy – The Young-Holt Trio
(Brunswick 55317 – 1967)
Thursday Evening 20 April 1967

"Fashion is a fickle thing. Predicting what will sell is a tricky business because it is unpredictable. There are no guarantees that a new line will sell." Alex Silvers had arrived with Nate at the MacKinnon's home. Effy and Grace had completed a new design ready for him to see. His parents were looking on as Effy modelled the dress in the lounge.

"It was interesting walking down Carnaby Street to see what they had in the shops. Much of what we saw was outrageous and flamboyant tat. Most of it's driven by pop music, but I don't think that'll influence the typical high street buyers. Carnaby Street has lost the plot. I can't see most of what they're offering taking off on high streets. Least of all up in the North." Mack commented.

"Mack's right." Effy joined in. "We thought the place offered nothing but tat for American tourists. It's had its heyday. When you see the gear they're selling, it's dismal. They're trying to live up that naff song about London swinging like a pendulum. Biba is selling what many young women want to buy. It has the right idea, make it affordable, and make it available. Let's be honest. Ninety per cent of young women our age can't afford Quant. Nor can they afford what Moods Mosaic sells. Your catalogue versions of my designs are a great idea."

"That's why using Moods as an upmarket shop window struck us as good," Mack added. "Nate's idea of using cheaper materials with minor detail changes, and going for the mass market, made sense. Selling inexpensive versions through catalogues has to be the way to go."

Alex and Nate reflected on their words. The older man rubbed his chin and furrowed his brows. "The secret of success in the fashion business is costing young man. Each garment needs costing to the last penny. So we have to have the right quantity of material at the right price. Then we need to factor in the pricing of the work by our machinists. The more work involved in making a garment, the more the final costs rise. Also, the margins the retailers demand to make a profit are another serious headache. In the rag

31

trade, it's all about keen competitive pricing. If we make a mistake with the choice of material or pattern, we're left with stock that we won't be able to shift. Perhaps not for a long while, but you're right. In effect, we suffer a financial loss."

"Let's not forget about the sizing too." Nate continued. "The larger the garment size, the more material needed so the cost increases. We need to equal out the price to the customers. Those buying the larger sizes should not have to pay much more. There's an obvious difference in the quantity of material involved in a size 6 than in a 12 or 14."

"Yeah, but the downside is the size 6 buyer pays for the larger sizes," Mack muttered under his breath with only his mother hearing.

"What we need in the North is somewhere like Biba. I should maybe consider renaming our shops in Manchester. Perhaps setting up in Liverpool and Leeds with outlets for an off the peg range? That way, we don't rely on the catalogues alone to push the younger market. What do you think, son?"

"That might be one way to expand the business. Perhaps we should rebrand our Manchester shops and restart the chain? Then we should look into opening new ones under the rebranded name. We could then control stock with greater efficiency. The demand is there, that's for sure." Nate responded, taken by the idea. "Meanwhile, what's your opinion of this design, Mack?"

"From a photographer's point of view, I can make this look good. I can give it a sunny background, and use filters and it'll look superb as summer wear. From a guy's point of view, it's easy on the eyes, and I imagine pretty and practical from a woman's. What do you think, Grace?"

Grace's response was enthusiastic. "I agree with Mack. I'm planning to wear this design, but I might try to make it in a blush pink or even apricot just for me. May suit my skin tone more."

"I like the choice of this tangerine and white bird's-eye polka dot pattern. The halter neck top makes it an ideal summer dress. It's different, and it's eye-catching, and it's cotton poplin. That will keep the costing down. Can we get this in enough quantity for a run?" Nate checked with his father.

Alex Silvers ran his hand through the thick thatch of grey hair. "I'll find out. I love the simple cut, too, one of your trademarks, Effy. Would any of the other colours or patterns do?"

"The white stripe on the French blue should prove popular. So too the hickory brown with a contrasting white hem, that would give it a Biba look. The faint turquoise with hints of sea blue in the fine sharkskin print would be perfect. Moods Mosaic clients would adore it." Effy's reply sounded decisive. She added. "I adore the softness and luxurious feel to the touch. That was the deciding factor in choosing the material. We women love the texture of the material as much as the design. If it is sensuous to the touch, it makes you feel sensuous too. So how a dress feels is as important as how it looks, but you already know that."

"Nate, make a note. We'll take Grace's pattern and get different sized patterns made up. Let our cutters in the workshops do one in the tangerine and get it costed. Ask them to make up two in each of the materials Effy mentioned as quick as they can. I want to see how the girls look in these. Mack, can you snap me some 8 x10s in colour and get them to me as fast as possible? Meanwhile, I'll check with our suppliers. We need to know about the availability and quantity of the print designs we'll need."

Jane MacKinnon interrupted his flow. "They all have exams looming. We've undertaken a promise to the girls' parents. We won't allow their education to suffer."

"As long as we can get these last designs completed, it should be no problem. If we can have these photographs from Mack on time, these should do. We should be able to get these into one or more fashion magazines for the next month or two. This one can go straight into our boutiques." Nate's diplomatic answer tried to sooth Mack's parents' concern.

"Oh, before I forget." Alex Silvers opened up his briefcase. "I have these cheques. One I've made out to Effy's design account. There are cheques for each of the girls for their catalogue work to go into the agency account. Also, a cheque to cover Mack's work and the studio hire costs. Our accounts department will be preparing a fee for the new young lady. Alison?"

"Oh, you mean Alice? Alice Liddell."

"Yes, Alice. That's the girl I meant. I want to see more of that young woman in Effy's designs. We've had a lot of interest from magazines keen to see more of her."

"Do you know where we can get some fashionable shoes cheap? Only we don't have enough different pairs for photo shoots?" Grace was both sweet and cheeky, making Nate and his father smile. "Also, we could do with some hairpieces and wigs?"

"I'll get it sorted for you, Grace. Just let me know all your shoe sizes and pass them on to Jane. I'll see what we can do. Hairpieces? Nate, do you have any ideas?"

After the Silvers had left, Robert MacKinnon removed his half-moon reading spectacles. Without a word, he passed over the receipts to his wife. Mack and the girls waited in bated silence. The open-mouthed expression was a comical mix of shock and subdued mirth.

"Am I seeing things?" Jane MacKinnon checked with her husband. "This can't be for real? The girls earn this kind of money? It's unreal."

"Oh, I forgot. I also received a letter today from *Petticoat*. There's a cheque enclosed for the snaps I sent them. The ones we took in the old parish hall. They want me for a job using models of my choosing. Here's the cheque, dad." He passed the envelope to him. "Feast your eyes on this and the letter. They want to negotiate a fee for a prospective shoot."

His father cast a glance over the letter and the cheque, and shook his head. Saying nothing, he passed them over to his wife, who gasped. "They can't be serious."

"Compared to what top snappers like David Bailey get paid, it's a pittance." Mack grinned.

"Some pittance."

CHAPTER 7

Yesterday's Papers – Chris Farlowe (Immediate IM 049 – 1967)
Tuesday 25 April 1967

"I picked up a copy of *Nova* from the newsagents this morning. The interview was interesting, and you came across well. To say how long the journalist spent with you, I'm surprised it wasn't longer. Some things you said were a touch daring."

Effy sat down on the sofa in the lounge, still wearing her school coat. Removing the brunette wig and fake glasses, she unpinned her strawberry blonde hair. The disguise didn't suit Effy. It helped her to avoid lurking press snappers and reporters outside the school. It was a drag getting into disguise. Pity Maria Sharpe had to give the game away to one of them. Despite the betrayal, she had given them the slip before they could get another photo of her. After today, avoiding them might become more of a problem.

"How's the bump behaving today? Kicking?"

Jane responded with a nod. "Must be another boy by the way it's trying to kick my ribs out."

It was a calculated change of topic, prompt too. The back door opened and closed signalling Mack's return. They heard chatter as the voices came nearer. "Guess which stray I picked up in the city centre? Thought I'd better give Grace a lift home on the scooter."

"Oi, you! Give up calling me a stray." Grace feigned annoyance. "I knew there'd be every chance you'd be down at Pearson's Records. Either there or Wood's. You're addicted to your little plastic discs."

"They're vinyl, not plastic." Mack retorted.

"Same difference. Anyway, what did you buy? Or is that another Mack secret?"

"1 found two 'A' demos by James and Bobby Purify. *I'm your puppet* and *Wish you didn't have to go*, on Stateside."

"Oh, I love those," Effy exclaimed. "So does Angie. Will you go back tomorrow and try to get them for her?"

"I doubt they'll have two demo discs, but I might be able to find two normal issues. Oh, and I got a promo copy of this just for you." He passed the 45 to Effy.

35

She giggled when she read the label. "*Jimmy Mack*, Martha and The Vandellas. Now you *are* famous."

"Yeah, okay. Let's have a read of the article."

Grace slumped down next to Mack and Effy on the sofa. He turned to the page with the interview. "I see they used your shot of Eff. You make her look so glam."

Mack read the interview, written as a series of responses to questions. He hadn't been present during the interview, so the content was fresh to his eyes.

"Fashion plays an important part in the lives of women. If we're honest, we always worry about what we should wear. It's an ever-present never-ending issue. What we choose to wear reflects who and what we are as individuals. Unfortunately, for most women, clothes have to fit in with the demands of society. This creates personal dilemmas for my generation. Should we dress to please society or ourselves? I believe we should always please ourselves but not deceive ourselves. Clothes are part of what makes a woman fascinating when it comes to attracting men. That's why clothes should always have an air of sexiness. Any young woman who pretends she doesn't dress to be sexually attractive deceives herself. Women compete and always will compete with one another in the desirability stakes. It's the great unspoken taboo most are too reluctant to admit."

"Strong stuff, Effy," commented Mack. "That'll get a few comments in the letters to the editor pages. Mind *Nova* isn't exactly conventional in its articles."

"Hey listen to this," Grace interrupted. "It's about the Cromwellian photo. *It's surprising how a teasing photo can fuel such outlandish speculations. We are young, and we were having fun when someone snapped us. Groundless sexual innuendos of all kinds are flying around since the photograph appeared. Mack is my boyfriend. We have been going steady for over two years. Angie Thornton is my dearest friend and his close friend. He is our photographer of choice. Thanks to his skill, Angie and I look amazing. We are his muses. Through his camera lens, he creates the best images of the clothes we model. In doing so, my designs come alive. Yes, we three have a special symbiotic relationship. It's nothing like the gutter press imagine it to be.* Wow, Eff. What does symbiotic mean?"

"It means Grace, the three of them depend upon each other. By working together with one another, they gain to their mutual benefits." Jane answered her question, then elaborated further. "Angie gains from Effy's efforts by modelling her designs and Effy gains by having Angie as a model. James gains by being their photographer. They gain by his photographs as the designer and models."

Mack reflected on his mother's words. They were more symbiotic than she could even guess. As the thought crossed his mind, he noted the peculiar look she gave him. His mother had stopped accusing Angie of stealing him away from Effy. She had begun to treat her with genuine warmth and friendship. Since returning from London, Mack had noticed a considerable further softening and acceptance of Angie by his mum. He little realized at that moment the reason. One day, it would become clear. Not that Angie had usurped Effy in his mother's affections. Effy was still number one. Somehow he knew this would never change. All the same, he was glad that Angie was no longer seen as a threat. Everyone accepted the two girls shared a close friendship. How would they respond if she knew what this closeness involved? It wasn't worth contemplating.

His thoughts went back to their contract on love. The brown-red smears under their signatures as he'd signed his name. "What are these marks?" he'd asked.

"We're blood sisters." They'd answered.

"What?"

Both had pricked their hands with a sterilised needle. They'd mixed their blood together, applying it to the contract.

"Nothing will break our friendship." They had declared. "Not even you."

CHAPTER 8

Watch Your Step – Bobby Parker (Sue Records WI-340)
Tuesday 25 April 1967

It was nine twenty by the time Angie returned home from her evening class. The sight of a woman with peroxide blonde hair and a crooked smile greeted her as she entered the living room. Gill gave her a warning glance.

"This is Mara Fisher. She says she's a journalist and wants to interview you. "

"I'm so sorry it's so late." The stranger began laying on dubious sweetness. "I've travelled up from London, and it took me some time to find where you lived. I'd like to do a quick interview if it's okay?"

Angie guessed she must be in her thirties.

"Could I ask where you got my address?" Angie's suspicion gland activated. How had this reporter found her? And why did she have a peculiar accent?

"Caroline Anstruther-Browne at Moods Mosaic is an acquaintance of mine. She gave me your details."

"Where are you from, I don't recognise your accent?" Angie asked, attempting politeness.

"I'm Australian, but I've worked in London for some years now." Noticing Angie's reluctance, Mara Fisher pressed on. "I do appreciate it's late and you've had a long day. If you could spare me twenty minutes or so, I would be ever so grateful."

Angie gave in to the request with reluctance. There was something about the woman she distrusted. This was more intuition than for any immediate or obvious reason. At first, everything the reporter asked sounded straightforward. The questions sounded innocuous. None appeared devious. How long had Angie been a model? How long had she known Effy, and how had they met? What could she tell her about Mack, their photographer? Angie guarded her responses. She revealed as little as possible while remaining polite and avoiding being indiscrete. Recent attempts at photographing Effy outside her school put her on the defensive. After the way the press attempted to present the three of them, Angie intended to let nothing slip. The scooter escapade had resulted in further publicity. It had

38

turned into a cracking piece of personal promotion. Then came a series of questions that left her cold.

"I interviewed a few people who were at The Cromwellian that night. According to eyewitnesses, they heard you and Effy Halloran saying, and I quote, *'We're good at sharing,* and *very close indeed if you get our meaning.'* They also confirmed that you made similar comments about the young man in question. You must admit, that photo does look explicit? Put together, it implies a somewhat unusual relationship between the three of you. Do the three of you enjoy such a *sharing arrangement*?"

Caught out by the question, Angie felt herself blush. A glance at her sister confirmed this unexpected predatory question had also ambushed Gill. How should she respond?

Angie faltered for a moment. "We were only larking about having fun. There wasn't anything serious going on just the three of us having a laugh."

"It wasn't then…?" Fisher let it hang for a second, "…but is it now?"

"What are you implying about my sister and her friends?" Gill intervened unnerved by the reporter's question. It was the momentary distraction Angie needed to sort the thoughts in her head.

"If, and I repeat if, anything had happened, it would be no one's business but ours. We behaved that way to keep men away from us. As for an *arrangement,* why not try to understand that we three are business partners? We have our own modelling agency. Effy's design business ties in with the modelling. Mack is our photographer. So yes, we are close as business partners and as friends. We work together all the time."

"How about as lovers?" There was a suggestive salaciousness in the look she gave Angie. "According to another source, you and your friend Effy shared a bed together."

"We were staying in a one-bedroom flat. So yes, I shared a bed for the three nights we were in London. Mack slept on the sofa, and no, we're not lesbians. Let me repeat that, so there's no misunderstanding, we are not lesbians. I imagine your source is that rat, Joe Silvers. He's a two-faced untrustworthy liar. Now, unless you have questions to do with modelling or fashion, then this interview is over."

Mara Fisher tried to resume the interview, but Gill made it plain it was at an end. She and Angie had found the last few questions intrusive and disturbing. The reporter didn't appear to take any notice continuing to press with other questions.

"Tell me about the fight on Brixton Road in the early hours of Sunday, 25th March?"

"What fight?" Gill looked askance at Fisher, she knew nothing about it.

"Exactly. What fight?" Angie's response was guarded and frosty. "The fight that took place after you came out of the Ram Jam Club. You went to see Geno Washington and The Ram Jam Band that night, didn't you?" Taunted the reporter. "What have you to say to that?"

"Yes, we went. Afterwards, we took a taxi back to the flat. As for a fight, what fight?" Lie and deny was her only option. Whatever Fisher was angling to find out wasn't the kind of truth Angie wanted raking up about them. This could hurt Mack, even Effy and herself. There was only one possible source for all this. Joe Silvers. This entire interview smacked of a setup, and this reporter was hunting for something, anything. Anything, as long as it was scandalous, and about the three of them.

Robert MacKinnon rose to answer the telephone, wondering who could be calling this late. Ten minutes later, he knocked on his son's bedroom door. Mack was still working on a history essay due in the morning.

"What's the matter, Dad?"

"Ever heard of a reporter called Mara Fisher?"

"No. Should I?" Mack put the pen down, giving him his full attention.

"One of Fisher's nicknames in Fleet Street is Digger, and it's not because she's Australian. The other is The Poisoner. Fisher likes to dig up the dirt on people for the tabloids. As reporters go, Fisher is a well-known scandalmonger. I suspect Angie and Gill didn't know that. Angie's phoned to warn us that Fisher will try to interview Effy tomorrow. Then you, or anyone connected to you three. She tried to do that tonight with Angie. She suspects you and Effy can expect a visit from her tomorrow."

It wasn't what Mack wanted to hear but was grateful for her warning. "Is she okay?"

"She sounded upset and asked could you call tonight before going to bed. They still haven't had the telephone connected by the GPO. At least she can take incoming calls. I don't like the thought of a young woman like her having to go to a public phone box this late at night."

"I don't suppose Angie had much choice if she was going to warn us. I know Gill did as you suggested and requested an urgent business line connection. Shame the GPO's so slow. I'll call her in a minute. She may

40

know more about the woman's plans. A penny to a pound, she'll be making tracks here to plague Effy and her sisters at the school gates."

"Nothing much we can do about the GPO. They can't seem to keep up with a demand for new lines. Angie strikes me as intelligent and able, a most personable young woman who means a great deal to you and Effy." There was a peculiar look in his father's eyes saying those words while studying his son. "Otherwise, I would never have entertained her as a partner in the model agency scheme you three concocted."

"Yes, Angie means a great deal to Effy and to me." Mack's tone was bland, non-committal, and intended as a conversation stopper. "Look, Dad, I need to finish this essay for tomorrow, and it's late."

"I'd better let you get on with it. Don't stay up too late talking to Angie on the phone." As he went out, Robert MacKinnon turned to his son, adding cryptically. "I hope you three know what you've got yourselves into?"

Was he referring to their fledgling careers? Or was it a comment about their mutual relationship? Did his father suspect what was going on between them?

"That looks like the reporter Angie described." Robert MacKinnon was quick to identify the bottle blonde reporter.

As the car drew up outside the school gates, he and Effy had spotted her. Fisher appeared consumed with note taking as she interviewed a delighted Maria Sharpe.

"Trust her to find big mouth, Sharpe," Ellen muttered, unable to refrain from anger. "All she'll get from her is tittle-tattle gossip."

"That's all it will be," Effy added.

"Before you go, girls," Rob MacKinnon turned to them, "be careful what you say to anyone. This woman reporter has a fearful reputation for writing scurrilous articles. Ones that often have precious little to do with the truth. In fact, she's notorious for twisting the least interesting fact to make it sell."

The girls left the car with resolute swiftness heading for the main entrance. It had become routine, almost comical. Each day lower school pupils parted in awe like the Red Sea as the three walked through the playground. Today they heard the clatter of stiletto heels pursuing them. The reporter was intent on catching the three as they reached the doorway.

"Can I speak to you for a couple of minutes?" Fisher asked, trying to get her breath. "I'll only keep you a few mo….".

"No comment." The three replied in impassive unison.

"…ments."

"Grace, follow me please," Ellen instructed her sister. Only sixth-formers enter the building before school started.

"Now is it true …

Nothing appeared to discourage the reporter. She tried to follow them into the building. Effy, verging on explosive anger, maintained an iciness managing to speak before Ellen. Turning to face Fisher, arms outstretched wide, she prevented the woman from entering.

"Are you a member of the school staff, or the parent of a pupil? Clearly not, in which case you are trespassing. You have no right to be on these school premises. I suggest you leave."

"… you and Angela Thornton have an unusual relationship with…"

"I'm sorry." Interrupted Bruce Mainwaring appearing to the rescue as if from nowhere. "Who are you?"

"She's a pushy, ill-bred, ill-mannered reporter, sir." Effy's response was icy and cutting. "One incapable of understanding the words 'no comment', Sir. She's on the school premises without good reason or permission."

Mainwaring ushered the girls inside. With the utmost politeness and tact, he prevented the reporter from entering. The woman's impudence left the sisters bristling. Even as they disappeared from Fisher's sight, they could hear her. She was still trying to pump information from the teacher. Angie had been right to warn them.

The office staff let Grace stay outside the deputy head's office. She stood there fuming until they allowed the lower school into the classrooms.

Meanwhile, Ellen and Effy exchanged interesting words with the Head of the Sixth Form. Miss Thorpe refereed the conversation. Fisher's reputation as The Digger or The Peroxide Poisoner was not so well known to everyone. Effy found it tiresome. Even as she listened to the teachers, she was unaware of what was happening elsewhere.

It hadn't occurred to her to ask Mack why he was going so early. He had plans of his own; one's he had no intentions of sharing. Some things were better kept to himself. Any friend of Joe Silvers was no friend of his and deserved what came her way.

42

Mara Fisher cursed as her Hillman Minx ground to a halt outside the Mecca Locarno, on Manningham Lane. The smell of burning tyre rubber had hit her nostrils as she emerged from the motorcar. The two nearside tyres had gone flat. This was no accident. On arriving, the AA man agreed. Someone had placed tiny pieces of road grit inside the valve caps. Once the vehicle set off, these had caused the tyres to deflate with unerring slowness. She'd left her car unattended in nearby Cunliffe Terrace, and some hooligan must have done it.

Mack was fifteen minutes late to his first class of the day. Apologising to Sugar Ray, he put the camera bag down and took out a ring binder. Settling to making notes on the Third Crusade, his face contorted in a fiendish grin. Mara Fisher's deflated tyres would be the least of her problems. The photos he'd snapped this morning would tell an interesting tale. This Aussie madam would soon find she was the news instead of the one making it. Effy confronting her at the entrance to the school would look as professional as the best any paparazzi could manage.

Angie sounded upset when he'd called. Mack wished he could have put his arms around her. He'd been on the telephone for twenty minutes before heading upstairs, the last to get to bed. Everything Angie told him pointed to Joe Silvers involvement. There were certain things only Silvers could have known. Mack had made a promise to Joe Silvers. That promise remained unfulfilled. The next time they were in London, Mack would get even. A beating would serve no purpose, and it would only aggravate matters. He needed to set up an impersonal revenge. Business always had to come first before personal satisfaction. A subtle mental kicking would be the best kind of punishment.

During the morning break, Mack took out his well-thumbed copy of Machiavelli's *The Prince*. He hunted for inspiration. One of the many underlined passages came to him at once. *The lion cannot protect himself from traps. The fox cannot defend himself from wolves. One must therefore be a fox to recognise traps and a lion to frighten wolves. Those who simply act as lions are stupid.*

"Are you planning to stab someone in the back?" Jersey leaned over his shoulder. "You're always dipping into that Machiavelli book."

"Not just yet, Jersey, not just yet. You need to be a man with a cunning plan to wreak havoc. To have the plan, you need to know your enemy." Cunning needed to be part of any plan to get even.

"I could do with a plan. Tim is still being a pillock. He won't let it go about me going out with Chloe. We used to get along, now he's narked with me."

"It's never a good idea going out with a mate's ex. Especially when she did the dumping. I don't think I'd like it. It seems Tim doesn't either. There's nothing much you can do about it."

"So why's he so narked about it?" Nice guy Jersey was clueless in so many respects. Chloe was his first girlfriend.

"If it was the other way around, how would you feel? Could you stand the thought of him snogging her and doing all the things you might do together now, eh?"

"Yeah, but I have to live knowing that's what she did with him before she went out with me. Is that any different?" Jersey queried.

"Think of it this way. Tim feels like a failure because she ditched him, not the other way around. He thinks he wasn't good enough. That makes you seem better than him. In his mind, he's failed as a bloke. Jealousy is tough on the old emotions. He's jealous and upset. If you go all the way with Chloe, when he didn't, that'll be worse. And if he did and now it's you doing the deed well.... Does that make sense?"

Jersey blushed. "We haven't…"

"…neither has he."

"How do you know?"

Mack tapped his nose. "He hasn't. But you might if you play your cards right."

"Chloe is not like that!" Jersey protested.

"Not yet. That will upset him if or rather when it happens."

Jersey reddened.

CHAPTER 9

Take Some Time Out For Love – The Isley Brothers
(Tamla Motown TMG 566 – 1966)
Wednesday 26 April 1967

"She called round this afternoon." Jane MacKinnon informed her son. "I told Miss Fisher neither you nor the girls were available for an interview. Nor would you be. What an annoying woman. I had to shut the door in her face. She even had the cheek to put her foot in the door to stop me closing it. The woman appeared incapable of taking no for an answer."

"Did she now?" Mack kept a straight face. "Maybe her *tire-less pursuit* will slow down if she gets nowhere fast."

His mother was quicker to cotton on, giving him a knowing look. "She mentioned somebody had let the air out of the tyres on her car. I hope that wasn't you? It's a mean thing to do to anyone. Even to someone like Miss Fisher."

Never tell an outright lie unless unavoidable. Admit to nothing. Misdirect your answers. Mack applied these golden rules in response to his mum. "I don't even know the woman. Are Effy and Grace home yet?"

"They're upstairs in their room. The school sent them home an hour early to avoid the reporter. I had a call from Effy's English teacher, Miss Thorpe. The school thought it wiser to let them go early under the circumstances. It's getting past a joke. Your father told me this morning the woman also upset your friend Angie."

"I'll nip over to see Angie and Gill to find out what happened."

"What about homework?"

"There's nothing important. My maths got done in a free period. A few notes need writing up in neat for history. I'll go upstairs and have a word with Effy and Grace about what happened to them."

Grace was pinning a new outfit on Effy. "That looks good. Is it one of the designs for the London boutique or the catalogues?" He enquired.

"One for London," Effy replied. Grace's had a mouthful of pins. "What a day we've had. That awful woman reporter! Well, you warned us. What a way to carry on? We never expected her to behave like she did. I dread to think what Maria Sharpe told her. What was your day like?"

45

Now was not the time to enlighten them on his nefarious activity. The two girls sounded as if they were over the morning's incident. That was more important. Engrossed in what they were doing, both looked as though their concentration was on dress. He gave Effy a peck on the cheek, telling her he was heading over to see Angie. Was it a carelessness brought on by distraction? Or was it something else? Mack wasn't sure.

"She'll be late getting back from her evening class. Why don't you stay over with Angie tonight and ride back in the morning? She could do with a kiss and a cuddle after dealing with that woman." The words came out with unintentional thoughtlessness as Effy concentrated on what her sister was doing.

Grace almost swallowed the pins in her mouth, hearing those words coming from her sister.

Effy went red in an instant, realizing the slip-up. She tried to correct herself in what she hoped would sound blasé. "I meant to say I could do with a cuddle before you go after dealing with that woman."

Grace looked at Effy and began sticking the pins back in a pincushion. "I'll leave you two alone for a minute."

"I'm sure Gill won't mind you staying over on the settee." Effy attempted to correct her gaff as Grace was leaving the room. "I didn't mean it to come out like that."

Taking her in his arms, he pricked himself on a pin and pulled back. "Ouch. I just got one of those stuck in my hand."

Effy could not stop apologising for the slip and was almost in tears. She wasn't thinking straight. It had all got to her today. What with the teachers getting involved? Publicity was important, but not the scandalous kind. Having an infamous scandalmonger on their tail was something else. How had the reporter found out about the fight in Brixton? This was troubling, and she told him so. Her breath tickled him as she whispered in his ear. "Stay with Angie if she needs you. It's not like her to get so upset. I'll understand. I'll try to explain it away, what I let slip to Grace."

"That might be a good idea." He whispered back, the softness of her hair against his face, the jasmine scent she wore arousing. "That was so awkward. The look on your sister's face…do I need to say more?"

"What?"

"What!" Grace confronted Effy after he left. "Have you broken up with Mack?"

46

"Goodness, no, not at all. We're still together and inseparable."

"Then what was that all about saying he should stay overnight to kiss and cuddle her?"

This wasn't going to be easy. Effy had no intention of offering her an explanation and attempted to laugh it off, pretending this wasn't what she intended to say. She tried to explain that he should give *her* a kiss and a cuddle before going.

Grace did not believe her. "Are you letting Mack cheat on you with Angie?"

"No. You can't be serious. Letting Mack cheat on me?" How could it be cheating if he had her permission to be with Angie? It was an honest answer. He wasn't cheating, and neither was she and nor was Angie. They were sharing.

"Because that's how it came across to me." Grace continued refusing to cease her interrogation. "I like Angie lots, and I know she's your best friend, but lending your boyfriend out to her is ... well, I can't believe it. I knew something weird had happened when you three returned from London. Even his parents think there's something strange going on between you three. The MacKinnon's are just too nice to say anything. Ellen thinks so, and so does Tom. I dread to think what Alice makes of you three?"

"Give over, Grace!" Effy tried to laugh it off. "Lending Mack out? He's not a book. Listen, It was me having a brainstorm. There are too many things running through my head at the moment. Don't go imagining things, sis. It came out wrong, that's all. Lending him out? Honestly, Grace, whatever next?"

"No one knows you better than me. Ma put me in our bedroom at three months old. I'm still sharing a bedroom with you fifteen years later. You can't hide anything from me because I *know* you."

Grace was right; she knew her better than her other five sisters, better even than her own mother.

Effy had pledged she would never admit to their three-way romantic arrangement. Not even if the truth about it came out into the open. They'd agreed that what they had between them would always stay with them. Grace was the closest to her in her family but excluded from the truth. Had it been a wise decision? Only Gill Thornton knew the truth, but could they hide the truth forever? Could she?

Waiting for Angie, Gill recounted word-for-word what passed between them and Fisher. She fidgeted the whole time they spoke. When Angie came home, Gill relaxed in relief. Angie needed more than a kiss and a cuddle as reassurances. No sooner did she return than they found themselves in bed. Angie confirmed everything her sister had told him.

When he phoned home around midnight, his father's voice gave nothing away. Mack explained he needed to spend the night in Halifax. The scooter had a fault, and it was too dark to see to fix. Angie squeezed up to him in the telephone box, a hand over her mouth. Her dark eyes shone, showing she wanted him. They had left the warmth of her bed to make the call. She was naked under the coat. When he put the telephone down, her face lit up in excited delight. Her hands cradled his head, her lips leaving a trail of tiny kisses on his face.

"Back to bed. I'll make sure you're up early." Her smile was contagious.

"You mean you're going to let me get some sleep?"

"Well, not for a couple of hours. Later maybe."

"Maybe?"

"I want to make the best of tonight. Don't you?"

CHAPTER 10

The Girl Can't Help It – Little Richard (London 45-HL-0 8382 – 1957)

Thursday 27 April 1967 – Effy's day

Gill woke them. "Your Mum's on the phone." Bleary-eyed Mack checked Angie's alarm clock. Six- thirty a.m.

Racing downstairs in his underpants sobered him. Mack was awake by the time he reached the receiver. "What's the matter, Mum? Are you okay?"

His mother's tone gave nothing away. "I'm fine, James. Your father says you broke down last night. Will you be able to get into school this morning?"

"No problem. I'll be able to see what I'm doing and I'll fix it." There was no other way to bend the truth. He disliked having to lie. "Let Effy know I'll pick her up as agreed in case we've got problems with reporters."

"It won't be necessary." She sounded curt, not her usual self. "Bridget has arranged for her solicitor boyfriend Greg to take them. He's going to drop them off and pick them up after school."

"Why?"

"So Greg can have legal words with any reporters harassing our girls. That's what Bridget let me know over the phone ten minutes ago. Ellen let off steam in his and Bridget's presence yesterday evening. Listen, James, I don't want you messing up your A-Level studies, so fix the scooter and get to school. Don't forget to thank Gill and Angie for putting you up last night. And take care riding back. Don't go racing and having an accident."

"I need to come home first to get my briefcase."

Our girls. Mack liked that.

The goodbye with Angie was brief, rushed, and apologetic. Not the romantic moment Mack had wished for before leaving. Pressing a tiny package into her hand, he left a kiss lingering on her lips and went without saying another word. It was only on the road heading to Bradford via Queensbury that Angie's last words struck home. "Don't forget to give my love to Effy. And for heaven's sake, make it up to her! Don't forget. You need to keep both of us happy."

Mack made it in time, grabbing the briefcase from his mother's hands. She reminded him not to dawdle after school. Nate Silvers was due late afternoon to see him and Effy.

Jersey and Tim Smith had still not resolved their differences. Mack doubted they could. If he sided with either, then it would have to be with Jersey. Chloe had made the wisest choice in going out with Jersey.

Hardacre, Hardcastle, and Hewitt's offices were quiet. Only Mr Hewitt of the three partners was in and busy dealing with his house conveyance clients. Whatever needed filing, she dealt with efficiently. This left her with nothing to do in reception except daydream. There had been little time for sleep. As hard as she tried not to keep yawning, Angie couldn't stop thinking about the sex they'd had. She kept reliving the night's lovemaking. After returning from making the phone call, she'd wanted him a second time. Neither he nor she needed any encouragement for more passionate sex.

The tender touch of his tongue on her nipples had tingled, causing her legs to spread, ready to receive him. Oh, how she'd wanted him inside her. She wanted to feel stretched and filled, his body pressing down on her. He'd penetrated her with gentleness, avoiding inflicting any painful stabbing. The sensation of dilating to accommodate him had released the tension. It was so pleasurable it was the ideal of how sex should be. The tingling had increased, overpowering her senses as he'd moved inside her. She could not stop herself crying out on climaxing. He had responded to her climax with his own. The sensual delight in remembering how eager he'd been the second time that night had left her elated. She'd clung to him as they slept afterwards. Now in the light of day, she revelled knowing how much he'd wanted her not once but twice. It wasn't only the sheer physicality of the sex. The tender loving words they'd exchanged filled her with joy. She was so in love, she couldn't help it. Yet she couldn't stop asking, how could he love her and Effy so much at the same time? How could she love him knowing he made love to Effy? Angie just knew he did. She could tell. The new promise ring on the third finger of her right hand signified he cared for her. It matched the one he'd given to Effy before they had become a threesome. It was his promise to love her like Effy. What a beautiful gift it was, and she was going to treasure it forever.

"What's the matter, Grace?" asked her classmate, Jean Sienkiewicz. "You seem to be in a funny mood this morning. What's wrong?"

Maybe it was nothing. Maybe she was imagining it all. Since the London visit, Effy's behaviour had become strange. Something about her sister left her disturbed. And not only her behaviour, Angie was different too. As for Mack, he had changed. Now he gave nothing away. What on earth was going on between the three of them? Whatever it was, it wasn't something Grace could confide in her friend Jean. They'd known each since infant's school, yet she felt too ashamed to share it with her.

"Oh, it's nothing." Grace smiled, keeping her suspicions to herself. "Did you ask your mum if you could come and work for Effy and me? We need your extra pair of hands."

"Could I? Damn straight, I could!" Jean responded. "My mum didn't mind. You blew my sister away when she found out you and your sisters were modelling. She couldn't get over you and Effy making it as fashion designers too."

"Thank heavens it's okay. It's urgent. We need your help. Now she's expected to model and design, it doesn't give Effy any time to help me with the cutting and sewing. When you come round, you'll have to speak with Mrs MacKinnon. She'll put you on the payroll. The whole thing's becoming a roller coaster ride."

"And what about the modelling? You're a star too."

"You would think so, but I don't much feel like one."

"Gosh, I wish I had your looks and figure, Grace. You and your sisters look so fantastic. Oh, and that friend of Effy's, Angie Thornton. She's so stunning. What beautiful girls, Effy, and Angie are, they look so fab together. Bet they have to fight off the fellas."

"Yes, Angie's beautiful. I wouldn't know about fellas. Angie never tells me anything, but I'm sure there's no boyfriend. Angie's too particular when it comes to boys."

"Oh, before I forget, my sister was friends with Caitlin at school. She'd like to get in touch with her again. Could I have her address? And phone number if there is one?"

No reporters or photographers hung around outside the school gate to Effy's relief. Greg Williams reassured her and Grace that it was no trouble driving them to the school. It was in everyone's interest. A few words from a solicitor might have the desired effect should the need arise to confront reporters.

Walking down the corridor to registration, Effy saw Chloe talking with Katie Fox. This piqued her curiosity. Since apologising Katie Fox had become more amiable. Maria Sharpe continued to snipe snide comments within hearing distance. Girls like Sharpe bullied others. They tried to destroy self-confidence in them to bolster their fragile egos. There was nothing Sharpe could do to intimidate Effy. Her sole concern was the lies Sharpe might have invented for the reporter's benefit. As she came closer, she could see Katie Fox's upset. What Katie and Chloe recounted next in whispers left her smouldering. It took all Effy's self-restraint not to seek out and hit the catty-mouthing gossiper.

During the lunch break, Katie Fox joined her and Chloe. To Effy's surprise, Katie uttered an apology. "I'm sorry for all the times I've said nasty things to you. They weren't at all nice. I hope you can forgive me." There was relief in Katie's face as the words tumbled out. Many truths came out during lunchtime.

"Katie's right," Chloe mumbled. "Before I knew you in the Sixth Form, those who had known you before thought you were standoffish. They said you were quiet and didn't mix. You always hung about with your sisters. That didn't help matters."

"And your looks," added Katie.

"My looks?" Queried Effy. "I don't get it."

Chloe and Katie exchanged looks. "Go on, Katie. Tell her why."

"Tell me what?"

"Effy doesn't see it, Katie."

Effy, bewildered, saw the looks exchanged between the two girls.

Katie blurted out, "You've intimidated most of us."

"Me?" Effy sat back, stunned. "How? I've never done anything to anyone in school."

"You never had to. You just had to be you, like some goddess among mere mortals. You're just too good looking for your own good," Katie added.

After a few moments, she continued. "When the rest of us had spots or acne, there you were with your perfect complexion. No spots, no blackheads, nothing. The only problems you had were the occasional bags under your eyes. Your hair always shines; it never has any split ends. Those fingernails, manicured to perfection, never bitten. You are always, always, so

52

neat with never anything out of place. For heaven's sake, how can anyone make our school uniform look elegant? Yet guess who does? When the rest of us went through hell with periods, you never appeared to have a problem. Have you any idea how annoying it was and still is seeing you? You made and make the rest of us feel inferior. Then to top it off, you're some brainy genius, a cross between the next Mary Quant and Twiggy. Then there's that awesome good-looking boyfriend of yours. My God! No wonder we're envious and bitchy. Your problem is you're too bloody perfect and successful, Effy Halloran. And the worst of it is you're such a lovely person."

Chloe shrugged and tried to bring a little levity to Katie Fox's words. "The girl can't help it." Moments later Chloe burst into the Little Richard songs with the same words.

Effy cut Chloe off, addressing the other. "It's not how I see myself, Katie. I've never seen myself that way. I'm just me. I can't help being me. I'm not perfect, and my life's not been perfect, far from it. Do you want to know what my life's been like?"

Hearing Effy's story about the tyrannical treatment she and her sisters had received from her father before his breakdown left Katie Fox and Chloe numb.

CHAPTER 11

With This Ring – The Platters (Stateside SS 2007 – 1967)
Thursday 27 April 1967 – Mack's day

The promise ring had been Effy's idea. "Give her a promise ring the same as mine to show you care. She loves you as I do. She deserves something better. Better than that cheap gold effect Lucite ring she bought in Woolies."

That record by The Marvelettes kept playing in his head. It had a mesmeric quality. *The Day You Take One (You Have To Take The Other)*. Effy was right. Angie deserved better, and it was up to him. Listening to Mr Gaylor's droning on about the sanctity of marriage in the RE lesson set him thinking. The two girls in his life were a constant. He hadn't asked to fall in love with both of them. Nor had he expected Angie to be so in love with him. If it had been a temporary infatuation, he might have understood, but it wasn't. Nor had he expected Effy to agree to share him with Angie, nor for Angie to agree to share him with Effy. Loving both was fine in theory but altogether something else in practice. He needed to do much better for the three of them if this was going work.

When Effy and Angie were together, he could tell how close their friendship had become. They had grown inseparable. Walking in front of him in London, he'd noticed how they linked arms. Chatting, smiling, giggling, exchanging whispered confidences, he'd felt left out. The way they looked to one another when talking told Mack everything he needed to know. They shared a closeness he'd only seen between Grace and Effy, the intimacy of sisters. A powerful mutual trust was at work. He couldn't fathom why, but he recognised it as an exceptional bond.

"According to the Church's teaching, and I quote here from the catechism, *Polygamy is contrary to conjugal love which is undivided and exclusive.*" Mr Gaylor announced to a disinterested group. At which point Mack debated with himself for a split-second: should he speak, or should he keep quiet? The last time he'd spoken in the class, he'd caused a theological uproar.

"What about polygamy in the OT Mr Gaylor? Didn't Solomon have hundreds of wives and concubines? He wasn't the only one either, was he?

Come to think of it I don't remember seeing JC quoted in the NT saying they'd banned polygamy."

Gaylor held his breath for a full two seconds. A look resembling panic appeared on his haggard face. Teaching RE was not Gaylor's favourite activity, more a matter of timetabling inconvenience. Mack watched him exhale, trying to control his breathing before stuttering out a reply. "Are you going to subject us to another theological rant, MacKinnon? Because if so, can I remind you this is a Catholic institution based on Catholic beliefs."

It was amazing how the group's interest level spiked the moment Mack spoke. A quick glance at Jersey's grinning face spoke volumes. Looking around the others, he could see they waited with bated breath for the sport to begin.

"I was asking a straightforward question, sir. If you like, for the next lesson, I'll turn up with all the relevant bible references on polygamy in the OT. Chapter and verse."

"If by NT and OT you mean the New and Old Testament, then refer to them as such. Furthermore, Our Lord Jesus Christ banned polygamy in the New testament.

"No, he didn't," Mack replied.

"Yes, he did, MacKinnon. Catholics don't believe in polygamy. Marriage is a sacrament between *a man* and *a woman*."

"That may be so, sir. But it doesn't say anywhere in the Bible that polygamy isn't allowed. Does it? Not in so many words. The Church pays lip service to the Bible to suit its own ends. Doesn't it?" Gaylor's emotional fuse went from lit to explosive anger in an instant.

"Has this anything to do with your own much-publicised harem MacKinnon?" Gaylor barked. "Presumably, you'd like polygamy legalised?"

There was an outburst of sniggering from the group.

"Mr Gaylor! Do I detect a hint of envy?" Mack shammed, stunned surprise. It was irresistible.

Raucous laughter broke out in the group.

It didn't go down well.

Later in the day, the Head of the Sixth Form pulled him up for his attitude in the RE class. Mack found it risible as he listened. The proverbial phrase about water and a duck's back sprang to mind. When told to apologise to Gaylor, he refused point-blank. Mack detailed the teacher's deficient scriptural knowledge. He mentioned Gaylor's insinuation that he was a polygamist. The teacher had implied he had his own personal harem. Well, it was true he supposed though he didn't think of Effy and Angie as his harem. Tired of verbal game playing and barrack-room lawyer tactics, the teacher reached a decision. Mack no longer had to attend RE lessons. Instead, he could take extra General Studies running at the same time. Once out of sight, Mack punched the air in triumph.

"You jammy twat! No more RE!" Jersey was envious when he found out. "Mind you, I'm not surprised. It'll be a relief for Gaylor knowing he's got shut of you. Looks like you've wangled a get out of jail free card."

Mack spotted Nate's Mini Cooper parked outside the house as soon as he and Effy arrived home. He heard his mother's laughter on coming in through the back door. Nate must have spent the time waiting by regaling his mum with amusing anecdotes. From her voice and his cheery tones, they sounded in good humour. Mack and Effy felt done in, the day had taken its toll on them both.

"Silvers Fashions needs you and the girls in Manchester on Saturday. They have an important fashion promotion to stage for a big buyer. Mr Silvers wants you to travel over on Friday evening."

"What? Grace too?" Effy looked concerned.

"Grace too. And Alice." Nate confirmed. "I know it's short notice, but we need all the girls on Saturday morning. I may even need to hire two extra local models. We've landed some new buyers. This one on Saturday is a big, big deal, a whopper in fact if it comes off. The buyer is American. She's coming from London keen to see the rest of our range, to be exact, Effy's. After seeing your shots in magazines, they've left quite an impression on our American. I'm heading back to Manchester by Halifax. On the way, I'll call at Alice's and Angie's okaying it with them. We've organised for all six of you to stay over at my place."

"You've got your own place?" Effy found it surprising.

"My father told me to buy the house last year as an investment. Property is the way to go. I've had it done up. It's not quite finished: only a few small jobs need doing. Some bedrooms are only part furnished, but they have beds."

"Am I needed?" Asked Mack.

"Bring all your camera gear. We'll want lots of shots, in colour."

"What about lights? If it's indoor work, I'll need decent lighting. Mine are too heavy to carry over."

"Our exhibition area is well equipped. It's not large, and it's attached to our main offices, but it should work for you. There are lights galore installed, and they're adjustable. We need to get everyone ready really early on Saturday morning. A dress rehearsal, before the buyer arrives at eleven. Then we want to do a promo shoot downtown outside one of the boutiques in the afternoon. We've started rebranding. Ring me at the works and let me know the time of the train you'll be on. I'll organise taxis to pick everyone up from Piccadilly Station. Just in case there's a problem, here's the address. My place is in Altrincham. Someone will let you in. My kid sister, as I'm likely to be working late, setting up."

CHAPTER 12

Happy Together – The Turtles (London HLU 10115 – 1967)
Friday 28 April 1967

Nate's house in Willow Tree Road was impressive. The four-storey Victorian red brick terrace with its grand bay windows surprised them. They had not expected Nate to live in something so imposing. The front door opened as they approached, their arrival expected. Diminutive, dark-haired, with an olive complexion like her brother, Nate's sister greeted them. Sara Silvers still wore her Manchester High School for Girls uniform. Mack struggled to work out how old she was. At a glance, she looked younger than Grace. As it was, she was the same age.

The journey from Manchester to Altrincham had taken longer than expected. The four of them squeezed into the single taxicab hired to fetch them. With all their bags and Mack's camera equipment, they'd only just managed. Sara let them know Angie and Alice were already here and upstairs. Effy and Ellen were to share a bedroom on the third floor with Angie and Alice next to them. She and Grace would be on the second floor. Mack would have to sleep downstairs in the main reception room. The enormous chocolate brown leather Chesterfield looked big enough to accommodate him.

"It's lovely to meet you. Have we stopped you from going to the synagogue?" Mack asked.

"No." Sara's face blushed with a shy smile, "we're not religious. My mum used to go when she was tiny, but me, my dad or my brothers and sister don't. I've been dying to meet you all. Nate and my father are always talking about you and Effy. They can't get over her designs, and they adore your photography. Nate thinks you're both brilliant. I think you girls are so gorgeous."

"Where is your brother this evening?"

"He's with my father and my mother at the Midland Hotel in Manchester entertaining some buyers from London. He told me to tell you he'll be late back tonight and we shouldn't wait up. That's why he asked me to act as hostess. There's food laid on. My mother prepared a buffet in the kitchen. It's set out when you're all ready."

"That was kind of your mother," Effy answered on their behalf. "Shall we see where we're sleeping and freshen up?"

Grace and Sara chatted about all sorts once they got into the room they were sharing. They had the smallest room, the one with two new single divan beds. The headboards still needed fitting and were stood in a corner. Sara told her she had helped to choose the wallpaper, as this would be her room when she stopped over. Patterned with small dark green daisy flowers on a pastel green, it was distinctive. Grace learned the decorator had only finished this room a day earlier. It still had that fresh, newly pasted, smell. A knock on the door brought their chatter to an end as Alice Liddell appeared.

"Are you two coming down to join the rest of us?" Asked the tall, super slim girl as she peered into the room. "We're all waiting for you so we can get a bite to eat."

Upon entering the main reception room, it was the expression on Ellen's face that struck Grace. A moment later, she realized why as her eyes were drawn to the Chesterfield. Angie was seated cuddled up next to Mack on his left. Her head rested on his shoulder. Effy, on his right, mirrored Angie. Her right arm rested on Mack's other shoulder. Immersed in a copy of Vogue, they hadn't noticed her return. Grace's heart began pounding. She could feel the blood rushing to her face, the redness forming in her cheeks.

Why wasn't Effy playing merry hell with Angie? Why was Angie behaving in such an over familiar way with Mack? Grace couldn't make sense of it. By her sister's expression, neither could Ellen. Even Sara seemed nonplussed. Only Alice showed no surprise. Grace wasn't sure which was worse? Seeing the three of them so relaxed and happy together? Or? Seeing Alice's cool indifferent acceptance of the situation?

Noticing Grace staring, Angie unfurled her long legs in a slow, smooth lissom motion. "Glad you finally came down, Gracie. We thought you and Sara had disappeared for the night."

Effy uncurled herself from Mack. "Aren't you hungry, Grace? Everyone else is ready for some supper."

It was so peculiar. Not only was it bizarre, but it was overstepping boundaries. Her sister didn't mind Angie draped over him in such an intimate manner. She had only seen such closeness between Effy and Mack before. Nor did he appear to mind treating it as quite normal with unbelievable casualness. If she were Effy, she would be so angry at Angie's behaviour. Yet here they were, the three of them. Happy, smiling with no hint of jealousy, it seemed inexplicable that this could be happening. Grace wanted to scream. "What on Earth are you three playing at? This is so wrong."

While the others were still eating, Grace and Sara went to the kitchen. It was on a pretext to make a pot of tea. Alice came to help. Grace found she couldn't hold it in any longer. Everything she was feeling flowed out in a torrent of hushed words. Alice gave her a strange and disconcerting look.

"Haven't you and Ellen figured it out yet?"

"Figured what out?" Alice's words puzzled her.

"It's so obvious. Effy and Angie are sharing Mack. It's a threesome."

"What?" Exclaimed Sara open-mouthed.

"What do you mean *sharing*? Threesome?" Queried Grace. "They can't be!"

"They must have agreed to become a threesome."

Grace and Sara looked at one another, speechless. After a moment or two, Sara spoke. "Well, that's different if it's true."

"Oh, it's true. It's the only explanation. If not for that beautiful friendship your sister has with Angie, it would have ended long since. How else do you explain their behaviour? Angie looks the happiest I've ever seen. Effy's not complaining or looking in the least bit bothered. I don't see her trying to scratch Angie's eyes out or tearing her hair out by the roots. They don't look jealous, do they? Sorry Grace, but you'll find what I'm saying is true."

"When I asked Effy if she was loaning Mack out to Angie, she denied it!"

Alice suppressed a laugh for a brief moment, before bursting out laughing aloud. "He's not an object to loan out silly. Listen, Grace, she's bound to deny it. The three of them must have agreed to share between themselves."

"But, she denied it!"

"Listen," continued Alice, "your sister's not going to admit to sharing, is she? It's not the kind of arrangement most people would regard as a normal relationship. The thought of it would shock most people. I imagine they don't want this becoming common knowledge. Besides, it's no one's affair but theirs."

"Wow!" Sara sounded amused and astonished, "Two girls sharing one boy. That's so out of sight! I've never had a boyfriend, but if I did, I'd want him to myself. I couldn't imagine sharing him with another girl."

"I'm going to have it out with them." Grace was a mixture of anger, sadness, embarrassment, and disbelief.

"No, Grace." Alice counselled. "Effy may be your sister. Angie and Mack may be your friends, but it's not for you to meddle or involve yourself. They won't thank you for interfering. I suspect they didn't go into this arrangement without talking it over. There's more there than the three of them will admit to you, me or anyone else. Whatever their relationship is, it's personal to the three of them. Let the whole thing rest, Grace. It's their life and their choice no matter what we or anyone else thinks. Besides, haven't you noticed something different that's the big giveaway clue?"

"What's that?"

Alice smiled that kind of irritating knowing smile that was her trademark. "Do you remember the first time I came to Mack's, just after my test shoot? They wore those Lucite rings and talked about how they were wedded to their business?"

"Yes, Angie kept teasing me. She said something like the three of them were serious."

"That's right. Did you notice they've stopped wearing them? Have you looked at the promise ring on Effy's third finger right hand? Of course, you have. Gorgeous, isn't it? It's almost as good as an engagement ring. Isn't it? I bet you didn't notice the same ring on Angie's third finger right hand? Call yourself a girl? What are you like? Buying rings like those must have cost Mack a bob or two. Why else would he buy them identical rings? Why would they wear them? They're not exactly cheap costume jewellery. We're talking serious money here. And they both *know* about each other's rings. Friends don't miss things like this. Seems like sisters do."

Grace flushed with embarrassment and annoyance. She ought to have noticed.

Later, before they went off to bed, Grace let Ellen know what passed between her and Alice. She mentioned the rings too. To Grace's surprise, Ellen sighed, admitting to having seen the rings. Yes, she and Tom suspected something was going on between them. Yes, they'd changed since their jaunt to London. Something strange had taken place to bring them together. Effy and Angie seemed okay with it, whatever it was they had going on together. Ellen confessed she didn't have a clue what to say to them, let alone even if she should. Tom had wanted to find out what the three were playing at, but the resulting slap down stopped him asking. Alice was right. They shouldn't interfere. It was Effy's choice, even if they thought it wrong.

CHAPTER 13

You've Got To Pay Price – Al Kent (Track 504016 – 1967)
Saturday 29 April 1967 – Early hours.

Mack wished he could have slept with Effy. The guilt he felt about having spent so much more time with Angie hit home. Perhaps he'd tried too hard to make up for all the heartache Angie had suffered. Now the difficulty of having two girls in his life was foremost in his thoughts. Trying to love two was proving harder to do in daily life. Mack needed both to know he loved them. Proving it wasn't so easy. He'd had to wait for an opportune moment to hug and kiss each of his girls on their own. Then there were the strange looks from Effy's sisters. Grace's shocked looks this evening didn't come as a surprise. By now, Grace must have worked out what was going on between the three of them? They weren't exactly hiding the arrangement any longer though not admitting it existed. Only Alice didn't appear shocked or surprised. Mack guessed she'd sussed out what was going on, and that didn't bother her.

The light in the room came on, waking him after what seemed like two-minutes. For several seconds he tried to recall where he was. Nate Silvers came in looking tired and tipsy.

"Sorry to wake you, Mack. I forgot you were sleeping downstairs." Nate slumped in an armchair. He began to loosen his tie and unbuttoning his shirt. "We've been wining and dining our American. Then my father insisted on doing the rounds of the city's cabaret clubs and casino. I hope it was worth all the effort."

Mack watched him slip off his Bass Weejuns and recline into the armchair. "Are the girls all tucked up in bed and fast asleep?"

"Yeah. They all went up about half-past ten to get their beauty kip for tomorrow. Sara's been an excellent hostess."

Nate shrugged his shoulder. "Sara's a great kid, isn't she?"

Before Mack realized they were talking long into the early hours. What surprised Mack was how open Nate became. This was the first time they'd had a proper man-to-man conversation.

"You know I'm a homo, don't you? Bent like a corkscrew, a regular nine-bob note?" The question came from nowhere.

"And?"

"You don't have a problem with that or me?"

"No. Should I?"

"Guys who aren't homosexual do. They find queers like me, scary. Sometimes, I try to imagine being heterosexual. Life would be so much easier if I was straight. I do even wonder what it might be like to fancy a woman? I am what I am. My private life is lived in the shadows. I hide my true self from everyone, except others like me. You, on the other hand, are a true *mensch* in every sense of the word. That's what I like about you, Mack. That, and the fact you don't give a damn about my being homosexual."

"The law is going to change. It won't be illegal by the end of the year." Mack commented.

For a minute, Nate lost himself in silent reveries. "Do you know what 'mensch' means?" He asked.

"A man?"

"It means so much more than a man. It means an honourable man, one who has integrity, and all the usual attributes of a man. I envy that, and what you have with Effy even though I don't have any interest in women. Mind you, I've always suspected something was going on between you and Angie as well as Effy. And I'm right.

Angie's eyes sparkle when she's near you. She's a good girl, funny, and down to earth. And you Mack, I liked from the first time we met at her party. Don't ask why. Anyway, we're none of us, as we seem. Know what I'm saying?

This dangerous dude who you see in me, the guy at the thick end of local crime? He can't exist anymore. There's no choice the way things are panning out in my life. In a way, Effy, Angie, and you, have become my saving grace at just the right moment."

Nate fell silent for several seconds then resumed. "Do you know I went to the original Twisted Wheel in Brazennose Street? I went when the Abadi's first opened the club. That was before this one in Whitworth Street. I'm twenty-two and the time's arrived to grow up. It's time for me to take on real responsibilities, more so since golden wonder boy was removed from the business.

Manny's now in London, so I'm needed more than ever to help run things here. If the business expands as planned, I have to step up and take my share of the responsibility. He'll expect me to run things in London real soon. There's no more playing at being a businessman; I have to treat the work with seriousness. It doesn't help to know that my father has a potential bad heart condition. We depend on him as the head of the family and the business. If anything happened, I'd be the one left to run it. The family business would have to come first because the family must always come first. Our family is the business."

"What about the pill peddling?"

Nate shook his head. "I don't know why I ever got involved. It must have been the thrill of doing something illegal and heading a gang. Guess I was sixteen when it started; it was a game in the beginning, and about playing the top tough guy. I just wanted to prove I was harder and tougher than my big brother. Joe was always the *wunderkind.* He was always seen as the sparkling future of the business. Turned out, he was nothing more than a polished turd, still full of shit on the inside. Joe was a greedy, avaricious swine, even when he was ten years old. A bullying bastard who beat me up whenever my parents weren't around. He knew I was *fegeleh,* a homo, and played on the fact.

After finding out how Joe tried to ruin the business and hurt the family, I had to change and he had to pay. The best thing my father did was to get shut of his swindling ways. For that, we have to thank you for helping. What you did wasn't easy and without the evidence, we wouldn't have had the proof. We, the family, owe you big time. Anyway, my dealing's days are now done. My former associates are running the local racket. Good luck to them. One day their luck will run out. The feds will come knocking but I won't be around when that happens."

"While you're mentioning Joe, I have a score to settle with him."

"Is this still about the fight outside the Ram Jam Club?" Nate chuckled. "And I thought I could bear grudges."

"There's that too. This is about a certain reporter. One called Mara Fisher and her connection to Joe."

"*The* Mara Fisher? The one they call Digger or The Poisoner?" Nate's interest seemed to wake him from succumbing drowsiness.

"That's the one. The Peroxide Poisoner."

"As reporters go, she's a prime example of a shit-stirring scandalmonger. Most reporters are just gossipers, but that one's in a league of her own. Looks like you three have a tiger on your tail."

64

"Fisher's a tiger about to get swung by her tail." There was real venom in Mack's words. "I'm expecting to see something in print real soon. Missy Fisher is going to need more than God's help when it goes to press. I made some useful press contacts that Saturday in London. I didn't know that at the time when I contacted her. The dope I have on Fisher gave the lady an orgasm over the phone. Her editor wanted what I had to offer them on Fisher as soon as I could get it to them in the post."

Nate perked, up grinning. "Okay, what's going on? What's the story?"

Mack then recounted the events involving the reporter. He related how she was in pursuit of any scandal surrounding him and the girls. Where the information had come from was obvious. Only Joe Silvers could have known about the fight. He was the one who organised it. And there had been the other slip-ups like the one about Effy and Angie sharing a bed. Nate listened, his brow furrowing the more he learned. There was a prolonged silence after Mack finished. Nate was weighing up how to reply. When he did, Mack found his comments worth hearing. The most interesting of which was that even bad publicity, could turn out as good publicity. When Nate knew about the photographs Mack had snapped, he liked it even more. This was a way to turn bad publicity into top-class publicity. Now he understood why Mack was so keen to get back at his brother. Joe deserved everything he got.

"Don't try beating the crap out of Joe. It wouldn't surprise me if he hired a professional hitman to retaliate. My advice, be real careful. Joe can be as nasty and as dangerous as a scorpion." Nate cautioned, making it clear he wasn't joking.

"No, violence won't sort him. I've figured that out. Sometimes a kicking just won't do. I suspect you're right about him hiring a hitman. Your brother's the kind of guy who would hire one. He's already got a major downer on the three of us. Anyway, he deserves a far more subtle and suitable punishment. One without my paw marks left behind."

Nate gave him a wicked smile. "Mack, I like your thinking. You're a young guy who thinks the way I do. You deserve to get even. As for my dear brother, Joe deserves everything coming his way. Anything I can do to help, just ask. There's no love lost where Joe's concerned. One day, I'll tell you how he tried to get me nicked by the feds, in the nastiest way possible. I can never forgive my brother for what he tried to do."

What Nate said next made Mack's ears prick up. Manny had telephoned in the morning. A girl had applied for a position at Moods Mosaic, claiming to know Mack.

"Tina Wood said you and the girls met her outside the Ram Jam Club in Brixton. She says she helped you to find a taxicab. Miss Wood is looking for a sales assistant's job at the boutique. She told Manny you might be willing to recommend her for the position. I said I'd check with you."

"Oh, yeah." Mack smiled, recollecting Ronnie Sykes's tiny sparrow-like girlfriend. "Cockney lass. Yes, I remember Tina. I can't say I know the girl, but she helped after the punch up. She seemed a pleasant sort if awestruck by Effy and Angie. Manny should give the girl a trial."

A moment later, Mack added, "Oh! Ask Manny for Tina's contact details. I promised to send an autographed photo of Effy and Angie but mislaid the girl's address."

The address part was fiction, as was the photograph part. Having a friend on the ground in London might prove useful. Tina Wood was Ronnie Sykes's girlfriend, and Ronnie and Tina could have contacts to get info on Joe Silvers.

CHAPTER 14

It's Growing – The Temptations (Tamla Motown TMG 504 – 1965)
Saturday 29 April 1967

The lengthy conversation with Nate had dragged on into the early hours. They roused him at seven. Head thick and thumping after only five hours of sleep, he had to wait to get into one of the two toilets hogged by the girls. Everyone rushed breakfast, the girls hardly touching food excited by the coming shoot. Mack found no chance to speak with either Effy or Angie, even after reaching Silvers Fashions.

The dark red brick Victorian building was in an area of Manchester populated by similar buildings. The exterior looked dismal. The interior defied expectations. To one side of the courtyard were modern workshops, the two-storey offices in the opposite corner. Once inside, Nate's father welcomed the group. Following Alex Silvers, they entered a large room next to the upstairs offices. This contained a tiny low-level stage and a short catwalk platform. There was insufficient room behind the powder blue velour curtains and changing room. So Mack didn't venture in there.

The seating area contained plush chairs and sofas in curtain matching blue upholstery. Adjustable installed lights made Mack's task easier. Using his light meter, he soon knew where to position the cameras. Sara helped him to set distance and focal lengths while the girls prepared for the showing. It didn't take too long to work out where to find the best angle shots. One camera was arranged on a tripod with a remote wired control. The other he intended for hand-held shots. They did a quick dry run-through for the thirty-minute display of Effy's designs.

The American buyer was not what they expected. They had been surprised to learn that it was a woman, not some fat, middle-aged, cigar-chomping businessman

Pearl Piper was nothing like they could ever have imagined. At five foot ten in heels, she was statuesque, elegant, with shoulder-length chestnut brown hair. She looked like a former model turned fashion editor. The kind Mack imagined he'd expect to meet in the offices of *Vogue* or *Queen*. Even the name suggested glamour. Piper, poised and self-assured, spoke with a slow lazy drawl. The kind he often associated with Western movies. The woman came from Texas, according to Nate.

Working for AIC-InStyle, Piper was seeking new lines and designs for the New York-based specialist fashion marketing and distribution group. With its statewide wholesale and retail operations, it functioned through numerous specialist sub-companies. It was the real big deal for handling imports and sales.

Piper was dismissive when introduced to Mack. She paid him no attention either before or during the showing. Not that it troubled him. Mack was too preoccupied with the technicalities of the photo shoot. Today's photographs he sensed would be terrific, and he was not wrong. The showroom was perfect for a fashion shoot.

Mack was on fire, even though knackered from a lack of sleep. The girls, strutting on top form, performed each walk on with sparkling fluidity. Switching outfits appeared slick, making the showing appear smooth and synchronized to perfection. Nate did the description of each outfit as they walked on. Effy's designs looked terrific. Grace and Alice amazed, giving him an, oh so bloody perfect performance shoot. Ellen, Angie, and Effy, classy and beautiful, wove magical spells as they paraded before them. They moved with glamorous flowing movements. The girls rocked the showing. He applauded them on the final group walk-on at the end, after the final click of the camera. The girls got better and better with each new shoot. Mack thrilled, knowing his coterie of models was so slick and so professional. None had ever set foot in a modelling school, yet were naturals, brilliant naturals. Ellen later confessed that the changing area was completely chaotic and was amazed to hear how smoothly it had gone out front.

After the show, the Silvers and Pearl Piper became locked in a lengthy discussion. Nate disappeared only to return with Effy scant moments later. More involved conversation followed with Effy giving brief responses. He was too far away to hear what she said. She had that determined look he knew well, and some negative shaking of the head accompanied it.

He left the room to reload the Leica with a fresh spool of film. The IIIf was perfect for hand-held shots. Mack knew the importance of having a new film loaded. These days he looked for potential new locations and backgrounds with his camera at the ready. Anywhere that could be used in the future, he snapped to remind him for possible future use. Storing the used spools of film, he returned to see Effy glancing over to him.

Something important was under discussion. Using the forefinger of his left hand, he tapped it below his left eye. Effy nodded, showing she understood he was taking in what was happening. Removing the tripod-mounted camera, he noticed Pearl Piper giving him brief hard glances. Nate broke away from the group and sauntered over to him.

"The lady will want to have a chat with you. Effy's sung your praises. She says she won't work with anyone but you. Nor will Angie, or the others."

Mack said nothing in reply. A sly wink was the only sign he gave Nate. Each understood the other. They needed no further words. He didn't realize it yet, but in Nate, he would have a friend and an important ally when things went wrong.

Close up, Piper had steel grey eyes. There was no subtleness in them or in her voice. If anything, there was something about the woman he disliked and distrusted almost from the first words they exchanged. She tackled him with the domineering bluntness of one who expected underlings to jump and say yes. Treating him like a pushover schoolboy proved the wrong tactic, making Mack smile. The type of smile Pearl Piper least expected. Trying to browbeat him on account of age was a serious misjudgement.

Changing tactics, Piper tried to appeal to Effy, "Boyfriends come and go. Top modelling career opportunities are few and need seizing when they arise. If you came over to the States, we could guarantee that you'd work with the best. The top fashion photographers like Avedon, Penn, and Devane."

Mack kept the tone neutral, non-confrontational, and diplomatic. He had no intention of playing the callow youth about to get trampled under this woman's stiletto heels. They would not go without him, and he would not go without his girls. Glancing, he saw Angie peering through the curtains. She was listening to everything. Mack snapped his fingers and watched as Angie stepped out on cue to stun the American.

"Miss Piper wants you and Effy to go to the States to model for her company."

"Just Effy and me?"

"Yes."

"Without you?"

"Yes."

"No chance. You're our photographer, and we're your muses." Angie responded with typical Yorkshire bluntness.

"A model needs a rapport with her photographer. That's what we have." Added Effy.

It looked choreographed yet appeared spontaneous. Effy and Angie each placed an arm around Mack resting their heads against his shoulders.

"It's the three of us." Angie began.

"Or it's none of us." Continued Effy.

"Take it or leave it." Added Mack.

Their impressive coolness and unity stunned Piper. Nate joined in the conversation. "Mack's the up and coming new young fashion photographer. You may not have heard of James 'Mack' MacKinnon yet, but all the fashion shots we've shown here are his." Surprise surfaced on Piper's face for a moment before disappearing. Alex Silvers listed the magazines where Mack's work had featured in recent weeks. Nate mentioned they had back copies in the office. Also the original studio photos for the catalogue companies. Would she care to see these?

"We'll leave you to talk." Effy patted Mack's rear as she left. This did not pass unnoticed by Piper. The girls returned to the changing area.

Piper studied Mack while taking in the Silvers sales pitch.

What was the woman thinking? Mack watched her mental cogs whirring. He could almost see her thought process at work. There was a kind of transparency about her. What he read left him with an unambiguous bad feeling. Miss Piper hadn't become an international buyer without being good at what she did. Wielding a powerful business clout meant this was a shrewd and tough businesswoman. He was certain she'd try to manipulate the three of them. That he wouldn't allow. Any game playing, and he would match it with his own brand of shrewdness.

What he lacked in experience Mack intended to do with all the cunning and deviousness he could muster. The only tune played would be of his choosing, not hers. The only game he played would also be one of his choosing. This was one Piper he did not intend paying. Nor of allowing his girls to vanish across the Atlantic without him. The Hamelin connection brought on a crooked smile. If there were any rats to sort out, Mack planned to do it himself.

The talking went on and until it reached a natural break. Mack expected Piper to engage him one to one. When it came, no preparation

70

could have foreseen the confrontation. Or the future fall out resulting from the next few minutes.

"If you cross me, they could lose this deal."

Mack left a long pause before replying.

"And this boat could sail if you're not careful." What Mack said next sounded like a bad line from a bad movie. "You won't be the only game coming to town."

Piper's smile was unpleasant. "Young man, you're a nobody, who doesn't even know what the game is."

"I'm seventeen, not stupid, *Missy* Piper." The insult was intentional.

"Ha! You're a minor not even old enough to vote, let alone represent anyone. I bet you don't even have a manager?"

"My father is our legal representative and authorised to act on all our behalves. There's a contractual arranged partnership linking our modelling agency to my photography. It's legal and formalised. All the girls here today are with the agency. We have our own financial experts too. My father is a banker, and my mother is an accountant. Effy's sister's boyfriend is a solicitor, or what you Yanks call a lawyer and our legal advisor."

"I see."

"No. I don't think you do. Effy and Angie are already in demand as models, so are her sisters and Alice. We're not tied to the Silvers for modelling, only for Effy's designs. If you want to sell Effy's designs, deal with Mr Silvers. If you want Effy or Angie as models, you deal with us direct. Threats don't intimidate us and maybe not even the Silvers. Something makes me think there will be other interested American buyers. In fact, I'd lay good odds on that."

"So, young man, do you want to play hardball?" Piper replied, a faint, unpleasant smile forming.

"Chess is my hardball game. Poker appears to be yours. I never gamble." Mack cautioned, returning a matching smile.

Piper believed she held all the aces, but this wasn't poker. This had nothing to do with gambling. Making calculated moves at the right time was how this game needed playing.

"Piper's a right snake," observed Angie later. " That woman's got a forked tongue. There's no way I'd trust anything coming from those lips. She even tried to get Effy and me disagreeing with one another in the changing room?"

"The woman's unbelievable thinking she could come between us," Effy confirmed. "What's more, I'd rather trust a real shark. A shame her fin doesn't show."

Angie turned to Mack. "What did you make of her?"

"The same. We'll let Alex Silvers sort the deal for selling your frock designs in the States. Meanwhile, we'll decide who does the modelling for who and when."

"Mack, please stop calling dresses frocks." Angie pleaded exasperated. "It's annoying."

"He does it to wind us up." Effy teased him with a quick kiss on the cheek.

"Don't encourage him. He'll keep on doing it. I'm not surprised Ellen gets irritated with him. Talk of the devil."

Ellen appeared from behind the curtain. "I heard that Angie Thornton! You're right about finding it annoying. He does it on purpose and thinks it's funny. Goodness knows why. Anyway, we've got a problem with Grace."

"What? Gracie causing problems?" Angie was genuine in her surprise. "Why?"

"Guess where she wants to go tonight?"

"Not The Twisted Wheel?" Effy groaned. "She's too young."

"Oh, no, I'm not!" Flared Grace, coming up behind her, "I can pass for old enough. Sara wants to go with too."

Effy complained. "You're supposed to go back to Bradford with Ellen this evening."

"I've to get home," Alice joined in, "count me out. Like Ellen, I've A-Levels coming up."

"I bet her dad says no." Mack tried to laugh it off. "Nice try, Grace."

"Nate said we could. In fact, both Sara and I have to go."

"How did you and Grace enjoy your first visit to The Wheel?" Nate asked his sister and Grace as they came back into the house. It had been necessary for Sara to stay over as his father and mother had taken an evening train to London. An elderly relative had died in Barnet.

"It was superb." Gushed Sara. "Me and Grace had a brilliant time."

"Loved every minute, Nate. I'm not surprised my sister and Mack love going. It was brilliant."

"Glad you enjoyed it. Now off upstairs for some shut-eye, I need to talk shop with Effy, Angie, and Mack before we go to bed." Sara and Grace looked shattered. Unused to stopping out so late, they went upstairs without uttering a further word.

Nate insisted they stayed over another night. This to allow him to take them through the deal they were working out with Piper. His late arrival at The Twisted Wheel was due to entertaining her at The Phonograph on King Street. He apologised for not taking them there. It was a club with a late-night boozing licence for over twenty-one's. Nate would have preferred to go to The Twisted Wheel. Business, however, was business and clients expected entertaining. The city's drunken professional footballers and visiting pop groups frequented The Phonograph. Nate managed to get down to the Wheel in time see The Drifters on stage. No sooner did the group finish than he'd ushered them out of the club. Not that the girls minded. After a long and exhausting day with only a few hours rest at Nate's, everyone felt drained.

The Temptations song *It's Growing* kept playing in Mack's head as he listened to Nate. Everything was snowballing, and where and when it would stop, nobody had any idea. Effy and Angie's expression changed from moment to moment. They veered between every combination of incredulous, excited, and panic-stricken. Silvers Fashions needed sunshine glamour shots, and these they wanted somewhere sunny and soon. Nate mentioned Spain. New York would have to wait until July. Everyone needed to get up-to-date passports as soon as possible. London was on the calendar for more Moods Mosaic showings. Clients wanted to see the new designs. Fashion journalists bombarded the office daily, wanting more and more information. The Silvers had already pressed Effy for a few more designs to add to the autumn collection. The clock was ticking. By the time Nate stopped, Mack was ready with a handwritten slip. He'd kept it on the back burner trying to decide what to do.

He read out the list of magazines wanting photo shoots with all the girls. Then there were a few advertising agencies keen to shoot Grace and Ellen. His mother had handed the list to him before leaving for Manchester. These had appeared in the last couple of days and the list was not short. Listening, he saw Effy's shoulders slump. Their eyes met, and each knew what the other was thinking. This was full-time work. Facing choices and decisions both realized they needed to reach a decision soon. Otherwise everything would implode from outside pressure. Nate called it a night telling the three of them to think everything through. Another decision now awaited Mack.

Effy and Angie both looked at Mack in expectation. With Ellen and Alice gone, each had a bedroom to themselves. Now Mack faced the greatest dilemma yet. Each wanted him to share their bed. *'Eenie Meenie Minie Mo'* was out of the question. Could life get anymore difficult? Mack needed to act with the Wisdom of Solomon. An inspired decision was what he needed, and it came to him.

With his arms around them, embracing both together, he kissed each one. "To choose one of over the other tonight wouldn't be right. I can't do that because I love you both too much."

Effy and Angie exchanged surprised looks with each other. They kissed Mack goodnight on the cheek. Then without a word, went upstairs side by side.

CHAPTER 15

You're My Everything – The Temptations
(Tamla Motown TMG 620 – 1967)
Sunday 30 April 1967

"You did the right thing. Angie thought so too. It would have been wrong to sleep with one and not the other."

They were leaving Bradford's Exchange Railway station, ambling towards the trolley bus stop. Effy held Mack's hand as they trailed Grace with deliberate slowness. Neither wanted to hurry home.

"Do you still love me?" Effy's tremulous anxiety upset him.

Mack stopped outside Carter's Sports Shop on Bridge Street. Dropping the holdall to the pavement, he turned to her. Balancing the camera bags over the shoulder, he took her in his arms.

"I will always love you. Never ever doubt it. Never. I get these moments of dread when I think one day, you might walk away and leave me." He heard the sound of her suitcase fall to the pavement as they kissed, making him hold her tighter and closer.

"Well, I'm scared too. Scared you'll end up loving Angie more and leave me."

Stroking Effy's cheek Mack found himself drowning in her beautiful emerald eyes. "Effy that will never ever happen, that's a promise. You're the heart of everything precious in my life. I would be lost without you."

"So is Effy's the heart of everything for you? You'd be lost without her, would you? Huh! Then why are you carrying on with Angie?" Grace had walked back unnoticed. There was an unfamiliar bitterness and sarcasm to her words breaking the spell.

Grace's continued her tirade, not holding back. "How could you? Isn't Effy enough? You're horrid. How I wish I'd never helped you meet her. James MacKinnon, I'll never forgive you! And you, Effy Halloran, how could you let him go with your best friend? Some best friend Angie's turned out. What's wrong with you two? What's wrong with Angie wanting to have your boyfriend?"

Effy burst into tears. Embracing Mack with an even tighter grip, her face pressed against his chest, she began sobbing.

"Stop right there, Grace. That's out of order. What goes on between Effy and me is nobody's business. What goes on between the three of us is also nobody's business. Got that?"

Effy pulled away from Mack, tears streaming to confront Grace. "Mack's right. As much as I love you, and no matter how dear you are to me, it's none of your damn business. We don't need to explain ourselves to anyone. And don't dare be awful to Angie. Angie is my best friend, she thinks the world of you and Ellen."

"Does Angie also think the world of you, Mack? And are you at the heart of everything in her life too?"

"You'll have to ask Angie. Why don't you call her when we get home?" He replied, more in irritation than anger.

"Mack!" Effy tugged at his arm. "You know what the three of us promised one another."

"Maybe we should stop pretending nothing is going on between us. Maybe it's time it came out in the open." He muttered, glaring at Grace.

"No. I will not have everyone judging the three of us. As for you, Grace… accept what we three have, a rather special love, that's all you need to know. The three of us are happy together. If you don't like it – lump it, little sister!"

Grace gasped at her response, turning she ran towards the trolley bus. When they boarded, there was no sign of her. Mack wanted to go on the top deck to see if Grace was okay. Effy forced him to stay, pulling him back. If Grace wanted to sulk, they should let her.

As the trolley bus reached their stop, Grace descended from the top deck, rushing past them without a word. They watched her dash across the road, disappointed by her reaction. On entering the house, they were in time to see Grace slam the telephone down and run upstairs.

"Great! As if we need that." He muttered.

"Take no notice." Effy tried to console. "Grace will come round in time."

"Will she? Are you sure?"

The telephone rang, and Mack answered. He knew who was calling. An unhappy sounding Angie was on the other end of the line. He listened, and then replaced the receiver without another word.

His mum appeared from the lounge. "Who was that?"

"Angie. She's popping over to see Effy."

"Why?" Jane MacKinnon looked puzzled.

"Effy, Angie, and I have something urgent we need to resolve."

Frowning, he and Effy exchanged unspoken words.

"How did the weekend go?" His mum gave them both a welcome home peck on the cheek.

"The weekend was superb, but you may not like what we have to tell you. There's more work on the way."

Angie arrived in tears. Before his mother could ask anything, they whisked her upstairs into his room. Grace's words had upset her so much she began to cry some more, the tears trickling down her cheeks again. Both he and Effy took turns to wipe the tears away with their handkerchiefs. After a while, Angie and Effy went up to the attic bedroom to confront Grace. Sometime later, Angie came back down to his room.

"It's done. Grace wants to see you. Actually, three of us, together." Mack rose from his desk and kissed her. "Let's go."

What followed wasn't easy. Grace was struggling to come to terms with what she was told. Acceptance wasn't easy. How could it be? Everything she'd ever known or heard or read about being in love had always been about couples, not a threeple. Grace's use of this new word, made the two girls laugh.

"Threeple! I love that, Angie!" Effy giggled. "I suppose we must be a three-person couple or threeple!"

Angie burst out laughing. "Threeple, why not. It doesn't sound as bad as threesome and what that implies."

Their smiles and laughter seemed to bring a change in Grace. Maybe it was the way the two girls had reacted to the word *threeple?* Or maybe it was something as obvious as the three of them sitting together on Effy's bed? Angie and Effy were leaning against him, their heads resting against his shoulders and their arms around him. Or maybe it was the way Effy and Angie smiled together, drawing strength from one another? Or maybe it was because the three of them were being open and honest with Grace? Whatever it was, it had the desired effect.

"I won't pretend it'll be easy for me to get used to it." Grace began apologetically. "I do understand why you don't think it would be a good idea to let everyone know. Thank you for being honest and letting me in on it. I'm glad you feel you think you can trust me. At least I can keep a secret."

It was a discreet reference to Ellen.

"You would have had to know sometime what was going on. It was unfair of us not to tell you." Mack added.

"You'd better not hurt either of them, James MacKinnon. Or else."

"There's no chance of that." He vowed.

Angie's invitation was unexpected. "It's May Day Bank holiday tomorrow. Gracie, why don't you come back with me for a sleepover."

"Why?" Grace was mystified but perked up in an instant.

"So you and me can have some fun together and get to know each other a little more. What do you say? I'll get you back by tomorrow evening."

"You're not just doing this because of what you've been telling me?"

"Yes, I am, but also because I genuinely would like to get to know my blood sister's sister better."

"You're what...?"

"I'll explain later."

"As we're all here, Angie, let's have that chat with my parents. I suppose they'd better know what the Silvers have planned for us in the weeks ahead."

Effy sighed. "Today's not going to be an easy day. I'm so tired I could fall asleep sleep now."

Angie left with Grace two hours later. Lengthy discussions had exhausted everyone. After they left, what followed became more stressful. His parents had said nothing in Grace's presence, waiting for Angie and her to leave. Mrs Ellis, their neighbour, had once again brought the Sunday newspaper to their attention. Spread across the scandal sheets centre pages was Mara Fisher's handiwork. Effy went pale then bright red as she began to read it.

Mack excused himself from the room returning, with a large cardboard envelope as she finished reading the item.

"I can't believe this!" She kept exclaiming over and over. "How dare she write something like this? Oh, Mack! She's trying to ruin me and paint a horrid picture of the three of us."

Lurid, filled with unsupported innuendoes, it offered little else. The article included Angie denying she and Effy were lesbians. This while mentioning they had shared a bed in London. The rest of the unpleasant piece about Effy came from quotes supplied by a girl identified only as M. M for

Maria Sharpe. Out of context quotes littered the article. Quotes like the one about her willingness to live in sin, uttered in the classroom. Fisher then described Mack as a *wannabe* fashion photographer and a vicious thug. James MacKinnon had beaten up another young man on the Brixton Road. How a visiting Yorkshire teenager became involved in a London gang fight was unclear. Written, as tawdry sensationalism, the article was nothing less than a deliberate vicious and smearing attack. Mara Fisher's writing aimed to appeal to the baser instincts of the paper's readers. Given the rag's reputation for scurrilous and sensationalist scandal, there was nothing more to add.

"You'd better look at the contents in this envelope before becoming too depressed." Mack passed it to his dad. "These are copies. Tomorrow, or maybe the day after, all this will appear in one of our favourite red tops. I posted them off last Thursday. The editors have copies of everything in the envelope plus more stuff of their own, so they led me to believe. Missy Fisher is about to become one unhappy lady. The reporter told me quite a few on Fleet Street have it in for Mara Fisher big time. Anyway, the editor said all of this would get used as soon as her item appeared.

His parents studied the photographs Mack had taken. They showed Mara Fisher harassing the girls and staff at the school. Besides the photographs, he had typed carbon copies of statements from eight girls. Mack also had the original handwritten statements. Chloe Johnson and Ellen had obtained these in the aftermath of Fisher's visit to the school.

Amongst the photos was one of Effy standing in the school doorway, arms extended wide, barring the reporter from entering. Grace and Ellen were behind her, looking upset. That made the photo superb. Another photo showed Mainwaring preventing her entry. It was all there, including what Mack considered his joint finest. This was one of Fisher, chasing after them, pushing some hapless schoolgirl out of the way. Capturing the little first former's shocked and terrified expression was an absolute corker! That had to be a prize snap! The photo looked worse than the actual incident at the time. Mack was so glad his new telephoto lens had arrived the previous week. This had been its second outing. Without the telephoto lens, the definition wouldn't have been anywhere as good. He had the bitch banged to rights with the rapid-fire shots. Among the snaps was one of Maria Sharpe that did her no justice. She looked like a fishwife, her mouth open and ugly. If you had to make a fool of somebody, then he'd achieved it with Maria Sharpe. If he never made it as a fashion photographer, he could always try his hand working as a paparazzi.

"My goodness. Those photographs are quite amazing." His mother responded. "These will not show Miss Fisher in a good light at all."

There was a momentary lull. His mother looked at him with one of those all too familiar looks she used to give him when she suspected he'd been up to no good when little. "You didn't let her tyres down, did you?"

"Moi?" Mack did his best to look offended. "By the way, they're going to pay me for each photo they use at the going rate. There's a catch, however. I had to promise something to the editor."

"What's the catch?" Jane MacKinnon wanted to know.

"They want an exclusive interview with Effy and myself for their Sunday supplement."

"Tell me you didn't agree to it?" Rob MacKinnon glanced up from the content matter.

"I didn't think there was a choice, dad. They wanted our side of the story in exchange."

"Have you any idea what they will write? Can you even trust them to write an honest account in response to what we've been reading?" Asked his mother. "There was no way I could let it pass mum. There are more than a few daggers ready to plunge in Fisher's back anyhow. It seems it harks back to one of their sub-editors having her family life ruined by Fisher. To quote the editor's words, *when we light the fire to burn this witch, it will burn for a whole week and more.*"

His parents voiced more concerns. It wasn't only the unpleasantness of the newspaper account. They expressed their other serious concerns. Mack and Effy felt frustrated and unhappy listening to them. Then they went on to talk about the detrimental effects on Mack and the girls' educations. And so it went on with concerns about Effy's parent's reaction thrown into the mix. No doubt the news would reach Ireland, if it hadn't already. This would cause upset when her parents read about it, given Effy's central role. The MacKinnon's were supposed to be in *loco parentis* looking after Grace and Effy, so this wouldn't do them much good either in the eyes of Halloran's.

Mack and Effy continued listening to everything said. It wasn't easy, and he and Effy offered little in response. Both knew his parents were right. After a short silence, Jane passed Mack's photographs and documentation to his father.

"Did you do all this using my typewriter?" His father asked, reading it through. "If you did, it's a fair job. It looks like the RSA typing class in the

Fourth Form wasn't an entire waste of a year. Reading it, I'm impressed. It's an object of clarity."

"Chloe got a few of the girls to sign some brief statements. Those are the handwritten copies." Mack pointed them out. "I paid to have them copied on a Xerox machine to send to the editor. It was worth the cost."

"Why have you kept all this from me?" Effy looked upset, staring at the pile of documents Mack had assembled.

"We didn't want you to worry," he responded, passing them to her. "Besides, we, that is Chloe, Ellen, Grace, and I thought it better if you didn't know what we were doing. We thought you'd stop us collecting comments from the other girls in school. So many of the girls have lovely things to say about you. Grace's friends were fantastic. Look what her friend Jean wrote."

"There you go again. I'm not some fragile flower." There was no hiding her irritation. "I can cope with whatever she wrote about me. You don't have to keep treating me like some defenceless princess in a fairy tale."

Sifting through the handwritten statements, it surprised her to find one. She reread it twice. "Katie Fox wrote this? Goodness. That's so nice of her to write those things."

"So when can we expect this next interview to take place?" His father asked.

Fisher's newspaper article had appalled his parents. They seemed at a loss at how to react. They didn't question Mack and Effy about the implied arrangement between them and Angie.

"We'll know soon enough. I don't think they'll be long before they get around to visiting us for an interview. It'll be fascinating to see what goes into print. They want Fisher reeled in, hooked and dangling high and dry. We are the bait to lure the readers to buy the newspaper." He enjoyed using angling terminology to make his point.

Mack could not have begun to imagine the savaging prepared for Mara Fisher. It even startled his parents. A serialised assassination, long plotted, rolled off the presses the next day and continued the whole week. Their own story disappeared under a welter of follow on stories dug up to disgrace the reporter. These vilified Mara Fisher as an unscrupulous liar. The paper exposed her for writing malicious manufactured articles about politicians. Her fondness for attacking celebrities and public figures was well known. The evidence stacked against Mara Fisher proved significant and in astonishing quantities. Her lies had been called to account. Her enemies had been a long time preparing for their own version of an Ides of March attack. The reporters' pen nibs had become sharpened knives for her assassination, honed to perfection. Fisher's unethical behaviour had flouted the rules. Even by Fleet Street's less than scrupulous standards, she was bad news. When the newspaper turned on her, it was like a pack of frenzied hyenas. Mack's lesson about Fleet Street and the media that week was one he would remember in the future. The press could make and break someone with ease and impunity.

CHAPTER 16

Do Right Woman Do Right Man - Aretha Franklin
Atlantic 584084 – B Side - 1967)
11 a.m. - Saturday 6 May 1967

"When looking through the lens of your camera, as you take a fashion shot, what are you looking to see in your model?"

"The clothes." Mack's succinct answer surprised the reporter.

The way they had arranged themselves on the settee for the interview was deliberate. Mack had posed them beforehand. Effy sat in middle, with Ellen to her right. Mack had placed himself next to Effy on the left. Angie was seated on the armrest next to him. Alice occupied the opposite armrest next to Ellen. Grace sat on the carpet, her legs tucked to one side, between Effy and Ellen.

"The clothes?" The reporter echoed.

"That's what fashion photography is about. The mistake would be to concentrate on the model, not the clothes."

"So, the clothes are more important than the model?"

"I'll answer that with a question." An enigmatic smile formed as he charmed the woman reporter. "Which is more important, the singer or the song they sing? The model or the clothes she displays?"

He let the question hang for tantalizing moments flummoxing the reporter.

"The singer without a song is no singer and the song without a singer is no song. Lyrics alone on paper are not enough. Without music, the song's magic can't happen. By analogy, unworn clothes on a rack have little appeal. Clothes need models, and models need clothes to bring them alive for buyers."

"I see." He wasn't quite what she'd expected. Nor were his answers and nor were these teenage models surrounding him. "So, what do you expect from your models?"

"Models need involvement in what they're doing. They have to *live* the clothes they're modelling. Otherwise, there's no affinity. To capture the affinity with the camera, I need to see and capture their emotional reaction to the clothes. Without that affinity, the magic can't happen."

Hearing a seventeen-year-old using the word affinity in its correct sense had June Nightingale smiling. This young man had an innate understanding of what it took to be a fashion photographer. He knew what he was he was doing.

"And if they don't 'live' the clothes they're expected to model?" She continued questioning.

"We don't make them wear anything they don't like. Relating to the clothes is all-important. That's the secret ingredient. Without it, there's no magic. We have a brilliant designer sat right beside me who knows what a young woman wants and needs from her clothes."

"From your point of view as a designer, what are your thoughts on the way James shoots your clothes?"

"It's Mack. Only his parents call him James. Sometimes I call him Jimmy Mack like in the song." Effy responded with a giggle after glancing at him. "What do I want to see as a designer? I want to see my designs worn and showing confident young women in love with what they're wearing. Mack looks for that through the lens when he does a shoot."

"You said *we*?" Questioned the reporter.

"Miss Nightingale, my sister Grace is my co-designer. Without Grace by my side, the designs wouldn't be half as good."

"So, Grace, you help design and model the outfits, too?"

"Effy exaggerates. She is the real designer. I'm just the seamstress."

"I see. As a fifteen-year-old, do you enjoy modelling?"

"Yes. It's great fun."

"Do you have a good working relationship with Mack?" June Nightingale asked, scribbling notes in Pitman's shorthand. James MacKinnon and the assembled young women intrigued her. She sensed a close relationship between everyone in the group.

"The best. When he's clicking away, I know Mack wants to make us look beautiful. Speaking for myself, he does just that. He's brill." Grace responded with youthful glee.

"Alice. I believe you're the latest model to join the group? Mack tells me that magazine editors are already seeking you out to appear in their pages. Tell me, what do you think Mack brings out in you?"

After a thoughtful pause, Alice made one of her strange comments. "I'm still trying to work out who I am and what makes me a woman. Simone de Beauvoir wrote in a novel *one is not born, but rather becomes a woman.*

Through his photography, Mack is helping me to understand how I'm becoming a woman."

"That's rather deep, Alice." Her reply had surprised the reporter. Returning to Mack, June Nightingale asked, "Are you helping Alice to become a woman?"

More enigmatic smiling followed. Alice was boxing clever, setting him up for some amusing game playing.

"When the girls see themselves at their beautiful best, it gives them insight. My photographs reinforce their identity, their sense of who they are as people. I want them to see themselves as I see them: strong, independent, go-ahead young women."

"And Angie? Do you feel that Mack's photography helps you to be a strong, independent young woman?"

"Most definitely."

"Does having a close relationship help, or is it a handicap?" The delving had to crop up.

"Yes, I believe it does. A close relationship is important." Angie's reply made Mack and Effy hold their breath, fearing what she'd say next. "Mack is a dear friend... so yes, we are close. Then again, Effy and I are best friends, almost like sisters. So it's not surprising we three share things as close friends do. Does being so close help when we're working together on a shoot? How could it not? As a model, I'm revealing things about myself that I wouldn't do under normal circumstances. All models do.

As a photographer, Mack has an intimate understanding of me as he does with all of us here. On a shoot, I'm relaxed. I feel safe knowing he will create the best images of me that he can. We all have bits of ourselves we don't like. These are things he teaches us to ignore and to see past. He focusses us on that which is the best of ourselves. It's important to me that Mack becomes recognised as the outstanding photographer that he is. He deserves the recognition. The way he's showcased Effy's brilliant designs speaks for itself."

June Nightingale's head reeled. Angie Thornton was no immature eighteen-year-old. None of them were, which made a refreshing change.

"Ellen, you've not said much so far." The reporter turned to her. "Does what Angie says apply to you too?"

"Yes, I suppose it does. Mack knows me well. As Effy and Grace's sister so he should. He always puts every one of us at ease when we work together. Listening to Alice, I have to agree. Mack makes you feel like a

85

natural woman. I know this sounds weird, corny even, but it's what he does. Mack has a flair for making us look and feel glamorous. He understands the feminine in us."

Turning to Mack once again, the reporter quizzed him. "You are quoted as saying, you're smart, sharp, and stylish. Is this all about being fashionable young Mods?"

"It depends on how *you* understand that word. If you mean how we dress, then yes. We are smart. We are sharp, and we are stylish. And yes, we are Mods. Mod isn't a word we use amongst ourselves. We know who we are. It's a term coined by the press to slot us into a category of youth culture."

"So how else should we understand those words?" June Nightingale studied Mack. She was intrigued by how he kept an unspoken interaction going with Effy and Angie. More had to be going on between these three than they would admit. Maybe Mara Fisher had been right all along? Adjusting her reading glasses, the interviewer went on. "Please explain."

"Smart and sharp? No one should ever underestimate us because we're young. We're brighter than some people think we are. We're quicker on the uptake too. We don't let anything or anyone get past us. Stylish? We don't confuse style with fashion. You know that song by The Kinks, *Dedicated Follower of Fashion*? Fashion is for followers, but we've decided we're not born to follow. We're about style and style expresses what fashion never can. Style speaks when words don't. Call us nonconformist chameleons. We never quite blend in with the crowd. You can always spot us if you look. We'll be the ones standing out and looking good."

Mack would have paid any price for the look on the reporter's face. As it was, it had come for free.

Turning to Effy, she asked, "What are your aims as a designer? What are you hoping to achieve with each outfit you create?"

"True independence for young women. These are designs for the under twenty-fives. No young woman of our generation wants to dress like her mother or aunt. Who wants to look like a junior version of a thirty or forty-year-old woman? Not when you're under twenty-five. Twin sets and pearls? You can keep them."

"Can you give me an example of how you want your designs to be different?"

"I'm interested in creating ultra-feminine little dresses, sexy girlie girl outfits. I design them, so they are simple, stylish, yet practical. It's as much about practicality as style. I'm not much interested or influenced by French or Italian fashion ideas. The knickers look from Paris this year does nothing for me. Nor do I imagine does it do much for most girls our age. Clothes need to be functional, flattering yet decorative."

"It appears you haven't attended any fashion colleges like the RCA. Or undertaken any fashion design courses. What makes you think you can compete against established designers? Dare I say, those who are more experienced than you? Designers I may add who have studied fashion and earned their qualifications."

"In all honesty?" Effy paused, an index finger on her lower lip. "This is something I never give any thought. Yes, I am self-taught and won't deny it. Which is not to say I'm not learning as I go along. You never stop learning. No, I don't let it worry me. In any case, the ultimate proof is what you come up with, not what diploma you have hanging on your wall."

"How do you approach your designs, what methods do you use?"

"These days, I start with the materials available to me. Thanks to Silvers Fashions, I have access to extensive fabrics and prints. I can tell from a swatch what will or won't work. The texture of the material is as important as its appearance. For me, this is central. From that point, I work out how best it should look when worn. My design aims are for practicality, affordability, and availability to the widest public."

"Yet your originals as sold in the King's Road are expensive. These hardly qualify as affordable." The reporter tried to pick a hole in Effy's statement. Once again, Effy surprised with her reply.

"Moods Mosaic is a shop window advertising my range. It exists for clientele who want an individual and exclusive, limited version of one of my designs. The important thing is that I'm contracted to produce designs for Silvers Fashions. They have the licence to make and sell my more affordable versions to a wider public through shops and catalogues. As a seventeen-year-old, I'm just happy to design for young women. I look at it this way. Anything bringing happiness and pleasure to someone's life, even if fleeting, is worth it. Isn't it?"

"How so?"

"We're the children of the Cold War, the Cuban missile crisis, CND, the Hydrogen bomb, and the Vietnam War. These confront us daily. Our lives could end without ever hearing the four-minute warning. Nuclear boms could fall, and that would be it. Life for teenagers like us may hold no future. We keep hearing Barry McGuire *Eve of Destruction* droning away in the background of our minds. So we live in the present, in the moment, trying to ignore what might happen. The constant shadow of nuclear annihilation darkens our lives. The present may be the only time we have."

"What exactly do you mean by living in the present?" June Nightingale was finding the heavy answers disconcerting. It wasn't what she had expected to hear or find. This interview thrilled and excited her. She contemplated the stupendous article she could put together for the supplement. These were not the usual empty-headed teenage pop idols and vacuous celebrities she had to interview. There was a true intellectual ability at work here among them. Nightingale watched Effy Halloran nudge her boyfriend, signalling him to takeover. They worked together as a team, knowing each other's strengths.

"Miss Nightingale, what Effy's trying to tell you is we can't change what's past. Thinking about the past only serves one purpose. That's to understand and to avoid repeating the worst in the present. As for the future, the choices made in the present will decide it. What others choose for the rest of the world we can't do anything about. Only the choices open to us as individuals count. All we have is now. Tomorrow may never come."

"I have to ask, and I apologise in advance, but a certain reporter raised the subject. Is there any truth to the rumour that you, Effy, and Angie are in a threesome relationship?"

Before Mack could respond, Grace went from seated to standing and confronting the reporter. What she said left the reporter stumped for a response.

CHAPTER 17

There's Gonna Be Trouble – Sugar Pie DeSanto
(Chess CRS 8034 – 1966)
Evening - Saturday 6 May 1967

"Ellen and Alice are unavailable now until the start of June. By then, their A-Level exams will be over. Alice says she's willing to take time out at weekends to do any modelling assignments for us. Ellen's unsure. I think we may talk need to talk her around, if only to do the same locally and only on a weekend." Mack explained. "As for Effy and myself, we'll be busy sitting end-of-year exams in June, and the same will apply to Grace. Our parents insist we don't leave school without qualifications. We do have a May half-term holiday looming next weekend. Effy, Grace, and I would have time to do the London shoots that week. Angie wouldn't have the time during the day without taking time off work, but she could make the weekend. Weekends wouldn't be an issue for her. I'm certain we can arrange things. As long as she's on the last train from King's Cross on Sunday evening, it should be okay."

There was a silent exchange between Nate and his father before Alex Silvers spoke. Shrugging his shoulders, the older Silvers seemed to accept what they said. It was not what he'd wished to hear, "Can we be guaranteed to have the autumn designs ready?"

Effy responded, sounding nervous. Yes, she already had a dozen designs ready, but she expressed concern. Fashion was fast-moving and about foreseeing new trends. She was expecting something explosive to materialize this summer. Magazines were filling with photos and articles on the flower power hippie movement. Already talk of LSD inspired psychedelic fashions had started. The fashions sported by pop stars on television reflected these developments. It could impact in summer on High Street fashions.

The conversation moved on to textile prints and the need to see what was available. Trying to describe what these fabrics patterns might look like was even more challenging. The Silvers weren't too keen on what they were hearing. They promised to consider it, to look into it and see what was taking place. Mack overheard Nate mentioned someone called Simon in a hushed exchange with his father. Alex Silvers nodded in approval.

Mack didn't dare tell the Silvers how many assignment requests he'd received. Third-party photographic sessions using the girls had reached absurd levels. Every day brought yet another enquiry in the post or over the phone.

If he and the girls worked every day full time, they might meet the demand. The three of them already knew that was impossible. Angie had already decided it wouldn't be long before she gave up her job as a receptionist and went modelling full-time. She'd told Mack and Effy it would be in less than a month. Effy was wavering and indecisive. She kept thinking about that potential Oxbridge future. Mack watched the scales of opportunity tipping daily towards him in one direction. The potential earning power was a strong temptation and had already more or less tempted Angie.

Leaving school to go into full-time fashion photography was a serious lure. Even in a few short weeks, they'd all earned money that had seemed improbable when they started. Allowing for tax, studio hire, photographic costs, his earnings were staggering. These were gross earnings for two months, although boosted by the newspaper payment. The newspaper had paid him a handsome sum for the Mara Fisher photographs. Even so, the money for his fashion photography work wasn't loose change. In the last two days, payment for his first two front cover photos had arrived. The teen magazine covers brought in two cheques for twenty guineas apiece. More cheques were on their way from other magazines and advertisers. Mack retuned to the conversation as Effy spoke.

"Can I thank you again for loaning us the Pfaff 360. Our old Singer was struggling. Having another sewing machine is so helpful. We should be able to do a better job with zips. And thank you for allowing Sara to stay over to show Grace how to use it. I didn't realize Sara was so expert." Effy filled the silence as they waited for Angie and Mrs Silvers to return from the kitchen.

Nate's father replied, smiling. "Everyone in the family has to know the essentials of sewing and the use of machines. I brought them up from being tiny to know how to do that. From the workshop floor up, there are no exceptions in this family, isn't that so Nate?"

Nate nodded. "No exceptions. We've all had to do it. Me, Joe, Simon, Sara and now, my little sister Leah."

"You have another brother and sister?" This surprised Mack.

"Simon's a student. He's away studying Textiles & Design in London. Leah is the baby of the family. She's eleven and out at a friend's birthday party this afternoon. So you see, Effy, yours is not the only large family."

Mrs Silvers entered carrying a tray with tea and biscuits. Angie followed with a second tray. Alex Silvers wife was a soft-spoken lady. Mack noted she said little but absorbed every word spoken. He guessed she must be fiftyish. Her immaculate coiffured hair suggested a bi-weekly visit to the best stylists in Manchester. Her two-piece looked as if it could be a Dior original.

Hannah Silvers wore her opulence well. Her husband had spared no expense at the jewellers. Effy noted her 18k gold Omega watch. Everything she wore was solid gold: the earrings, the necklace, and the bracelet. Even the rings on her fingers were chunky with impressive stones. One, in particular, had a massive Ruby.

Mack noted Angie was doing her best not to look upset. Something had happened when she had been out of the room. On her return, she came and sat beside him when before she'd been beside Effy. It was a defiant move and a clear gesture to Mrs Silvers. Effy noticed it too.

Pouring out the tea, Mrs Silvers question came from nowhere. "Sara was telling me, Mack, that you, Angie, and Effy have an unusual relationship. Is this why the girls wear identical eternity rings?"

It was a heart-stopping, jaw-dropping moment. Nate's father looked embarrassed. "Now, Hannah, I'm not sure we should ask."

"Why not?" Hannah Silvers was curt cutting him off. "After all the publicity and notoriety? I'm intrigued. Call me a nosey parker. Is it true? Are the three of you romantically involved?"

Angie's pale complexion coloured, and Mack noticed so too did Effy's. Taking Angie and Effy's hand, he went eye to eye with Mrs Silvers. "What you see is what you see. How you choose to see it, we'll leave with you. We are close. How close is for us alone to know. Take it from us - *Close*. Call the three of us a *cooperative*. Let's leave it at that."

Pregnant silence.

"A cooperative." Hannah Silvers smiled, embarrassed. "What an interesting description."

It wasn't quite a conversation stopper...

"I think you three should give yourself a brand name. Something that sells you as a unique identity." Nate suggested as the four of them walked towards The Twisted Wheel from the car park. Zoot Money's Big Roll Band was performing that night.

"A brand name? What brand name?" Elicited Effy, puzzled.

"You should call yourself *The Cooperative*. It's perfect. Mack nailed it when he put my mother in her place."

"The Cooperative?" Mack repeated, puzzled. "Why?"

"It's exactly what you three and your sisters and Alice make up a cooperative. You are a team, a tight-knit crew working together. A trendy name like that would get decent publicity and establishing you as a brand in the fashion biz."

"The Cooperative." Mused Angie. "I like it. What a great idea. We should use it. What do you think, Mack? Effy?"

Nate stopped walking, causing them to do likewise. "You three own the model agency. It serves Mack's photography and Effy's designs. It enables Angie to model. Now Angie's primed to take on running the modelling side, it's the logical next step. You are the ultimate kind of partnership in this business, covering it all. You are the *new breed* taking on the fashion world."

"I like the sound of that better." Rubbing his chin Mack looked at the girls. "The new breed. Yes. A new breed, something not encountered by the *fashionistas* so far."

"A co-operative new breed in more ways than you can imagine," Effy uttered. To her surprise, Angie linked arms when she caught those scarce audible words. The worried frown on her face upset Effy.

Later, finding a quiet place, they spoke.

"All I've done is to make you unhappy. I'll break it off with Mack rather than cause you any heartache or trouble." There was no disguising, Angie's upset. Effy knew her friend too well.

"Don't be silly, Angie." Effy paused. "The way I am at the moment has nothing to do with the three of us. As far I'm concerned we're fine but tell me something? Do you get jealous when I'm with Mack? You know what I mean, don't you?"

"Honestly?"

"Yes, Angie. Honestly. Tell me the truth."

"I won't lie. I do get jealous. A little. But then I know I shouldn't and stop myself because I believe it's wrong of me. I can't explain it any better. What about you?"

"Believe it or not, I'm the same. I try not to get jealous. It's not easy, but you need to know it's getting easier. It will take time for us to adjust. We'll get there because we both love him. As long as we love one another as friends, everything will work out. That's the important thing. So please don't break it off with Mack. Not because of me. I'd hate that to happen. We wouldn't cope without you as a part of us. It's hard, but we need to stick together. We are something special, and neither Mack nor I want to lose what we three are together. Don't forget we're blood sisters too. Anyway, this isn't the reason I'm down. It's everything else."

Effy confessed the pressures of designing, modelling, and studying were spiralling. It left her wondering how much longer could she could cope with everything. Silvers Fashions were demanding more and more in what they wanted from Grace and herself. Mack wasn't finding it easy, either. Then the whole issue of everyone prying into the relationship made life harder. It wasn't something they could ever be open about. Her mum's forthcoming visit didn't bode too well. She worried about how that would go. Effy's words reassured Angie, now she understood what had troubled her friend. She hugged Effy.

"Look, Angie, I don't want you to think we'd hold you back with the modelling. You need to know that," Effy paused to let her words sink in before explaining further. "Everyone's insisting we stick it out and do our A-Levels. Neither of us knows what to do. Mack's tempted to kick the Sixth Form into touch. He's fed up with the place treating him as an intruding Eleven Plus reject. He doesn't want to let his parents down because they want him to succeed where Adam didn't. It doesn't help either with all the work pouring in and the money he's getting paid. It's a huge temptation to leave. Mind you, the money we're making just from photo modelling isn't petty cash. It's so tempting, and I'm tempted too. Don't let us hold you back from going full time. Who knows? You might finally make up our minds for us to join you."

CHAPTER 18

Because They're Young – Duane Eddy (London HLW 9162 – 1960)
Wednesday 10 May 1967

Mack read and reread the letter Rósín Halloran had sent to Bridget. "Phew. Your mum doesn't sound a happy lady. I suppose all the newspaper items had to find their way to Ireland sometime. Those *Opus Dei* pals of your dad, the Monaghan's, you can bet they had something to do with this letter. Their creepy son is in the Fifth form at Bede's."

"Don't lose any sleep over it. I'm not." Effy sighed, trying to sound dismissive. "What's the worst that can happen?"

"Our mother may want you and Grace to move back to Whites Terrace. Under Bridget's or my supervision," Effy's eldest sister chuckled.

"Huh! There's no chance, Aileen. If Ma thinks we'll go back, she's got another thing coming. If the MacKinnon's said we couldn't stay any longer, we'd move in with Angie and Gill in Halifax. Better still, I've enough money now to set up on my own. I'd take Grace with me." Effy tried to erase the thought of the missed period from her mind.

"Hush yourself sis," Aileen's warm gentle smile touched Effy. Since leaving the convent, Aileen's happiness shone through a constant smile. "Caitlin and I have already talked the matter through with Bridget. We've spoken with the MacKinnon's and it won't come to anything so drastic."

"Did you go behind our backs?" Effy sounded miffed but with a hint of relief.

"Don't get annoyed, Effy. We have your best interests at heart, as did Bridget when we talked over Ma's letter. The three of us are so proud of you, Grace and Ellen. What you've accomplished in so short a space of time is remarkable, nay almost a miracle. Jane has told us how hard you and Grace have worked, and what incredible talent you've shown. That's left everyone staggered. And as for little Grace, she's such a gorgeous model, our Ellen too. No. Your three older sisters won't let Ma and Da ruin it for you three. You're young adults now, not children. Besides, if the worst came to the worst, I now have a job. I'd take care of you and Grace, but I doubt you'd need me."

"A job, Aileen? Since when?" A pleased look of surprise appeared on Effy's face.

"Mr MacKinnon has taken me on as a teller at his bank. I had savings that I could never make myself give up on joining the novitiate. Something must have told me the novitiate wouldn't work out. So we three would manage. Anyway, there's nothing to worry about. Your big sisters will deal with Ma. We have your backs. Our parents have done enough damage to their daughters. We'll not allow them to do anymore, be sure of that. You deserve better. Leave it to us. Meanwhile, keep working hard. That means you too Mack because you're the glue holding everyone together. You're the one who makes everything work."

That last comment left Mack nonplussed.

"Besides," Aileen added, "the MacKinnon's are fond of you and Grace. Jane confessed she'd miss you girls. With the baby due in weeks, it would be helpful if you were around."

Tom Catford appeared at his bedroom door. His cousin was a welcome distraction from the Economics essay. Mack was struggling to write an answer to the question. The subject bored him to mindless distraction. Thinking about the monopoly powers of nationalised industries in Britain defined dullness.

Tom had taken the driving test that afternoon, having kept the date secret from Mack. He'd travelled over to meet with Ellen pass or fail, though that wasn't the only reason. Like Effy, the letter had upset Ellen. Tom knew he'd better show.

"You know how women are? Anyway, I passed my driving test this afternoon. First time too. Beat you to the punch Mack! I'm having a good gloat when I see Angie. Remember what she said about my chances of passing the first time, eh?"

"Well done, Tom! Brilliant! I'm sure Angie will find something to say. You can bet she'll find a way to take the mickey too!" The news disappointed Mack. He'd hoped to pass his driving test before Tom.

Ellen appeared at the door. "Is Tom bragging about passing his driving test? That's all we'll get out of him for the next few days. Do you know what he did in W.H. Smith's this afternoon while checking out LPs? God, you can't go anywhere without him behaving like a hooligan. You won't believe this."

No. I'm sure I will." Mack grinned. "Go on, El, you know you want to tell me."

"What I couldn't understand was why he kept looking at classical LPs? When he asked for a biro, I should have guessed he was up to no good. Your cousin brazenly defaced an LP album cover. He scribbled on *Bach's Organ Works,* so does mine."

Tom sniggered. Mack burst out laughing. Typical Tom.

"It's not funny. You're so childish, Tom. I can't believe I'm going out with someone so juvenile…"

"You've got to admit, that's funny, El." He and Tom were still laughing.

"Oh, grow up the pair of you. I'm surprised at you, Mack laughing at his vandalism."

"So who legged it off school this afternoon, Ellen Halloran? Tut-tut young lady." Mack retaliated, still chuckling.

"I needed some time to revise. Not that I got much revising done."

"You kept your driving lessons quiet," Mack tried to make his cousin feel guilty for saying nothing.

"Ah!" Tom began, "Adam made me keep it a secret. I didn't want you getting all jealous and upset. I didn't even tell Ellen to keep it a surprise if I passed."

So the truth was out. The business Tom and Adam planned with Benny and Mick Jenkins, needed Tom with his own driving licence. It made sense; a mechanic who couldn't drive was useless. Adam had taken Tom out for extra lessons in his old Anglia. Mick Jenkins had also given Tom extra driving lessons in his Austin A40. They needed him to pass his test as soon as possible. When Tom qualified and passed his City and Guilds exam, Adam and Mick needed him ready to leave the garage where he worked. Suitable premises on Canal Road were available for the new business. Finalising buying the spot would enable the three to establish a new local car dealership. Tom wasn't prepared to say which motorcar dealership they had in mind.

Ellen looked upset. Mack could see why. She had wanted to go to college in Huddersfield. She had planned to move to Halifax to live with Angie and Gill to be near Tom. Instead, she might now need to stay in Bradford. Life wasn't getting any easier for them. If Ellen had realized, she would have applied to Bradford's Macmillan College. Or to the one in Bingley to be nearer to him.

"Interesting how Grace stuck up for you three in that article. I suppose she had a point." Tom continued to make himself comfortable on

96

Mack's bed with Ellen reclined by his side. "We don't understand what's going on, but we *know* what's going on."

"There's nothing to understand. Believe what you want to believe."

"Listen, Mack. Have you any idea how this has affected Angie? No, I bet you don't. Angie's not one to talk. It's not gone unnoticed. She never comes out in the week like she used to do," Tom continued. "It's as though she's avoiding answering questions about you three."

"Angie has her reasons, and these have nothing to do with Effy or me. Try asking, Ellen why." Mack didn't see the need to mention Angie's night classes at Tech.

Tom gave Ellen a mystified look. Ellen avoided his gaze, knowing why Angie kept herself busy on evenings. He continued. "Linda, Stingray, Alan, and others keep pestering Angie. They all want to know what's going on. Even those who don't know you like we do. They've noticed Effy and Angie wearing the same rings. Alice has tried putting everyone off the scent by saying it's a PR job. We've tried to laugh the whole thing off. What surprises me is that your parents have said nothing, because my mum's said plenty to Aunty Jane."

Mack shrugged, dismissing Tom's words. So his parents knew.

"Oh, knock it off Mack," Tom pulled himself upright on the bed, propping his back against the headboard. "The way Effy and Angie look at you when you're together. The way they're always snuggling up to you. And when you're alone with either Effy or Angie, they behave exactly as if you were their one and only. You must think everyone's blind and taking no notice. I've got news for you, cuz. I'm not blind, and they're not blind. I bet even Ray Charles would have noticed by now."

"What is it about the three of us that so fascinating? I can't understand why you and everyone else are so damned interested? Why the hell does it matter to anyone?"

Ellen poked Tom in the ribs with a forefinger as she snuggled up to him. "Mack's right. If Effy and Angie are happy, who's anyone to say anything? The girls have never looked happier unless they're pretending, which is most unlikely. Leave it, Tom. Grace was right, and so is Mack. It's no one's business but theirs. So stop being nosey. Just pretend they are like some weird married... well, can't say couple..."

"How about a threesome?" Tom muttered., unhappy with her words.

Ellen changed the topic. "A girl in my registration group loaned me a copy of that pop magazine. The one in which they interviewed you as one of the up and coming young photographers. Effy's reading the magazine right now. They've described you as the 'baby face' of a new wave of snappers. I still can't believe how many of your photographs are already in newspapers and magazines. It's a wonder you've got time to do anything else. I'm amazed the finger that does the clicking hasn't worn out."

"I'm getting a massive callous on it." Mack loved pulling her leg.

"Wow! Let me see?"

"Jesting Ellen, jesting, although, after two hundred clicks, the index finger aches."

Effy burst into the room, giggling and waving the magazine at Mack. "How's my baby faced photographer? Spearheading the new wave of snappers? *From obscurity to headlines in only four months*. What a fantastic write up that reporter has done."

She sprang on to his lap without warning to deliver a smacker of a kiss. The chair wobbled, tipping backward as her arms wrapped about him. Mack had to steady the chair. "Angie must read this article. Let's buy her a copy. Angie loves reading everything written about you."

Mack tried to recall what he'd said in the interview.

"From nowhere to guess where and elsewhere in three months." Effy teased, "The future's looking bright."

"Lets not to get blinded by this article," Mack's cautioned. "Okay, go on, read the article to me?"

"This is the best bit, I love this," Effy giggled then began reading it aloud. "*I ask him why do you like fashion photography? He replies, what's not to like about working with beautiful young women? Are you in love with any of your models? I ask. All of them, he replies, all five – I've been in love with them ever since we started working together. As a photographer, you need that personal rapport with your models. Call it a love affair between the photographer and his model captured on film.*"

Ellen smiled. Sitting up on the bed, she winked at Mack, preparing to wind up Tom, "Yeah, I have to agree. You're so right. Models and photographers have to have that *special* relationship, and I suppose it is like a love affair. We have to be in tune with one another."

Tom grunted, annoyed by her comment. After a moment or two, he added. "Gawd Mack! You and El sound so corny. It would have sounded better if you'd said something like. *I just love snapping five fantastic, fuckable females in fashionable frocks*. Then…"

Sitting back chuckling, Mack didn't intervene on his cousin's behalf. He watched Tom laughing like an idiot as he disappeared under Ellen and Effy flailing slaps.

CHAPTER 19

The Kid – Andre Brasseur (CBS 202557 – 1967)

Friday 19 May 1967

Sara Silvers greeted them at the penthouse door.

"Wow!" Overwhelmed and overawed Grace struggled to take in the apartment. Turning to Effy she said in a lowered voice, "This is awesome."

Effy recalled the party they had attended here when it was Joe Silvers place. It wasn't a pleasant memory, but it made her smile as she recollected the way they'd bushwhacked him.

Nate was relaxing in an armchair, his stocking feet on a grey ottoman footstool. Mack noticed that the ottoman matched the suite. The suite was new. On closer inspection, it was two identical three-piece suites helping to fill the cavernous room. Most of the furniture and furnishings looked new. Later, from Sara, they learned how Joe Silvers had trashed the place. When told to leave, he had wrecked the furniture in a berserk rage. No one in the family had heard from him since.

Nate and his sister had arrived earlier from Manchester. He had instructed Manny and his wife to meet Angie at King's Cross and to bring her to the apartment. Mack wondered about the sleeping arrangements. Nate picked up on his unasked question. He explained he'd arranged to stay elsewhere with *a friend*. Grace and Sara could share the bedroom with two single beds. Mack, Effy, and Angie could decide between them which of the other bedrooms they used. Mack considered the choices. Angie had to return on Sunday evening while he, Effy, and Grace stopped over until Thursday.

Nate set out the work schedule for the week as they sat over coffees. Mack's inputs on the week's locations specific to Silvers Fashions requirements went unchallenged. They considered more suggestions from Nate for other magazine shoots.

Effy's low-cost design range was the priority shoot this week. Angie's modelling assignment was first on the list. Without Ellen and Alice available, Nate had hired the services of a Twiggy like model. This was someone they'd used before who they knew. She would join the line up at the beginning of the week. Working with a total stranger for the first time could prove a challenge, but it didn't daunt Mack. He relished the prospect of meeting and working with a well-known model like Hester Clayton.

Nate had booked a studio for a two-day shoot. The studio had a darkroom facility attached. He expected Mack to use the darkroom after seven each evening during the coming week. Nate wanted all film spools from the daily shoots developed on the day. Everything Mack would need was there, ready and waiting. An incredible sense of urgency permeated his and Nate's discussions.

Mack had always realized he was living through fast-changing and exciting times. His new life was proof of it. Tremendous social changes were in the air. Accepted forms of thinking and behaving were being discarded and binned like yesterday's newspapers. There was an escalating, frantic scramble in search of all things new. Keeping his mind and eyes open, Mack could see this was no fairy tale change for everyone.

Staring out of the train window, he'd seen how much more familiar and widespread was the world of most working people. It wasn't just Bradford and Halifax or the other Northern towns and cities. Depravation was everywhere. The suburbs of London looked just as blighted and as squalid as the ones in Bradford. There were still too many decrepit Victorian slums. They hugged the sides of the railway lines running into the capital's centre. Bombsites from the war years could still be spotted, nasty scars on the cityscape. Yet here he was in a rich man's penthouse in one of London's most exclusive neighbourhoods. The contrast was stark.

His parents had never hidden the world's inequalities from him. If anything, they had encouraged him to learn about them. He'd seen the poverty first hands when visiting the homes of less fortunate school friends. At eleven, Mack knew how fortunate his life was relative to his school friends. A promise of better times ahead was the fervent hope of many toiling on low wages. Life was bound to get better as years of post-war austerity receded into memory, and standards of living improved.

The future held out prospects of better times ahead for the many trapped in poverty. Yet was all this promised change for real? Or was it more illusory wish-fulfilment foisted on people by politicians? Mack despised the so-called wealthy hereditary elite. This ruling class manipulated the nation to favour their own. It perpetuated inequality through their public school chosen. The old school tie repressed society working against the interests of the many for the benefit of the few. Now they were seeing the rise of a new moneyed elite: the pop stars, the movie stars, the fashion photographers, the models, the wealthy entrepreneurs of media and advertising. The old decadence was being joined by the new. Mack had no intention of allowing himself to become like them when he succeeded.

The daily newspapers were filled with tales of the licentious and degenerate behaviour of the Rolling Stones. Jagger and Richards were facing trial for drugs in Chichester. The tale was occupying column inches in the press. Not one to believe all he read in the tabloids Mack felt antipathy towards the pair. Their alleged behaviour struck him as stupid and senseless. He'd passed the newspapers to the girls to read. If that's what mixing with the wealthy and the celebrated led to, they could stuff it. As for the female involved, it was obvious who she was. He had smiled hearing Effy berate Grace for saying the Stones drug and alcohol partying was cool. Grace, unlike Effy, was still impressionable. Mack felt he had a responsibility to watch out for her in the future. Nate's sister seemed more level headed, but at fifteen, what did Grace and Sara know? He'd seen enough of the effects of drug-taking among some of the Halifax and Bradford crowd. The thought ran through his mind that he would have to protect the girls.

By the time Angie arrived, he and Nate had finalized the entire week ahead. This included all the location shoots around the capital. A hectic week loomed starting in the morning. The first job was a shoot for a weekly teen magazine using Angie. Mack planned to photograph Grace at the same time in the same surroundings. He would alter views by judicious and subtle changes of angles and backdrops. These he hoped would do for other magazines. Effy, he would shoot in an exclusive at Moods Mosaic down the King's Road. This would have to be in the afternoon after her morning in the Silvers London workshops.

CHAPTER 20

Can't Take My Eyes Off You – Vikki Carr
(From the LP 'It Must Be Him' - Liberty LBL 83037 – UK – 1967)

Saturday 20 May 1967 – Early morning.

Hester Clayton appeared as Mack was shooting Grace by the fountain in Sloane Square. Preoccupied with ensuring Grace's pose was right, he didn't notice her. Neither did Angie, standing close by shivering, and waiting for her turn in front of the lens. It wasn't the warmest of days, and though Mack didn't rush the shoot, he'd realized the need to work quickly. Both girls wore lightweight summer dresses under their coats. Sara was with them acting as a volunteer assistant, carrying his camera bags. She was also helping Grace and Angie by holding their coats while they were in front of the camera.

They had set off at six o'clock after hurried coffees to avoid rush hour passers-by. So far, the shoot had gone well. Perfect light conditions made Sloane Square an ideal spring in the city location. As a well-known London landmark, the spot allowed him to get creative. Shooting in colour with the Leica, Mack used the second-hand twin-lens Rolleiflex he'd picked up for the black and white shots. Exchanging the Leica for the Rolleiflex, he heard a cut-glass voice from behind. Not one he recognised.

"James MacKinnon?"

Without turning, focussed on taking the next shot, Mack replied in a disinterested voice. "Who's asking?"

"Hester Clayton. I'm booked for a Silvers Fashions modelling assignment you're shooting on Monday."

Looking her over, in three seconds, he took in more than most did in a minute. Hester Clayton was a true blonde with a Twiggy style bob. He could see no giveaway dyed roots, so her hair was her natural colour. Shorter in height than Angie or Grace, the young woman had striking hazel eyes. Her features were symmetrical, with high cheekbones. Hester Clayton was a natural beauty born to model. Her diminutive figure was difficult to assess under the fluffed white fur coat. Was it fur or synthetic, he wondered? He'd seen her in several magazines and from memory recalled her gamine figure.

The patterned magenta stockings made those graceful legs eye-catching. He understood straight away why Nate had hired this elfin model.

Remaining polite and professional, Mack did his best to avoid sounding brusque. "I'm busy right now and need to stay focussed. You must excuse me, but I don't like distractions while working. Stop and watch Miss Clayton. We can talk when I've finished."

Returning to Grace, he called out. "This is a three-quarter shot. I want the 'S' shape. Left hand on hip the other on the head. Excellent, now turn with your chin up. Unclench the hand, Grace. Remember you're having fun. That's it! Keep your eyes looking upward on the first click, on the second towards the figure in the fountain. Excellent."

Several camera clicks followed.

"Now turn to your left. Good. Place your right hand on your hip; use the left to pretend to sweep your hair to one aside. Turn towards me. That's great. Hold it. Brilliant."

"She looks so young." Hester Clayton commented to Angie as they watched.

"Grace is fifteen," Angie answered, absorbed in what Mack was doing.

"What sensational red hair, what sensational legs too. Is this for a teen mag?"

Angie turned to her. "Sorry, I need to stay focussed when he's shooting to see what Mack may want from me. He's almost done with Grace."

"Oh! I'm sorry, I didn't mean to distract you. He takes what he does with professional seriousness, doesn't he? I've heard he's only seventeen? Is this true? His photos are amazing for someone so young."

Her concentration broken, Angie turned to the intruder. "Mack's a genuine wiz with a camera. He knows how to make models look good in whatever they wear. Hi, I'm Angie Thornton."

"Yes, I know. You've appeared in a few magazines recently. As you say, he has an eye for shooting superb photographs. Nate Silvers calls you Northern girls and your kid photographer, *The New Breed Co-operative*. Is that true?"

"As labels go, it's accurate enough. We love working together," Angie responded, studying the interloper. "Mack understands us, and we understand Mack. So yeah, *The Co-operative* is a good name. As for Mack, take my advice. Never underestimate him and never call him *a kid*. At seventeen, he's no kid. Mack's more of a man than most men you'll ever meet. As for his talent with a camera, let's just say, when Mack's mediocre, Mack's outstanding. When Mack's good, Mack's brilliant."

After a brief pause came an unexpected question, shaking Angie by its bluntness.

"So is it true? You and Effy Halloran are both sleeping with him? Is he that good in bed?"

Angie, stunned, replied with an unmistakable glare, eyes flashing.

"Angie. Coat off, you're on pussy cat." She heard him call.

The timing couldn't have been better. Angie's irritation edged on explosive as she walked away. How dare she! Without another word, she removed her coat, giving it to Sara.

Passing Grace, she muttered. "Be careful what you say to that nosey cow."

Nodding Grace acknowledged Angie's words watching the newcomer approach.

"Hi. I'm…"

"…Hester Clayton, I know." Grace acknowledged in her friendliest voice, pre-empting what the gorgeous young woman would say. "You're in loads of magazines. What are you doing here at this ridiculous hour? How did you know we'd be here?"

"I didn't. I'm here by accident. Daddy owns an apartment close by, he lets me live there." Hester's confidence struck Grace straight away. The young woman added airily. "I was returning from a party when I recognised who you all were. So, I thought I'd stop by and say hello. I'm supposed to be working with your sister this week."

"What, from an all-night party? One of those swinging Chelsea parties? I'm curious, and I can't help wondering," Grace changed the subject continuing unabashed, "your surname, Clayton? Are you related to the famous Lucie Clayton of the model school fame?"

"Good heavens, no! Not to my knowledge." Hester Clayton looked astounded at the suggestion as though it was demeaning. "My family is one of the South Surrey Clayton's. Pure coincidence let me assure you."

There was a momentary lull in the conversation before the interloper continued. "Is James MacKinnon always so focussed when doing a shoot?"

"Always. You've seen his work in magazines and the newspapers? He's the best."

"Wait until you have to bookings with one of the top men like Bailey, Donovan, or Duffy. They could get you on the cover of Vogue and other top magazines abroad. That's my ambition. I want to be on the cover of Vogue. That's when you've made it." Hester declared.

"Well, good luck with that. We've only ever worked with somebody else once, and that wasn't a great experience. Besides, none of us are into Vogue. To quote Effy and Mack, that's not our target market. I don't think we're too interested in Vogue and high fashion at our ages. We'll stick together and work with Mack. One day we'll get round to Vogue."

Hester Clayton was open-mouthed at Grace's assured cockiness.

Observing him, she became impressed. This smartly dressed young man worked like a professional Svengali. Weaving with methodical slowness around the object of the hunt, he sought that elusive moment to shoot. His movements were those of a cat stalking prey. There was an indefinable quality to his voice too captivating and rhythmic. The way he elicited responses from Angie Thornton was extraordinary. The girl was under his spell, succumbing to every instruction as though mesmerised. Watching the interaction made Hester aware of what an incredible rapport existed between the two. There was a dream-like entrancing quality to what she was seeing. She experienced a peculiar sensation of wanting to respond to his voice even though she was a bystander. When he finished the shoot, Mack approached her strolling with purpose. His eye to the viewfinder, he snapped off several shots.

"That's unfair..." she flustered.

Stony faced, he cut her off before she could think about how to respond further. "Unbutton your coat, please, Hester. I want to see what you're hiding under it."

Open-mouthed, Hester did as Mack asked. Had she fallen under his spell too? "How tall are you, Hester?" Without waiting for an answer, Mack continued, his tone thoughtful yet detached. "Five foot four? That looks like a Quant frock. Magenta with the orange strip backing a ring ended zip halfway down the front, and a border white hem. It is Quant, isn't it?"

"Why, yes, it is." She stuttered.

"Love your choice of patterned tights. Sara, can you give Nate and Effy a call at the workshop? Let them know we will need to make alterations to Miss Clayton's outfits for the shoot. If we want her showing some thigh, the hemlines will have to be higher. Seeing as she's modelling the trapeze

106

dress designs, these will require doing beforehand. You're the seamstress, Grace. What do you think? Am I right?"

Grace looked her over. "Hang on a sec. Sara, can you pass me my handbag? I think I've got my tape measure with me."

Out came a tape measure to Hester Clayton's amazement. She passed the handbag back to Sara. Grace made a quick, slick, professional check commenting in a low thoughtful voice. "Yes. Right as usual, Mack. God, you've got a great eye. Well spotted. We'll need to have them altered. These three dresses won't look right otherwise. We'll need some clips to tuck in the backs, or the dresses will hang like sacks. Either that or we ask the workshop to put some real tucks in while shortening the hems. And I thought I was skinny."

Turning to Mack, Grace added. "Effy will insist on shortening the hemlines if Miss Clayton is to model them. I've made a mental note of how much we'll have to take off or tuck in."

Hester Clayton began to fasten her fur coat, embarrassed.

Grace unwittingly needled the model. "Do you know you've got what looks like a red wine stain on your dress? And there's something starchy or snotty on the front left thigh? I should get it to a dry-cleaners before it's ruined."

Mack and Angie burst out laughing. Hester Clayton went bright red in an instant.

"You're gorgeous looking, Miss Clayton," Grace continued, puzzled by the laughter and the model's reaction, but carried on regardless. "It's a shame you're a bit on the short side. You could do with being two inches taller."

Hester Clayton's cheeks began to tinge a fetching rose shade. "I've never been so insulted. I've got a good mind to chuck this assignment."

Mack went eye to eye, his voice soft yet betraying a steely edge, "That's your choice, Miss Clayton. Let's get something straight. I'm getting paid a great deal of money to do this assignment, as are you. Our job is to make the dress designs look good. So good that young women working for a tenner a week wage will want to buy the dream we're selling. Now a tenner may not seem much to you. For factory girls working forty-hour weeks in dead-end jobs, it's a big dip in their purses. So let's not forget whose money pays for our time. We're lucky doing work paying this well. Modelling is a fabulous way of earning a living. Far better than sitting in a typing pool. Or standing around in a shop, or getting bored mindless on some factory production line. As for me, well, I get to snap gorgeous-looking young women like you. What's not to like?"

He let the words sink in then continued. "Besides, there is a definite upside to working with me. You've seen what I can do. I'm better than good. Once I've worked my magic, even more photographers will fall over themselves wanting to use you. Your booking agent will struggle to find enough time in your diary for all the assignments. Now, if you don't like the sound of that, fine. Grace can always step into your shoes, and we won't even need to make alterations. It's no skin off our backs. Your choice."

Mack's ambiguous smile and those penetrating hazel eyes beguiled and bewildered her. Twenty-year-old Hester Clayton found herself provoked yet wholly captivated by his assured masculinity. She could not stop looking at him. The more she looked, the more she loved what she saw. Mack's deep, velvet-soft voice had sent peculiar, thrilling, and pleasing shivers through her body. This young photographer was nothing like anyone she had ever encountered in her modelling career. Surely, he was too good to be true? It wasn't the most lucrative paying assignment. She'd worked with some top names in the recent past for far more money. At her friend's insistence, she'd agreed to take on the assignment. Now instinct told her this was an assignment opportunity not to miss.

Almost as if it had slipped his mind, as he walked back to Angie, Mack turned. "And never call me kid, Miss Clayton."

After she'd gone, Grace turned to Mack and Angie, puzzled. "Why were you two laughing? She looked embarrassed. Was it something I said?"

They both sniggered with Mack shaking his head. "Angie, you can explain to Grace about the 'starchy' stains. It might be better coming from you rather than me."

CHAPTER 21

Peter Gunn Theme – Henry Mancini (RCA 1134 – 1959)
Saturday 20 May 1967 – Later

The studio was in Lansdowne Walk near to Holland Park tube station. On the top floor of a converted terrace, its deceptive size took Mack by surprise. It impressed Grace and Sara. They had tagged along volunteering to help Mack in the darkroom. Nate's sister seemed eager to come along with Grace. Mack had promised to show her how photographs were developed.

Mack estimated the studio was twenty by thirty feet long. It had high ceilings painted a stark pale grey throughout. Kitted out with the latest and best equipment, it left Mack awed. Bowler's Bradford studio was a cramped hole by comparison. Every piece of equipment he could have wished for was here. On the back wall hung a massive paper roller for backdrops. The best of it was that there was a large selection of different coloured paper rolls. Checking the studio further, he saw an umbrella diffuser and a choice of reflectors. There was also a photoflood and a photo spot as well as a barn door light. Shooting full length would be no problem. His new short 85mm telephoto lens could get the desired results. Mack need not have brought his folding tripod. The studio possessed two.

One of three small side rooms boasted one of the best darkrooms he'd seen. It contained everything he wished for, including a sophisticated safelight box and an enlargement facility. Nate informed them there was a changing room for models downstairs. This had a dedicated professional makeup area like the ones found in theatre dressing rooms.

"So, what do you think?"

"Nate, this studio is amazing. I wish I had this place. Who owns it?"

Nate's response was cagey. The studio was company-owned, but no further enlightenment was forthcoming. Without more ado, Nate trotted out that tired cliché that time was money. He told Mack he needed to develop today's shoot straight away. Mack attempted to explain, each coloured roll would take about an hour. There were four rolls of black and white too. Each of those required between fifteen and twenty minutes. Then they'd only have the contacts but not all the full sized photos. Thanks to Sara's intervention, Nate gave in to her.

They hadn't eaten all day surviving on coffee and biscuits. Sara insisted that her brother should take them out somewhere for a decent meal. Her insistence went one step further. She begged him to get a reservation at Gaylord's Indian restaurant in Soho. As Angie was heading home tomorrow evening, Nate relented and conceded they deserved a break and a treat. He agreed to let Mack work through Sunday evening and caved into his sister's request. It had taken some persuasion. Nate settled for the morning's coloured shoot and one of the afternoon's black and white spools. He agreed to collect Effy and Angie from the apartment and to pick them up around eight.

"Okay. Let's get started and introduce Sara to the dark arts of developing film. We can train her up as number two assistant."

The facility was so well equipped he finished developing with fifteen minutes to spare. They managed to print out full sets of contacts.

The Indian restaurant was off Regent Street. Nate referred to the area as Fitzrovia. Neither Mack nor the girls had experienced Indian cuisine. Sara had been to the restaurant once before with Nate and her parents. The Indian meal proved a novel experience. Mack decided he could get a taste for Indian dishes. Only Grace and Sara enjoyed the meal. Neither Angie nor Effy enjoyed the food. They didn't share his enthusiasm finding it too spicy. Sara and Grace loved what they chose. Mack found himself drawn into more business talk. Nate was keen to make Angie the focus of a particular range of outfits and coats in the morning. While they were deep in conversation, trouble came calling.

Effy and Angie found themselves accosted as they returned from the women's toilets. Hearing Angie's strident voice alerted Mack and Nate, and they became aware of a commotion, though hidden from view. Both were on their feet without a word to see what the fuss was about. A waiter was trying to intervene as they arrived. Nate indicated to him he should leave.

Mack found Nate pulling him back. "No, you don't, Mack. I wasn't expecting this to happen here and now. This is a setup. Stay out of it. I know who these guys are, and what's going on, so leave this to me. Whatever you do, don't, and I mean don't, start a fight. It's what they want. It's why they're here."

Angie looked furious. Two men had backed her and Effy against a wall. Angie slapped away the wandering hands of the dark-haired one.

"You've got some balls, my little chickadee." Mack heard one of them laughing.

"Balls? Huh!" Her voice was hard and sharp as she squared up to him full of anger. "My balls are bigger than yours. They're on my chest to avoid friction, you ugly wanker. Bet you're hung like a fucking peanut, anyway."

"Why don't you find out?" He egged her on with an all too obvious display.

"Why don't you piss off?" Came her fiery response.

"You heard my friend." Effy intervened, stepping in front of Angie, acting like a shield. "Leave us alone. Go on, piss off."

"You heard the young ladies, Griffin. Leave them be. Tell Barker to back off too. Pick on someone like me instead. You know you want to." Nate stood a good six inches shorter than both men.

"Or what?" They turned round to confront Nate and Mack. Neither appeared surprised to see him. "Well, well, can you Adam and Eve it! If it ain't Manchester's baked bean his self. Brought your boyfriend with ya, ya big woofta."

"Long time no see, Billy." Nate eyed him up and down, ignoring the insult. "Listen, Griffin, you and Barker are in the wrong parish. You should leave right now. Our Maltese cousins aren't big on you Stepney boys coming onto their patch. Start something now, and you won't be around long enough to see the end of it. Or have you forgotten what happened to 'Big' Eddy?"

If it came to a fight, Mack had worked out already how to take the one with the brown hair called Griffin. The silent one with the balding head called Barker would be a problem. He looked like Mick McManus's double without hair. Someone you'd expect to see in the wrestling ring on Saturday afternoon TV. The typical bruiser you'd watch wrestling The Giant Haystack or Shirley Crabtree. He was huge.

Nate continued unfazed. "So, Joe's up to no good again, hiring you two. Whatever my ever-loving brother's game is, you shouldn't be playing along with him. Where's the photographer? Hiding somewhere outside, is he? Ready to snap you two handing out a beating? Tell Joe I'm on to him. While I'm at it, you should remind him. He's in our Maltese cousins' naughty book. Joe doesn't want his health taking a turn for the worst, and neither do you."

111

As Nate spoke, Angie and Effy had sidled away to join Mack and Nate. Two men entered the restaurant, one holding a camera. "We found him lurking and took his toy away."

"Where is he? Still outside somewhere?" Nate checked with the guy holding the camera.

"Mike's keeping him safe so you can have a word with him."

"Yeah. I'd like a word or two with him."

Griffin's giant pal made an aggressive move towards the two men stopping short. Both pulled open their suit jackets. Mack spotted handgun butts peeking out of their trouser waistbands.

"Tsk, Tsk," Nate smirked, "Truth is Griffin, your pal Barker's a hard man all right, hard but not bright. You should know by now that my family uses bodyguards here in London after what happened. If you're smart, you'll forget any deal you've made with Joe. Joe's yesterday's man, just like in the song."

Outsmarted, Griffin grunted unhappy with the situation. Barker shuffled like a caged gorilla glancing in Griffin's direction for Plan B.

"Mack, be a gent, take care of our young ladies. I need to have a few more words with our unwanted visitors in private." Nate's smile suggested there might be more than just words. "There's nothing to worry about. There's not going to be a problem, is there Griffin? Sara will explain about the bodyguards while I'm having a cosy chat with these two *gents*."

In Nate's absence, Mack questioned Sara as the girls listened. What Sara revealed shook them. Two years earlier, there had been an attempt to assault her father. It had taken place here in London. The attack had failed because Nate was there with a friend to prevent it. How they'd thwarted the attack, she didn't offer to explain. Sara hinted Nate's friend's presence had been enough. There were reasons behind the attempted assault, but Sara was reluctant to tell them more. Sara claimed she didn't know the full story. Since then, her father had hired bodyguards. They followed at a discrete distance whenever they were in the capital. Sara said she didn't think Joe would try to do anything to her or her brother Simon, but he might to Nate and his father.

Later, Nate enlightened Mack further. They intended the assault to pressure his father and his business interests in London. Nate was vague, almost evasive, about it. Mack worked out that an East End mob must have wanted a slice of the Silvers business in a protection racket attempt. The family's Maltese associates had intervened.

112

"So, you were you expecting trouble?" Mack questioned Nate.

His reply came as no surprise. "I know my brother. He's shallow and not as smart as he thinks he is. His girlfriend's even shallower and none too bright. We've been keeping close tabs on her, so we know what Joe's doing. There are one or two people who owe my dad favours. They've kept us informed about Joe's activities. The way he's carrying on, it's not going to end well. Since my father kicked him out of the family business, he's lost it. There are things he's doing that can only end badly. The less I mention in that respect, the better. The man's a fool to himself. From what we've heard, he's also been yapping his mouth off about you and the girls. He didn't much like the way you and they treated him. I've been told he took your promise as a personal insult, and as a real threat. As for the way the girls spoke to him, they pissed him off. Not getting his way with Effy infuriated him, but not as much as you did tell him to stay clear of her. Some comment about cutting his balls off and making purses out of them for the girls didn't go down at all well. You also upset one of his close pals. That one's been baying for blood ever since she lost her job because of you and them."

"Friend?" Then it came to Mack like the proverbial flash. "Mara Fisher?"

"The one and only. Let's say no more. You know all you need to know for the moment. Careless talk costs failed plans."

"And Caroline Anstruther-Brown? Is she still working at Moods?"

"Not for much longer."

"You're putting Manny in charge, is that it?"

"Manny is a behind-the-scenes man. He keeps an eye on the boutique and on our other local workshops and suppliers. He's a cousin who also has family ties with our local Maltese associates. They help to keep our activities safe, smooth-running, and legitimate. We kept Caroline on as the token manageress because of her clientele contacts. Also, that way, we could keep tags on my brother's activities. Caroline's not the most discrete person. Tina Wood, who we hired on your recommendation, is shaping up as Caroline's future replacement. In the meantime, we've persuaded Tina to keep tabs on Caroline on the QT. She's a smart cookie, according to Manny."

That proved unexpected. When he next spoke with Sykes's girlfriend, he would need caution. Whose side would she take? His or her bosses the Silvers?

Mack learned something surprising. The Silvers family history was interesting. They were not a typical Jewish family. He'd assumed their

113

origins were in Eastern or Central Europe or else of long-standing in England. They weren't. A few generations back, the family had lived in Malta. Their Italian connections stretched even further back. This explained the family's Mediterranean olive complexions. There were still ties to the island and to the Maltese community in London. Over time, the family had anglicised their surname to Silvers from Silvetti.

CHAPTER 22

Show Me – Joe Tex (Atlantic 584096 –1967)
Sunday 21 May 1967 –1.30 am

"I thought we'd agreed."

"We did," Effy responded coolly. "I'm willing to make it an exception tonight. After what's happened, Angie's needs you. So you two sleep in the double bed tonight. She could do with some love and attention after what happened. Since she's going home, you sleep with her. After all, I'll have you all to myself for the rest of the week."

"I'm not happy doing that. Not with you in the single bed next door. Then there's your sister and Sara across the way…"

"Well, I never!" Effy smiled as she embraced him. "I never thought you'd be such a prude. Don't go assuming. Angie may not want sex. And if she does, I'm coming to terms knowing we share having sex with you."

"I'm still struggling with that," Mack replied, squeezing her while trying to control the hardness awakening in him. "Don't look at me like that with those eyes, Eff. You know how much I love you, how much I want you. I know how much you love me too. This only makes it worse."

"So, you're struggling trying to love two? You knew it wouldn't be easy. Angie and I always thought you'd find it tough. Funny, isn't it? We thought we'd be the ones who'd find it hard, the two of us loving you. Yet here we are. Still close friends, still sisters in compromise, sharing, and loving you."

"Do you two talk about sharing me?"

"Of course we do, silly. Our friendship wouldn't survive otherwise. This will sound weird." She paused, gave him a long soft kiss as she stroked his cheek, before continuing. "We girls share our thoughts and feelings. This is how we're avoiding jealousy. Angie's the insecure one, not me. She tries not to show you, but she frets. Behind that cool tough image, Angie's frightened of losing you. I'm the secure one who doesn't worry. She's the worrier. She thinks that one day, you will walk away and leave her. Angie believes you'll find it too hard loving the two of us. She loves you as much as I do, but Angie needs most reassurance."

115

Mack felt chastened. After a moment or two, he asked. "How do you cope…with sex? That worries me a lot. How do you deal with it?"

Effy let out a long, enormous, heartfelt sigh. "It's a purely physical thing. Don't misunderstand, I love the sex, but I don't let sex confuse me about why I love you. There's so much more than sex going for us. I'm learning to keep sex in a separate room in my head different from the room with the emotional side. I love sex, it's brilliant, but it's not the be all that keeps you and me together."

"Does Angie see it that like that too?"

"Why don't you ask her?"

When he and Angie were lying next to each other, an hour later, he asked. She answered in almost the same words as Effy. It didn't ease his conscience, hearing her response. That phrase Effy had used, *sisters in compromise*, stuck in his mind. What had she meant? It all hinged on how Effy and Angie understood the word compromise. Relieved the bed didn't creak, he and Angie uttered no sounds knowing Effy was in the next bedroom.

Staying silent was something neither girl did during sex, but tonight was an exception. Mack's lovemaking was tender. His hands and lips explored her entire body with more than usual gentleness.

The pale moonlight shining through the window illuminated her satin-soft nakedness. Angie's body had a lustrous porcelain quality in the semi-darkness. When she climaxed, it was in silence, biting on his should. She responded to his emptying in wave after wave of contractions clinging to him. Afterwards, they spooned until dawn broke.

Mack awoke with a start on hearing a gentle tap on the door. He tried to slip out from under the sheets, but Angie refused to let go holding on to him. "Don't get up just yet. Cuddle me for a few more minutes. There's something I need to say. It's important."

"I'm listening." Mack felt her warm breath in his ear as she spoke in a whisper.

"Please, Mack. I'm begging you, don't go looking to get even with Joe Silvers. I know you. So does Effy. Whatever you're planning, don't. Joe Silvers is too dangerous. Both Effy and I fear what he'd do. You're seventeen and a half. Think about this, and don't be stupid. As tough and as brave as you are, you'd be no match for a hired gunman or professional thugs. If anything happened to you, imagine how it would affect your parents. It would break mine and Effy's hearts too." "Has Effy put you up to this?"

"No. We talked it over and agreed. I told her I'd speak to you," Caressing him, her hand moved with tender lightness backwards and forwards on his chest. She added, "We want you safe and sound. No, we *need* you safe and sound."

"So, the ganging up on me continues?"

"We're serious!" Angie tweaked the skin on his chest, making him wince. "Treat this with seriousness, Mack. Not just for me, for Effy too."

A sharper rapping on the bedroom door interrupted them. It was Grace, "Oi, you two! Get up! There's a full day of work ahead."

"Promise me, promise Effy, you won't resort to violence, Mack."

"Promise."

"Cross your heart?"

"Cross my heart."

"…And not just getting physical. That'll you stay well clear of Joe Silvers altogether. Effy, and I know you too well. The way you play word games."

Mack promised to stay away from Joe Silvers once more. What he intended was avoiding any direct contact or confrontation. *He would act on his worst instinct if it were demanded,* as Cesar Borgia had once said.

Nate had arrived while they were still sleeping, rousing Effy and the girls first. By the time they all sat down to have breakfast, it was six-thirty. It was a rushed affair, and Mack found himself the source of giddy laughter. Sitting between Angie and Effy, he somehow managed to splash milk over himself instead of the cornflakes.

"Honestly, Mack. We can't take you anywhere without you making a mess." Effy's sternness was comical as she and Angie tried to clean him up using a tea towel.

"Oh, for goodness' sake, MacKinnon." Angie fussed. "You'd better get changed. You can't go out with your clothes in that state."

"And while you're at it, put your underpants in the laundry bag." Added Effy. "I'll have to get your stuff washed before we go home."

"Effy, do you want me to put these in the wash now?" Angie asked. "You might as well use the front loader while we're here."

The girls' spontaneous reaction caused Nate to slop his coffee as he burst out laughing.

"What's it like having two mum's fussing over you?" Sara giggled.

"Now he's got some idea of what it'll be like with two wives." Jibed Grace.

Angie and Effy blushed at the reactions. Red-faced, Mack went to change into fresh clothes. Muttering under his breath, he gave Grace a dirty look as he passed. Putting on clean kit, he smiled to himself. Angie and Effy's responses were spontaneous, reassuring, and so genuine. At that moment, he understood what Effy had meant by *sisters in compromise*.

CHAPTER 23

Groovin' – Book T and The MGs (Stax 601018 - 1967)
Sunday 21 May 1967

Onlookers proved the downside to shooting in popular locations. Even at eight o'clock on a Sunday morning, they gathered to see what was happening. When the girls were relative unknowns, they had excited little interest. Now it was extraordinary. Though not everyone recognised them, people stopped to stare.

Arriving at seven, in Piccadilly Circus, he took thirty shots around the fountain. During their first London trip, he'd scouted the location together with Effy and Angie. He'd looked for good angles. At the time, he'd learned from Effy that Eros wasn't Eros. It was Eros's twin brother Anteros, and the statue was aluminium, not bronze.

Though Angie was the principal model today, Mack snapped Effy and Grace too. There was no point in wasting good opportunities. Photo shooting the sisters together and in separate sequences proved a smart decision. Those extra photos would earn them a great deal of money from several other magazines.

Angie's Piccadilly fountain photo would appear on the front cover of a French teen magazine. Silvers Fashions would syndicate a second to a Dutch fashion magazine. That would also appear on the front cover. The editors would credit both Mack and Angie. Two of Effy and Grace together would find their way into West German fashion magazines. Continental demand for the girls as models would not only snowball, it would avalanche.

They tried to avoid onlookers and passers-by in the background. It soon became increasingly more and more difficult to do so. The streets of London were never empty during the day, not even on early Sunday mornings. Mack tried posing Angie and Effy with Tower Bridge in the background. This proved time consuming and exasperating as passers-by intruded unintentionally.

When it got to midday, strollers on The Embankment proved too great a nuisance. Even allowing for growing numbers of people, the results justified their efforts. Though they quickened the pace of working, it became obvious, they would need to return to some of the planned locations. Other

119

locations proved less suitable. Today's session had challenged but not overwhelmed. Good location photo shoots depended on the light and the weather for the best results. Mack had made the best of both.

Grace couldn't believe it when a group of teenage girls recognised her. Gathering around, they asked for autographs. This left her elated for the rest of the day. The same girls then recognised Effy and Angie. Inevitable disruption followed.

"I know you. You're the ones in that picture with him, aren't you? You know… that photo of you three coming out of that club. It was all over the Sunday newspapers, wasn't it?"

"Can I have your autograph?" Another of the girls asked Mack.

He nodded, distracted by the interruption. He remained polite.

"Oi! Guess who this is?" Another girl called out. "This is 'im, 'e's the cool Mod on the scooter wot stuck two fingers up at them reporters. I've cut that photo out and got it on my bedroom wall."

Mack grinned, shaking his head, reminded of the incident. It ended the session on the embankment. Angie had a small notebook. Tearing leaves from it, he took some and signed a handful of autographs. He took several impromptu shots of the girls together with his three models. It was too good an opportune situation to miss.

As they walked away, the girl who had recognised Mack ran after him and said. "Ta. My mates think you're a diamond geezer. I do too. See ya."

"Gawd," Grace exclaimed. "Once they knew who you were, they were all over you like a rash. I could see you as another Alfie if you weren't Effy and Angie's boyfriend."

"Wait until I tell, Nate, what's happened." Sara sounded excited. "I hope the photos you took just now look good. You could make use of them for publicity."

"We'll have to wait and see what comes out of the development tank," Mack winked.

Grace recalled in an instant the wink outside Church. The one Mack gave Effy outside the Church. That's when it had all begun, this wonderful new life they were now living. Grace still struggled to understand how her sister had ended up sharing Mack with Angie. Yet she couldn't stay angry with Mack. Grace would have loved a brother like Mack. As for Angie, she was like another big sister and a true friend. There was no way Grace could ever dislike Angie for what happened. Everything Angie felt for Effy and

Mack was genuine; it was in her every action when with one or both of them. Grace wanted to be like Angie: strong, confident, cool, smart, and kindness itself. She hoped the three would stay together forever.

Her new friend Sara was shy in Mack company, less so with Effy and Angie, but in awe of all three. Grace suspected perhaps a little of herself too. Quiet and introverted, Nate's sister was the opposite of Grace.

Sara could not conceal the shock of what had taken place in the restaurant. This was something that had not passed unnoticed. Grace had watched Sara talking to Nate afterwards. Speaking in hushed voices, whatever passed between the two, Sara kept to her self. She hadn't looked happy. Grace thought it wiser not to ask but mentioned what she'd seen to Mack in a quiet aside.

Leaving the Embankment, the group crossed to Whitehall. Mack used the mounted Horse guards as a backdrop for a photo of Angie and Grace as they passed. Once again, tourists stopped to ogle what was taking place. Having been on the go for hours, the five walked back to Soho. Sara led them to a coffee bar in Old Compton Street called the 2i's. She had been here once before with Nate and Simon. It was hallowed ground for Rock and Roll lovers, but it didn't matter.

Refreshed, Mack thought about the work ahead in the evening. He'd taken over a hundred shots, and developing these would take time at the studio. Angie was keen to get back to the penthouse. She wanted to make sure she was packed and ready when Manny called to take her to the train station. As they left the coffee bar, Grace and Effy spotted the two bodyguards from the restaurant.

"Didn't you notice them hanging around before?" Mack smiled. "They've been with us all day. There are two more."

"Two more? Where?" Mack's observation surprise Effy.

"They don't make it too obvious. Look to your ten o'clock, fifty feet by the large black doorway."

"Oh! Have they been following us?"

"Ever since we set foot outside this morning. They've been discrete. Time to get the taxicabs. Might as well head back. We've done for today as far as I'm concerned."

"What do you think? Have you some good shots?"

"We'll see when I develop them this evening."

On their return to the apartment, they found Manny and his wife waiting. In their absence, she had been busy in the kitchen preparing an evening meal. A young man they didn't know was with them. Sara beamed the moment she spotted him and dashed across the room to hug him. Mack knew who he was before Sara introduced him. Simon Silvers resemblance to family members was plain, but the brother-sister likeness was striking. At a guess, he was nineteen and dressed in the sort of clothes sold in boutiques like *Granny Takes A Trip*. Simon Silvers floral jacket was outrageous, its ostentatiousness grating on Mack's eyes. He wore his hair long, reminding Mack of Dave Davis of The Kinks. What Mack liked less was the way he eyed Effy when introduced.

Mack had seen this instant smitten ogling in too many guys' eyes. It now went beyond irritation, often turning to resentment. He had grown to expect blokes lusting over Effy, but it didn't mean he cared for it. When he discovered the reason Simon Silvers was here, Mack liked it even less.

After the meal, Angie packed her few things for the return journey to Halifax. She seemed reluctant to go. Before leaving, Angie took Effy to one side. They had a short, whispered conversation filled with intermittent giggling. Angie then took Mack out of sight of the others in the hallway entrance.

"I want to remind you."

"What about, Angie?"

"Joe Silvers and staying away from him. You've made a promise to me, and that means to Effy too. We expect you to keep it." Angie's appeal to him had an added earnestness, "Don't go looking to get even. If I were you, I'd pay more attention to Mr Temptation over there."

Mack understood her warning. "Have I something to worry about?"

Angie stayed silent.

"Well? Have I?"

"Probably not, but take nothing and no one for granted, least of all anyone who might fancy himself a smooth operator. This one does, I've met his sort before. Remember, I love you no matter what. I can't wait for the weekend. I'll miss you so bad until then. Don't forget to call me after-nine thirty. Oh, and watch out for Grace as well as Effy. From what I've experienced of the Silvers so far, the only innocent among them is Sara."

Her words left a chill. Seeing his expression alter, she embraced Mack. Leaving a trail of small kisses all over his face, she pressed her body against him. Before letting go, she kissed him on the lips as if it was their last kiss.

122

Manny and his wife took Angie to catch the train as Nate arrived. He'd disappeared for the entire day, where he didn't say when he returned. Nate had arranged Simon's visit but had neglected to mention it. His brother was a student at the Royal College of Art studying Fashion. Simon's specialist interest lay in fabric print designs. Nate said his brother was here to discuss a company project with Effy. Unique fabric prints they intended to have run off for the sole use of Silvers Fashions. These they would make from Simon Silvers artwork. The exclusive print designs would only be for Effy to use and for her to create original designs.

Annoyed, on learning he had to work alone in the studio, Mack prepared to set off. It wasn't as though he didn't trust Effy. He disliked the thought of her left alone for all those hours with Simon Silvers. The guy's wandering eyes reminded him too much of his older brother, Joe. Effy didn't put his mind at ease when he passed a hushed comment. Her response came like a splash of cold water.

"Don't tell me you're jealous? Afraid of the competition?" There wasn't even a hint of teasing in her voice, no smile. A curious hard edge to her words left Mack hurt and unhappy. This was so unlike her, so strange and out of character. Effy had never spoken to him like that. What made it worse was her frozen expression of irritation. Mack bit his lower lip, turned, and walked away. The sensation of hurt was so physical, so intense; it was as if his life force was draining from his body. His heart pounded. He felt sick.

Sara and Grace were in no mood to help him in the studio. After tramping the streets of London all day, they'd had enough. Nate tried to persuade them to go but to no avail. It had been a long day, and Mack understood their reluctance. All the girls wanted to do was to crash in front of the television. Sara protested so much Nate gave in, allowing them to stay. In one way, it pleased Mack. With them, in the apartment, he'd feel better knowing Effy was not on her own with Nate's brother. Developing the spools of film would take hours without the girls' help.

Nate dropped him off at the studio with the keys leaving him to it. By the time he'd completed developing and getting prints made, it was near midnight. Phoning for a taxi, he returned half an hour later, finding the apartment in darkness. No one was in.

CHAPTER 24

I'll Never Stop Loving You – Ketty Lester
(London HLN 9698 – B Side – 1963)
Monday 22 May 1967 – 0:05 am – 8:30 am

Mack attempted to read *Capturing Character* in the March edition of *Amateur Photographer*. Unable to keep his eyes open, he fell asleep on the sofa. Effy's last words haunted his sleep. The worst thing about dreams was how real they could seem. An angry Effy kept shaking him by the arms repeating over and over and over, "Jealous? Afraid of the competition?" Waking with a start he found Effy shaking his arm with a gentle touch.

"Come on, sleepy. Let's get to bed," her voice soft, sweet and tender, "you look worn out."

"Are you still angry with me?" He yawned, rising from the sofa.

"Not really. Leave it be. Let's get into bed. We can have a lie-in until nine. We don't have to be at the studio until ten-thirty. Oh, I changed the sheets on the bed earlier this evening."

"Where did you go tonight?"

"Sara wanted us to go to a club, so she twisted Nate's arm, and he ended up taking us to The Tiles club in Oxford Street."

"Not with Simon?"

"Simon? No. Why would I go anywhere with him? I looked at his designs, discussed which ones I liked, and he left after an hour. Listen, we're both tired. I'll tell you all about it in the morning. I just want to sleep in your arms."

There was no sex during the night. By the time they got into the bathroom and finished, they were both too tired. Effy slipped between the sheets in only her briefs. He slept naked as normal spooning with her just as he had with Angie. Both girls favoured the same spooning position. It was impossible for him not to make comparisons.

Effy's hair and skin had a distinct and different scent to Angie's, more of a jasmine scent compared to Angie's musky sandalwood. Blindfolded, deprived of the sense of smell and hearing, reliant on touch alone, he might have found it difficult to tell them apart. They were almost like twins. Same height, same build, same bust shapes, and sizes. Not even

124

the areolas of their breasts felt different. Even the texture and thickness of their hair felt the same now both had bobbed hairstyles. Yet there was one crucial physical difference that set them apart. Mack could tell by touch alone which one he was next to in the dark. Their earlobes were different.

Effy loved him nibbling her ear lobes, as foreplay. Angie didn't like her ear lobes touched, but she liked to talk dirty in his ear to arouse him. Yet both enjoyed and insisted on his tongue running loose on their nipples as a way of intensifying arousal. Audible responses to foreplay and orgasm were different too.

Did he enjoy sex with Effy more than Angie? No. Mack loved the variety he experienced with both. Each responded to their needs in distinctive ways. Mack loved the different noises they made climaxing. When it came to sex, there was no restraining Effy. Effy would try anything once. While Angie was not averse to trying different positions, she was less adventurous. Angie preferred to lay spread-eagled, feeling the downward pressure of his body pinning her. This turned her on the most she confessed. Twice in a night was normal for both girls. The limited opportunities for intimacy demanded it.

A waft of coffee in the nostril woke Mack from the darkness of a dreamless sleep. Effy's smile filled his eyes. A kiss on the forehead followed. "The slave driver's here checking the contacts printed off last night. Here, drink this."

"Is Grace up yet?"

"Not yet. She and Sara are still sleeping off last night." Rising from the bed, Effy took off the bathrobe and began to dress. "I'd get in that bathroom real quick before they do. Otherwise, you'll end up busting for a pee and taking a shower in cold water. Remember how long they took when we stopped at Nate's?"

"Why were you mad with me yesterday?" Mack needed to know. "Because you were so don't deny it."

"Listen, Mack..." Effy paused. He knew that look on her face. The one Effy had when deciding what to say next. "It's ... well, when I saw your expression as I spoke to Simon. There was no reason for giving me that look. I dread seeing it because it warns me your dark side is coming out. I saw it with that guy at the party, the rugby player. I saw it again with Scooby and Sykes and then in the fight in Brixton Road. I saw it at the restaurant the other night. It frightens me, and it frightens Angie too. After you left for the studio, I overheard Nate warn Simon to stay away from me. He said that making a pass at me was a dangerous idea. He frightened him off by telling him about the violence you were capable of carrying out. Anyway, I told Simon he could take me on a conducted tour of the RCA to show me around in case I want to apply. So don't get mad at me, or him. Grace will tag along. It might be somewhere for her to think about applying in the future."

Mack couldn't believe what he was hearing. Embracing him, Effy gazed into his hazel eyes. More came tumbling from her lips. "Mack, there's no need to get jealous. You are the only one for me, and you will be the only one for me. I've told you before, and now I'm promising you once more. I love you, and only you. Now our faces are becoming known, it will happen far more often, and it will get worse. As a model, my looks will attract male attention. You'll have to live with that. Men will try to chat me up. But no man will get lucky with me except you. Knowing Angie, and how she feels about you, she'll be like me. So behave yourself for both our sakes. All jealousy will do is prove you don't trust me, or Angie. If you don't trust me, then what kind of love do we have?"

Her words left him almost dumbfounded. "Well, that's me told."

"Listen, you're going to have to chat up Miss Clayton this morning. I might be the one who ends up jealous." She playfully tweaked his nose then continued dressing. "You'd better hurry. I hear them stirring. You don't want to be waiting to get into the bathroom again."

CHAPTER 25

Sweet Talking Guy – The Chiffons (Stateside SS 512 – 1966)
Monday 22 May 1967. Morning.

Hester Clayton arrived at ten-thirty. Unlike some models, she was a professional when it came to timekeeping. The photographers she'd worked with rarely took the time to talk to her. If they did, it was often cursory and to the point telling her what they wanted. Often she felt like a piece of meat dressed up and served as some kind of dish of the day. Today was a different experience. Something so peculiar it bordered on the extraordinary.

At first, it seemed like an elaborate chat-up line. When Effy Halloran joined them, she realized it wasn't. It was genuine and intended to put her at ease with him and his girlfriend. He wanted to know all about her. He asked about the trivial things, too, such as where she lived. Did she share her flat and with whom? Hester noticed how he kept checking out her sense of humour. His amusing anecdotes and jokes made her smile and laugh. She enjoyed talking with him more and more the longer they spoke. The way he defrosted and relaxed her had an undeniable charm and maturity. This young photographer had warmth and knew how to talk to a woman like a real person.

Her past experiences of seventeen-year-old males were of immature youths whose brains dangled between their legs. Like most young women, she had come to believe older men were more mature. Yet this young Northerner was so different, so exceptional, and so mature for his years. He was contrary to her expectations, engrossing, and charismatic. Those hazel eyes of his were compelling, and his voice had a soothing, hypnotic gentleness. His smile left a strange warm emotion running through her. Angie Thornton was right. James MacKinnon was no kid. Now she began to understand why she had said he was more of a man than some men she'd met.

An ex-boyfriend used to irritate her playing an old Blues record. The title came to mind as they talked. *Mannish Boy*. That strange title summed up James MacKinnon. That's what he was, a mannish boy. All the time they talked, Effy Halloran sat in silence by his side. She was occupied drawing in a sketchpad.

Once in front of the camera, Hester found herself at ease and responsive to his instructions. Mack had a transistor radio tuned to Radio Caroline playing in the background. She could hear the sound of Martha and the Vandellas singing *Heatwave*. Right there, right now, whenever he used her name, she felt a peculiar sensation, and her heart began to skip beats and race. During the session, he had her giggling, then laughing at his jokes. His compliments brought smiles to her face, even blushes. The occasional provocative comment achieved gasps eliciting unexpected changes of expression. His way of working was unusual. Yet she enjoyed the informal and unconventional way he did the shoot.

Most photographers asked for a standard range of predictable clichéd poses. They usually asked for them in a prepared set order, so it became the artistic equivalent of modelling by numbers. With him, it didn't. The longer the session went on, the more she enjoyed it. His method of working felt so natural and easy. No wonder his photographs were so creative. He knew how to capture a model at her seamless best working as though by instinct. Taking a pause, the sound of Frankie Valli's voice singing *Can't Take My Eyes Off You,* filled the silence. Hester found the lyrics triggering a strange set of emotions. Watching him changing a new spool of film to the song's words made her heart beat even faster. She was overcome with an inexplicable sensation of weakness.

Working with his girlfriend in front of the camera was another revelation. There was a kind of intimacy between them bordering on the telepathic, identical to the one she'd seen with Angie Thornton. Hester was right to anticipate the end results. She even wanted to own the dresses she modelled, a rare occurrence. This young woman was a designer with flair about to make a significant name for her self. As a model, she would soon be up there with the best. This MacKinnon and Halloran pairing could become another Bailey and Shrimpton.

Hester Clayton envied Effy. Her stunning model looks, natural gracefulness, and talent as a designer left her feeling inferior within minutes. Knowing her powers of attraction had no effect on Effy Halloran's boyfriend, didn't help.

She would have loved to seduce him, but Hester knew she couldn't compete. That young woman owned him body and soul. Before the session started, while chatting with Mack, she had watched as Effy Halloran had sketched an amazing pencil portrait of her. Drawn with a swift, economical, and effortless precision, she caught glimpses of it taking shape. Stopping only to sharpen the pencil, Effy had then sketched a new dress design. The only time she spoke was to show him the design. A silent exchange passed between the two as they studied the sketch and her.

"Could suit Hester." Her tone had been businesslike, lacking emotion. "What do you think? I'll suggest it to Nate, shall I?"

"Why not? Let's see what he says."

After the shoot, Effy gave her the sketched portrait. This came as a surprise since Effy had exchanged few words with her. She'd signed it Effy H and dated the picture. In years to come, this would have pride of place in Hester's home.

"You are incorrigible!" Effy shook her head. "I could not believe how shameless you were pumping her for information. You should work for MI6 interrogating people."

"Don't you mean, MI5?" Mack countered with a smug smile and chuckle.

"I used to think your cousin Tom was Mr Smooth, the sweet-talking guy. It seems I was mistaken. It looks like it must run in the MacKinnon sides of the family. No wonder you and Tom have all the females falling for you."

Mack tried to suppress chuckling. "Blame Tom for teaching me how."

"After what I heard, you could teach Tom a thing or two. You're both as bad. Whatever the male equivalent of a shameless hussy is, you're it."

Effy's shirty retort made him chuckle even more, "Now, now, Effy anyone would think I was trying to seduce her."

"Huh. You'd have had no problem there. She was all doe eyes and gushy. If I hadn't been here, she'd have tried to get you inside her knickers in no time."

"Just as well you were here in that case."

"Miss la-di-dah Hester Clayton's no innocent, she knows all about sex and seduction. Angie told me all about the *starch stains* on her dress. No wonder Grace went red when Angie explained it to her. I'll be keeping a beady eye on Missy tomorrow."

"I can't help wondering why you gave her the sketch? Why were you so nice to her?"

"You know that saying you always use?"

"Which saying is that?"

"Keep friends close, but your enemies closer."

Chuckling Mack shook his head. "A rival, maybe, but she's no enemy."

Effy leaned in, rubbing her nose against his. "Okay, I'll keep *all my rivals* close. So, how much longer do we have to hang about waiting for Nate to collect us?"

"I'll give him another thirty minutes. It's five-thirty now. If he's not here by then, I'll call a taxi. We could do with something to eat. Apart from instant coffee and tea, we've had nothing since breakfast."

"Can't we cut down on the taxis rides?" Effy swept her bobbed hair back. "It's costing you a fortune."

Effy was right. It was an expense but not unaffordable. They could walk to Holland Park and take the underground to Bond Street. Then it would be another short walk to Grosvenor Street. A taxi would be far quicker. Whichever way they chose, it would mean travelling in the rush hour on a busy underground. Rain seemed imminent too. No, it would have to be a taxi. Hunger aside, he wanted to sit down and rest, to assess what he was doing. He also wanted some time alone with Effy and called for a taxi.

There was no sign of Nate when they returned. They waited for a further-hour. Sara tried phoning Manny to find out where her brother was but without luck. Hunger got the better of them. Sara knew a place down the King's Road where she'd been with her parents and Nate twice. She left a note letting him know where they were going.

The restaurant wasn't quite what they expected. The bistro was a dinner and dance spot near to Sloane Square. A sign announced, *Down this alley you will find Buzzy's Bistro*. On entering, there was a reception area with a cloakroom for guests to leave coats. They were refused entry at first because they looked underage. That was until someone recognised Effy and Grace. Then there was no problem, even being underage.

Reached by steep stairs, *The Bistro* was in the basement. Entering by the black-painted doors, they found a small circular dance floor surrounded by tables. Candles in wax dripped straw bottles decorated table tops covered in red and white checked tablecloths. Sara had been here once before for lunch with her parents together with Joe. That had been the previous summer. She had seen Ringo Starr here. He was a regular diner at the bistro. Paul McCartney sometimes came here, too, with his girlfriend. They ordered and relaxed, the girls chatting away non-stop while he listened to his stomach grumbling. It was worth the short wait. Mack enjoyed a medium-rare steak in pepper sauce.

The place was quiet. It was a Monday night. There weren't too many people getting up to dance. Most of the records the DJ played were up-to-date releases and latest-hits. Sara and Grace enjoyed every minute of experiencing the novelty of a dinner and dance restaurant. It was not Mack's idea of a great place, but what did it matter. All four were enjoying the time together.

Settling the bill took most of the remaining funds he'd brought with him. It was the inevitable consequence of eating out and taking taxis. A quick visit to the bank in the morning to cash a cheque for the first time would be necessary. Going to a bank was a real pain when you were under eighteen. He hoped his driving licence would be enough ID to cash a cheque. The teller might not accept this as enough ID. Just in case there was a problem, he'd brought his Post Office Saving's Book along. In October, he would be eighteen. Then there would be no more problems withdrawing money. His mother had told him to make sure he and the girls kept receipts for every out-of-pocket expense they incurred. As their bookkeeper and accountant, she would make sure these would become tax-deductible expenses.

Returning to the Grosvenor Street apartment, there was still no sign of Nate. Sara began to fret. This was not like her brother. The phone rang just after eleven-thirty making her jump and grab the receiver. The relief on her face was palpable.

When she replaced the receiver, Sara looked puzzled. "Nate said not to worry. He wanted to make sure Grace, Effy, and you were at the studio tomorrow morning for ten. Oh, and something about you should forget about keeping your promise Mack. He told me you'd understand. Does it make sense?"

It made sense. He wondered why?

CHAPTER 26

She's Looking Good – Rodger Collins (Galaxy 750 – US – 1966)
Tuesday 23 May 1967.

When Hester saw Mack's photographs, she could tell at a glance, these were her career-best. He'd captured her essence, making the clothes appear amazing. The photographs were perfect; from the way she was lit to the way he'd posed her. Most of all, it was her eyes. There was intensity in them she'd never seen in any of her previous photographs. Mack surprised her further. Using a magnifying glass, he showed how he had imprinted his image behind the camera in each eye. Amazed, she asked if it was accidental? Grace answered for him. No, it wasn't. Mack often did this with close-up shots. Hester's hope of working with him strengthened when he smiled. Her heart beat faster. James MacKinnon would be up there with the best.

There were further upsides to the day. Hester sensed a greater acceptance by them. Working with Effy in front of the camera was an amazing experience. Grace Halloran was in a far friendlier mood. So too was her sister though more restrained and businesslike. Even Sara was more talkative. Grace's sense of humour made her giggle. She enjoyed watching Grace tease Mack with remorseless tenacity. Shaking his head, he would grin biding his time. When it came, it always caused hilarity. Mack knew how to put Grace in her place. As the shoot went on, Hester loved the feeling of belonging to the group.

The clothes for the day's sessions had arrived before they had. They were hung on a rack in the changing room, ready for the shoot. Manny had pinned a note to the protective sheaths of the dresses Hester was to model. The hemlines had been altered as per Grace's instructions. Slight tucks had also been sewn in the backs for a better fit. There would be no need for pegs to clip the backs.

Before Mack photographed each outfit, Effy and Grace double-checked it. Hester had worked with top designers. These two teens were as professional if not more rigorous. Everything about their mode of working left her impressed. Even though she was older, they were so adult they made

Hester feel she was immature. Mentioning this brought about smiles. Mack passed a strange comment. "Wait until you meet Alice."

Hester liked James MacKinnon's unspoken implication. This so-called *Co-operative* was stoking flames in the fashion world ready to set it alight. They would be the next big thing, the way Twiggy was now. Surrounded by a bevy of talented teenage beauties, James MacKinnon's *Co-operative* couldn't fail. With his photographer's eye, Effy's brilliant designs, nothing was surer. They were different, exciting, and vibrant, a mysterious new breed. *New Breed.* The description suited them better. She wanted in with the New Breed.

There was still no sign of Nate Silvers.

Sara's concern about her brother's absence increased. Although she said nothing, helping them on the shoot, she looked worried. Whatever he'd said to her, she wasn't sharing. Mack suspected he'd not told her much. Nate arrived a few minutes before midday. His usually immaculately pressed suit was a creased mess. Yawning and pale, Nate looked in need of some shut-eye.

Taking Mack and Effy aside, in hushed apologetic tones, he said, "Guys, I'm sorry about this. I have to move you two downstairs to the small flat. Grace can still stay with Sara. My parents are arriving with my sister Leah in tow. They'll need the double bedroom and Leah the single. I didn't think you would mind bedding together downstairs. I can't imagine my mother would be too keen on letting Leah see you two getting fruity and sinful. Manny's missus is moving your things downstairs as I speak. She'll leave the keys with the concierge for you to collect. I'll talk to you about the reason my parents are here when I see you next. It's complicated, and I'm in a rush, and Manny's waiting downstairs in the car. Show me later what you've snapped. Meanwhile, I'll be busy, so don't expect to see me until late."

"Oh," Nate turned as he was leaving adding, "if my parents ask… I've slept in the apartment. I don't want them knowing I was at my friend's."

"Meaning I kipped on the sofa," Mack replied.

"You got it," Nate grinned and stuck his thumb up in approval.

Whatever was going off had to be serious; it was something Nate's agitated state couldn't conceal. Giving his sister a hug and a few whispered words he left.

Mack had the shoot wrapped up by two o'clock. Effy had taken matters in hand concerned about Mack paying for them to eat out. Even

133

though he was keeping receipts to claim as expenses, Effy had insisted on preparing sandwiches for everyone. Sara, who had kept hot drinks coming all morning, brewed the tea once more. They sat relaxing in the changing room eating.

Sara was a bright girl. A willing worker eager to learn every aspect of what they were doing. The teenager's help had been invaluable during their time in London. Mack had even overheard her asking Hester Clayton what she thought of them? Did she think they were amateurs?

The model had replied, "Amateurs? They were the best damned professional amateurs with whom I've worked."

Hester had added she hoped to work with Mack and Effy again. She had nothing but the greatest respect for Mack, Effy, Grace, and Angie. The girls were amazing models. Alice and Ellen, Sara told Hester, were awesome models too. As Hester left, she gave Mack her phone number and address. She insisted they all went down The Marquee club that evening. Cream would be on stage, and she could arrange for them to get in to see the group. Pressure from Grace made Mack and Effy agree to go.

It was the final day's shoot in the studio. With insufficient chemicals and photographic paper, Mack couldn't finish developing all the films. Only two rolls came out of the darkroom. Using the remaining stock of silver bromide paper, he produced thirty-two prints. The results surpassed expectations. These would come in handy at tomorrow's appointments.

CHAPTER 27

I Feel Free – Cream (Reaction 591011 – 1966)
Tuesday 23 May 1967 - later.

Effy's ears were ringing. She was perspiring when they emerged from The Marquee club. It was a relief to be out in the street in the night air. Packed to capacity, the atmosphere inside the club had become too oppressive and unbearable. The experience was unpleasant. Something she imagined not far removed from a steam drenched Turkish baths filled with an ear-splitting racket.

They were fortunate to have got into the club. Hester had the right connections all right, ensuring entry without question or the need to queue. Otherwise, there would have been no chance of getting into The Marquee. On arriving, they found they were treated as VIPs, which also came as a huge surprise.

As they entered, Mack heard one bouncer saying to another the queue now stretched back to the 100 Club on Oxford Street. Mack hadn't rated their chances of getting in having seen the queue outside. Some of those queuing had recognised the girls as they passed them on the way into the club. Anyway, they'd got see Clapton twang his guitar, Baker bang the drums and Bruce do the vocals. Leaving the suffocating club for the freshness of the cold night air had brought instant relief. Grace had wanted to stop to get the group's autographs but found herself outvoted.

Mack noted his girls had warmed to Hester. The young woman was working overtime to make friends with them and him. Mack could guess why, finding it flattering. She invited them round to her place, but it was late. They needed Grace back in the flat, or the Silvers would worry. Depending on how tomorrow went, they'd try to make it before returning to Yorkshire. Tomorrow would be another busy day.

Nate had done them a favour. They were glad to be alone in a small flat. Mrs Silvers wouldn't have appreciated her eleven-year-old daughter becoming exposed to their sexual antics. After a torrid bout of noisy sex, they lay wrapped in each other's embrace. Mack lay drifting in half-asleep post-coital bliss. Effy's words brought him to full consciousness in a split second.

"I missed my period."

"What?"

It was like being plunged into ice-cold water. Mack sat up in shock.

"Or thought I did," Effy paused for two or three seconds that felt like an eternity before adding, "I was two weeks late. I started on Sunday, only for a day or so. It was the shortest period I've ever had."

"You didn't bother to tell me you'd missed?"

"I didn't want you to worry, just in case I was late. Being on the pill can mess up your periods, and it seems to have done that to me."

"But you're okay now?"

"Yes, I am." There were several seconds of awkward silence. "What would you have done if I had been pregnant?"

"I'd marry you as soon as I could. You know I would. It's what we've both said we'd do when we're old enough."

"Supposing I didn't want to get married?"

"What? Why not?"

"Well, you'd be free to carry on with anyone, maybe even Hester Clayton?"

"No. Don't be daft. I've got you, and you're who I plan to be with forever. And there's Angie too. I don't need more women in my love life. You two are more than enough."

"She is, sexy though, isn't she? I bet you were fantasising about her. Wondering what it would be like with her between the sheets?"

"Well, Effy, here's a surprise. I don't want to have sex with every girl I meet, no matter how gorgeous they look. Nor do I have fantasies about them either. You and Angie are enough. My name's not Tom Catford. Just because I'm photographing her doesn't mean I want to leap into bed with her. Besides, she's twenty. Why would someone her age be interested in me?"

Mack hoped it sounded convincing because the thought had crossed his mind, but only as a thought. Perhaps it was the Catholic teaching they'd tried to indoctrinate in him? The one about not sinning in thought, word, or deed. There would never be a deed. He would never cheat on Effy or Angie. The thought part he found illogical. He couldn't see the connection. Imagining was not the same as premeditating. Mack found Hester attractive, and his imagination had been active.

"Anyway, you like older women, don't you?" Effy giggled. "Angie's an older woman."

"Yeah! Right! Angie's a year older. That hardly makes her an older woman. Besides, it's different between the three of us, and you know it is."

Effy gave him a squeeze.

"You were joking, weren't you? About not wanting to get married?"

"What do you think?"

He didn't know what to think when Effy was in this somewhat disconcerting mood. Nothing ever sounded like he thought it should. He hoped he was imagining doubt in her voice. Consciousness slipped away without warning as sleep overtook him.

The dream was as peculiar as dreams went. Strange and convincing, it seemed a deceptive clone of the real world. The strangeness of knowing he was asleep yet in a dream made it even more peculiar. Camera in hand, he found himself in a studio for a fashion shoot. The studio resembled a surreal blend of the one in Bradford and the one in London. To the side, he could see Angie and Effy reclining on individual red velvet chaise longue. No matter how hard he tried, he couldn't hear their conversation. He didn't know why, but he found this upsetting and unsettling. The other side of the studio opened up without warning. Transforming, it exposed an auditorium with cinema seats. These were filling up with everyone he knew. Not only were Effy's sisters there: so too was his brother, Adam, his parents, Effy's mother, and his Aunt Ellen.

Tom and friends from the Mod scenes rushed through the doors appearing as if from nowhere, pushing and jostling to get seats. Behind them came stern teachers from the grammar school with sixth-formers. The school chaplain followed them. Dressed in a weird multi-coloured high-mass vestment, he swung a thurible above his head as if it was a lasso. Clouds of choking incense spread everywhere, blanketing the place in a sinister mist. Emerging from this mist, behind the priest, came his grandmother and the Silvers. The studio began to change in a slow, crazy surreal kaleidoscopic manner to become a movie set.

Hester Clayton appeared from out of the clouds of wafted incense. Wearing a Twenties vamp dress, she took to the centre stage. Whirling and twirling with incredible speed, she danced towards him. Clicking away, he tried to photograph her. His camera metamorphosed into an ancient box brownie. Sara appeared in a flash of smoke, a genie dancing around him dressed as a magician's assistant. With each click of the camera, Sara attempted to distract the audience. At the same time, Hester peeled off an item of clothing in a burlesque dance that became a speeded up striptease.

137

The discarded items of clothing were thrown into the audience. Rapturous applause greeted each arriving item together with wolf whistles and catcalls. Effy and Angie, still deep in conversation, appeared oblivious to everything going on around them.

Glancing in a mirror, Mack saw himself flush with embarrassment. His clothing vanished item by item to leave him stark naked. The wall with the photographer's backdrop metamorphosed into a cinema screen. The studio cum cinema darkened and cloaked the audience. This super-wide screen, bathed in garish Cinemascope colours, filled his vision. A movie featuring himself and the girls as the stars of *Carry On Modelling* started to play. Without understanding why he joined in the riotous laughter of the audience as he watched himself on the screen. He was laughing, but it was not the laughter of someone amused. The movie came to a sudden end. The credits rolled over an image of his doppelganger staring back at him. He didn't like his twisted, evil grin but couldn't stop laughing. That's when he awoke with a start, Effy shaking him.

"What the hell's so funny?" Half asleep, sounding grumpy, she added. "You've been laughing in your sleep like someone demented."
The travelling alarm clock said seven twenty-two. He fell back into a deep dark sleep for another hour, waking to the sound of the flat door buzzer.

CHAPTER 28

The New Breed – Jackie Wilson (Coral 72467 UK – B Side -1963)
Wednesday 24 May 1967.

Grace was still in bed when they came up to the penthouse. Nate's parents had left for the police station early, leaving Sara in charge of Leah.

Mack suggested walking to the magazine's offices. It was only about a mile and a half or thereabouts. Grace overheard his words outside the bedroom door. Pulling the bedcovers over her head, she refused to get up. She showed a determined reluctance not to leave the bed. A poor night's sleep after The Marquee had left her tired, grumpy, and in an uncooperative mood. Effy lost patience with her sister seeing how late it had become. When soothing polite requests to get up failed, Effy reacted less lovingly.

Yanking the bedcovers clean off, Effy harried her sister into the bathroom. Then she made Grace her breakfast. Afterwards, she ensured Grace's appearance was perfect, attending to her makeup, hair, and clothes. She made a point of reminding her sister how much they were getting paid as models. Sara and her little sister looked on startled by the frantic rushing. Mack sat on one of the grey sofas smirking as he waited. Grace stuck her tongue out at him when she finally appeared ready to go. He came to her and inspected her appearance. Nodding approvingly, he took her by the hand and gently spun her around, giving Effy a wink. "Grace, you look gorgeous."

It never ceased to surprise him how a compliment always worked wonders.

Manny was unavailable once again, so it was a case of walking or taking a cab. Nate had left a note with Sara. He apologised for leaving them to go it alone. It further read that the police had arrested, Joe. He and Effy re-read the note and exchanged looks, thinking it wiser not to say anything further. The news was and wasn't a big surprise after what had happened at the Indian restaurant. Nate was going with his parents to Hampstead Police Station. They needed Sara to stay in the flat to mind Leah while they were out.

As it was approaching the time the magazine expected them at the offices, they took a cab. No one wanted to arrive hot and messy, rushing on foot. Getting there on time was the priority.

Today they were on their own.

First on the agenda was a visit to *Rave* magazine offices on Southampton Street in Covent Garden. The taxi dropped them outside Tower House. It was an imposing building in a prominent position on the corner of Tavistock Street. The editorial staff made them welcome on arrival. One commented on how Mack had a vague youthful resemblance to a fashion designer. Someone called Halston. Who Halston was, he didn't have a clue. Effy did. Halston, she whispered, had designed the pillbox hat made famous by Jackie Kennedy.

Rave wanted to spotlight Effy and Grace as the new faces of teen fashion and modelling. By the time this appeared in print, it added to the mystique surrounding her. One of her comments became much quoted. *Style and fashion should never be confused. One is eternal, the other ephemeral.* Then Mack found himself interviewed for an article at the same time. That hadn't been part of the plan.

Whatever the editors had arranged or agreed with the Silvers, the talks went much further. Job offers independent of Silvers Fashions arose during conversations. How would Effy and Grace like to appear in photo shoots with pop groups? The editors mentioned several top names. The possibility of appearing with groups such as The Small Faces left Grace thrilled. They asked Mack if he would take commissions from the magazine. He hinted he would consider it without making a firm commitment. He omitted mention of a meeting with *Petticoat* magazine's editors in the afternoon.

While there, they saw a preview of what was appearing in the June issue. A double-spread feature on the American pop group The Monkees was in preparation. The editors were toying with 'Monkeegram' as a title. A comprehensive article on a group called Pink Floyd was also in preparation. The article still needed completion, but they saw the photographic layout for the next edition. Everything taking place at the magazine impressed them.

On leaving Grace complained the slingback straps of her shoes were rubbing her raw. They took another cab to spare her the discomfort and their ears her complaining. Although only a mile or so from Tower House, it would have been an awkward route to walk to Fleetway House. In the taxi, it was an all too short journey. En route, they passed the Strand and Australia House. Further on, they saw another famous landmark in St. Clement Dane's Church. Fleet St. home of the nation's daily newspapers was a disappointment.

During the short journey, Mack couldn't help wondering if he could ever live and work in this hectic city. The same thought was crossing Effy's mind. Did she really want to leave school and move here? Grace, lost in daydreams of life in London, loved the idea and kept talking about it.

Fleetway House was a brash block located a mile or so on Farringdon Street. Arriving early, they looked for somewhere to get a sandwich and drink close to the offices. Mack and Effy asked Grace about Joe Silvers arrest. What did she know?

She shrugged her shoulders in response, cupping her chin in her hands. "Nothing. They were talking about him last night as I went to bed. I didn't hear what they were saying. They went quiet when I was around. Sara wouldn't tell me anything either. All I can say is she was upset and embarrassed."

Mack and Effy exchanged expressionless glances.

"Must be serious for his parents to come down," Grace added. "What's he like? I mean, I know you two aren't fond of him. Did something happen when you met him?"

Mack and Effy exchanged a second set of expressionless glances. Grace understood her sister's response too well. Saying nothing said everything. Something had happened. Grace also knew there wasn't any point in pursuing an answer. Not yet.

Mack had already sold photographs to *Petticoat*. He'd made connections at Moods Mosaic on their first London trip. Plenty of handshaking greeted them on arrival. As the meeting went on, offers of further commissions surfaced. Was he prepared to work with other models the magazine liked to use? Were Effy and Grace and other girls in the *New Breed* willing to work with other photographers? Would Effy object to other models wearing her designs? Could other photographers do her shoots? Would their tie in with Silvers Fashion create problems?

Listening, they made mental notes of everything the magazine editors said. They took care not to make promises or commitments.

Nate must have been pushing the *New Breed Co-operative* label. The editorial staff kept using it over and over during the meeting. If nothing else, it was creating a brand image. Effy could see it benefitting them and whispered it in his ear.

Mack showed them a sample of the last two days shoots, including some featuring Hester Clayton. These photos had the features and fashion editors excited. They were proof he could work with other models. The longer the talking went on, the more everything became transparent. If they were to work for the magazines, there was an implied expectation. They would have to be in London full time. It was an inescapable conclusion.

Chancery underground was a short walk from Fleetway House. On the Central line, it was a straightforward return journey back to Bond St. and then to Grosvenor St. They stopped off at a corner shop as they walked from the underground station. Not having eaten since breakfast, Effy did a bit of a food shop.

Back in the flat, she made sandwiches for the three of them. Grace stopped a little while longer before going up to the penthouse. She returned less than ten minutes later with Sara and Leah in tow. Sara's parents were upstairs with Nate's solicitor. They didn't want them listening to whatever was going on. Grace didn't fancy staying closeted in the bedroom with Sara and Leah, so they came down. It was too early for children's TV, and there was nothing for Leah to do.

Keeping Leah entertained wasn't hard. Once Grace took the situation in hand, Leah sat wide-eyed in awe listening to her. Grace's account of the visit to *Rave* and *Petticoat* held the eleven-year-old spellbound. Grace had gone from some silly child to a sensible young woman in the past few weeks. The change these past months had been swift. Since things had taken off, she had begun to show the same kind of maturity as her older sisters. Glancing at Effy, he caught her smiling as they observed Grace. Their eyes met, and each knew the other was thinking the same.

The telephone rang, interrupting Grace. It was his mother. She went quiet, exchanging glances with Effy. Mack said little, grimacing, at what he heard. After a couple of minutes, he indicated Effy should take the phone. She remained impassive, responding with quiet guarded politeness. Cupping the phone mouthpiece, Effy returned it to Mack. "Let's not bother going back."

He gave her a strange look. Their hands held the phone for a full three heartbeats before Effy released it to him. Grace held her breath. What she heard him say next over the phone made her gasp.

"We may stay until Friday, or even until Sunday. We're even considering not bothering coming back if that's her attitude. Okay, Aileen, see what she thinks of that. Can you pass my mum back?"

Grace listened, stunned, and opened mouthed. She couldn't believe what he'd said. Watching her sister rocking in silent laughter, she tried to work out what was going on. Mack and Effy's eyes had locked in silent agreement. Whatever his mother was saying, left him smiling. That annoying smile of his was something Grace could never decipher.

"No, we'll be back like we said unless we need to talk to the people at *Honey*. We're still waiting to hear if that meeting is going ahead. Effy and Grace are going on a conducted tour of the Royal College of Arts tomorrow morning. Nate's brother Simon is a student there." Longish pause. "He's designed some unique fabric pattern prints for Effy to use in her designs."

As soon as the phone call ended, Grace asked what was going on?

"Our ma's back from Ireland. She's thrown a bit of a strop. Aileen, Bridget, and Caitlin have had to have words with her."

"Oh, no! Why?" Grace exclaimed, looking to Mack then to her sister and back to him.

"Seems the Monaghan's have been telling tales again." Mack seethed. "You know what happened the last time they did that, don't you? They stopped Effy from seeing me for a whole year. It seems they've been filling your mother's head with tales of debauchery and orgies. Wait till I get my hands on that short arsed runt of theirs. He'll look like a panda when I've done with him."

"So she's thrown a wobbly?" Grace's eyes welled up. "Is she going to stop us from modelling?"

Mack went over to the window. Staring out over Grosvenor Street, he scanned the skyline. After a moment or so, with a dramatic aplomb, he chuckled. "There's no chance of that happening, Grace. No chance at all. Not even if a squadron of pigs flew over London in Battle of Britain formation to the tune of the Dam buster's March."

143

CHAPTER 29

The Cheater – Bob Kuban and The In Men (Stateside SS 448)
Thursday 25 May 1967. Morning

They arrived ten minutes late. Effy's decision to walk from Grosvenor Street to The Royal College of Art took longer than expected. They had made their way to the Dorchester and then crossed over into Hyde Park. Skirting the Serpentine, the girls needed to ask for directions from other walkers. An elderly gentleman took them along the right path near to the edge of the park. On reaching the Albert Memorial, he directed them to the nearest crossing.

Once across the road, they made for the Royal Albert Hall following his directions. By the time they arrived at the Modernist Darwin building, the walk had taken fifty minutes. They were late.

An impatient Simon Silvers was waiting for them at the front entrance. Grace spotted him pacing up and down, glancing at this wristwatch. His relief when they approached was obvious. Effy excused their lateness, explaining they didn't realize it was such a long walk. The weather was in their favour, overcast but dry. They were fortunate it didn't rain; otherwise, the sisters would have had a soaking.

Grace found it disconcerting the way he kept staring at her sister. Effy didn't appear to mind or notice his efforts at flirting and paying her over-familiar attention. She couldn't figure out how Effy could miss these glaring signals. They were so blatant. Surely, Effy couldn't be that oblivious to his charm offensive? She was behaving like her usual smiling and obliging self thrilled by the opportunity to go around the RCA.

Simon Silvers behaviour made Grace smirk. Grace wanted to laugh at the way he dashed to open doors for them. It seemed so false and forced the way he danced around them. He was trying too hard to impress. When Mack opened doors, it was an instinctive act with no show.

As for his dress sense, it was *The Top of the Pops* pits. He looked like an escapee from a Carnaby Street clown show. This had to be his best-dressed sartorial worst. Someone must have tailored the jacket from an old skinned Victorian sofa. The beige and brown classical leaf fabric pattern was hideous. The jacket was a dreadful double-breasted Dandy affair from the Nineteenth Century. She'd seen one like it on the cover of a trashy Barbara

144

Cartland novel. The floral shirt and neckerchief clashed with everything he was wearing. As for the crushed plum-coloured velvet trousers, they left her sniggering. Pity, because otherwise, he might have passed for handsome.

From what Grace saw of the students on the fashion courses, many of them appeared no better dressed. Garish outlandishness appeared to be the order of the day. Effy's comments were gracious and diplomatic and without any critical comments. It was interesting, she said, the way students were experimenting with colours and vivid prints. Grace's sniggering snort echoed down the corridor as she tried to suppress laughing aloud. Mack would wet himself if he could see this bunch of weirdies. Effy gave her one of those glances telling her to behave.

The atmosphere in the college was of laidback enthusiasm. The Women's Wear rooms of the Fashion Department looked amazing. Grace could imagine herself as a student here.

Everywhere they went, it seemed most students knew who Effy was but not why she was here. They appeared astonished to see her walking around. Most stared in amazement when she passed them in the corridors. Effy's reputation had preceded her visit before she'd even set foot in the RCA.

A few stopped to chat with her and Simon. Grace found they also knew her too. This was still a new experience, the realization that she was a celebrity. The most flattering moment came when she overheard two students passing a comment.

She heard one female student say to another, "They look even more gorgeous in real life than in the photographs."

"They are a treat for my eyeballs. Real stunners," Admitted her male companion in an Afghan coat, eyeing Grace. "So that's what top models look like in real life. God, they're beautiful."

When they came to a common room, she overheard a female student say, "He's setting his sights high again. Does he think he can bed a top model like her?"

Her friend sniffed. "Simon Silvers thinks he's God's gift to women. He's tried it on with most of the girls in our department. That one fancies himself too much, the no-good skirt-chasing Casanova."

Grace wasn't sure if Effy had heard the comment, *no good skirt-chasing Casanova*. Hearing those words brought on an immediate feeling of distrust. From that moment, she experienced an overwhelming sense of leeriness. Simon might be Sara's brother, but what she'd heard didn't please her. She began to feel concerned for Effy. Then she noticed the subtle changes taking place between her sister and him.

They lost count of the number of students he introduced them to as they walked around. On learning that Effy might consider becoming a student at the RCA came as a shock to most. Throughout the visit, her conduct was self-effacing and quiet. She said little, leaving Simon Silvers to extol her talents and abilities. During the college tour, Simon introduced them to one of the Senior Staff who was passing. Neither she nor Effy took to her initial frost cool comments.

"I see you've brought the replacements for the Shrimpton's and the Boyd sisters to visit us, Simon. How good of them to deign us with their presence."

Effy's remained pleasant, polite, and tactful. It was not how Grace felt like answering. Simon explained that Effy and her sister were considering coming to study at the RCA. This brought a change in the woman's attitude.

"Do you think there is something we can still teach you?" The lecturer studied Effy's reaction.

"There's always something new to learn," Effy replied in a quiet, personable voice. "Anyone who stops learning stops progressing. Nothing stands still. Nothing remains a constant, least of all in fashion."

The lecturer smiled with a tiny nodding of the head. "You may be right, Miss Halloran. And what about your sister? Grace, is it? Tell me, do you have ambitions to work in fashion wear design?"

"I don't have the artistic talent and the vision of my sister. I'm more practical with patterns and pins and scissors. If it involves making clothes, that's what I'm good at doing."

"My sister's too modest," Effy defended her.

The conversation returned to Effy once more. The woman could not believe that Effy had yet to take her A-Levels. The woman was even more surprised when informed that Effy could expect to get an Oxbridge place. The even bigger shock to Grace came when Effy told the woman she had no great desire to go to Oxford or Cambridge. This was news to Grace. Effy told the lecturer that if she chose to go into higher education, she would consider applying to the RCA. This left the woman looking speechless yet delighted. There was a peculiar look on Simon Silvers face, one that left Grace with the unhappiest sensation she had yet felt in his presence.

146

It was like the sudden lifting of a mist as Grace now paid closer attention to him. His infatuation with her sister was unabashed and designing. He was trying hard to get her interested in him and to snare her.

Grace noticed how he kept sweeping his long shoulder-length hair back, trying hard to catch her eye. Maybe it was as well Mack wasn't here. Grace didn't think he would like him at all. Now she began to think there was something about him that was scheming and a bit creepy. He might be Sara's brother, but the way he was fawning over Effy made her sick.

They went for a coffee after the tour. That did even less to charm him to her. It was the way he kept prancing so attentively around her sister. What was worse, Effy appeared to be enjoying his attentions? She kept playing with the ends of her hair, giggling at things he said, looking at him. While Simon was at the counter buying the coffees, Grace let Effy know what she thought of the way she was carrying on.

"He's chatting you up, Effy. Trying to make an impression."

Effy gave a small nervous laugh. "Don't be silly, Grace. He's doing nothing of the sort. He's being nice to me, that's all."

"Huh." Grace stared into Effy's eyes. "You know damned well he's chatting you up. He's flirting with you. What's worse, you're letting him. What's even worse than that, you're flirting back. What game do you think you're playing?"

Effy went red, turning away from her sister's glare. "Stop it, sis. Nothing of the sort is going on. Nothing. Stop talking nonsense, stop imagining things."

"So why are you blushing? And why are you so defensive? Don't treat me like I'm stupid. You've got into a habit of doing that with me too often of late. What's gotten into you?"

Effy rose from the table, pushing her chair away with unexpected exasperation. "I'm going to the toilet. Nothing is going on, Grace. Nothing. Stop it off. When I come back, I don't want you saying anything to upset him."

Grace scowled at her sister. Effy walked away without another word. "Where's your sister gone?" Simon asked returning with the coffees.

"The loo."

"Oh." He sat down.

Grace had no intention of staying silent. "You do know Effy has a long-term boyfriend, don't you?"

"Yes, that friend of hers with the cameras. Long term? She might want a change soon." His cocky tone made her angrier. So that was his game.

"I wouldn't waste your time flirting with her. Mack is *more* than a boyfriend. They're as good as engaged. Besides, he's not someone you should annoy. You wouldn't like him if he got angry. Making him jealous would be a bad idea, a dangerous idea. If I were you, I'd think twice about it. He isn't someone you want to mess with. If he found out that you were trying it on with my sister, I wouldn't want to be you."

Grace didn't appreciate the real truth of her words. She'd heard tales of Mack's involvements in fights, but she knew nothing much about them. It did no harm to intimidate Simon Silvers by making the suggestion.

"So, it's serious between them?" He queried.

"Yes. As serious as it gets."

Grace enjoyed watching Simon Silvers deflate before her eyes. His brother's words reminded him of the warning to stay clear of her. Warning's Grace knew nothing about, but which reinforced his brother's words. Her comments left him slumped and stumped.

When Effy returned, they drank the coffees in silence. Grace's looks made her displeasure clear to them both. She felt a deep sadness, unable to comprehend her sister's strange behaviour. Surely, Effy couldn't be tiring of Mack, could she?

The girls took a taxi back to Grosvenor Street. Neither said a word during the journey, avoiding looking at one another. Before going up to the apartments, Effy turned to Grace. "Nothing was going on. He was flirting with me, and I thought I'd flirt back a little. That was all it was, nothing more. Believe me, Grace, I wasn't serious."

"Are you sure, Effy? Because it looked serious enough to me."

Effy hesitated before dismissing the suggestion. "I'm only interested in one boy, Grace. You know which one. Do I need to say anymore?"

CHAPTER 30

I Fought The Law – Bobby Fuller Four (London HLU 10030 – 1966)
Thursday 25 May 1967. Evening.

"Joe's arrest could damage our reputation as a business. My father is trying to find legal ways to lessen the potential fallout." Nate was towing the family line. "He's gone round to Simon's flat to let him know about Joe. Simon doesn't know yet."

Mack could see that Nate's face was a bizarre mix of displeasure and delight. The potential repercussions to the family business were in the balance. How it affected business, was of vital importance to the Silvers. Mack understood that Silvers Fashion meant a great deal to Nate and not only to his father. Yet getting even with Joe seemed like a moment of personal triumph as well as disaster. For a moment, Mack recalled his father's situation and his grandmother's business affairs in Edinburgh.

"Anyhow," Nate continued, "it's not your concern. We'll ride it out no matter what happens. As long as the publicity doesn't get back to the firm, we should be okay."

"So, what has Joe got arrested for doing?"

It was quite a list.

Mack gave a long low whistle when Nate stopped. Joe Silvers arrest charges were extensive. They included: fraud, bouncing cheques, and drug dealing. The worst charge of all involved hiring a hitman to kill someone. Not any *someone*. This involved a member of the aristocracy well known in society circles.

Allegedly, this celebrity figure had tried to cheat Joe out of a large sum of money. There were other offences too involving a notorious East End gang. Scotland Yard was enjoying its success. Luckily, they had caught the hitman at the scene, firearm in hand, before he could commit the murder. An unnamed female had tipped off the police to prevent the shooting. The hitman had confessed at once implicating Joe Silvers in the hopes of a lesser charge and sentence.

The charges against Nate's brother were serious. Involvement in a conspiracy to plan a murder made jail a foregone certainty. When the beak finished with Joe Silvers he'd be somewhere like Pentonville for a long time. Effy sat in silence, horrified.

Nate became silent. He spent a couple of minutes examining Mack's latest batch of photographs and Effy's sketches. Seeing the results cheered him, and he approved of everything they had laid out before him.

"It was an acid test." Nate smiled at Mack. "My father wanted to see how you got on working with a known model you didn't know. Well, when he sees these, he can show Piper you're good enough to work with the best. If these pics don't impress her, nothing will." "Is she still keen to get Effy over to the States?"

"Pretty much. Are you up for going, Effy?"

"Only if Angie and Mack part of the package."

"Angie is a definite and has to go. She wants Grace and Ellen too. Also, Alice." Nate gave Mack a funny look, one of those Mack now recognised. He knew more but had but no intention of sharing, at least not for the present.

For a moment, Mack had a bad feeling about this proposed trip to the USA. He dismissed it as Nate continued. "Have you got your passports sorted?"

"With luck, they should have arrived by the time we get home," Effy added, the prospect of New York brightening her.

"Looking at your calendar of dates, I'm planning to send you to Spain to do a shoot. The Yanks might want to see the sun, sea, and sand as backdrops. Good news, Effy. We've negotiated some of Simon's fabric prints for limited runs with a well-known manufacturer. Simon's running off some other samples for you to create a limited handful of dresses. I'll show you the samples later this afternoon. While you're in Spain, we'll be sorting your work visas for the States with Mack's father. He'll have to go on the trip with you. Effy smile broadened on hearing the news.

"Spain?" Mack queried.

"Yeah. A spot called Benidorm. Have you heard of it? The place is going to become the next big tourist resort on the Med. It will only be for four days. We need you to get some exotic shots of Effy's range. I take it you're up for it?"

"Definitely." Mack responded.

"You'll fly from Heathrow to Valencia on BEA. Then you'll travel down to the town by coach

"How many of us?" Effy asked, sitting back on the sofa, her hands together covering her mouth in a prayer gesture.

"Everyone of you plus Hester Clayton. You may need one of your older sisters to go as a chaperone, seeing as Mack, you and Grace are under eighteen. Can you arrange something? We'll need a responsible adult if they can't go. Any suggestions?"

They exchanged bewildered looks. Caitlin was out. Bridget and Aileen would both be working, but one of them might take her holiday leave and go with them.

"Aileen has an up to date passport. She took one out when she went on a trip to Lourdes." Effy offered.

"Good. Let me know who you can persuade to go as soon as you can. I know your mum's expecting to give birth real soon, so it will be tricky."

Mack sat back on the sofa, taking a big breath.

"Oh, and can I persuade you to stop another day? The people at *Honey* want to meet with you and Effy. They want Effy to do a shoot for them with one of their regular models and wonder if they could interest you?"

CHAPTER 31

Sticks and Stones – Ray Charles (HMV POP 774 –1960)
Saturday 27 May 1967.

They expected a major confrontation with Effy's mother on their return. It didn't happen. Seeing her two youngest daughters again overwhelmed Róisín Halloran with joy. Ellen and her older sisters had worked together, calming her worries and concerns before she saw Effy and Grace.

Ellen became incensed with what the Monaghan's had been telling her mother. She took it on herself to visit them and gave the Monaghan's a stinging piece of her mind. Ellen threatened them with legal action if they persisted in making further slanderous accusations. They tried to deny it but were unconvincing in their denials. To make it real, Ellen persuaded Tom to telephone them. He pretended to be Bridget's solicitor boyfriend. His scary impersonation of Greg's voice appeared to have achieved the result. When her mother visited the Monaghan's, they greeted her ashen-faced. Their reluctance to say anything untoward came as a surprise to Mrs Halloran. She had expected to hear terrible things.

Mack faced a different homecoming. His parents were not happy with what he told them. They could see the demands of the magazines would mean him leaving school and not finishing his A-Levels. It also concerned them because it would affect Effy and Grace too. Grace still needed to do her GCE's. They knew Twiggy had left school without sitting any exams. Her mother remained unconvinced that Grace should do the same. In this, Rósín Halloran's had Jane MacKinnon's support. Both believed the same about Effy and her academic reports. The money they were earning was an immense temptation, as was the lure of travelling abroad. Mrs Halloran's question was, how long could a career as a fashion model last? A year or two, and then what would the future hold for her daughters?

When Effy showed her mother how much she had earned, a gasped exclamation tumbled from her lips. "Jesus, Mary, and Joseph! I'll be seeing things I'm thinking? All this money in a few short months?"

It didn't quite render her speechless. It did leave her struggling to argue in favour of carrying on with their schooling. Effy and Grace could not believe how Aileen and Bridget had defended them to their mother. Later

Caitlin had added her words to their cause. Róisín Halloran found herself swamped by this deluge of support for her youngest daughters. The trickiest moments came when she confronted Mack. Was he carrying on with this Angie and taking advantage of Effy?

Answering was both a moral and ethical dilemma. Though he disliked lying sometimes lying, was necessary to evade the truth. Loyalty and commitment to both girls were the bedrock of their relationship with him and his with them. Effy's mother provided the loophole. In an almost legalistic manner, Mack used it. Angie and Effy shared him by mutual consent. *Ipso facto* the expression *carrying on* didn't apply to Angie. So he answered, no. He was not *carrying on* with her. The truth would never have been understood nor appreciated. It did not fit the norm. Nor would trying to persuade Mrs Halloran be anything but a complete disaster. When confronted by her mother, Effy had used the same reasoning.

No matter how hard he tried to dance around matters, his parents had him figured. Convincing them was something else. They listened to what he had to say about his future and that of the girls. There were lengthy discussions that led nowhere except into a mutual zone of frustration.

"Not all paths in life lead to somewhere you may want to go. This is what makes our choices intriguing. There is only now, and we have to decide because the past is gone, and what happens next is unknowable." His mother's words left him haunted.

"I'm pleased to hear that Effy and Grace took the time and the trouble to visit the RCA. It would be a logical avenue for both to pursue art and fashion design further if their interests lay there. And what about you? You've worked so hard this year. Despite the incidents with the RE teacher and chaplain, your other teachers appear pleased with your progress. You appear to have made a big impression on Mr Robinson, your history teacher. I've read most of your essays myself, and they are first class. Your maths is exemplary, even your father admits, you could study Maths at degree level."

"I could do it, but I'm just not interested in Maths. I enjoy history, and I suppose I'm good at it, but…"

"… but you could never make a career studying or teaching history." His father finished the sentence for him. "So what security do you think you have as an untrained self-taught fashion photographer? How long do you think you'll last in such a competitive field? What happens when they expose your limitations?"

153

"What limitations? Look, Dad, every time I point the camera and shoot, I improve. I have an eye for it. Don't forget. I'm reading lots of articles too. Those photography magazines aren't there to while away the hours. I'm learning from them. Most of all, I learn from the girls. Every time they step in front of the camera, they teach me something new. Call it learning on the job. With one big difference, I'm my teacher. You and mum know the bottom line. They wouldn't pay me the money they do if I wasn't good enough. For someone who didn't have much of a clue six months ago, I reckon I've got a good handle on it. Now I've worked with a top model, like Hester Clayton, the magazines know I can definitely cut it. If I can work with someone like her, not just Effy, Angie, and the girls, I can work with any of the top women models."

"Don't get too cocky, James." Robert MacKinnon looked to his wife for support.

Jane remained impassive, refusing to say anything. Her concern was in part elsewhere. Rubbing the enormous bump, she listened to the exchange between father and son. James was right. The magazines and the Silvers wouldn't be paying him unless he was good. With reluctance, she conceded her son was better than good. Dealing with the inflow and outflow of money into and out of his account alone was the obvious proof. Last week, the cheques arriving had amounted to over two hundred pounds. Further sums were due with the monthly invoices. Then there were all the girls' earnings. These grew with each new shoot.

Taking phone calls from Alex and Nate Silvers was one thing. Dealing with all the other enquiries was time-consuming. The enquiries alone now demanded someone to take on the work full-time. While James and Effy were in London, she had invited Angie Thornton round one evening. The time was approaching when Angie had to shoulder more of the burden.

Agency bookings were getting out of hand. The stock of composites was running low. Advertisers required detailed individual information on each girl. On each composite, the photo now also contained a printed footer. The footer detailed each girl's statistics and other important information. Everything was included: name, age, hair colour, eye colour, height, bust, waist and hip measurement, shoe size, and so on. The composites could be re-ordered quickly enough at Sean Halloran's printing business. It was the constant telephone calls and the visits to the post office that wore her out. Angie would have to take on the work, but she had a full-time job, so how could she? Perhaps it was time they had an office and hired someone to take over.

Jane never wanted to take to this dark-haired beauty with the dark eyes. She feared for Effy and her son's relationship. Effy was like the daughter she always longed to have. She could see her as a future daughter-in-law. And yet the more she knew Angie, the more Jane couldn't help liking this young woman. Angie was more of an open book than Effy. One thing was certain. There was no escaping the mutual attraction the three shared.

When she met Angie during the week, the truth had emerged. The ring on the third finger of Angie's right hand may only have shown the band, but Jane could tell what it was immediately. Even though Angie had turned the ring to conceal the setting, it was obvious. She could tell the design from the band. It was the same as Effy's. So the rumours were true. Thinking back, the three of them had neither denied nor confirmed what was going on. Jane had tried to put the suspicion aside at the time. Now thinking back, it all made sense. Her sister-in-law had been right all along. Like it or not, this threesome was what it was. Jane tuned back to her husband's voice.

Robert MacKinnon was reluctant to admit to his son that he had an extraordinary talent. Each new photo he'd viewed confirmed it. There was a freshness and originality in the way he captured young women in his photographs. Though he wanted his son to go to university, it was looking unlikely. It would be a shame if he didn't complete his A-Levels and try for a university place.

Looking back to their childhoods, Robert MacKinnon often felt ashamed, ashamed of the way he'd treated both sons. A compulsive first child syndrome had driven him to neglect the younger one. Robert MacKinnon knew he was trying to make amends. Maybe it was not too late. There had been precious little guidance or example from his father. Perhaps that was how it was in life? You only learned to be a parent as the years went by.

Jane Mackinnon broke into the conversation. "Who will be the adult chaperone on the Spanish trip?"

CHAPTER 32

Getaway – Georgie Fame and The Blue Flames
(Columbia DB7946 – 1966)
Wednesday 21 June 1967 – Spain

It was the sweltering heat that hit them first as they emerged from the aeroplane into an unbelievably bright sunny day. The incredible blueness of a cloud-free sky surprised all but Hester. After clearing passport control and customs, they boarded a coach hired just for the eight of them. The journey from Valencia to Benidorm was longer than the flight from London. A new airport had opened near Alicante, but it could not yet handle international flights. Arriving there instead of Valencia would have cut the transfer time to Benidorm by hours. The journey to the resort was long and tiring.

There was no motorway, only a narrow coastal road that threaded through the countryside, passing endless olive groves and orange trees. The coach interior was hot and stuffy, the air blowing through the windows having no cooling effect. A stunning Mediterranean coastline with its mountain backdrops formed a continuous scenic consolation.

Their parents had been unhappy about them flying following the Stockport air disaster. The crash had happened at the start of the month, killing seventy-two passengers and crew. Alice's widowed mother, tearful and wringing her hands, didn't want to let her go. There was nothing they could say to stop Mrs Liddell fretting, nor his parents. Even Gill, Angie's sister, had voiced her concerns.

Travelling on the twisting coastal road, Mack now wondered what all the fuss had been about. There was far more chance of the coach crashing the way the driver attacked bends. Careering over one of the long drop ravines or to the sea below looked more likely than dying on the aeroplane ever had. Notwithstanding that possibility, they were all excited and happy to have arrived. The girls were laughing and giggling as if they were on a schoolgirl's outing.

Mack loved being among his young women. Occasionally, he yearned for some male company. He wished that he had someone like Tom or even Nate along with him. Smiling to himself, he recalled his cousin Tom's words.

"You know your problem and mine, don't you? You're like me, a woman's man. The plain fact is we just love having women around and being with them. We love their company. We love everything about them. Given the choice of standing around in a pub, supping pints and shooting the shit about footie with the guys, or being elsewhere with a girl, which would it be? There is no competition where we're concerned." The memory of that conversation made him grin. Tom had admitted he envied him. "You must love it, being the only cock among all those hens."

Tom hadn't intended it to sound lewd, but they had both cracked up laughing like idiots. His cousin had begun doing an impersonation of a rooster. Strutting around his bedroom, he'd given vent to singing the Rolling Stone's *Little Red Rooster*. Grace had opened the door as she passed by, wondering what was going on in his bedroom. Did Tom stop or show any embarrassment? No, he pounced on Grace going cock-a-doodle-doo causing more hilarity. So here he was in Spain, the only rooster with seven hens, the idea made him snigger but also worry.

"What's so funny?" Asked Grace turning around from the seat in front.

"Little Red Rooster." He replied grinning.

They had the coach all to themselves, along with the extra suitcases packed with the clothes for the assignment. Other clothes had already been sent ahead and should have arrived at the hotel. Mack had mental fingers crossed that the shipment had made it there. There would be real problems if it had gone astray. He was here to shoot advertisements planned for the Australian and New Zealand summer months. Mack's earlier photos of Effy's designs taken in London were already in American magazines. That was according to Nate, though Mack had not yet seen copies of these. Alex Silvers told Mack, before they left for Spain, that the Americans were orchestrating a sales campaign for Florida and California. The climates in these states were more temperate in winter. Nate though the Spanish shoot might still be used for these campaigns by the Yanks.

He found himself thinking back over the past few weeks as he stared out at the window at the passing Valencian countryside. It had been an amazing time with so much happening.

There had been one further visit to London since the first. This had involved a fashion shoot at the Lansdowne Walk studio. During the short stay, he'd even met up with Tina Wood and Ronnie Sykes. He had hoped to make use of any information they might have. It hadn't proved fruitful, but

Mack found both keen to stay in touch. Ronnie even treated him like a long lost brother. Considering he had given him a merciless beating, threatening to cut his ear off with a flick knife, didn't seem to matter. To Ronnie and Tina, he was now *The Mack*. It was heartening to see Tina exerting such a positive influence over the one-time hard case.

On returning to Bradford, he'd taken and passed his driving test the first time. That was a big relief, but buying a motorcar would have to wait. Although the money was flooding in like a torrent from the photo shoots, he had other plans for it. These involved the real possibility of leaving school and moving to London.

All the girls were now in demand for assignments. How he and Effy had got through the past few weeks, he couldn't figure out. Revising and sitting the summer exams filled not only his but Effy's spare hours. They were still undecided about what to do next. Uncertainty over their futures had led to a constant discussion between them and Angie. They had only made one decision. They'd agreed that Effy should only model her designs.

The name of the game was to sell herself and her clothes. Modelling other designer's clothes was a definite no. It didn't prevent Effy from doing perfume and cosmetic ads. Those were fine, so too were ones for jewellery or accessories. As long as assignments didn't involve wearing designs belonging to other fashion designers, that would be fine. They had stipulated that in those ad assignments, she would wear, only her designs.

Turning down work was something none of them wanted. There was no choice as more offers arrived daily. They had more work than they could handle. When Effy turned down assignments, Angie recommended to the clients that they might like to work with Ellen or Alice. The excuse was she was already booked up for the foreseeable future. Often this worked.

Since finishing A-Levels, Ellen and Alice had undertaken quite a lot of jobs in London together. Neither relished working alone, so the two always travelled together. Hester Clayton let them stay in her flat, and they appeared to have become quite good friends quickly. It was as well they went together as a pair and never worked alone. They returned with whispered tales of sexual harassment. Both had soon earned a reputation for standing up to men who tried it on.

Ellen had told Mack and Effy of having watched an incredible and unbelievable scene. One photographer had been on the receiving end of a black eye for his efforts. He'd attempted to molest Alice after he persuaded her to go into a side room for some reason or other. His intentions were unclear, but according to Alice, he'd tried to get her to undress for a topless shot. Ellen had heard her shouting obscenities that would have made navvies blush.

Rushing down the corridor, wondering what was going on, she'd forced the door open. She was there just in time to see Alice in action, and that had been astonishing. Alice, boxing like a man, was punching the photographer's lights out. She had him up against a corner. A flurry of combination punches with a right-handed uppercut to the jaw sent him crashing to the floor. Alice stood over him like some awesome female bare-knuckle boxer. The bloke's lip was cut, and his left eye had swollen like a balloon. Ellen couldn't stop laughing, retelling the story. At the time she was so shocked and open-mouthed she couldn't believe what Alice had done.

The photographer hadn't dared to complain or say a word afterwards. His reputation as a seducer would have ceased to exist after getting knocked down by a girl. Ellen had approved of Alice's action. She still had a vivid memory of the rape attempt at Osborne's hands.

Though they had become close friends, Ellen had always thought there was something a little strange about Alice. When she asked her how she had learned to box like that, Alice had given her a bizarre reply. She had told her something about having been the regimental lightweight boxing champion. Mack and Tom reckoned Ellen had misheard her. Alice must have meant her dad had been one and had shown her a few boxing moves.

Then the big event had happened.

Three days before the trip to Spain, his mother had given birth. Now he had a sister and his mum, the much-longed-for daughter. His brother had teased his father with a complete lack of mercy. Mack couldn't help laughing aloud, thinking about Adam's words to his dad. "I didn't expect a cigar, seeing as it's a lass, but not even a Woodbine? You tight-fisted Scottish git…"

Effy had wanted to stay behind to help, but Caitlin had turned up and told her to get on the plane to Spain. She'd be there to look after her mother-in-law. Mack's parents planned to christen his little sister Fiona Grace Ellen MacKinnon. So not only was his Aunt Ellen included in the naming, but so too was Effy's sister, Ellen. Choosing Fiona came as a complete surprise and honour, as it was Effy's forename. Including Grace in the names said such a beautiful thing about the way the MacKinnon's regarded them. All the girls had been so excited by the new arrival.

The jaunt to Spain was for four days. It was their first overseas assignment. Angie had to be back for the following Monday. She still had to sit her final GCE exam. There would be no staying over on this all-expenses-paid trip for Silvers Fashions. This was going to be a taste of what was to come. They were all looking forward to flying to New York. In the meantime, Mack was on a tight schedule to complete the shoot.

Finally, the journey's end saw them arrive in time for the siesta and lunch. It was a relief to be inside the hotel's cool interior. The management was on hand to personally greet the party. They may have thought they were unknowns when they arrived. This was not the case. The hotel staff knew exactly who the visitors were and why they were here.

Greeted like international stars, it made Mack feel like a real celebrity for the first time. Once registered, they were shown to their rooms on the third floor. For convenience, they had all been located close together. Each room had a recessed balcony with a fantastic open beach and sea view.

Les Dunes was an imposing white, L shaped building. It overlooked a long sandy beach and glistening sea. The reception area and lobby were located close to the beachfront drive. There was an outdoor pool for the hotel guests with a shady poolside bar behind. To the side of the pool, an area set aside for sunbathing. As it was the hottest part of the day, many of the guests had taken to staying indoors.

Information supplied by the hotel stated that it was among the first to have been built in the resort. The hotel had been the idea of Miguel Martorell, who took enormous pride in the place and had been on hand to meet their party. This year he was celebrating the tenth year of Les Dunes opening. Nate had warned them that this was a high-class hotel. They could expect to meet all kinds of celebrities, including politicians, movie actors, entertainers, and international jet set travellers. He had advised them to take appropriate evening wear. The hotel insisted that guests dressed formally when dining in the restaurant.

Except for Hester, none of the girls had ever stayed in a hotel. Mack had stopped in one a long time ago when he and Tom were about eight. They'd gone to Bournemouth with his Mum, Aunt Ellen, and Granny MacKinnon. Les Dunes was everything the staid British hotel had not been. His memory of the Dorset hotel was of a staid frightening interior resembling a Hammer House of Horror's movie set.

Later that afternoon, he learned other celebrities were also staying at the hotel. A famous Spanish actress and a popular French teenage Ye Ye singer were vacationing at *Les Dunes*.

Business, Mack understood, was wherever you found it. *Kerching*! Before arriving, these celebrities had learned of a fashion photographer and his models arriving from London. They had expressed instant interest in meeting him. Almost as soon as they had arrived, both women had inquired if Mack would be willing to shoot promotional photos? *Kerching, Kerching*. It became even more interesting when they learned that Effy was a dazzling new English fashion designer.... *Kerching, Kerching, Kerching*! The doors of opportunity opened unexpectedly. He would make money from this stay, and as a result of a lot of trouble too.

Aileen had come along as their chaperone. As Ellen was eighteen, she could have been the chaperone, but Róisín Halloran had insisted on Aileen. Otherwise, she would have refused to grant permission for Effy and Grace. So here he was, the little red rooster with his hens. His father had warned it would not be easy managing all these young women. His son's youthful inexperience might turn the trip into a complete shambles. A lot of responsibility rested with him. Robert MacKinnon need not have worried. The girls behaved like true professionals and Mack, like a born manager and leader.

Hester was an experienced traveller. Mack thought that as the oldest, she might pose the most problems. This proved unfounded. Hester enjoyed her role as the worldly-wise traveller and guide to the group. Aileen found her delightful, and Hester's travel experience was going to prove invaluable. Mack was surprised how well Aileen and Hester got on with one another. Almost as soon as they met, the two hit it off. Alice also appeared to have made a particularly close friendship with Hester. Her frequent stay overs, together with Ellen, had led to the three bonding. Angie's attitude towards Hester had also begun to change, as they became better acquainted. Like Effy, Angie remained unsure of Hester's romantic inclination towards him. He couldn't avoid detecting a hint of possessiveness from both Angie and Effy, whenever Hester was near.

After unpacking, everyone took a rest, meeting in the lounge before the evening meal. The hotel had reserved a part of the restaurant for their party. So many beautiful young women created a dramatic stir among the male patrons as they took their seats. It was more formal than they had expected, and there was some nervousness as they successfully managed to maintain an illusion of sophistication. An a la carte menu was available, but dishes could also be prepared and served to meet personal requirements.

The girls fussed as they struggled to decide what to order. The restaurant's etiquette confused them. Hester, with quiet dignity and whispered suggestions, eased the difficulties. While he waited for his meal, Mack concentrated on prioritising his next steps. He would need to find great locations almost straight away. It didn't help, not knowing the language and having so short a time in the resort.

He learned that the hotel was on Levante or the sunrise side of the new end of the town. On the far side of the old town, lay another beach that stretched several kilometres southward. The locals called it Poniente. After the evening meal, he decided to explore the town. Only Alice and Hester wanted to go along with him. They left without telling the others where they were going.

Hester had visited Spain several times though not in the past three years. Her father owned a villa at Juan-Les-Pins on the Côte d'Azur in France. When she was younger, she and her sisters spent their summer holidays at the villa. Her father would drive along the coast, taking them with him, to stay with a maiden aunt in Sitges. Hester spoke reasonable schoolgirl French and had acquired a useful smattering of Spanish. Neither he nor Alice spoke any Spanish, although he intended to try with the aid of a Collins phrasebook he kept in his back pocket.

What he liked about Alice Liddell was her absence of fear and assured confidence. It was as though she'd gone through much worse. Maybe having died and revived did this to someone? Hester, he found confident, though he thought this was more of an act.

The old town was a mile or so from the hotel. Walking along the beachfront on Levante, they took in the new apartment tower blocks. More appeared to be springing up on the road behind the front. Reaching the old town, they found a warren of streets with small bars and places to eat. The old clashed with the new builds they'd passed. They made their way through the narrow streets heading for the church on the promontory. Passing under a decorative archway, on which a colourful poster advertised a bullfight, they found the steps leading to the blue-domed church. Not far from the church stood another hotel on the promontory overlooking the sea. On the way up, Mack had noticed the fading name, Hotel Planesia.

Beyond the church was an ancient library building. At the far-end, a balcony viewing point reached by steps led to the end of the rocky promontory. The second beach stretched away to another headland. Poniente beach, as this was called, looked almost empty compared to Levante. Building work was taking place, but this beachfront still had fewer buildings. Wandering down some steep steps, they came to the quaint harbour with its umpteen fishing boats. Further on, there was a wooded area. They found one of the few British bars in the resort not far away. At Alice's suggestion, they stopped off at Vincent's Corner Bar. The humid heat had taken its toll. They needed a rest and to buy a drink.

Mack didn't drink wine or spirits but made an exception on this his first evening to Spain. The three got through a whole bottle and then ordered a second. Time seemed to pass at a leisured tempo. Unused to alcohol, his head soon became woozy. They stayed forty minutes, perhaps fifty. Mack engaged a waiter in conversation about the best places to get good photographs receiving some excellent suggestions. One local ex-pat suggested a location that struck him as of special interest. A tiny chapel building called L'Ermita sounded promising. Found at the end of Poniente, near the top of the next headland, it had exceptional views. Given the distance, it would involve a couple of taxis to make the trip.

Hester and Alice proved excellent company on this evening excursion. It made a surprising and pleasant change to talk to these two young women. From her conversation, Hester, at twenty, was a woman of the world. Her tales of modelling in London, Paris, and Rome, and all the wild parties she'd attended held their interest. So too did her accounts of staying in New York. Mack enjoyed her company more and more, as the evening wore on and dusk turned to night.

When they were alone for a few minutes, Hester became unexpectedly serious. She would be in New York on an assignment at the same time as Mack when he travelled over in July. Taking out a slip of paper from her handbag, she passed it to him. There was a New York telephone number on it. Should he experience any problems at all, no matter how great or how small, she wanted him to contact her immediately. Hester was insistent that he should do this, and on no account fail to do so. She would be there to help him as a friend, but she *insisted* that he keep this secret from everyone, especially from Effy and Angie. There were good reasons why, but Hester refused to tell him. What she said to him next left him mystified. Hester refused to say any more when Alice returned.

Their presence soon attracted attention in Vincent's. An intoxicated middle-aged London woman recognised Hester. They were glad to leave as the over loud women let all and sundry know who they were and what they were doing in Benidorm.

Unlike England, you paid as you left. This was something novel to Mack, though not to Hester or Alice. It surprised Mack how far the pesetas went when he paid. The wine was incredibly cheap compared to England. A whole bottle of red wine cost less than a glassful in a British pub, assuming the pub sold wine. Mack felt himself swaying as they left. Alice and Hester fared better, although Alice confessed it had gone to her head too.

On the way back, they came across a Jewellers shop called *Amor*. They stopped to look, with Alice commenting that diamonds were a girl's best friend. For some peculiar reason, this caused the two mildly intoxicated young women to go giddy and start laughing. Settling down, the three of them examined the window display, hypnotised by the glitter. Mack saw something that grabbed his attention. There was a gold chain with a heart locket that would look good on Effy and Angie. He wondered if the shop had two? If he could get two, they would make a surprise gift for each of his girls. If the locket were the only one in stock, he'd look for something else that Angie might love and cherish. She didn't have a bracelet or bangle, well not a gold one, so perhaps he could find one for her as an alternative? He made a mental note of the streets name, *Avenida Martinez de Alejos*.

British travellers were restricted to a maximum travel allowance of fifty pounds since last year. He had enough funds to buy something pretty for each girl as a souvenir of their first trip overseas together. Although breaking the law, he had squirreled another thirty pounds with him in case of emergencies.

Their lengthy absence had caused concern. Aileen, Effy, and Angie were waiting in the lounge for their return like agitated mother hens. Where had they been? Why were they gone so long? That all three returnees were tipsy didn't help. Aileen felt obliged to lecture Mack about underage drinking. To which Mack replied, this was Spain, not England. Then he received a further lecture from Effy that was more tongue in cheek than serious. Mack couldn't avoid noticing how his two sweethearts became cool towards Hester. Worse for wear and tired, he asked reception to wake him at seven in the morning. That night he slept alone from choice but not until he'd had quiet words with Effy and Angie. Hester didn't deserve being treated as if she had done something wrong. If they didn't believe him, they should ask Alice who had gone with them.

164

Rising early, he went out of the hotel within ten minutes of getting out of bed. He returned an hour and a half later, having taken a taxi to scout the suggested locations. After collecting his room key, he met Angie coming down from her room. His words from last night must have affected her. She apologised for her coolness towards Hester, receiving a passionate kiss. At the restaurant doorway, a Frenchman waylaid them.

He introduced himself as Henri Fournier. That's what it sounded like to Mack's ears. Between the Frenchman's limited English and Mack's minimal schoolboy French, they managed a brief exchange. Angie's French was no better than Mack's having forgotten most of what she'd learned. Between them, they thought they understood that the man was the manager of someone called Micheline Queneau or Charmaine. Charmaine was a teen pop star, a YeYe singer from France. She was on a short holiday break. As they conversed, she came to join them.

The singer was a demure and dainty brunette. Charmaine, the manager informed them, was a big star on the French pop scene. She looked younger than Grace, but he learned later the singer was older than Angie. Mack assumed he'd understood everything. He hadn't. They agreed to meet later in the day to talk business. That's how the conversation appeared to go. Effy's French was good, as was Hester's. The girls might strike a deal for him to photo shoot this Charmaine. No one could have foreseen how this would impact on him and the girls.

Mack and Angie found themselves accosted once more. This time in the lounge as they came out from breakfast. One of the English-speaking staff persuaded him and Angie to meet Eva de Santiago. The famous Spanish actress wanted to be introduced to them. Out of politeness, they agreed to say hello. Mack guessed she had to be in her late thirties. Striking, beautiful, and glamorous, the lady spoke broken English after a fashion. They agreed to talk to her later in the evening. Explaining he and his models were working this morning.

An air of hectic rush greeted him on the corridor with their rooms. Aileen was already busy fussing over her sisters in Grace's room. She was applying lavish quantities of Ambre Solaire to Grace. On Hester's recommendation and urging, they had brought a supply of suntan lotion on the trip. Now her warnings about the intense sun made sense. Hester and Alice needed help, so Ellen did the honours. Effy and Angie helped one another. Then they insisted on applying the lotion to Mack. Giggling, they made him strip to the waist. It was unnecessary, since he would be wearing a tee-shirt. Teasing him, they massaged the lotion all over. He wasn't about to complain, enjoying the sensation of both their hands on his torso. Within seconds he had gone hard, and both girls knew they had aroused him, teasing him even more. Across the corridor, he could hear Aileen fussing over Grace. She was reminding her not to get sunburnt again, the way she had in Morecambe when ten years old.

Mack wanted the shoot to take place before nine-thirty, avoiding the midday sun's brightness. It was closer to ten before they were ready to leave. Another cloudless deep, blue sky greeted them as they stepped out of the hotel. Everyone donned sunglasses to cut the glare. Two taxis took them to the far headland at the end of Poniente along the coast road.

L'Ermita was up a steep lane. It wasn't at the top of the headland but three-quarters of the way up to the crest of the mount. The view across to the town from the mini chapel was breathtaking, but it lacked shade. The girls did well in the heat of the burning sun. Hester had brought a broad-brimmed floppy hat with her. The girls wore silk scarves to keep the breeze and the sun off their hair. Aileen stood by with a hairbrush and clips during the shoot as a warm breeze enveloped the group. With a striking coastal backdrop to one side and mountains to the other, they were in business.

Avoiding over-exposed photographs was a major problem. He had to make constant adjustments to the camera settings using the light meter. Picking the right angles became critical. It was a relief knowing he'd bought films with him of the right ASA to cope with the conditions.

Hester had warned him to get them back indoor as soon after midday as possible. Sunstroke could be a real problem. He didn't need the girls suffering headaches and getting sunburnt. Another issue arose with the suntan lotion. It was staining some of the pastel outfits already.

On wrapping up the morning's shoot, they learned how the local taxi drivers were laid-back with timekeeping. Their taxis arrived much later than requested. With so little shade, the girls found the burning sun and the heat wearisome and uncomfortable. Concern mounted for Grace with her red hair and pale skin. Hester exchanged her broad-brimmed hat for Grace's headscarf. By the time the taxis arrived, tempers were fraying, with Mack feeling reluctant to give the taxi drivers a tip on returning. Hester advised him to do so, in case they needed them again.

Back in the hotel, all the girls wanted to do was drink iced water and take an early siesta Spanish style. Even Mack found himself on his bed in only his underpants. Angie and Effy materialised in his room. Stripping

166

down to bra and briefs, they flaked out on the double bed either side of him dozing off after a few words.

Around four in the afternoon, they woke up to the sound of Aileen knocking on his room door. He didn't bother to get up and called out for her to come in. "So, that's where you two girls got to?" Aileen averted her gaze away.

"Nothing's happened, Aileen." Effy's drowsy response followed with an excuse. "Mack's room was shadier and cooler."

"I think I'll take a shower," Angie muttered, unable to stir. "An ice-cold shower."

Aileen left without another word or admonishment forgetting to close the door. Effy slumped back on the bed, her head resting on his chest. Angie rolled over, placing a hand on his right thigh. In what seemed like brief moments later, there was another knock on the open door. "Come in!" All three chorused in near-perfect unison. Without looking up or opening their eyes, they half expected to hear Grace or Ellen.

"*Oh!*" There was a gasp of surprise and a titter. "*Excusez-moi! Je suis désolèe pour cette intrusion. La porte était ouverte. Vous avez dit que c'était bon d'enter.*"

They raised their heads in silent embarrassment. It had to look compromising, two girls in their underwear, embracing an almost naked young man on the same bed. Their dresses lay discarded with careless abandon on a chair.

"*Qui es-tu?*" Effy raised her head, still only half awake.

Angie slid her legs off the bed in a matter-of-fact manner. "It's that French pop singer. The one Mack and I met in the lobby."

"*Ce n'est pas ce que tu penses voir.*" Effy tried to explain.

If the French girl felt embarrassed, she didn't show it.

"*Pas de problem Mademoiselle.*" Mack sat up, rubbing his eyes, responding in his limited French.

The singer was about to leave when Effy invited her to come back. They carried on a brief conversation that neither he nor Angie could follow. Something about photographs was all he could make out.

Charmaine turned and smiled at him with one of those *knowing* looks. Giving him a wink as she left, she said. "*Désolé je n'avais pas realise que tu étais occupé autrement.*"

"What was that she said?" Mack asked, his eyes narrowing.

Effy gave him an irritated look. She appeared not to have seen the wink. "What do you think she said? She said she was sorry for catching us unaware. She didn't realize *you* were *otherwise* occupied."

Angie started giggling, then spluttered. "Bang goes his status as a virgin."

It took a moment for Angie's words to make sense. Then Effy gave way to a fit of giggling.

"Hahaha, Angie, hilarious or as the French would say, *très drôle.*"

He pronounced it *trezz drowl.* "Anyway, you two should think about getting prepped. So should Hester and Alice. We have to do that shoot about six-thirty or so on the old town promontory. I'll have the sun behind me and that wide open beach and sea so I can get that sun, sea, and sangria pic as per orders."

"And you'd better get a move on and book those taxis. I'm not walking there to end up hot and sweaty." Effy warned.

"Don't forget the sunglasses we're supposed to be advertising," Angie reminded. "I want the first pick. Where did you put the box with the selection, Effy?"

It was a co-promotional shoot. There were plenty more of these in the pipeline. Tomorrow, except for Effy, the girls would model swimwear and sunglasses. While there, they would advertise a famous brand of suntan lotion at the same time. Effy would do a separate sunglasses product shoot early tomorrow morning. She'd wear one of her summer dress designs. Mack intended to do this as a balcony shot with an amazing sea view.

The evening shoot would produce some of the best photos yet. They forgot the bedroom incident as they climbed into the taxis heading for the town. Like most incidents, they never suspected there might be consequences. For the present, it disappeared from their heads as their thoughts turned to the evening's shoot. By the time they had finished, it was late."

That evening, with Effy and Hester's help, they organised a special evening shoot for Charmaine for the following day. Using a local Spanish notary, she and her manager signed a witnessed agreement. Fournier had organised the deal. They paid Mack cash in advance in French francs. An English-speaking member of the staff had translated for them. Fournier was sure the photographs would appear in *Paris Match, L'Officiel,* or *Age Tendre.* This was an unusual way to do business. Mack could do the shoot in the hotel.

It looked even more promising when they learned that Charmaine had opened a boutique in Paris. She was looking for fresh designs from trendy England to sell alongside her own fashion line. That's when he and Effy realized how successful Charmaine was in France. It was not just another *kerching*. The future potential sales potential was there. The singer was keen to see Effy's range and indicated she would travel to London when her forthcoming continental tour was over.

The infamous photo taken outside The Cromwellian had appeared in French and continental magazines. The three were already a minor *cause célèbre* across the Channel even though none of them knew it. Worse would follow. Sometimes *kerchings* came with huge price tags, and this particular shoot would cost them more than money. Thinking no more about it, her manager asked to take a photo of Charmaine with the three of them. They gave no mind to it. It was just a personal memory snap of the four of them together as a keepsake for Charmaine.

Their meeting would lead to adverse publicity with unforeseen consequences.

CHAPTER 33

Walk On The Wild Side (Opening Title Theme & Credits)
Elmer Bernstein & Orchestra
(MGM 1164 – 1962)
Monday 10 – Saturday 15 July 1967 – New York

They planned well in advance, to get work visas for the USA. Finding responsible adults to go had created a few problems for Mack and the girls. They were underage, requiring adults to accompany them to the States. Pearl Piper's people in New York agreed to pay for Bridget to accompany Effy and her two sisters. Robert Mackinnon took his annual holiday leave. He was unhappy forsaking his wife and newborn daughter for two weeks, but what choice did he have? Someone needed to be there as another responsible adult to ensure the safety of Alice and Angie as well as Mack. There was no one else, and there were other important reasons for him to go.

Robert MacKinnon disclosed he had formed a private limited company on Effy's behalf with her full permission. Greg Williams had submitted the paperwork for the company's registration. It was vital for his father and Greg Williams to be on this trip.

Greg was needed in a legal capacity to help his father understand the legalities of any deal that would be signed. With powers of attorney, the two men had serious responsibilities. The associated deals and contracts that would come flooding in, alongside the main one, would require careful vetting. The potential sums of money being mentioned staggered everyone. While they were away, they would have some respite from the British press. The Benidorm bedroom incident had made the news pages.

Charmaine, the French singer, had given several interviews on returning to Paris. She had revelled in telling the journalists all about meeting Mack and the models. How the singer described what she had seen in his bedroom made for lurid reading. It was the last thing they needed.

The published French versions of her accounts sensationalised the encounter. The keepsake photo had appeared in at least three magazines along with the publicity photos he'd shot. How Mara Fisher found out about these reports in France remained a mystery? Somehow, Fisher contrived to interview the French singer, or so she claimed. It didn't take her long to get back into one newspaper editor's favours. The next thing they knew, the story was out. Fisher's salacious trashy gossip appeared in one of the red tops along with Charmaine's keepsake snap.

Trying to explain this incident to his parents hadn't gone well. His mother didn't help matters. An exchange between her and Effy ended with neither speaking to one another for two whole days. Both refused to tell him what they'd said, leaving him annoyed with them both. Whatever passed between the two had shaken Effy, leaving her in tears. Despite Aileen's explanation of what had taken place, it left an atmosphere of unpleasantness. It took all of Angie's persuasiveness to convince his mother nothing untoward had gone on. Saying nothing was one thing. Giving him long, peculiar stares, was something else and uncomfortable. Far more was going on than he realized.

Effy remained upset even after Aileen and Angie's words placated his mother. Mack found Effy did her best to avoid talking to him about anything remaining distant. Had he done something wrong? Perhaps, keeping details of the new company secret was what had worried her? Whatever it was, it appeared to involve him. He hoped things would pick up once they arrived in New York. How wrong he was.

The trip was to prove a nightmare. Almost straight away, Mack found himself sidelined.

Pearl Piper's company men at AIC-InStyle had made the local arrangements. The girls ended up in the St. Regis hotel on 2 East 55th Street. Mack found himself alone five blocks away. They had lodged him in a tiny apartment with Alvin Young, one of Piper's assistants. Their excuse was the hotel was fully booked, and there wasn't a room available. The girls, in the meantime, enjoyed every minute staying in one of the city's finest luxury hotels.

Mack found himself walking the streets wondering what was going on, and why no one was contacting him, not even the girls. It wasn't until the Thursday that he found out what was happening. When an unexpected little bird left him a message.

It came courtesy of a phone call from Alice who had struggled to get hold of him, being denied his location. There was a conspiracy to keep his whereabouts a secret. Alice believed something evasive and untoward was taking place behind his back. He should respond to this message immediately by ringing the phone number she now gave him. He did, identifying the number as soon as he wrote it down. He rang the number. The call left him numb.

What he learned sent an icy shiver down his backbone. He began to shake, experiencing a sudden loss of his legs from the shock. Sitting down, he tried to make sense of what he'd heard. Then the adrenaline began to kick in, and so did the fury he felt. Ignoring the advice over the phone his anger for once got the better of him.

He walked the seemingly endless city blocks to the hotel, hoping to control his outrage before he reached there. He failed. His fury intensified with each stride. He exploded as he confronted Effy in the hotel lobby. His anger shocked Angie and Grace with the awful accusations he made. Angie tried to calm him down without success. His uncharacteristic behaviour reduced her and Effy to tears. Effy turned and fled weeping and trembling, followed by a dismayed Grace. They dashed past his father and Greg, who happened to be talking to Pearl Piper nearby. Mack pursued her, demanding answers. Coming across Piper, Greg, and his father, he stopped and unleashed hell in public.

His acid, verbal attack, on Piper left the Texan woman physically flinching from his scorn. Unused to having home truths hurled at her with such ferocious precision, she went white as blood drained from her face. Mack, driven by a calculated, incandescent fury, didn't stop. As public humiliations went, he delivered a master class.

Greg and his father had to drag him away from an ashen-faced Piper using force, fearing he might physically assault her. Robert MacKinnon had never in his entire life seen his son in such a dark, vicious, and violent mood. Nor could he ever have conceived his son capable of destroying and humiliating someone in public without mercy. It was a deliberately executed assassination of Piper's character for all to hear, and it horrified his father. Attempts to calm Mack by both men met with utter contempt as he snarled shaking free of them. Robert MacKinnon knew then he had made a horrible error of judgement.

His son's words showed furious defiance. "You knew, the pair of you knew, and you said nothing. You've both been in on this from the start, selling your souls for the shekels." Breaking free, Mack left the hotel seconds before security guards arrived to eject him.

Later that afternoon, they summoned him back to the hotel. To ensure he returned, they had sent a company limousine for him complete with an escort. He returned because he thought they might have changed their minds. Deep down, he knew it was a forlorn hope.

Meeting in a conference suite, they subjected him to a verbal mauling as he listened to the assembled grown-ups. Piper wasn't present, which didn't surprise him. Instead, two AIC-InStyle suits had taken her place. Everyone in the room ganged up against him, except for Nate. Nate said nothing, unhappy with what was taking place. When he tried to say something in Mack's defence, Alex Silvers told his son to shut up. Nate had no choice but to leave the talking to his father. He wasn't pleased, and Mack could see the sudden resentment there.

Alex Silvers then gave Mack a stern telling off abetted by his own father and Greg Williams. In effect, they wanted an apology from him to Pearl Piper. Mack conceded in his head that it had been a vicious butchering on his part. It just hadn't gone far enough. Under the circumstances, he felt no regret for what he'd said because now he understood the nature of this game. He just didn't feel he'd been harsh enough with the home truths. Next time he would go for bust.

What it all amounted to was straightforward. Alex Silvers didn't want the deal on the table collapsing, and if it meant selling him out, so be it. Mack was told in no uncertain words he had to accept what was happening. It was a *fait accomplit*. They had signed and sealed the contracts. The girls would do shoots with other top fashion photographers in the city and not with him. He would be here with his thumbs doing the proverbial twiddling, and he'd better make the best of it.

That hadn't been the deal IAC-InStyle had promised. Behind his back, they had conspired to renege on it. Mack had expected to sign on the usual dotted line when he arrived. Instead, they had deliberately sidelined him. This explained why they'd kept him isolated from everyone. All those tenuous excuses about the hotel being fully booked up with no spare rooms, they had made it up. Piper had claimed it was only temporary. Temporary for the entire trip.

One of the quiet Americans, Pyle, informed him his isolation was a deliberate company policy. *Mistah* Pyle's condescending Deep South accent grated on Mack's ears. He resented the 'quiet' American even more because he kept referring to him as 'sonny' in every sentence. Pyle made it worse by saying it was in everyone's best interest. Whose best interest, Mack asked? It was not in his best interest, and he informed them so in his most colourful and unforgettably explicit way.

What upset him most were the reasons they gave. AIC-InStyle wanted to avoid any scandals during the stay. The last thing the Americans wanted was another Benidorm incident to flare up in the home press or TV. Piper's corporate bods at AIC-InStyle were averse to all unfavourable publicity. Mack told them he wanted to see all the girls immediately.

They told him he couldn't. He'd caused too much upset already. Mack replied he hadn't even begun to cause upset yet. They would know all about it when he did. Pyle then told him that after he left this room, he would not be allowed in the hotel again. The security guards outside the door would escort him out. The hotel had instructions to prevent him from returning.

How dare they try to keep him from seeing Effy and Angie?

The hurt experienced was profound. Knowing Effy's involvement in this betrayal had felt like a knife stabbing him in the heart. Even before they'd travelled, she had known he would not be doing the photo shoots. Effy had sold out to Piper and Silvers. She had known what would happen when they landed. Why? Why would she have done something like this to him? What part had Angie played in all this? Had Angie known too? Had all the girls?

More hard words were exchanged, but Mack proved unrelenting. He'd come over to shoot fashion photographs of the girls. He was not here to end up sidelined by that double-dealing Texan sidewinder and her bootlicking associates. Pyle and his associate began to lose their cool demeanour. He knew he'd hit the intended nerves, sticking in and twisting the verbal knife. When his father told him to quieten down, Mack spat out the word *Judas* followed by, "I bet you got paid your thirty pieces of silver or whatever the going rate is in dollars these days."

Robert MacKinnon went pale, hearing those words from his son.

Mack's parting words dripped with a strange poisonous menace. "You think you've fucked me over, don't you *Mistah* Pyle? You'll wish you'd done a better hatchet job when I get even with you and Piper. And I promise, I will. When I do, you won't forget it. I'm a young man with a bullet. You have two days to reconsider your options. If you don't, the gloves are off. After which, I won't even need a fan to cover you and your fucking sidewinder boss in inch thick shit."

Pyle and the other American began laughing in disbelief. To them, he was a seventeen-year-old kid full of bravado, making empty threats. Pyle was still laughing when Mack leaned over him. Eyeballing Pyle, separated by just enough breathing space, his menace was real and intimidating. He mocked him with an exaggerated Deep South accent, "Yeah, have a good laugh, *Mistah* Pyle. Let's see who's laughing last."

"Are you threatening me, *sonny*?" Pyle spat out the word sonny. "Carrying a gun at your age in New York is illegal, *sonny*."

"You dozy ignorant wanker, Pyle. A bullet is a bullet point describing a hot hit climbing up the Billboard charts. I'm heading to the top as a photographer, with a bullet, you ignorant fuck."

"I don't like your manners, *sonny*. Nor do I appreciate your use of foul language or your threatening behaviour. " Pyle snarled.

"No, *Mistah Pyle*, this is not a threat. It's a promise, and I always find a way to keep my promises. Bad publicity? You all have no idea how bad I can make it, or will make it. You ain't seen nothing yet."

He didn't wait to leave, or to be escorted by the security men waiting outside the door. Mack walked out of the meeting without another word, laughter echoing in his ears. His father tried to stop him, but his son broke his heart, "Fuck of Judas."

The words rang in Robert MacKinnon's ears.

Their mistake, they shouldn't have laughed. The price tag for laughing had just gone up.

Mack vanished from sight for the next thirty-nine hours.

He became a ghost.

What happened during those thirty-nine hours would remain a fateful mystery.

Mack intended to play this game of chess his way, with two Queens on his side of the board.

When Mack did turn up at the apartment, after going missing, Alvin Young telephoned his father. The young American informed him that he was back and packing his suitcase. He'd have to hurry over or miss him. Robert MacKinnon rushed over just in time to catch him. Young left the two together to talk.

The relief on seeing his son safe proved too much. Robert MacKinnon gave his son a powerful hug, almost squeezing the breath from his lungs.

"Where the hell have you been, James? I've been sick with worry. I didn't dare phone your mother. Effy's been frantic and hysterical, Angie's not been much better. We've filed a missing person's report and had the police getting ready to look for you. The stick I've had to take…"

175

Freeing himself from his father's grip, Mack tapped the side of his nose. "Where have I been? That's my secret. You're not the only one who has secrets. Is there a return airline ticket waiting for me, or perhaps a change of mind?"

Before his father could answer Mack sneered, the cynicism marked and heavy. "Neither it seems. Not a great surprise. A pity, but never mind, Missy Piper and her friends have an unpleasant surprise heading their way. The lot of you deserve everything that's coming."

"What are you on about, son?"

"You'll know soon enough. I only came back to pick up my passport, suitcase, and spare film spools. I might as well shoot a few more snaps and earn a few bob over here before heading back across the pond."

"Listen, son, let me explain..."

Mack remained impassive, saying nothing. His father attempted to spell out why things had panned out as they had. His son's silence unnerved him. Robert MacKinnon realized he didn't know his son anymore. Something had broken. He stopped explaining, it was fruitless. Picking up the phone and using a scribbled a number on a piece of paper, he rang the hotel. Leaving a message for Bridget with the reception, he wanted her to let the girls know he'd found James safe.

"Promise me you won't go walkabout again?" Robert MacKinnon tried to extract a response from his son as he finished packing. Mack noted his father's anxiety with a wry smile.

"What? Promise? Like the promise, they made to me? The promise Effy knew about and then said nothing to me, knowing what was going on? You knew too, and you did nothing and said nothing. I might have expected Alex Silvers to fuck me over. That wouldn't have surprised me and didn't. Business, as they say, is business, and big money is at stake for him. It goes with the territory, but I expected better from her and you. I can't believe she wouldn't tell me. When the person you love deceives you, it goes beyond hurt. As for you, talk about backstabbing. You, my father, in on it the whole time. What could be worse? A word like worse doesn't come close to describing what you did, does it?"

"It wasn't her fault." His father sighed shoulders slumping. "They made Effy keep it secret. It wasn't what she wanted. Nor was it what I wanted. What you said to her in the hotel lobby was awful. No wonder she ran off."

"Well, there you are. Nothing hurts like the truth."

"Your words were hurtful in the extreme when Effy already felt overwhelmed with guilt. You should know two facts. First, she knew nothing about you being cut out from the deal when she signed. She only found out after the signing and then by accident. Second, she threatened to pull out of the deal altogether. Except, by having signed binding contracts, she couldn't for legal reasons, without incurring serious penalties. She was *made* to keep quiet. That little girl came here, to this apartment, to see you with Angie, so she could beg your forgiveness. Let me repeat that so it sinks in with you. *To beg for your forgiveness.* I've never seen a girl in such floods of tears and remorse. They waited in this apartment for a whole afternoon, hoping you'd come back. We had to drag them away when you didn't turn up. When she learned you'd disappeared without a word, she and Angie became frantic. The two of them were ready to go scouring New York to find you. Bridget and I had to stop the pair of them."

"Did Angie and the other girls know about this rotten deal?"

"No. We thought it wiser not to tell her or the other girls. Angie was furious when she found out. She's refused to go along with the deal, contracts or not. I understand Alice, Ellen, and Grace, were angry with Piper. Alice and Grace told Piper to her face what they thought of her. They said they would have refused to come if they'd known what she and Alex Silvers had planned. The girls are all loyal to you. They even told Alex Silvers and Piper to their faces they would never work for him or InStyle again unless they re-instated you."

"And I bet that did a fat lot of good. So was it all just business for you? Coming even before your son? And I thought I knew my dad. And telling me this… do you think this would make everything right between you and me? It doesn't." There was no disguising the hurt in those words. Robert MacKinnon collapsed on to the couch as he watched his son doing a final check on his suitcase. It was the closest he had ever seen his father almost reduced to tears.

"Business is business, after all." Mack's icy words hit even harder. "You've taken after your father, the ruthless, scheming, Edinburgh businessman without a conscience? He gave you your lessons for life, didn't he? I can see it's a family trait. If you want to see how ruthless I can get, see what happens next. Oh, and as soon as I'm back in England, I'm moving out. I've enough of a reputation as a photographer to work for at least two well-known magazines in London. They made me offers, I just didn't take them up at the time."

"Son, calm down. I understand you feel betrayed. If I could, I would turn back the hands of time to change it all, I would. Look, do nothing. Listen to what Nate has to say before you do anything. He wants to speak to you.

His father should have listened to him and heeded his advice. Nate was on your side. He tried to persuade his father not to agree to the arrangements brokered with Piper and AIC-InStyle. And your two lovebirds deserve better, don't they?

You owe Effy a chance to make it up to you, and Angie is blameless in all this, as are the other girls. You can't throw away everything you have going with each other and with Angie. Oh, yes, I know all about your 'arrangement' with both girls. I can't say I approve of how the three of you got yourselves into such a messy situation. I don't pretend to understand it, but you owe it to Effy to let her and Angie see you."

Mack softened. Now the truth was seeping out, he regretted the words spoken in the hotel lobby. On reflection, no wonder she had avoided talking to him. The guilt of knowing what she had done, even if unwittingly, must have preyed on her conscience. How on earth had they persuaded her to sign? Piper and Pyle must have buried the details deep in the small print. She could not have known until too late. It was the same for Angie and the others. They hadn't known either placing their trust in Alex Silvers and Greg Williams.

Greg must have read the small print? He must have known. Why had he not warned them about what they were signing? Did he not realise? No, that wasn't possible, he had to have known. Greg was too sharp and too astute. He and Alex Silvers had let him and the girls down. The big question he wanted answering was who, of the two, was the one most guilty? The finger pointed straight at Greg Williams.

Mack said he would try to contact Effy, but didn't reveal to his father what was planned. Today he had no time as he had a meeting arranged. Where and with whom he refused to say. "I've left a note thanking Alvin for letting me stop here, but given the circumstances with his employers, I'm moving out. I don't need one of Piper's underlings spying on me and what I'm doing."

"Where are you going? You don't know anyone in New York."

"You'd be surprised. I'm stopping in Greenwich Village, that's all you need to know. That Texan bitch is about to find herself well and truly fucked. By noon today, things will look really ugly for *Missy* Piper and *Mistah* Pyle."

"Are you living in cloud cuckoo land, son? Why would she or InStyle do that?"

Mack tapped his nose again. "You'll find out. Remember the name Eugene Henderson. On second thoughts, don't. Let it all come as one massive nasty surprise for Piper and co. I'll be in touch soon enough after the fall out starts to settle. In the meantime, I'm staying with someone I can trust not to sell me out."

Something in his son's face told him he was being taunted. For several seconds his son's crazy words worried him. Had he completely lost the plot and suffered a breakdown?

No. This was crafted craziness. James really was up to something.

After his father left, Mack made two phone calls before leaving. One was a message for Nate left with hotel reception. The second was for a taxi. Mack dropped the apartment keys on the kitchen table and then left with his suitcase and camera bags.

CHAPTER 34

Let Your Conscience Be Your Guide – Marvin Gaye
(From the LP 'The Soulful Moods of Marvin Gaye' - TM 21 1961)
Saturday 15 – July 1967. Mid afternoon, New York

Tompkin Square Park was about a mile and a half walk from Bleecker Street to what was the East Side. Locally, it was becoming known as the East Village. Hippies, as they were labelled, seemed everywhere. The park had become their gathering point.

This was the Summer of Love, according to the press and the media. He had been hearing about it since arriving in New York. Now here he was in its midst, capturing it with his camera. Not only did he look out of place, but he felt out of place. In contrast to their long hair, multi-coloured gaudy fashions, he dressed like an alien.

In stark contrast to the long-haired hippies, his brown hair was cut short to a half-inch with a razored parting. His was the quintessential look of young British Mod in casual mode. He stood out amongst the gaudy fashions wearing Levi sta prest trousers and a short-sleeved Ben Sherman shirt.

Taking his time, he put the camera to work. A first successful photo book would result. So too would a major exhibition of his work. These would feature the photographs taken today. They would capture the social history of these moments in time. During this trip, he would take a further three hundred photographs. These excluded the ones he'd already taken of Hester and other models in as yet undisclosed fashion shoots.

It was as humid as it had been in Spain. A thermometer outside a drugstore showed 82° Fahrenheit as he hunted for interesting images. Stores selling TV sets kept showing coverage of the Newark's Race riot. The rioting had gone on for the past two days and didn't look like ending anytime soon. This alternated with footage from the war in Vietnam.

Mack worked his way round to the place where he was meeting Nate. It was the corner of East 7th Street and Avenue A at the entrance to Tompkin Square Park. The guidebook told him it was close to the Bowery, on the edge of a district called the Ukrainian town. Somewhere nearby, he heard the sound of The Doors *Light My Fire* playing. It had reached number one in the hot one hundred charts.

180

"Fuck me, mate. Why did you choose this part of the city? Couldn't you have picked somewhere civilised, like Times Square or the UN building? These hippy types freak me out."

"I'm here earning a crust since your old man did me out of work."

Nate shook his head, getting straight to the nitty-gritty of their meeting. "You weren't kidding, were you? Those AIC-InStyle suits thought they had it all sewn up tight. I don't think they're laughing right now. Still, you were a touch over the top with the melodrama. It was a bit too Lawrence Olivier for my taste. Next time try Paul Newman. He's a lot cooler."

After a brief pause Nate added. "Do you know something? Maybe you should. Acting may not be a bad alternative. I do think that's where your true vocation could lie. Either acting or as a politician."

"I've heard that said too."

"Not that you're not a good photographer. I happen to think you're gold, and among the best in the business right now, with the potential to be the best."

"Nice of you to say so."

"Which is why I'm on your side. Well, young fella, you've got the Yanks at AIC-InStyle in a tizz. God knows what kind of wobbly Piper's throwing right now. You've got that Texan tiger by her tail. What's more, you're swinging her round faster than a racing car at Brand's Hatch. Now what? Are you planning to let go?"

"Get ready to duck when I do." Mack chuckled.

"Listen, I'm staying out of it and leaving this one to my dad and Piper to sort out. They created the mess; they're responsible for what's come their way. My father should never have agreed to cut you from the deal. Piper should not have insisted. It's all her fault. That's where the real blame lies."

Mack knew more than he wanted to reveal to Nate at this moment. What he heard next surprised yet did not astound.

"Looks like our Hester did the unexpected." Nate continued. "She pulled out the biggest gun in her armoury, a huge howitzer in fact. You have a lot to thank her for, young Mack. She's done you a massive favour. How is Hester? I take it you're staying with her?"

Mack remained impassive for several seconds, considering how to reply. Nate had used him like some puppeteer to further his own plans. "How did you know I was staying with Hester?"

181

"We planned it. Or rather I did. Hester came to New York because I thought it might be a good idea. I didn't like what they had done to you, but I couldn't say anything either. If I had, this trip would never have happened. You and the girls would have pulled the plug. Then I would have been in deep shit. So I told Hester you would need a good pal when you learned about the backstabbing. Besides, she digs you. The girl's got the majors for you, poor kid. Neither of us wanted your trip to become a total washout. We agreed to try and make it work for you somehow, the best we could."

"So that's what she wasn't telling me. You were involved from the start."

Nate changed the subject. "Has Hester finally bedded you?"

"Not for the lack of trying. Otherwise, we've become the best of friends."

"I asked Hester not to say anything, and only if necessary. We didn't know how you'd take it. It was a lot worse than we expected. Most of all, I didn't expect Hester to use her connections in the way she has. She buggered up my plans and improved on them to her credit. It's turned out far more entertaining. She must think a hell of a lot about you to have connected you to Henderson. Hester wouldn't do that for just anyone. I'm sure she wouldn't even do it for me, so you must have a special place in her heart."

Mack scratched his head. "I reckon you're right, Nate. She must like me a great deal when you put it like that. The more I get to know Hester, the more I like her. A guy could so easily fall in love with her if he wasn't careful. Once you get past that Cheltenham Ladies front, there's an adorable person behind it. Is there anyone she doesn't know? She seems so well connected everywhere. Thanks to her, I've made a few more important connections here. I take it you know she related to Eugene Henderson?"

"Oh, I know, believe you me," Nate acknowledged with a puzzling smile, "the girl's a social goldmine all right. So? Are you two staying in Greenwich Village?"

"Yeah, I'm sleeping on my own, desperately trying not to get laid."

"Her powers of seduction must be slipping. Let me take my hat off to you two. Piper must be well pissed right now, and likely as not bricking it. The pair of you nuked the lady's life this morning, according to my father. You've certainly brought him closer to having a heart attack. She deserved it. Piper should never have messed with a good thing." Nate clasped both hands behind his head and leaned back to stretch himself. "Our American lady got it so wrong. She looked at you with a glass eye."

182

"Eh?" His comment puzzled Mack.

"You need both eyes on the prize. Not just one. And if you do only have one, then it shouldn't be a glass one. Being single-minded is fine as long as it doesn't blind or blinker you. In your case, she didn't see you for who you were and what you were capable of doing. All she saw was a teenager with a camera. She failed to see a mean, determined bastard capable of waging a vendetta. I knew you had balls, but after what's happened, I don't think I'd ever dare cross you myself. That's where she got it all wrong. She didn't realize you were the mongoose to her snake. I have no time for people who lack vision. It smacks of a kind of ingrained one-track-minded stupidity."

Mack chuckled. "Shame Piper never read *How to win friends and influence people* by Dale Carnegie."

"I'm guessing you did?"

"When I was fourteen. I borrowed it from the local library."

"I've never been much of a reader myself. Got to respect you for that, Mack."

They strolled over to a nearby coffee house. Relaxing in the cool interior, ordering coffee and bagels. Scott McKenzie's *San Francisco* was playing on a jukebox in the far corner.

"I can't stand this crap. To be honest, Mack, from what I've read about these hippies, they don't impress me none. Strikes me they're out of touch with reality. Peace and love and all that flower power shit. Cute ideas, but it's not the way the world works."

"Yeah. I got to agree. I've spent more than an hour or two photographing them. I tuned in to a few of the conversations. What they're spouting is a load of drug-addled rubbish, but it's got me lots of interesting snaps while wandering around. Most of these hippies need a serious reality check. Anyway, down to business. So give me the low and the why? What made your Pa go along with Piper to steal my deal?"

The explanation was lengthy. It was personal, also about him but not about his photography. The Spanish shoot had produced some of the best fashion shots to date of Effy's range. The top photographer Piper had in mind was her lover. She wanted him to break Effy as the new hot designer and model from England. The money this guy would earn was a major factor because of his recent divorce settlement. His alimony payments had involved scary sums.

As for Silvers Fashions, this was their biggest deal. If it came off, it would be the most lucrative the business had ever made. Everything depended on how it was handled. If that meant giving Piper what she wanted, then Alex Silvers had been prepared to give it to her.

Nate explained the hard realities. The Silvers were following a trail blazed by the likes of Mary Quant, and most recently, by Twiggy. Twiggy had conquered the States as a model and as a purveyor of her range of clothes.

In the States, advertising was everything. Selling was reliant on marketing skills. Once in the stores, everything was in the hands of the sales staff. If all went well, you made the money. The sums involved raised Mack's eyebrows. AIC-InStyle was the key to the operation. No matter what animosity Mack might have towards them, they were the most skilled to make it all possible.

Whoever InStyle determined was best equipped would get the contracts for the advertising campaigns. The Effy Halloran fashion range had the potential to become a massive seller. Her designs were what young women wanted. Not only that, her gorgeous looks made her face a major selling asset too. Thrown into the mix was the modelling talent Mack had assembled around her. Angie, Grace, Ellen, and Alice were stunning young fresh faces in a burgeoning youth market.

This was a lucrative package for InStyle. It was a crass shame they hadn't appreciated Mack's talents too.

Adding a known name like Hester Clayton to his roster had excited the fashion editors in London. And not only in London, but now he was hearing in Paris too. For whatever reason, Hester had not been on Piper's list. Nate suspected there were good reasons that only Hester was aware of but unwilling to share. That's why Nate had planned for him to work while in the Big Apple, with Hester. What Nate told him next had Mack rubbing his chin.

In London, he had already garnered fans in a number of the top fashion and teen magazines. Nate repeated himself. Mack was pure 24 karat gold, with a startling intuitive understanding of fashion modelling. What it had taken the top names to accomplish in years, he was doing in a few short months. Yes, he was as technically proficient as the best in the game. His creativity now rivalled the best too. According to Nate, the big, *however,* was that he had no track record. To the Americans, he came unproven.

Mack found he was laughing at what Nate said next.

"Mack, you are being described as a prodigy. An *enfant terrible*. I didn't know what the French meant until an editor at *Nova* explained. MacKinnon, she said, is young, unconventional, controversial, and possessed of an incredible gift. He is Effy Halloran's other half. The editor nailed it. You two are like the teenage equivalents of Bailey and Shrimpton. Effy's talent as a designer is an added huge plus in her favour. You are the new *enfants terribles,* but it comes with a caution. While you can get away with your threesome shenanigans in England, you can't in the States.

Three minors sharing sexual relations could prove offensive to large sections of conservative America. Your little threesome may even break more than a few states' laws over here. The age of consent in many states is eighteen, not sixteen, as in England.

It may be the Swinging Sixties back home where anything goes. It's different here. Teenage *La dolce vita* doesn't go down well with everyone.

Bible Belt America holds sway over sizable chunks of the population. You haven't forgotten about Lennon's big mistake, have you? When he mouthed off about Jesus and The Beatles being bigger? American businesses are wary of offending Middle America. Middle America is nothing like cosmopolitan New York. Nor is it anything like the hippy wonderland we're seeing here and on the West Coast. It's conservative, and in some places, it's hard-line conservative.

Piper suspected there was far more going on between the three of you. Give her credit; she was right. That's why, my young friend, she wanted and wants *you* out of the way. Given the Benidorm bedroom fiasco coverage in France and back home, are you surprised?"

"So I was out, sacrificed and sidelined to avoid scandal?"

"Bang on. As for my father, well, he needed to tread with care. The firm has a potential scandal brewing. Joe will face the beak at the Old Bailey before long. My father doesn't want to give AIC-InStyle any excuse to pull the plug on Effy and on us. She is our gateway to becoming a truly global brand. He'd do anything to please Piper and the Yanks. That was why he sacrificed you to get the deal. Your dad understood where my dad was coming from when they decided. Think it through and try not to get too angry with your old man. Your father was keen to protect Effy's business interest separate and distinct from yours. What you need to realize, he was also trying to protect your long-term interests too. Effy's interests are the priority at the moment. Yours are secondary. What she does and what you do affect all of us: me, my dad, my family, Angie, Grace, Ellen, and Alice. Like

185

it or not, we are all tied into this together. What none of us want is for you two to get torn apart by it. Piper failed to understand that we *need* you. She's come close to wrecking everything because she made it personal between you and her."

"Spain was no big deal. Even if the press could prove anything about the three of us," Mack tried to explain, pausing to accept a refill of coffee from the waitress, "who'd be that interested in three English teenagers in a Spanish hotel? And anyway, my dad let me down. He could have made a better effort on his own son's behalf."

Nate shook his head. "You ought to know better than that. The press only needs half a story, and the rest becomes damage limitation. Neither he nor Greg Williams wanted to do the dirty on you. Piper convinced them otherwise. She said if you were involved, there would be no deal. The thing with Greg was, he and Piper did a deal of some kind on the side. Whatever it was, he's the real Judas, not your old man."

"So, Nate, will the deal still go through as things stand?"

"Depends on what Eugene Henderson does next." Nate let out a long sigh. "Involving Henderson was like using a steam-hammer to push a drawing pin into a display board. There was no need for it to end up this messy. You and Hester put the kibosh on things somewhat, but not in the way I expected. Perhaps, in a better way, we'll see. I should have given you and her more credit. Look, Effy's on a morning TV talk show tomorrow doing a promo interview. She'll need you there in the wings to give her your support. Effy's broken up over what's happened between you and her. You two need to kiss and make up, for both your sakes and for everyone else's. It's too, too easy to blame the kid for what she did. Lay the blame with the right people. You now know who they are."

"Nate, you make one weird Cupid. So, where is she now?"

"Doing a shoot all today over in Lower Manhattan."

"So, will they let me see her?"

"I've had words with Piper. She says you can see Effy this evening. They'll allow you fifteen to twenty minutes before Effy leaves for this big society do tonight."

"Fuck that! Putting me in a time slot to see, Effy! That sidewinder can stuff it. I know what'll happen. I'll turn up, and Effy will suddenly be unavailable. They must think I'm some sort of simpleton. Anyway, I already know where the party is anyhow. I don't need an invite, I've got one. My

186

spies have been keeping me informed. Let's just say that Hester has struck again. I'll play along just to keep the pretence going."

Nate looked staggered

CHAPTER 35

I'm A Man of Action – Jimmy Hughes
(From the LP 'Why Not Tonight' – Atlantic 587068 – 1962)
Saturday 15 July 1967. Late Evening, New York.

Mack and Hester arrived at the party. Except it wasn't quite gate crashing, more a statement of their last-minute invite. They were the unexpected expected.

A celebrated socialite, Amy Lee Fitzgerald, was hosting the party. The gathering was in her townhouse on East 56th Street. They'd taken a twenty-minute taxi drive from Greenwich Village to reach it. The soiree was taking place in their hostess's red brick six-storey period house. Mack discovered the spot was round the corner from the St. Regis Hotel as they drove there.

He wore his grey three-button mohair suit with a white silk hanky in the breast pocket. Mack had chosen a lightweight white cotton roll neck in preference to a shirt. A Manhattan party was not a Manchester Mod club. He hoped his attire would pass with cool stylishness among New York's elite. Hester drank in his appearance with her sparkling hazel eyes. Smiling her approval, she'd passed judgement with a single word. "Sleek."

He raised an eyebrow as she added, "You will make me look super cool. I'll be the envy of every woman there."

Hester was every inch the consummate blonde fashion model. Dressed in a stunning black and gold Lurex sheath mini dress, she appeared to shimmer as she moved. Her legs in patterned gold sparkling tights added to the glittering effect. Black open-toed kitten heel slingbacks and a finger ring purse completed the look. Hester was an arresting vision so sexy he wondered how he had managed to resist her charms. They were coming to this soiree on a war footing, dressed to kill.

Hester was his accomplice, a partner in war, and a guide for the evening. As his newfound confidante, she knew more than a few of the important faces in the New York fashion world here tonight. She was his beautiful, distracting camouflage for what was planned.

Two burly security guards were on the door. Hester smiled and gave them her name. A young woman acting as the meet and greet directed them

188

upstairs. Everywhere his eyes wandered confirmed that the owner had spared no expense. Hester told him their hostess had one of the finest collections of antique Colonial furniture. Mrs Fitzgerald, the hostess, was by the main salon door. As they walked in, arms linked, Hester received a greeting reserved for long lost nieces. Later he would learn Hester and Mrs Fitzgerald shared a close connection. Pleasantries exchanged for several minutes they went through into the huge salon. Mrs Fitzgerald was keen to catch up with Hester telling her she would seek them out in a few minutes.

Groovin by *The Young Rascals* was playing in the background as they entered. The salon, filled with the sight and hum of guests holding polite conversations, was impressive. He tried to take in everyone present, but the crowded room made it difficult.

He caught sight of Angie, surrounded by a group of three men. Unaware he'd arrived, she looked distracted and anxious. Her hands toyed with a half-empty champagne glass. The men appeared interested in only one thing as they competed for her attention. Angie looked as if she wished she were anywhere else than at this party. Mack almost succumbed to launching a rescue mission, but he knew he couldn't. It wasn't part of the plan. Angie's job would be to sneak Grace, Ellen, and Alice out of the building when the time came. When that time came was another matter. The plan had to wait for Eugene Henderson's arrival. Angie would then persuade Effy to go to the powder room. Instead, they would make their getaway downstairs. Meanwhile, Mack and Hester would distract Piper and everyone else. Then Henderson would intervene to make Piper's day complete.

Alice and Ellen were standing near to Angie. He overheard them talking and giggling with one of the elegant blue-rinse ladies present. They hadn't noticed his arrival, and neither had Grace. She appeared to be in personal heaven, talking to a young man with shoulder-length blond hair. Mack couldn't be sure who he was but thought he'd seen his face in a copy of Billboard he'd purchased on arrival.

Looking around, he couldn't see Effy anywhere. His heart beat faster as he searched for his girl in distress. Everything Alice had told Hester over the phone sounded unbelievable. Piper and her suits were treating Effy like a prisoner. The other girls felt the same.

Mack's quarter of an hour visit to see Effy hadn't happened. Nor had he expected it to happen. It hadn't surprised him. Piper's people had no intention of allowing it. That fifteen-minute window of time allocated for Effy to see him had vanished. Vanished, without warning, or explanation.

They'd made sure that due to an *unexpected schedule change,* she was *unavailable* when he called at the hotel. By stopping Mack seeing her, Piper had once again revealed her hand and intentions.

Before leaving Greenwich Village, Mack spent several minutes giving a thought to a quote. Sun Tzu said, *attack the enemy when they are unprepared, appear when you are not expected.* Well, he'd arrived, unexpected and prepared. He intended his appearance to threaten and disrupt their cosy evening. They were about to get taught a lesson. No one was going to parade a captive Effy like a product for sale. He was going to irritate, mystify and mislead them. To win in warfare, deception was everything. And he was waging war, not playing a game. Everything planned and arranged late this afternoon now came into play. They only needed Henderson to appear as promised. In the meantime, they were here to keep Piper and company watching him and Hester. Battle plans seldom went as expected, and did this one was no different. The deviation would prove so much sweeter.

Mrs Fitzgerald came looking for Hester. A wealthy divorcee, she had extensive fashion world connections. The jewellery she wore came from the exclusive jewellers like Tiffany's. Hester confided in a whisper that their hostess's necklace could buy a small apartment in Manhattan.

Mack knew he had a way with young women. There had been a growing realization that he also had a way with older women too. Mrs Fitzgerald found him charming and kept looking him over. On learning who he was and why he was in New York, she became excited. She insisted on him meeting one of the editorial staff from *Seventeen.* One introduction followed another. They found themselves introduced to more leading luminaries of the Big Apple's fashion world. A few Hester already knew.

There was a subtle adroitness to Hester. She possessed levels of self-confidence rivalling him; hers were attuned to social interaction. Three years older than Mack, she had mastered how to create a social spider web of connections. He couldn't help admiring her.

As they moved from one person to another, she held onto his arm as Effy and Angie did, and this worried him. The way she looked at him left him uneasy too. They spotted Effy in a far corner by an end window, but not before Pearl Piper had seen them first. Her face was a complex expression of puzzled shock and annoyance. Mack acknowledged Piper with a nod of the head, smirking as he did so. She responded with an ugly scowl. He hoped with sincerity that his words in the hotel lobby had left her with a searing

190

mental scar. If not, he was ready to let her hear more, not yet having scraped the bottom of his barrel of vindictiveness.

An entourage comprising Piper, Alex Silver, Pyle, and the other man from the meeting surrounded Effy. Some other guy, in his late twenties or early thirties, was talking to her. Effy was listening to him, her face taut and sullen. They had her surrounded. With her back to a window, they wanted to control her movements to prevent her from circulating. She was on show and guarded like a prisoner. His father, Greg, and Bridget stood nearby. He detected real irritation on his father's face. Something didn't seem right. Bridget, always so calm, looked furious. She kept nudging Greg with short sharp poking motions of her elbow. Whatever she was saying to him did not appear well received. Greg looked equally furious with her. Alex Silvers was somewhere, but he hadn't spotted him.

Mack knew Nate would not be present this evening. Knowing Nate, he was probably up to no good planning his next devious move. Then Effy caught sight of Mack as she glanced in his direction, and everything changed.

She could not stop herself. A wink from Mack reminded her of that day over three years ago. She winked back. Like an omen, the faint sound of The Turtles *She'd Rather Be With Me* was playing in the background. Piper, her face contorted in an ugly mask, watched him while spitting out words to Pyle. It got interesting. The timely arrival of Eugene Henderson couldn't have been better.

Hester whispered in his ear. "I wish for many things in life. Right at this moment, I wish I could be her. That girl loves you so much. Effy is lucky to have you." She squeezed his arm as she finished speaking. Hester was reluctant to relinquish her hold but knew she soon must. There was a momentary heartfelt glimpse of sorrow as he saw her become misty-eyed. Neither he nor Hester had time to dwell on it. The plan, as conceived, underwent an interesting and drastic change of direction.

Effy broke free, taking her guards by surprise. Weaving through the crowded room between groups of chattering people, she made for Mack. Pyle followed her snatching at Effy's arm but missing. Mack understood exactly what he needed to do. Sweeping Hester behind him in a gentle motion, he reached out to Effy grasping her wrist. In a balletic move, he pulled her behind him to join Hester. In a deliberate action, he allowed the champagne glass in his left hand to fall. Mack dropped to one knee. There was no chance of catching the glass, nor was that his plan. He did it to mask his true intention, to deliver a concealed uppercut punch straight to Pyle's groin. Rising, bent forward, he caught the man under his jaw with the back of his head as he straightened. It hurt, but those watching would see this as an unfortunate clash of heads. Pyle staggered back senseless, clutching his groin almost knocking Piper off her stilettos. Mack rubbed the back of his head. It was painful, but worth the retribution inflicted on Pyle.

Hester came round to his front, pretending to see if he was okay. As she did so, she stamped her heel on Pearl Piper's open-toe shoe. There was an agonising screech as Piper hopped on her one good foot. Hester may have gone to Cheltenham Ladies College, but sometimes behaving like a well brought up debutante didn't work. While turning, she had also 'accidentally' caught Piper in the midriff with her elbow. Offering profuse apologies, she kept a contrite though mocking expression. Effy meanwhile had grabbed his left arm gripping it with both hands. She held on tight to make sure nobody could pull her away from him.

"I'm staying with Mack, my boyfriend. I'm not going back with *her,* and *no one* will make me."

Eugene Henderson could not have chosen a more opportune moment to appear and intervene. He was only five foot five, grey-haired, and scrawny. At a guess, Mack put him in his late fifties or possibly sixty. Although Hester had refused to disclose her exact relationship with Henderson when they'd met, Mack thought he'd detected a resemblance. Now he was convinced of the likeness.

"That was an unfortunate accident, Pearl." Henderson's voice was soft, deep, and mocking.

Turning to Hester, he enquired, "Are you okay, honey?"

The strange endearing way he spoke to her set Mack's mental cogs whirring. It left him unable to dismiss the thought from his mind.

Turning to Mack, Henderson winked, asking if his head was okay. He didn't miss a trick.

Robert MacKinnon and Greg Williams had made their way over to the commotion. It had taken everyone by surprise. Mrs Fitzgerald had glanced over to see what the fuss was about. Seeing Henderson she beamed and blew a kiss to him turning back to her group of socialite friends.

Piper, confronted by Henderson, was shaken and confounded. Henderson was the last person she had expected or wanted to see this evening. What had passed between Henderson and Piper earlier today Mack had no idea. Whatever it was, it must have been quite something. As she gathered herself, her attention turned to Mack. She glared at him. He could see the pent up fury rising ready for unleashing. Henderson placed himself between them, knowing she would not dare to have a go at him. Donovan's *Sunshine Superman* had started playing in the background. Mack cheekily mimed the song lyrics at her over Henderson's shoulder. It was the bit mentioning Superman and Green Lantern not having anything on him. That infuriated Piper even more. She would have taken a swing at him but for Henderson's presence. For Mack, it was all about sticking the knife in rather than the gloating. He hoped it had gone in up to the hilt.

Reprimanding Piper, in the slickest most consummate manner Mack marvelled at Henderson's technique. It was not what he said, but it most definitely was the way he said it. How he sounded so urbane, so polished and polite, yet showed such immense displeasure, was the consummate art of communication at its finest.

"I'm staying with Mack." Effy blurted out in desperation for anyone and everyone around to hear. "No one will treat me like a prisoner again. They've kept me away from my boyfriend. I'm in love with him, and he's my photographer, and they've treated him with disgusting unfairness. I'm not going back to the St. Regis. Not with her, keep that horrible Piper woman away from me. They've kept me a virtual prisoner since I arrived in New York, stopping me from seeing him. And not only me, the other girls too."

Henderson exchanged glances with Hester and Mack before turning to Effy. "That's okay, Miss Halloran. You are quite safe now. Hester honey, you and the young women we discussed earlier, should stay at my place for now. Pearl, you went against my wishes when we met earlier today. You have chosen to ignore my instructions. This is no longer a request. Monday morning at eleven-thirty, you, Pyle, and I will talk about the way forward in the board room."

The words made Mack wonder if Piper would still have a job after Monday.

Henderson continued, "Mr MacKinnon will go with Miss Halloran to the TV station tomorrow, Sunday morning. So, too, will *all* the other young English models. I will be present to ensure that the interview takes place the way it should. After the TV interview, I will see Mr MacKinnon Senior and Mr Williams. We will then schedule a further meeting with Mr Silvers *and* his son *viz a viz* the contracts."

To Robert MacKinnon, he said. "I will renegotiate the terms with Mr Silvers and Miss Halloran. The ones Miss Piper drew up with Mr Pyle's connivance are not acceptable. I believe they need amending. I am also

193

unhappy at the way they treated your son and young Miss Halloran. This will need remedying too.

Turning to Piper, he gave what amounted to an order. "Pearl, you and Pyle, and whatever his name is over there, you need to leave. *Now*. Make your apologies to our hostess as you go. She is one of my oldest and dearest friends, so don't make a scene. In case I haven't made myself clear, from now on, you will have no further dealings with Silvers Fashions on behalf of InStyle. Nor will you speak to or contact Miss Halloran again. Nor any of the other young English models in her party. At the end of the evening, my chauffeur will take Miss Halloran, and the other young ladies to my penthouse. Hester, could you please ask their chaperone, Miss Bridget Halloran, if she would like to join them? I will ensure the hotel brings their things over from the St. Regis during the night. They will be my guests for the rest of their stay in our city."

"You can't do this..." Piper tried to protest. Henderson dismissed her with a wave of his hand. She continued her voice lowered. "You have no controlling interest on the board to do this, and you can't tell me what to do."

"You forget yourself, Pearl. Together with Jordan Baker, I can outvote the entire board. I can, and will replace Phil Connor as the CEO and you too if necessary. In the next day or so, I will have a full controlling interest in AIC-InStyle. I have agreed to buy Cathcart's stock in the company today. This means I won't even need to ask Jordan Baker for her backing. You know she would support me without hesitation. As for you, Pearl, I will be brutal. You have disappointed me. Everything I heard earlier from Miss Liddell and Miss Thornton, confirmed by Miss Halloran's sisters, has appalled me. Your interference in Miss Halloran's private life has been shameful. You and Pyle could face a charge of wrongful restraint, even abduction.

If Miss Halloran chose to press the matter with the police, you could face serious charges. Her treatment, as a guest and potential client, has been lamentable and an utter disgrace. If it became public, IAC would look like abductees or even kidnappers and exploiters of young women. Our reputation might never recover. Until now, I never questioned your skills as a buyer and junior VP of the corporation. Your undisguised favouritism for a certain photographer is all too well known. His part in this affair and yours will not be without consequence."

The Texan was about to reply to Henderson but bit her bottom lip. The livid look she gave Mack spoke murderous intent.

194

Turning to go, she heard Mack call to her. "Miss Piper! It's not whether you win or lose, it's how you play the game... it's got to be the right game. Chess not Texan hold'em poker. King takes Queen. Checkmate."

CHAPTER 36

For What It's Worth – Buffalo Springfield (Atlantic 584077 - 1966)
Sunday 16 July 1967 – Morning, New York.

Effy Halloran interview with Randy Pryor on Channel 7 broadcast July 1967. Transcript. Typed on the day from the audio recording made in the studio on a Philips EL3541 cassette recorder.

RP. This morning we have a talented young lady joining us in the studio, seventeen-year-old Miss Effy Halloran. She is one of the youngest and brightest fashion designers and models to come out of Swinging England this year. How are you enjoying your stay in the Big Apple?

EH. It's been most interesting and not at all how I expected my stay to be.

RP. Yes, New York, New York it's a hell of a town. I guess you'll find it is very different from London. What do you think of our amazing skyline?

EH. Impressive. I've never seen so many skyscrapers before.

RP. I understand you are here as a designer and also as a model. Which do you enjoy most, the designing or modelling?

EH. I think of myself as a designer. The modelling happened more by accident. I enjoy both.

RP. They tell me you are still at school back home? Do you plan to continue with your education? I'm told you could be eligible to go to one of England's top universities like Oxford or Cambridge.

(2 second pause).

EH. I'm undecided but giving it a great deal of consideration.

RP. The temptation to leave school must be considerable? Are you tempted, now that you are enjoying such incredible success?

EH. It is tempting. I've dreamed of being a fashion designer since I was ten years old.

RP. Could I ask you to stand up for our audience at home? So they can see what you're wearing? I understand it's one of your designs.

EH. It is.

RP. Don't you think your dress pushes the boundaries of acceptable shortness? It's what, five maybe six inches above the knees?

EH. On this dress, it's nearer seven.

RP. Surely such short dresses and skirts, like yours, take something away from feminine mystique? Aren't they too revealing?

EH. Mystique? Like the name of the newly launched fashion magazine? (Giggles) To answer your question, no, I don't believe it takes anything away from a woman's mystique. Women have more freedom of movement in a short skirt or dress. The way we dress should be practical, comfortable while hinting at sexiness.

RP. Such short hemlines can't suit every young woman? Not all women can boast a figure like yours or even legs like yours? Is fashion like this only for young women with good figures?

EH. Fashion is always a matter of taste and practicality. When it comes to defining your personal style as a woman, you have to choose the clothes that suit you best. That will depend on your age and circumstances. If a woman of forty has the right figure, there is no reason why she should not wear one of my designs.

RP. The mini is decried by the older generation. They say it to encourage the worst kind of male attention. What are your thoughts on that?

EH. Some men need to rethink their attitude towards women. Women do not exist simply to satisfy men's lust. We are not living, walking, talking dolls - toys for the pleasure of boys. Every woman is a person not a mindless sex object without thoughts or feelings.

RP. Those are strong words. Do you regard yourself as a women's libber?

EH. I suppose I do if it means I expect men to treat me with respect and as an equal.

RP. What do you think makes your designs so appealing to young women?

EH. Practicality, comfort and allure, that's what I have foremost in mind when designing. I try to create dresses and skirts with the fewest seams possible to ensure the most comfort and ease of fit. For me, the choice of fabric is of vital importance, too. Above all, clothes must be practical. A girl should be able to run down the subway stairs to catch the train or to reach the bus stop in time. Women couldn't do this wearing the restricting clothes and girdles of our mother's generation. Nor wear shoes with those ridiculous heels. We need to feel at ease in clothes that make us feel good. Finally, and most importantly, I don't want any young woman looking like a junior version of their mother or grandmother. I want them to look and feel as if they belong to the new generation.

RP. Okay. We're now going to take a look at some designs from your collection. So our audience at home can see for themselves what we are talking about.

(Visuals)

RP. Well, they look amazing. And of course, so do the clothes. I can imagine a lot of our young women viewers buying these dresses. Thank you, ladies for such a glamorous display.

EH. Thank you for allowing us on your show.

RP. There is something I have to ask. (Pause). It seems that you have been the target of scandalous press gossip in Britain and Europe, especially in the French press. Were you involved in a highly compromising situation with your photographer and your best friend? Would you like to say anything about that?

EH. There's nothing to say. The press has blown it out of all proportions.

RP. So is it true the French pop singer discovered you in bed with your photographer and your friend?

EH. (Laughing). Not quite. We were in a Spanish hotel taking a siesta after doing a shoot. The heat of the day was humid and oppressive. Quite a lot like it is here in New York. My friend and I came into his room to talk. Yes, we were on his bed with him but not in it. And we most certainly did not do anything inappropriate.

RP. So is it true that he is your boyfriend?

EH. Yes. We've been together for two-and-a-half years.

RP. And is it true that the other girl, your friend, is also his girlfriend?

EH. (Two-second pause). Yes.

RP. And is she aware that you know she is?

EH. Of course, I know. (Giggling). She's my best friend, like one of my sisters.

RP. And does he know you both know?

EH. (Giggling) Of course, he does. We three are close friends.

RP. Friends?

EH. Yes, we are very, very close and very, very good friends.

RP. Intimate friends? A threesome?

EH. Well, Mr Randy Pryor! I see you are well named Pryor: Pryor by name, prier by occupation.

(Laughter)

For what it's worth, we are close. We work together, day in and day out. So we are, yes, relaxed with one another, as friends are. So much so it becomes too easy to get the wrong idea. It's flattering but sad that there is so much speculation about how close we are. Why does anyone care? For what it's worth isn't the war in Vietnam more important? Or what about the race rioting that's happening? In Newark, and now Detroit? Aren't these far more important news than what supposedly happened in a Spanish hotel to three young people? I can tell you right now. Nothing of a sexual nature happened that day. And that is the truth, for what it's worth.

RP. Thank you for clearing that up. It's been fab meeting and talking to you this morning. We're coming to the commercial break. I'd like to thank you for sparing the time from your busy schedule to be on the show today. May I wish you every success during your stay in our wonderful city. After the commercial break...

(Transcript ends).

CHAPTER 37

The Day You Take One (You Have To Take The Other)
The Marvelettes
(Tamla Motown TMG 609 – 1967)
Monday 17 July 1967 – Morning, New York

Seated on the spacious rooftop terrace, they relaxed in the early morning sunshine. Gazing at the view across Central Park to the Upper West Side, they enjoyed being together. High above the hubbub of the street life below, they were escaping the world if only for a brief while.

Angie turned to Mack and Effy breaking the silence. "I saw Hester giving Henderson a hug and a kiss. He returned the kiss. I didn't know he was her sugar daddy."

"On the cheek?" Mack took a sip of ice-cold orange juice. "Or the forehead?"

"Hester kissed him on the cheek. He kissed her on the forehead. Why?"

"Haven't you figured out why?" Reaching over, he took her hand in his giving it an affectionate squeeze.

"Go on," Effy nuzzled his ear her warm breath, sending an erotic shiver through him as she sat on his lap. "Tell us what you know that we don't."

"He's her father." Both girls looked at him open-mouthed. "Haven't you noticed the family likeness?"

"Hester told us about her family in Surrey. Don't you remember that day in the studio? During her first session with us at Lansdowne Walk?" Effy pressed her cheek against his.

"I suspect that her father in Surrey is her stepfather and Henderson, is her real dad."

"How?" Angie asked.

"I'm not sure. Maybe her mother married him, and they divorced. Or maybe she had an extra-marital fling and got pregnant. Anyway, he's her biological dad I'm certain. I'll bet you your last dollar."

"Hah! No chance." Angie returned a reassuring squeeze of his hand. "You forget. Effy and Tom have told me all about your nickname,

Superintendent Lockhart. I don't know about you being a photographer. Scotland Yard detective might be a better career choice."

"Do you still love both of us?" Effy's question took him aback."

"You know I do, I couldn't stand the thought of ever losing either of you. I will love you and Angie forever; you two are my everything. You two are the best thing that ever happened to me."

"If I didn't see and hear it for myself, I would not believe it." Hester's voice took them by surprise. "You three really *are* together. So it is true."

Angie turned to her. "You must have suspected?"

"I wasn't sure until I just saw and heard it for myself. I still thought it might be some kind of gimmick or elaborate game you three were playing to get publicity. Now I see it's not. It's genuine. You are all involved with each other."

"Whoa there, girl! Effy and I are not involved with each other. We're not lezzies, Hester."

"Definitely not, Hester," Effy gave a light shudder. "We're not like that. We both love him, and he loves us. So we have an arrangement. We're happy together."

Hester seated herself on the opposite side of the table. "And you make it work?"

"We don't *make it* work. It's the way we are." Effy added.

"How do you not get jealous of one another? I mean you must get jealous?" Hester looked baffled. "I couldn't stand the thought of another woman with a man I loved."

Angie raised her sunglasses onto her hair and looked at Hester. "That's because we're not you nor like you. I love these two with everything that's a part of me. I know they love me the same way. There's nothing I wouldn't do for either of them."

"And there's nothing I wouldn't do for Angie and Mack. We're not just friends and lovers, *we're family.*" Effy slipped off Mack's lap. She came over and put her hand on Angie's shoulder. "You haven't walked in our shoes, so you can never understand why we are as we are. The ties that bind us are unique to us."

"So, do you all sleep together?"

"Why does everyone assume we have sex together? Mack chuckled. "I respect Angie and Effy, too much. So no, we definitely *do not* have sex together. Yes, we have slept in the same bed once or twice because there was only one bed. There was definitely no sex involved. You need to understand Hester. I love these girls for who they are, not because we're into kinky sex. For us three, it's the real thing."

"You must think the three of us are weird." Angie giggled. "We're not. It's our beautiful compromise. We agreed to it. Most people couldn't deal with an arrangement like ours. Then again, we're not like most people. "

"We share him, and he shares us," Effy explained. "So it's unusual, so what? I'm as close to Angie as if she was one of my sisters."

Angie added a moment later, "And Effy is *like* my other sister. She *is* my best friend too."

Exchanging glances, the two girls spoke at the same time. "We're blood sisters."

"Blood sisters?"

"Like in the Western movies. When the Indians cut each other and mixed blood to become blood brothers... we've done the same. We swore to always stay that way. Nothing will come between us in our friendship. *Not even Mack.*" Angie explained.

"So you see, Hester, we're in deep with one another. I wouldn't want it any other way. I love them and I can't imagine my life without Effy or Angie."

"The three of us are in this come what may." Effy's winsome smile left Hester reflecting on her own love life. There wasn't one.

Hester's life was one of too many brief ephemeral affairs. She had never experienced true romantic love. No man had loved her in the way Mack loved his two girls. She envied them. They seemed to have that elusive love she craved and could never seem to find. In that fleeting moment, she knew she was lost in a forlorn love for him. Superficial romances were all she had ever experienced and known. Always brief, empty, emotionless, and unfulfilling, each new relationship like the last. Was she fated to keep ending up as notches on men's bedposts? Was that all she was worth? Doomed to be yet another man's sexual conquest? Hester was desperate to find love and to have a love like Effy and Angie. For a love like theirs, she would share if she had to. Glancing at her wristwatch reminded her of the errand.

"My father would like to see you and Effy in the library. And you're right, Mack. I don't know how you found out, but yes, Eugene Henderson is my real father. I didn't and don't want anyone to know, especially back in England. Can I please ask you to keep it to yourselves?"

Effy and Angie exchanged knowing looks then nodded confirming they would.

The library was on the middle floor of the penthouse below the roof terrace. Books filled two sides of the room from top to bottom, these looked like legal tomes and company reports. The only free wall was tiled in pale Italian marble panels. On it hung an enormous portrait. Hester's parentage revealed itself in an instant, leaving no doubts. The library served as Henderson's office. His desk faced the portrait of the woman who had to be Hester's mother. The resemblance was uncanny.

The view from the library was the same as from the roof terrace with the same unbroken vista. Mack compared the library's dimensions to his own home in Bradford. At a guess, he estimated the lounge and the kitchen would fit in the same space as this room occupied. Henderson, seated at his desk in the corner, finished dictating to his personal secretary.

"Would you like me to stay?" Hester asked.

Pointing to the sofas in the centre, he indicated she should.

Joining them, he enquired if they'd slept well. Alice and Effy's sisters were sharing a guest apartment several floors below. They would join them later, so Henderson could talk to them all in the afternoon. Right now, he wanted to talk to Hester, Effy, and Mack about a special assignment. Could Mack do a special shoot in the penthouse? Mack replied that it would depend on the assignment's brief. Doing an interior shoot required studio lighting. On the terrace, depending on the light and time of day, it was workable.

The assignments were for Bvlgari and Tiffany. Effy would model for Bvlgari while Hester would do the Tiffany shoot. The jewellery photos would appear in select coast-to-coast magazines. The companies would also place them in a few foreign fashion magazines. Henderson didn't specify which. Mack asked what the brief was from each of the companies.

Snapping his fingers, Henderson summoned his secretary. "Veronica, please bring me the assignment details from Bvlgari. Mr MacKinnon needs to read their brief to see what they require."

Veronica, tall, bony, with mousy hair in a tight French plait, crossed the room. Dressed in a severe grey two-piece suit, she looked an elegant woman who had to be in her late fifties. She passed him a blue file. Mack watched as he sifted through the contents. Henderson pulled out two typed pages stapled at the corner. Glancing through them first, he then passed the details to him without a word.

Mack was still trying to reconcile himself with what was happening. Bvlgari and Tiffany were familiar names, but he knew nothing about them. All he could bring to mind was Angie saying she wanted to visit Tiffany's. She'd loved Audrey Hepburn in *Breakfast at Tiffany's* and wanted to see the place. He promised he'd go with her there later today. As for Bvlgari, he had a vague recollection of seeing ads for watches in the colour supplements. Aside from that, he had shown no interest in either brand. Reading the Bvlgari brief, his mind began working out how to do a shoot with Effy and Hester in the penthouse.

Henderson passed him the coloured photos of the jewellery for the shoot. "Tiffany's will let us have details of their items this afternoon. The shoot has to take place here, for security reasons."

Mack finished reading the brief. Turning to Effy and Hester he said, "Whatever you two do, don't get any spots, cuts, or bruises on your faces between now and when we shoot."

The jewellery, in the Bvlgari brief, included bracelets, bangles, an arm clasp, necklaces, earrings, rings, and watches. Then without taking a breath, he returned to Henderson. "I'll need lighting. I'll make a list of what I'll need. The girls will need a hair and makeup stylist. I hope the budgets are good."

"They're among the best. The girls will receive $400 each for a day's shoot as they are still relative unknowns here in the States."

Mack did a quick mental calculation. It amounted to about one hundred and seventy pounds. He'd read somewhere a police constable on the beat earned eighteen pounds a week. This was almost the same as ten weeks' wages for a day's work. Angie's job at the solicitor's had paid seven pounds ten shillings a week. No wonder she had opted to quit and model full time after Spain. Even at English modelling rates, she was earning more than that for a day's work. In the week before flying out, she had earned forty guineas. Six times more than what she would have earned as a receptionist. In America, the pay was stratospheric in comparison. Mack refocussed on what Henderson was saying.

"The same applies to you as a photographer. You are fast earning a reputation back in Britain. Over here, we still have to see what you're capable of doing. Last week, speaking with Miss Clayton, I took the liberty through my contacts to arrange these shoots and pulled in some favours for them to happen so quickly. I'm putting a great deal of trust in your capabilities based on what Miss Clayton had told me. Also based on what

205

I've seen of your work so far, so don't disappoint. If they take your photographs, this is what you will get paid." Henderson scribbled a figure on a piece of paper and passed it to him. "A good fee you'll agree for someone of your age and experience. I had to negotiate hard to get this for you. It's not my usual practice to involve myself at this level. Since Mr Pyle and Miss Piper let AIC-InStyle down, I've taken steps to handle this deal myself.

I regret that we cannot cancel a contract with a certain photographer. The girls will have to accept this. It would be a considerable injustice not to allow you the opportunity to work over here."

AIC-InStyle will ensure you have plenty of opportunities here in the States in the future. That should please your young lady friend Miss Halloran too. She is likely to be in demand here as a designer and model. Now I have other pressing business to attend to this morning, I still need to deal with Miss Piper and Mr Pyle. Veronica, my secretary, and PA will arrange anything and everything that you may need. The jewellery shoot for Tiffany's will be tomorrow. It's short notice, but Hester is available.

Miss Halloran, I've cancelled the photo shoot for the day after tomorrow. Your sister, Miss Ellen Halloran, will replace you. The Bvlgari shoot is far more important and must take precedence. You will still have to take the assignment scheduled for tomorrow with Miss Thornton and Miss Liddell. The photographer feels you three will be the right combination for what he has in mind."

Effy looked relieved. The cancelled shoot was the one with Devane, Piper's ex. Henderson stood up, smiled at Hester, and left the library, followed by his PA. Ellen would need a chaperone. Her sister's experience with Seth Devane was as bad as her own. Bridget would have to be present and maybe even Mack's father."

"Well, that's was unexpected and amazing." Turning to Hester he said, "It looks like we have so much to thank you for Hester. You're responsible for putting your old man up to this." It was a statement, not a question.

"Believe it or not, Mack, I'm a lot more like you than you think." Hester rebuffed him. "I've always prided myself on trying to achieve success on my own without his help. That was until I came here to help you and Nate."

"Effy's brows furrowed. "To help Nate?"

"Yes, him, you, Mack, Angie and the others, except I didn't stick to Nate's plan. When Nate told me what was happening, I decided I'd spill the beans to my father. I knew he was a big wheel on the board at AIC-InStyle and one of its biggest shareholders. Now I guess he owns it on account of what happened to you. Anyway, what are friends for if not to help?"

Effy, seated next to Hester, gave her a spontaneous hug.

CHAPTER 38

Lee Morgan – The Sidewinder (Blue Note 45-1911- 1964 US)
Monday 17th July 1967 – Evening, New York

Bridget was tearful as she spoke with Mack. The falling out with his father had not been the only one. At Henderson's request, she'd left the St. Regis to move in with Ellen and Grace. Bridget had broken up with Greg over his conduct during and after the deal-making. She blamed him for the underhand methods used to seal it but refused to blame his father.

"Robert," she told Mack, "was doing his best to protect Effy's interests. "You need to understand and not get angry or hold it against your father. Piper, Pyle, Alex Silvers, and Greg lied and pressured him for the sake of completing the deal."

Mack listened, unconvinced at first. Bridget provided him with a more detailed picture of what had taken place. His father wanted to ensure Effy's deal would not fall through. Piper and Alex Silvers had convinced him that any scandal surrounding Effy would prevent InStyle signing. His father knew nothing of what had passed between his son and Piper in Manchester. He was unaware of Piper's personal vendetta against Mack.

If Robert MacKinnon had known this whole affair might have been handled so differently. By then, it was too late. Piper had already isolated and sidelined him. Lodging him in a distant apartment, she had planned to keep him away from the girls. There were tissue-thin excuses in the beginning. Busy schedules for the girls, without Mack present, ensured she got her way and her revenge. Remaining vague about his whereabouts should have alerted suspicions. The awful incident when he'd turned up at the hotel had upset everyone. That's when matters began to come to light.

It was only by coincidence that she had learned from Angie what had happened in Manchester. Spite had motivated Piper for what Mack had said to her. Cutting Mack out of the deal wasn't down to his inexperience as a photographer. It was Piper getting personal; it was intentional, and it was poisonous. The realisation of what the woman was up to and had planned all along with Alex Silvers unfolded. The truth of the situation emerged thanks in part to Angie.

Angie had read an item in a fashion magazine on the flight to New York. The item in question had proved interesting but not important at the time. It mentioned Seth Devane, a leading New York fashion photographer. His notorious reputation for womanising was public knowledge.

Pearl Piper's role in the affair with Devane led to a much-publicised divorce. A divorce that had ended in demands for huge alimony payments from Devane's ex-wife.

Angie's suspicions became aroused when she found out that Mack was not at the St. Regis. Piper and her associates appeared deliberately vague as to his whereabouts, which was not only strange, but stupid raising instant suspicion. When Angie and the girls learned that Devane would photo shoot Effy's design range, the awful truth dawned. That was when the last jigsaw pieces finally fell into place, completing a picture angering Angie and the girls.

Accusations of betraying Mack had followed with Angie and Alice forcing the truth from a desperate and miserable Effy. That had been distressing, seeing their friendship almost disappearing before everyone's eyes. Only when Effy confessed that she had been blackmailed into silence did the truth emerge.

Angie had then turned to her to confirm if this was true? That her friend had been silenced and deceived? She had approached Alex Silvers and Greg about the deception. The two men had *ordered* her not to rock the boat. Bridget's job was to be a chaperone and nothing more. This was none of her concern. They didn't want this deal jeopardised. Furious, Bridget had told them they could forget *ordering* her to do anything. Who did they think they were? That was when he'd pulled his disappearing act for two days. Mack stayed silent, not offering to explain to Bridget where he'd been or what he'd done.

Bridget had worked out for herself, that Hester must have been the one to contact Alice, at the hotel. How Hester knew where they were staying in New York remained a mystery. Why Hester was in New York, was an even bigger mystery. What Alice, Angie, and Hester discussed Angie refused to confide in her. Looking back, Hester Clayton's arrival, now appeared deliberate. Mack smiled, as he listened.

Angie and Effy had refused to work or do anything until he was found safe. Effy was so distraught, she had blamed all the adults involved in the deal for making her sign it. This had been said in front of Alex Silvers, Greg, Piper, and her cronies, as well as the girls. Piper had threatened Effy, and them, with dire financial penalties if they didn't to the photo shoots. She had even resorted with threats to sue them. Angered and reluctant, the girls agreed to fulfil their contractual commitments. They had all told Piper, they would never work for her or InStyle in the future, once the contracts were fulfilled.

Although she had not been present, she had learned later, that Grace and Alice had confronted Piper. That confrontation had resulted in Alice calling Piper, " *Devane's amoral tramp.*" Piper had tried to slap Alice across the face but she had been too quick. Alice had pinned her against the wall muttering some more ugly truths. There were no witnesses to see it, which was as well.

Piper had turned to Grace screaming, "You saw her! You saw her attack me! I want you to be a witness when I report her to the police! "

Grace had apparently laughed in her face telling her to, " 'Eff off you 'effing bitch, before I land you one myself."

After that Piper kept her distance and avoided all the girls except Effy who she persisted in targeting.

Angie and Ellen had also tackled Alex Silvers. They had given him a mouthful too, threatening never to work for Silver Fashions again. Nate had to take them to one side to calm them down. Once all the girls knew the full extent of what had taken place, the atmosphere became poisonous. Angie spat on the floor every time she passed Alex Silvers.

The person responsible for allowing this legal deception was her now ex-boyfriend, Greg Williams. Why he did, Bridget wasn't sure, but she suspected they'd made him a lucrative offer he couldn't turn down.

Bridget then recounted the serious difficulties the girls experienced dealing with this Seth Devane character. Since she often chaperoned Grace at other shoots, she couldn't be present with the others. All the girls had experienced various degrees of sexual harassment with that man.

During the two days he was missing, a meeting had taken place between Seth Devane and the girls. Ellen said he was trying his smooth chat up lines on Effy from the moment she stepped through the door. On the quiet Devane tried pawing her, but she'd stormed out of the studio. Effy refused to be left alone with him. Backed up by Alice and the others, Angie confronted Devane and told him to keep his sticky mitts to himself. Devane treated it as if it was some kind of joke. Models, he said, should expect to sleep with their photographer. He claimed this was perfectly normal and an accepted way of working. Alice's reply to him was unrepeatable but made her laugh as she recalled what Ellen had told her.

During a later photo shoot, despite the warning he'd received, Devane had tried it on with Effy again in the studio's changing room. That, Effy had told her, was even with one of his assistants present. Effy refused to be alone in his presence, insisting on Angie or a chaperone being present at all times. After that, the girls made a point of staying together in pairs when dealing with him. Angie was Effy's constant bodyguard refusing to leave her alone with him. Effy did the same for her. Ellen and Alice made it their job to watch over one another because she was always with Grace. When Devane tried it on with Ellen, Alice had picked up one of his ultra-expensive cameras and casually smashed it on the studio floor.

"Ooops. Dearie me." She had said. "Try it on with her again or me and it won't be a camera next time."

Piper had turned up at his studio during another session. She'd tried to separate Angie from Effy but with no success. The two refused to be apart, even going to the toilet together. Piper had even attempted to persuade Effy to go on a date with Devane. She was keen that he and Effy ought to get to know one another better. What she meant was, he and Effy should sleep together. Devane had thought it an excellent idea, according to Effy. He'd even suggested it to her, saying it would *ease the tension between them*. That was when she understood what game Piper was playing.

If Piper thought she'd swoon like some overawed teenager, she was mistaken. Devane repulsed Effy. She'd told him straight she had no intention of joining his list of conquests. Piper's reasons had become clear. She wanted Effy seduced to cause a total breakup with Mack. It was a sick and perverse form of power ploy revenge. Effy had confided the whole awful tale to her. All this, she now recounted to Mack.

He listened intently concealing all emotion.

At the party, Devane had continued to flirt. There was no mistaking his intentions towards Effy. Worse still, it happened in front of everyone she knew. He'd tried to imply that Effy had already had sex with him, which was a falsehood. Bridget had wanted to intervene to put an end to this farcical travesty. So too had his father who by then had finally realized that this was not right. Greg had pulled Bridget back, cautioning her against doing something silly. He'd tried telling her it was simple male banter and nothing more. Besides, he'd warned, they shouldn't cause a fuss as guests at the party. It hadn't sounded like banter to Bridget, and it wasn't. The end of their relationship happened there and then.

Matters between her and Greg had not been good for some time. There were other long-standing reasons for its ending, but she felt unable to share these with him. So, this proved to be the final push-button moment ending their relationship.

His father had been about to ignore Greg and intervene when Effy had broken free and rushed towards him. Although Bridget had not expected what happened, she delighted when it did. She still believed it had all been an accident when Mack had collided knocking Pyle senseless. Bridget had found Pyle to be disingenuous and as distasteful as Devane. A revolting man were her exact words.

Mack knew some of what Bridget had told him but not all of it. Angie and Effy had not mentioned the incidents with Devane. He could guess why. They knew exactly how he would react, fearing what might happen if he knew. They were right, and this was not over. Even as he listened to Bridget, his thought turned a blacker shade of dark, and a plan began to evolve.

Without thinking, she let Mack know where Devane's studio was located.

Bridget's next comment caused him to roll his eyes and groan. There was another problem now. This one involved Grace. At the party, she had met the lead singer of Zorro's Mask, a West Coast group recording in New York. Richie Miller was nineteen, and Grace was fifteen. Teen lust had sparked at first sight when they met at the party. On learning she had left the St. Regis, the singer knew where Grace was staying. Having contacted her, she'd sneak out to meet him without a word to anyone.

CHAPTER 39

I Put A Spell On You – Nina Simone (Phillips BF1415 – 1965)
Wednesday 19 July 1967 –New York

"Nothing happened. We didn't do anything. Well, I gave him a peck on the cheek when he brought me back. We went for a walk in Central Park and sat near the Balto Statue, that was all. Richie was lovely; we just talked. He told me all about the story behind the statue. Then he asked all about me. Then I asked all about him. He's from Los Angeles…"

"You shouldn't have gone off like that, Grace. What were you thinking? Disappearing without a word." Effy sighed. "It was bad enough after what Mack did to me and Angie. The thought that something might have happened to you made me feel sick again with worrying. You're only fifteen."

"And how old were you when you sauntered off that Saturday afternoon to meet Mack? When he was working at Benny's scooters? You were as young as me."

"Grace, I'd already met Mack at the library, and you were there with me when I did. We knew who he was and where he lived. I didn't saunter off in one of the world's largest cities, on another continent, with a stranger, without telling anyone."

The stylist put the last touches to Effy's make up for the shoot. She had been unable to stop smiling, listening to the two sisters. Finishing, she showed Effy the results in a large mirror.

"That's it. You're good to go." She looked pleased with her work as she let Effy see herself in the mirror.

They'd had to find a strapless dress, something suitable and upmarket. With help, they'd located one that had appeared in Vogue they could hire. It was an elegant long white dress with pearl and gold embroidery by Susan Small. Effy took her bra off and stepped into the dress, allowing Grace to fasten her in. They needed two clips at the back to make the front fit. After they photographed the jewellery and before returning the dress, he planned to take full-length shots. Dressed like this, Effy looked good enough for Vogue. Wearing someone else's design on this occasion was a necessity.

213

They needed something upmarket. Still, he only planned to shoot above the midriff focussing on the face and jewellery.

"I was reading about Richie Miller and Zorro's Mask in Billboard. It looks like they could become even bigger." Mack had finished setting up in one of the penthouse's bedrooms. The wall there was perfect as a backdrop for head and shoulder shots. "His voice is okay, I suppose. Can't say I'm that keen on their music. It's all that hippy psychedelic folk-rock like The Byrds."

"Just because it's not Soul music or Motown doesn't mean it's no good," Grace pouted as she and Effy made final adjustments to the dress. "It's different. Anyway, he wants me to go along to the studio where they're recording an album. He wants all his band members to meet me. He also said you could come along with your camera."

"Did he now?" Mack gave Grace a wry smile. "Did he also suggest Effy, Angie, Alice, and Ellen should come along too by any chance?"

"How did you know? Are you a mind reader? Yes, he did." The surprised look made Mack want to laugh.

"No. I'm not a mind-reader just a bloke, and I know what blokes in pop groups want."

"What's that?"

"Booze, drugs, and sex with beautiful young women. Come on, Grace, they're all horny, sex-mad, and just want to get laid by famous models. Don't you read the news? When they're not pissed out of their heads on booze or doped up, they want sex with some famous bird to bolster their egos and standing."

Grace blushed, turning away from him, with her hands clenched. "They're not all like that."

"Yeah, right. Have you forgotten about the Rolling Stones recent escapades filling the newspapers? You know? The mad drugged up party? And the Mars bar girl?" Smirking, he added, "Yeah, okay, I'll go. First sign of booze, drugs, Mars bars, or attempts at an orgy, and they won't be playing any venue for a while."

"Why?"

"Best not hear the answer to that, Grace." Effy grabbed him by the arm and pulled him away towards the door. "Come on, we have a lady with expensive jewels waiting for us to do the shoot. Remember what Angie said. We don't need anymore Osborne or Brixton Road incidents."

"Why? What incidents? What happened in Brixton?" Grace called out after them.

214

"Ask Angie." He laughed as Effy pushed him out of the room.

"Don't!" Effy warned, closing the door behind her.

The jewellery was in a metal security case. An undistinguished looking older lady had brought it to the penthouse. They had chained the case to her wrist. An armed bodyguard in a dark suit accompanied her. Mack estimated she had to be in her late fifties. It had been stipulated both would be present at all times the jewellery was out of the case and worn. Henderson's secretary would also be present to make sure nothing happened to it.

"You're not the photographer? Are you?" The lady from the jewellery company addressed Mack, astonished by his appearance. "But you're so…"

"Young? I hear that a lot." He frowned, muttering aloud. "Just don't call me kid or sonny."

How much the contents were worth was problematic. Glancing at the woman, she received a nod acknowledging it was okay to start wearing the items. They placed them on the dressing table in readiness. Effy picked out the emerald and diamond necklace first. Then came the matching dangling, chandelier earrings, the bracelet watch, and the ring that was a size or more too large for her fingers. Some cotton wool padding on the palm side would sort the problem, and it wouldn't show. There was also a snakelike clasp armband. Even if she could have afforded any of the items, she would never have considered buying them. None of the jewellery was to her taste. It was all too clunky and large. Effy loved dainty items. Mack's comment had made her smile. He'd described it as over the top opulence for super-rich people with more money than sense.

Studying her reflection in the mirror, she wondered who this was? She no longer knew this young woman staring back. Whoever this person was, it was no longer her. This stranger in the mirror had stolen her life and her identity.

Yesterday Mack had done the photo shoot with Hester in another room on the lower floor of the penthouse. That had gone beyond his best expectation. Henderson had even arranged for him to use a nearby photo developing facility. There seemed nothing the man with the money couldn't arrange. Today would be more challenging. He needed to avoid repetition to ensure that both ads presented the two models in different guises.

"I'm looking for that Mona Lisa touch, that indefinable smile moment."

"I'm flattered you think I can carry it off." Effy allowed a faint ambiguous smile to escape, the kind he wanted to capture. He took a final light meter reading before going behind the tripod-mounted camera.

"I have every confidence in you, Eff. Keep listening to what I'm saying. I need you to make only the slightest, tiniest inclination of the head and hand on hearing the clicks. Don't forget about the hand. I need to see the ring and the watch too. Keep your eyes focusing as if you're seeing the memories or in a daydream."

"As we've done before?"

"*Exactement ma belle*. As we've done before." Click.

Then he began to weave a hypnotic spell drugging her and the others in the room with the sound of his voice and words. Working with a mesmerising slowness, he held them captive. Spellbound, Effy drifted from memory to memory as if sleepwalking. She relived those precious personal moments as though for the first time. Each new click captured a desired facial reaction.

All the recollections were so intense, so personal, so emotive and so moving. Yet here they were sharing these memories with strangers as he awakened them in her. That first shy exchange outside the library when they'd looked into each other's eyes. His look of sheer delight when she'd kissed him on the cheek. Once more, his words returned her to their first summer together.

She was strolling once more through Shibden Park. A cooling summer breeze tempered the heat of the August sun on her face. The scent of Mack's Old Spice aftershave was with her once more. Its fragrance reminded her how she had nuzzled his ear as they'd sat under a tree that afternoon. That was almost a year ago. The texture of his cheek had felt so smooth as she stroked it.

The memories continued to float in out of her consciousness as he spoke. She was on the crowded dance floor in The Plebs, his hands on her hips. They were kissing as *My Guy* by Mary Wells was playing. More and more memories reawakened. The tender way they'd made love that morning came flooding back. The sensations of his hands exploring her nakedness seemed so real. She remembered how his masculine scent and the feel of his body enslaved her in the night. His touch had sent a paroxysm of pleasure flooding her body, leaving her weak. Time ceased to have meaning as she listened to his voice anew, adjusting her head and the hand on each button click.

His words were foreplay so she could make love to him and his camera. Mack was seeking to capture her passion, her desire for intimacy with him. Yes. *He was really saying something.* The Velvelettes song struck her with incredible poignancy. He was her world, and she was his. He was her night and her day and she was his sunlight. Some things were just meant to be. Then from nowhere, Simon Silvers drifted into her head. She tried to extinguish his intruding face from her thoughts. Why did he have to spoil it by making an uncalled for appearance?

Then it was over, the magical spellbinding ending without warning. Approached by the older woman, Effy heard her say, as she took off the jewellery, "You're both so lucky my dear. Whatever you do, don't lose what you both have. I've never seen a couple as enchanted with one another as you two are. It's been a genuine privilege to watch you two work together. I think he will have captured that Mona Lisa moment and perhaps more."

Closing and locking the jewel case, the woman exchanged a few quiet words with Veronica. Then she came to have a word with Mack.

"I apologise for thinking you were too young. In the past, I have been present at many photo shoots. I have watched some of the top professionals at work. Seeing you working today was a unique experience, unforgettable, and such a privilege. I look forward to seeing the results, and perhaps watching you two at work again."

Silent and smiling, he said nothing responding with a polite inclined nod of the head.

Turning as she went through the door a last glance sent her heart beating faster. The girl was now by his side, her head resting against his shoulder. Their arms were around one another, their faces revealing a story needing no words.

CHAPTER 40

Just For You – Jerry Butler (Sue WI 4009 – 1966)
Thursday 20 July 1967 – New York.

"The answer is still no."

"Why, Bridget? You'd be there. Give me a reason?" Grace protested.

"Prince Charming doesn't exist. He's a fairy tale. Ask yourself why a nineteen-year-old young man would be interested in you, a fifteen-year-old girl?" Bridget demanded. "Now you give me a reason."

"She has a point." Effy conceded. "He's much older and…"

"He wants to send her home with her knickers in her handbag."

Effy closed her eyes and shook her head on hearing Mack's words. Bridget glared at him.

"What?" His mock deadpan puzzlement only made it worse.

"Like you did with my sister!" Grace snapped.

"Let's get something straight. I wasn't underage. No one pressured me. I wasn't with a stranger. I was with Mack, who you set me up with him the first place. And if it's not obvious to you, we've loved each other from the start, and that has never changed."

"Yeah, and since then, he's added, Angie. Is Hester going to be added to the collection as well?" Grace's snide remark struck home. Then Grace reminded her, in a low barely audible, voice. "And you don't mind flirting on the side, do you? I haven't forgotten about you and Simon Silvers."

Effy shut her eyes tight, putting her hands to her ears. Grace's reminder of her flirting with Simon on that visit to the RCA was uncomfortable and disconcerting.

"Okay, we'll go. It would be unfair not to let her see him again." Effy colluded, hoping Grace's words had not been heard. Mack appeared not to have heard her sister's words.

"We'll go all right. I'll even take my camera. For the before and after shots." There was a terrifying blandness to the tone of his voice that Effy knew. "I'll want Angie with us. We ought to take Alice for her boxing skills."

"What?" It was Grace's turn to look puzzled. "What do you mean before and after pictures? Boxing skills?"

"One wrong move from him or any of his bandmates and they'll end up with a wild party none of them are expecting, or will forget."

Effy shut her eyes again, her lips tightening, her stomach knotting. She empathised with Grace. She could understand how excited her sister was at the thought of meeting Richie Miller again. At the same time, she was freaking out inside, hearing Mack's words. He could mete out swift and horrifying violence if things went wrong. She'd seen how lethal he could be. What had happened at the party was no accident. Pyle's punishment was light. Mack thought she didn't know what he'd done to Osborn either.

The story had turned into a legend in the re-telling. Two of her classmates had heard from those who'd seen what had happened. Beating Osborn to a pulp and kicking him down a road for trying to rape Ellen had seemed like justice. Since then, she'd heard even more horrific stories and rumours about how he'd dealt with Ronnie Sykes.

Those rumours had spread along the grapevine. They had circulated amongst the Halifax and Bradford Mods before reached her. Graphic details mentioned knives and nail guns being used with a nail being shot through someone's foot. After the incident on the Brixton Road, she'd seen for herself what he could do. It frightened Effy. She had every reason to feel scared. It would need Angie's presence for them both to rein him in if any trouble started.

Moneywise this American trip would be successful beyond belief. They had involved Nate in the new renegotiations. Alex Silvers let him do the fine wheeling and dealing. Nate, at last, had the opportunity he'd been after to make his mark. Afterwards, Nate, his father, Mack, and Greg Williams had met with her to go over the fine print. A final meeting with Henderson and his lawyers saw them sign a new deal. The sums involved were staggering.

On a personal level, it had been disastrous. Bridget's relationship with Greg had crumbled away to nothing in front of everyone's eyes. Almost as soon as the trip had begun, problems had arisen. Even before details of the deal emerged, Bridget had seen sides of Greg she'd never suspected. They weren't married, and he wasn't divorced. Nor was the divorce even on the horizon. Maybe it was for the best.

Then there was Mack. Oh, how she loved him, but would he ever trust her again? Knowing she'd kept the details of the deal from him still haunted her. Then Simon Silvers kept intruding into her thoughts for no good reason. She couldn't stop wondering why? She had Mack who loved her passionately but had anything happened between him and Hester when he'd gone missing? Had he been unfaithful? He refused to tell her or anyone anything about those missing two days. Was he punishing her for not telling him about the deal they'd made her sign?

When she confided her worries to Angie, she had told her to stop filling her head with silly doubts and nonsense. Hester might have a thing for Mack, but Angie was certain nothing had happened. Mack still loved them both. To cap it all, he'd fallen out with his father.

That so solid relationship between the two had disappeared. If she'd had the strength to tell Mack the truth, they could have avoided it. Now it was too late. She could not undo what she had done. Worse was the haunting guilt for the consequences of her failure to say anything. That damned contract was exacting too high an emotional price.

Effy began to wonder? What if she were to stop designing? What if she stopped modelling? What if she gave it all up? For five minutes, it seemed the perfect solution. Then it unravelled, as she considered the implications.

Mack had found a direction and a purpose with a future. So, too, had Angie. Alice had gone along with the modelling to help her widowed mother. She too had found an unexpected career. Ellen would soon earn enough for her and Tom to consider their long-term future together. Would Ellen still want to become a teacher after experiencing the high life? Grace was her big concern. She was young and impressionable. Handling all this fame, fortune, and pressure might have damaging consequences.

There were more than a few predatory males in the fashion world as she was discovering. Then there were the celebrities. So many top models seemed to become involved with pop musicians or movie stars. At fifteen, Grace was too young to let fame and money turn her life upside down and inside out. At seventeen, it was bad enough facing these challenges her self. The way things were now, she couldn't help seeing herself as someone's pawn on life's chessboard.

She hated feeling this way. She wished she had Mack's strength and confidence, something Angie shared with him. They took everything in their stride, not like her. America had wrecked her.

Jane MacKinnon's words never seemed truer. She'd written them down in her diary as a reminder following a long and intense conversation with her. *"Life is like looking down a path leading somewhere. You think you know where it's going to take you, but you get fooled. It takes you to places you never expected and where you didn't want to go."*

Then there were Miss Thorpe's words bedevilling her. *"You do have an eye for fashion and dazzling talent for design. But it's not all you have to offer."*

If she took an Oxbridge scholarship, where would that lead in the future? She enjoyed maths and literature, but she couldn't see herself any careers involving them. Maths was fine, and she enjoyed it as a recreational challenge. The thought of working as an accountant or actuary repelled her. As for literature, even with an Oxbridge degree, did she want to work for a publisher? Or become a magazine editor? Journalism? That was an even bigger no. None of these appealed. When it came to art, this was her singular passion, and that passion tied itself to fashion.

Maybe going to study at the Royal College of Art in London was the choice? It had felt right. Simon Silvers had made a big thing of the possibility. She would breeze it, he'd said. With her reputation, they'd welcome her with open arms. There were still things they could teach her to make her a better designer. Going to live and work in London, it seemed, was inevitable.

Angie was more and more intent on working in London. Even Alice was considering the same though she didn't want to leave her family in Halifax. Then she realized. Here she was in America, and they'd want her back. Where else would they expect her: Paris, Rome, Amsterdam, and Tokyo? Life wouldn't be simple again. Life *could never* be simple again.

Anger brewed inside her as she considered all the options. Wherever they wanted her to go, Mack would have to go too and vice versa. They were the whole package. Whoever wanted one of them would have to take the three of them or leave it. How would Angie take it? They were a threesome or as Grace had put it, a threeple. Angie would have to come too. They couldn't split them up, and they wouldn't split. No one would split them unless they did it to themselves.

CHAPTER 41

I Don't Need No Doctor – Ray Charles (HMV POP 1566 - 1966)
Friday 21 – Saturday 22 July 1967 – New York

Midway, through take five of a new song, *Different Drum,* their arrival had brought the recording to a stop. It was a song the band was considering for their new album. The moment Grace walked through the studio door, Mack could see Miller was smitten.

Ellen had been reluctant to go to the studio from the start. On hearing what Mack had to say, she feared the worst and decided not to go. Though she wouldn't say it, Ellen had a bad feeling about it. Bridget's shoulders had sagged listening to what Mack expected to see. Ellen's stern warning to Grace wasn't well received. It didn't help when Effy thought it wrong to deny Grace the chance to see Miller again. They should have heeded his warnings. Mack reluctantly gave in. It was time for Grace to learn her first hard lessons about male conduct.

Alice grinned, doing a boxer's pose. "If any of them try it on with Grace, they'll be in for a surprise."

Watching Alice's impression of Mohammed Ali, they'd laughed.

Yes, she would go along with them to protect Grace. Alice made it clear she had no qualms about defending Grace's virginity. It sounded hilarious, and they began to laugh. Mack didn't, and Alice noticed. They should all have noticed. His face remained expressionless, but not his eyes. Out of Effy and Angie's hearing, Alice whispered to him, "You have *carte blanche* to kick their arses good and proper if they try it on."

Bridget overheard and gave Alice a freezing glare.

Zorro's Mask was a five-piece band. How Richie Miller had come to front this bunch of misfits, mystified Mack. Steve Maguire, the bass player, was a recent addition to the band. Older than the others, he appeared out of place. Quiet and reserved, Maguire struggled to take his eyes off Bridget the moment they met. He seemed okay.

Mack did the obligatory studio photo shoot of the band recording. The atmosphere was desultory with little enthusiasm on show. Miller lost interest in recording the moment Grace stepped into the sound engineer's booth, his face brightening on seeing her. Only two of the band looked sober.

The bass player's stony features said it all. Mack took in the jaded and dissolute scene. He was witnessing the end of the band. It was the last ever take of the last recording session of this line-up of Zorro's Mask. He snapped the photos, knowing what they would show. This would be an unambiguous visual tale of the group's self-destructive dissolution. Later that day, he would bring it about though it wasn't intentional. The studio photos would make Mack a mint of money. The end-of-party snaps would become legendary and make him even more.

It went as Mack expected it to go. They found themselves hustled over to the band's Chelsea hotel suite on 23 West Street. He'd read enough in the music press about the group's antics to know it would not end well. Three of them were out-and-out louts. That they ignored him wasn't an issue. Mack preferred to go unnoticed when doing out of studio shoots. The girls stuck close by him. This wasn't popular with three of the members of the group. They appeared under the illusion the girls were here to offer sexual gratification.

The drummer, Brady Emerson, had deluded notions of being America's answer to Keith Moon. He displayed ego, but none of Moon's reputed swagger or panache.

Jack Torrance, the guitarist, fancied himself as the lady-killer and the group's top dog. The keyboard player, Jim Colby, was weird but not in a good way. One day they would lock him away in a mental institution, his brain scrambled and frazzled from LSD.

These three *Mal Amigos*, as the press labelled them, had well-publicised reputations. Their outrageous antics made for popular red top fodder. Infamous for drinking, womanising and troublemaking, they were a public menace. Wherever and whenever they appeared in public chaos and damage followed. Whoever had interviewed them for the article Mack had read wasn't wrong about one thing. They were prize assholes

So-called groupies were already in the hotel suite when they arrived. Wrecked furniture and a smashed TV set were the first things Mack spotted. Torn drapes were next. A beer-soaked carpet, stained and used as an ashtray, competed with the ripped sofas, summing up the state of the room. The expensive hotel room resembled a squat, not a five-star hotel suite. An expensive four-track tape player hooked up to an amp was playing a weird selection of pre-recorded music.

More and more hangers-on arrived along with the band's drunken roadies. Other musicians rolled in looking drunk or high. Several lesser-known intoxicated movie starlets and artsy types followed. The record producer was there too, along with the sound engineer. Alice later claimed she'd seen Andy Warhol and Edie Sedgwick pop in for about five minutes. The party was on full steam ahead with a Casey Jones train wreck disaster in the offing.

Steve Maguire and Bridget seemed to hit it off straight away to Mack and Effy's surprise. They became inseparable that evening, standing next to Richie Miller and Grace. Mack noticed how Bridget's eyes sparkled as she listened to Maguire. Playing with her strawberry blonde hair, she was doing some serious flirting. Even Effy and Angie commented on the way she'd sidled up close to him. Her bust kept poking his arm, and it didn't look accidental. She looked interested in a way none of them had expected. Had Greg Williams been present, he would have known this signalled the end for them as a couple. Bridget entranced Maguire. He couldn't keep his eyes off her. Their reaction to one another was spontaneous and unexpected. Something between the two had most definitely clicked.

Even though Effy had her arms entwined through Mack's, Jack Torrance took no notice. There was no disguising who he wanted. Either Effy or Angie would do, it didn't matter. Oblivious to the obvious, he treated Mack as if he didn't exist. Arrogant, he began making an immediate play for Effy suggestively stroking her arm. Gripping Mack's arm tighter, Angie informed Torrance that Effy was with her boyfriend. Effy sensed Mack tense, communicating trouble. Angie sensed it too, glancing at Effy.

He gave Mack a look of disgust, passing a comment about him being some friend of Dorothy's and an Ivy League faggot. The reek of Bourbon and cigarettes on his breath didn't do him any favour. The ripe nose curling locker room body odour made it worse. He stank, his tee-shirt needed to visit the laundry bin. Angie turned away, waving her hand under her nose. Her signal was explicit and intended.

Mack had his arm around Angie's shoulder as Torrance turned his attention to her. Angie informed him that she was also with her boyfriend. He directed his words at Mack, having taken an instant dislike to him earlier Torrance couldn't understand how a faggot fruit like him had two gorgeous girls on his arm, let alone one. The guitar player didn't like it when pretty women rejected him. Effy and Angie made their feelings known by looking away. Treating it as a joke the snubbed guitarist slapped Angie's behind as she kissed Mack on the cheek.

Her response to Torrance was strange. "You get that one for free. The next comes with a price tag."

Torrance should have taken her advice. Slapping her behind again a little harder, he joked. "How much, baby? Love you a long time for a dollar."

The words had scarce escaped his drunken leering lips when Angie gave him her response. A sound reminiscent of a whiplash followed as Angie's slapped Torrance's face. The power behind the blow sent him reeling and stumbling backward.

"How about that much?" She snarled.

The surprise slap had taken Torrance off guard. An angry red hand mark appeared etched through his unshaven stubble.

Grace, dreamy-eyed, stopped talking to Richie Miller, surprised by the sound of the slap. Everyone nearby turned on hearing it wondering what was happening. Bridget missed seeing the actual slap, but she caught sight of the ugliness in Torrance's face. Later she told Angie and Effy it was the same as watching a car crash about to happen.

The guitarist's features hardened. Alice's loud laughter didn't help. Chatting with the record producer and studio sound engineer, she'd seen the whole incident. Alice recounted, afterwards, it was one of the funniest things she had seen. It was like a Charlie Chaplin slapstick scene. Except it wasn't. It enraged Torrance in seconds.

Worse for wear, his Jack Daniel's consumption left him in no mood to look a fool. Fired up, he was ready to hit Angie. Mack anticipated what was coming. Stepping between him and Angie, he joked. "You should have asked her for the price first."

The Californian was tall and muscular with greasy long blond hair. Torrance had once been a promising high school football Tackle. Not making it on the gridiron, he'd become a rock-and-roll star instead. Used to full contact on the football field, he regarded himself as a tough cookie. No one would slap him around, definitely no Brit chick. Notorious for his bad temper and barroom brawls, it was as though a light switch went from off to on.

There was sporting violence, and then there was Mack's brand of violence. 'Thirty Seconds Lenny' had taught Mack the no-nonsense methods of handling brawlers. Since then, Mack had picked up a few more techniques. Plenty of witnesses saw what happened next. It went against everything Lenny had taught him. *Do unto others before they do unto you. But do it first.* Mack knew at this moment that he couldn't make the preemptive strike. It had to look like self-defence. He would have to take the hit and the pain before reacting.

Intercepted the punch on the cheekbone, he shielded Angie. Turning his head just enough, it became a glancing blow. A direct punch would have been serious.

The heavy skull ring on Torrance's fist could have chipped or fractured his cheekbone. For a moment or so, he saw spark-like stars. The ring broke the skin with an ugly slicing cut. The impact hurt like hell, jarring his teeth sending him reeling sideward. Effy tried to stop him toppling while Angie did the sensible thing. Stepping aside, she avoided him staggering back into her. The damage such a punch would have done to her delicate features was too dreadful to think about. Snatching an empty tray, Angie planned to use it either as a shield or weapon.

Though dazed, Mack's reactions went into rapid response. There wasn't time to think, only to punish viciously. Springing back upright, his left foot snap kicked Torrance's knee. In the same move, he slid the edge of his shoe the full length of the guitarist's shinbone, applying full force against it. Reaching the ankle, he stamped on his foot while elbowing him in the gut. This didn't deter Torrance even though he gasped in pain. The drugs and alcohol must have had an anaesthetic effect. Pulling back, he swung his fist at Mack. Doing so left his face open like a bull's eye target. Using the heel of his palm in a Jack-in-the-box motion, Mack broke his nose. It bent to one side with a faint crack spurting blood.

The Californian couldn't or didn't understand that Mack had beaten him. Making a last lunge, he lost control attempting to strangle him. Mack grabbed his left wrist. Driving fingers deep into the soft underside, he swivelled the wrist around. A sharp pain shot through the gripped hand. It disabled the guitarist for a moment. It was all Mack needed. With cold clinical precision, Mack dislocated three fingers in a single snapping motion. His punishment was calculated callousness. The guitarist would have to pay the price for attempting to hurt Angie. Any man capable of striking a woman deserved nothing less.

Mack took pleasure in what he'd done. A cold ugliness was at work. It was an injustice for an injustice. He carried it out as a self-appointed judge, jury, and executioner. Torrance fell to his knees. Clutching his hand, he howled like an injured wolf. Staring in disbelief, he watched his dislocated digits swelling like balloons.

Mack's politeness was eerie and chilling. "Jack, you should have checked my price first. You're lucky I'm only charging you mates' rates. Taking a swing at me comes at a price. Taking a swing at my woman comes with serious payback."

The swift violence numbed those witnessing it. Talk petered out as horrified gasps filled the air. The sound of Aretha Franklin *Respect* sounded louder than it had as background music. It seemed to fill the room.

Pandemonium broke loose. Jim Colby, drunk, slurring and staggering, picked up a chair. Planning to hit Mack from behind over the head, Effy saw him raise it high. Shoving Mack to one side, the chair hit the floor where he'd been standing almost hitting her arm. Angie, still holding the empty metal tray, smacked Colby with the flat side square in the face as hard as she could. The tray sang out a distinct gong-like note as metal met flesh. Dropping to his knees, Colby wavered for a moment. Then keeled over and hit the floor semi-conscious.

Emerson, the drummer, freeing himself from three groupies, launched himself across the room. Drunk and disorientated, he came crashing through the crowded room in his effort to reach Mack, causing further havoc. Alice, acting with cool aplomb, stuck her leg out, tripping him. Unable to stop, he stumbled, losing what little balance he had and fell face-first onto a glass-topped coffee table. The glass broke but didn't shatter on impact. It was a mess, and so was the drummer. Their manager lost it and began threatening to sue everyone in sight. Angry, he and a roadie rushed over to the carnage. Maguire tried to prevent the roadie from reaching Mack.

"Stay back, Billy!" He ordered. "This boy's lethal. He'll chew you up and spit you out."

The angry roadie disregarded him. He should have listened. A precision Glasgow kiss met him. Then an elbow to the face came next, followed by a knee to the groin. It was all over in five seconds. The roadie was clutching his crutch, making peculiar whimpering noises and lying in a foetal position. Blood flowed from his shattered nose.

Mack checked to see if anyone else planned to have a go. No one did. The room had gone silent. The sound of Aretha Franklin's *Respect* began to fade out. The recording was two minutes and twenty-six seconds long. That was all the time Mack needed to take them out. Turning to the manager with casual politeness, he pointed to the floored band members. "Please shut up, or you'll have you join them."

Their manager thought about what he'd seen. Looking away, tight-lipped, he shrugged his shoulder. He backed away without another word. The Beatles latest release *All You Need Is Love* came on next.

Alice, with incredible coolness, picked up his camera case. She took out the camera. Attaching the flash unit, she handed it over. "Make some money, Mack. Snap these idiots. The newspapers will love it."

She slapped him on the shoulder as they exchanged grins.

"Well, what are you waiting for?" Alice prompted. "Shoot!"

"You heard the girl." Prompted Angie, shaking with anger.

After the doctor left, they told the manager the four were lucky not to be facing arrest for assault. Mack could press charges against them if he wished. Miller and Maguire warned the manager that assaulting a young underage man while drunk and on drugs would see the three jailed. The young man had acted in self-defence. They'd got what they deserved. The resulting publicity would do the group no good. It didn't. It was better left at that. Matters then took a further strange turn.

Richie Miller informed the manager that was it, he was quitting. He'd had had enough of the band's wildness. The soft-spoken bass player joined him. He was quitting too. Six months on the road with these lunatic was enough. Maguire told the manager he would rather go back to being a session musician.

Both Miller and Maguire apologising for what had happened. Maguire told Mack, it was about time they had learned a lesson. Mack had taught them a damned good one, one they had coming for a long time. Going by what he knew of their past in Bakersfield, the three had always been a bad bunch. He and Miller were not part of the original group. Since the money had come rolling in, things had escalated out of control. Although he didn't know it now, he and Maguire would hit it off and become good friends in time.

Mack didn't need any medical attention. The cheekbone, although bruised, was not broken. The cut required a Band-Aid but no stitches. In the suite's palatial bathroom, Effy cleaned it, and Angie applied the Band-Aid. Effy was silent, and her hands trembled. Richie Miller looked on amused with a tearful Grace by his side. She couldn't stop apologising for Mack's violent response and for ruining the evening. Angie became annoyed, explaining what had happened. After hearing Angie's words, Grace gave Mack an apologetic kiss on the forehead.

Miller and Maguire proved to be genuine old-fashioned gentlemen. Miller, trying hard to impress Grace, ensured they returned to Henderson's penthouse without trouble. He promised to come and see her after tomorrow's shoot. The final bombshell of the night came when Bridget went off into the night with Maguire. She wouldn't return until late the following morning.

CHAPTER 42

Pick Up The Pieces – Carla Thomas (Stax UK 601032 – 1967)
Saturday 22 July 1967 – Early hours, New York

"What is it with you?" Effy became angry with Mack and Angie. "I can't understand how you keep getting into fights. And as for you, Angie, why couldn't you have told Torrance to piss off? All you had to do was say leave me alone. Why did you have to slap him forcing Sir Galahad here to go to your rescue?"

Mack had never seen Effy so angry with Angie. It was startling. They'd returned to Henderson's penthouse without speaking. They were about to sit down at the enormous white breakfast table when she exploded. He'd known by Effy's silence and tight facial expression she was seething. So, too, had Angie. Both had exchanged glances knowing it was inevitable.

"Effy, you're out of order." The softness of his voice did not conceal his irritation. "Angie had…"

"…No man will ever take advantage of me, Effy. No man. I won't let any man abuse me again. Do you understand me? Never again! How can you, my dearest friend, not understand? You know what happened to me. Not even Mack knows. I swore I'd never let another bloke hit me again as long as I lived, and I meant it. I thought you of all people understood."

Effy recoiled from Angie at the returned outburst. She watched her friend burst into tears.

"For fuck's sake…" He tried to step between them.

"Don't swear!" They both hollered at him, pushing him away and squaring up to each other.

"Stay out of this, Mack," Angie warned him. "Effy has a point. You're a menace, and you always keep ending up in fights."

"So what was I supposed to do? Let him hit you? That punch would have landed you in hospital needing a plastic surgeon to fix the damage. Do you think I would let that happen?"

Turning to Effy, he gave further vent to the anger inside, "I warned you what to expect. You wouldn't listen. Oh, she only wants to see him again. We can't let Grace not see him again, blah, blah. Well, next time

230

maybe you'll credit me for getting it right. Maybe, you *might* realise that I *might* know what I'm on about."

"Oh, yes. You always know better, don't you?" Effy snapped back. He was right, and she loathed having to admit it.

"You didn't have to break the guy's nose and fingers, did you?" Angie now joined Effy. "The violence was over the top. You were savage."

"And you didn't need to smack the other guy with the tray and knock him out cold." Mack retaliated. "They deserved what they got. Torrance needed a major reminder of how not to treat women, most of all the girls I love. And for your information, I only dislocated his fingers. I didn't break them. He should have stopped when I bust his hooter. He insisted on coming back for more. What the hell did you expect me to do? Let him strangle me?"

"You went over the top." Effy sobbed.

"For fu...goodness' sake! They attacked me! I didn't attack them! And you have the cheek to have a go at me?"

"We're not talking about defending yourself. It was the violence you used. You were enjoying what you did." Angie continued. "That's what was so shocking."

"I should never have asked to go. It's my fault. If we hadn't gone, it wouldn't have happened." They heard a small apologetic voice. Grace stood with Alice and Ellen. Unnoticed they'd come in listening to the exchanges.

"What's wrong with you two? Bickering and having a go at Mack?" Alice's resentful words silenced them. She had followed Grace into the room, hearing what they were saying. "You ought to be proud of him for handling it the way he did, instead of having a go at him and each other."

Both stared at Alice, open-mouthed as she berated them further. "Mack warned you what would happen if we went. You didn't want to believe him. It turns out he was right. He knew what to expect. What a pity you didn't want to listen. Maybe next time you will. If I had a fella like him, taking personal care of me the way he takes care of you two, I'd be proud of him. I wouldn't be bollocking him."

Walking over to them, she pushed Mack aside. "Don't forget. I've no memory of what I was like before I died in hospital. Since coming back from the dead, I've had to learn all about being a female. Let me tell you it's not been much fun. Most blokes seem to think we only exist for sex. Or to get exploited as household drudges. Or to become low wage slaves in dead-end jobs. You're damn lucky to have him. Every one of us here is damn lucky to have him. He's not like most guys. In his eyes, we're his equals. Mack treats women like all men ought to treat women."

"It's just the violence he used that was frightening..." Effy voice trailed away. Something about Alice's glance warned her not to say anymore.

"I saw every moment of what happened. They were drunken lecherous animals deserving of everything they got. I'd have done the same in his place." Alice defended him lecturing Effy and Angie.

"But..." Angie tried to protest.

"No, buts! I expect you two to kiss and make up with one another, and then with Mack. The three of you need to pick up the pieces before everything falls apart. Appreciate what you have shares in, you three. Prince Charming he's not, but he's the closest to one you two will find. He's the only young man I know capable of keeping you two happy." With those words, Alice hugged him. The orange blossom scent of her perfume filled his nostrils. Whispering in his ear, she added, "You kicked their arses good and proper. I'm proud of you, young man. You were brilliant. We need more guys like you around."

That sounded so bizarre. She was only a year older than him, if that. Calling him a young man?

"We've never told you all the problems Alice, and I had in London," Ellen joined in. "Some of the photographers we had to deal with were trying it on. One even wanted to get nude shots of me for a porn magazine, so don't just think its only Devane who tries it on. Now you know what you can expect if you get involved with pop groups or movie actors. You wouldn't believe the unprofessional things we had to deal with in London. So don't be a fool Effy. After what happened be glad Mack was there to deal with it."

"It's all my fault." Grace sat down at the table next to Angie, head in hands, tears running down her cheeks. She looked miserable and despondent.

"Don't blame yourself. It wasn't your fault. Besides, Richie Miller strikes me as an okay kind of guy." Mack softened, placing a hand on her shoulder.

"Yes. Richie seems so nice. It's not about what you did. I don't suppose you had any choice. He would have hurt Angie. They weren't very nice men. No, it's Bridget. She told Alice and me not to wait up. She said she wouldn't be back tonight."

Everyone looked at everyone else without a word. "If I hadn't made you all go, she wouldn't have met that Maguire and gone off with him."

What could they say to her? The level-headed and grown-up sister, the sensible one, had behaved uncharacteristically. They were stunned by her act.

They slept in the same bed that night. Sex wasn't on their minds. All three needed to find solace and comfort in one another. The events of the party had affected them in different ways. They talked in hushed voices for a while before tiredness overcame them.

Mack found sleeping with his two girls less than restful. Both clung to him, preventing any movement. Even with air conditioning, it was too warm, and they slept with the covers thrown back. He woke feeling exhausted when Hester knocked on the door.

There was a shoot to do in Times Square. Angie had a photo shoot with Ellen and Grace later in the morning. Effy was going with his father, Greg Williams, Alex and Nate Silvers, to a business meeting at InStyle. They would then attend another to discuss fabrics and pattern designs. Only Alice had the day off, and she planned to go exploring Macy's and other stores.

Hester was already up. Dressed and make up on, ready to go, she waited patiently while Mack downed coffee and toast. They had to set off early to catch the light and avoid crowds. After a final check of his cameras, he went to wake Effy and Angie, giving each a kiss.

CHAPTER 43

The Way You Do the Thing You Do – The Temptations
(Stateside SS 278 - 1964)
Saturday 22 July 1967 – Midday, New York

"We've both come a long way in a short time." Nate took the hot dog from the street vendor. Mack and Hester had agreed to meet him by the Flatiron building.

"How can you eat that crap?" Watching Nate chomping away, he heard his own stomach rumble. He hadn't eaten since setting off to the location shoot, but that had been hours ago.

Nate shrugged his shoulders in response studying the Elastoplast on Mack's cheekbone.

"Don't ask," Mack told him. "You'll hear all about it soon enough."

It was midday, and the heat was getting to Hester and himself. This was the last shoot of three organised in secret by Hester and Nate. The other two had taken place during his missing thirty-nine hours. This morning's shoot was for *American Girl* magazine.

They'd been out since six in the morning together with another local model. The temperature had soared as the sun had risen over Manhattan. A heat haze hung over the skyline with a temperature gauge displaying 83°F by the time they met Nate. Mack was sick of the taste of Coca Cola and hungry. Hester looked drained. Both needed something better than a hotdog.

"Can we go somewhere cool?" Hester pleaded. She was complaining of feeling faint and light-headed, the sun and the heat were the most likely cause. They made for the cool refuge of a nearby diner.

The air-conditioned coolness brought instant relief as they settled in a booth. A jukebox was playing easy listening music in the background. Mack could hear the smooth, soothing sound of Tony Bennett singing *Smile.* They ordered cold drinks, then food and coffee to follow.

"Okay, Nate, Hester, 'fess up. What's the story with you two? And what game have you two been playing?" The question did not appear unexpected.

"We all have our agendas, Mack. You have yours, Hester hers, and I have mine. But we all have mutual self-preservation interests, so to speak. Let's look at ourselves as a kind of mutual self-preservation society."

"Explain." Mack sat back, putting down his half-eaten pastrami on rye on the plate.

"Hester's mum and mine knew each other from their time at Cheltenham Ladies College. Both were models before we were born."

"My mum married Eugene." Hester continued. "She divorced him and remarried, which you worked out. There was one slight problem, me."

"My mother kept in touch with Hester's mum over the years. They were old schoolgirl chums who became models. In fact, being more or less the same age, we met as kids more than a few times, didn't we Hez? Remember when we used to sit in Harrods eating ice creams as kids while our mum's gassed away? Understand Mack, it's about who you know not what you know. It's about the right connections. That's the way the world works."

"Yeah, I'm getting a fine appreciation of that this trip." Mack's face gave nothing away. "Funny how things look to fall into place like pieces in a jigsaw puzzle. Is the flat in Sloane Square your American dad's?"

Hester nodded, still looking washed out exhausted from the sun and the heat.

"And was it a coincidence, you and Caroline Anstruther-Browne sharing your flat? Or was that planned too?" The comment was blunt and intended.

"No, it wasn't. That was pure coincidence." Hester sounded tired and past caring. "We knew each other from Cheltenham. One afternoon I bumped into Caroline shopping down the King's Road. Caroline was looking for a place, so I suggested she might like to stop with me. She's well-intentioned enough, there's no real harm in the girl. Caroline is just rather vacuous with a mind like a chocolate aero bar. Hooking up with Joe was a coincidence."

"You know how it is, mums like to gossip." Nate winked at Mack. "My mum mentioned she'd been talking with her old school friend. She told me Caroline was dating Joe and staying with Hester. The rest you've figured out already."

"For auld lang syne," Mack's sarcasm made Nate grin.

"For auld lang syne," Nate repeated.

"I've never forgiven Joe for what he tried to do to Nate." Hester yawned. "It was vile. Joe deserves everything coming his way."

"Oh?" Mack expressed interest glancing at Nate. "Tell me more."

"Well, you might as well know." Nate sat back, staring at the fan in the ceiling whirring around. "Joe, my dear brother, tried to get me arrested during a... shall we say... compromising situation. The whole thing was a deliberate setup. Lucky for me, I got out as the police raided the place. Others were not so lucky. Joe wanted me out of the way, jailed and discredited. He saw I was better at running the business than him. He also knew I suspected him of ripping off the business."

"So you needed Joe out of the way? Why help me and Effy?"

"Ah, that's complicated." Nate stared at Mack. "You know why. You are the man with the golden camera. Effy's the girl with the golden touch who knows how to make young women look fabulous."

"And Effy's so beautiful she makes me ache with jealousy every time I see her." Hester's sadness took him by surprise. "Worse when I see what you two have together, or should I say what you three have together. I still can't figure out how you make that work. You and your girlfriends make me feel so inadequate."

Patsy Cline's song, *Crazy,* began playing on the radio. The conversation paused. The lyrics seemed to affect Hester.

"Well, we shouldn't, you're gorgeous too, Hester." Mack meant what he said. "If I wasn't in love with the girls, I'd probably do more than look at you twice."

"Which is why I was keen to have you photo shoot Hester and help me out. Hester is beautiful and not only the parts on show.

Look. At the risk of repeating myself, my father's deal broking was sloppy. His body was here, and his mind was back in London, worrying about Joe. Since Joe's arrest, his mind hasn't been at the sharp end of the business. What makes it worse he's not well. This is a serious concern for the family and myself. If I should have to take over running the business, it's got to be in the family's best interests. We depend on the company for everything we have. Besides, any deal we sign up to has to work in everyone's favour. Including yours."

Nate paused, rubbing his chin.

"My father couldn't understand you three. He didn't realize what an unbreakable, and unshakable combination you three made. He thought you

236

would all roll over and do what everyone wanted. You were just a bunch of kids, after all, talented, but kids. This was something I couldn't make him understand. You weren't just a bunch of kids. No one knew better than me, you wouldn't buckle.

He also underestimated your influence over the girls and their loyalty to you. When they said they would never work for him in the future, it came as a bombshell. My plans, for you three and the others always was and still is for the long haul."

"Why?" Mack knew the answer.

"You know why. How often do you get to find your kinds of talent wrapped up in a package? I'll tell you when. Whenever there's a blue moon in the daytime sky, that's how often."

Nate's words struck a chord. Another Tony Bennett song started playing. Mack recognised it. He'd heard it on one of his father's latest LP purchases. It was that Anthony Newley song, *Who Can I Turn To (When Nobody Needs Me)*. They fell silent as the words drifted through the room.

Mack watched Hester's eyes misting once more. Hester had that longing look as she contemplated him. Maybe he'd said too much, and maybe he'd sent her the wrong message. Maybe the words of the song were somehow speaking to her.

Nate must have noticed what was passing between him and Hester. He broke the silence. "For heaven's sake, Mack! Do everyone a favour. Just screw the poor girl and put her out of her misery."

Hester blushed bright red. She slapped Nate across his arm twice in rapid succession without uttering a sound. Nate laughed, fending off her attack. Hester gave him an angry glare. Glancing once at Mack, she lowered her eyes into the half-finished iced-tea.

Effy had once quoted a line from John Milton's *Paradise Lost* when she'd caught him staring at a young woman. *Seek not temptation then, which to avoid were better*. That moment returned with such instant vividness.

They had been working in the reference library. She'd been studying a passage from the A-Level set text. Listless and fed up with the economics essay he was writing, his attention had wandered. He'd felt awful then and was feeling much the same now. It was uncomfortable, and it was tempting. It was also wrong. His mind recalled how he, Effy, and Angie had gone through a personal hell. The girls were still getting over that wretched party and the fight. No, he could never do it to Angie or to Effy. They loved him, heart and soul. Also, they shared him. That had to be an incredibly difficult thing for them to do.

No. A fling with Hester was not on and could never happen. No matter how tempting, and she was tempting. No. It would be so wrong to mislead and hurt Hester no matter what they both felt. He wasn't prepared to use her knowing how she'd felt about him. She deserved better. Having sex with her would be a cruel, destructive act. There was also the single important fact that he loved Angie and Effy.

Hester composed herself, behaving as though nothing had happened. Mack was half listening to Nate and still observing her. The time they'd spent together in New York had brought them closer. Under all her assertiveness lay fragility and vulnerability. The self-confidence was there but as a mask. Yet they all wore masks concealing their true selves behind them. The older he became, the more he was seeing what was going on behind the masks people wore.

"You need to make it up with your father, Mack." Nate's words broke into his stream of thoughts. "Even if it's only as your banker. Forgive your old man. He's a decent, honourable guy. From Effy's sister Bridget I know he's not taken your falling out well. You need his experience at the helm until you're old enough. Not only you, all the *New Breed*, so smoke the old peace pipe with him." Mack nodded. "Maybe you're right, maybe I should."

"You should. AIC-InStyle has agreed on a deal with us. Effy's non-refundable advance alone over three years is thirty thousand dollars. What's more, this guarantees her designs and AIC-InStyle as Silvers American buyer and distributor. The licencing agreement will protect her designs and our business. My dad's already agreed to let me do all the future wheeling and dealing over here. You'll need to chat with your dad about Effy's new company.

From here on in, it looks like he'll have to take on a new full-time job. Looking after Effy's business and yours. Which means the modelling agency, too. If you're ready to flee the nest and move down to London, we'll talk more when we're back in England. But it will have to be the whole package, the full *New Breed*."

This information came as a stunner, his father giving up his safe job and taking a risk? Nate had to have got that wrong. The whole package?

"What, even Grace?"

"No, we can work something out where Grace is concerned. You, Effy, Angie, Ellen and Alice we'll need in London. You'll also need a supervising adult full time for foreign travel, and to supervise photo shoots. Also, a full-time adult PA."

"You mean someone like Bridget?"

"Bridget would be excellent. Aileen did a good job in Spain, didn't she, Hester? Perhaps, we should consider her too."

Hester nodded. "Aileen would be great. I liked her. We got on so well together. Keeping the business in the family would be a sensible idea."

"Yeah, she might consider it. Coming back to the situation here. The Big Apple a revelation. I'm not so sure I'd want to live here. I don't drink, but not getting served alcohol until I'm twenty-one would be annoying. What else will they stop me from doing because I'm a minor? I know naff all about American laws, none of us do. As for moving to London, there are issues we need to resolve.

For a start, I don't have a studio, and I don't have the money to set up from scratch the way I'd like. Going by London prices, it's going to be a touch expensive.

Effy is still deciding what to do about her A-Levels. Then there's the whole Oxbridge possibility. She's the key to everything.

Angie's on board for making the move, she's already jacked her old job in and taken assignments in the city. But here's the nitty-gritty, I won't go unless Effy does and if we don't go, Angie won't move without us. It's down to Effy.

As for Ellen, I couldn't tell you. Will she still want to be a teacher after tasting the high life and earning the big bucks? Somehow, I don't think so. She and my cousin, Tom, need to sort things out first if they can.

Alice? God knows what she thinks. She's a one-off. I love her dearly, and she's great but strange. She's made her mind up. I understand Alice is moving in with you, Hester?"

Hester nodded. "She is. I think we'll get on well."

Mack continued. "Grace is the big worry. Tasting the high life she's experienced here could go to her head. Now we have the added distraction of Richie Miller sniffing around her skirt. That's a serious concern. Bridget has mentioned he's thinking of coming to England. It looks as if he has the hots for her."

"Don't worry about a studio." Nate's answer was smooth. "If you like Landsdowne Walk, you could rent it. We can make arrangements. If

239

Effy is the key, then you and Angie need to work on her. We can plan for Effy to do her designing in our London workshops. My brother Simon is there and creating print designs. It could all work out for the better."

Hester seemed about to say something when a look from Nate stopped her.

"Even if, and I mean 'if' we came to London we'd need somewhere decent to rent. There's no way we'd slum in some Notting Hill Rachman type dive or hippy squat."

Nate grinned. "The money you three will make will buy flats in Mayfair or Kensington in no time. It won't be easy money; making money is never easy. What you've earned over here is a taste of what you will make in the long run. Effy will make us all rich. She is the key at the moment. You and Angie have to work on her, and Hester too. Persuade her, though I suspect that won't need much doing."

"Get thee behind me, Satan!" Mack joked.

Nate leaned across the booth table. "I have to tempt you. It's in my nature."

Hester touched his hand. "How much have you earned over here in the last few days, A thousand dollars?"

"About that. Why?" He let her keep her hand on his. "That's what... just over four hundred pounds in a week? That's not bad going."

"The girls have earned between a hundred to two hundred dollars for a day's shoot since they started. The snappers over here are falling over themselves, especially for Grace and Alice." Nate incentivised. "British models are in even bigger demand since Twiggy arrived here. The girls are tail coating on her success. Hester's had a chat with Alice, haven't you, dear? How much did Alice say she'd earned this week?"

Hester stared straight at Mack. "Alice has worked five out of the last seven days. She did two sessions a day when not working for the AIC-InStyle shoots. Angie made them pay Alice forty dollars an hour before going for a whole day fee. She insisted the girls got paid by the day, even if they only worked part of it. She demanded that Grace, Ellen, and Alice be paid two hundred a day, and she got it. That's eighty-odd pounds."

So far, Alice has earned eleven hundred dollars. Grace has earned more, thirteen hundred and fifty dollars. That's five hundred and fifty pounds. That doesn't include the money they're getting paid for the AIC-InStyle promo work."

"Angie's sharp and a tough negotiator. She's done most of the wheeling and dealing for the girls over here. You should see her in action negotiating. The only deal she didn't negotiate was the one Hester's father made for Effy with Bvlgari and Hester's with Tiffany. Wait until you chat with your dad." Nate purred. "Wait until you hear about the cosmetics deal for Effy and the one Angie's landed with a rival."

"You could rent a decent place in somewhere like Earl's Court until you were ready to buy something more permanent," Hester added, the sadness in her eyes clearing. "We could all be near each other."

Nate continued to sell the move. "Quite a few of the local ad agencies are already seeing you as the first teen superstar snapper on the block. You've already got the connections in London. The next step is to do more photo shoots here. You could work with all the local greats, like Cheryl Tiegs, Colleen Corby, and Ali MacGraw. Don't forget the movie stars and starlets. They always need promos for magazines and newspapers. Your foot is in the door, and no one is trying to shut it. Not here in the Big Apple, not in London. I'll bet not in Paris or Rome by next year."

Mack sat back, looking up at the fan for a moment. Picking up the remains of his pastrami on rye, he took a bite.

CHAPTER 44

Danger Zone – Wilson Picket (Atlantic 584023 B – 1966)
Sunday 23 July 196, New York - Monday 24 July - London

Hester knocked on Mack's bedroom door. The voices inside sounded serious. "Don't bother knocking Hester and don't be surprised by what you see," Ellen, standing behind her, pushed the door open. "There's no orgy going on."

Hester's eyes opened wide. The king-size bed was full. Mack was sitting up between Effy and Angie as they snuggled up to him. Alice, reclined and relaxed, lay stretched out in a languorous pose across the bottom. Her legs gave the illusion of being longer and more perfectly shaped than usual. Grace was seated cross-legged on the covers next to Angie. Effy patted a space by her. "Join us. The New Breed is in conference. As an honorary member, we'd like your advice."

"I hope there are no French singers outside." Hester joked. "Should I strip to my undies just in case?"

"You can for me," Mack joked, raising a smile from the girls.

Slipping off her shoes, Hester sat down beside Effy and made herself comfortable. "Okay. Now what?"

Ellen pulled up a chair. "They've decided to move to London and need your help."

"They?" Queried Hester.

"I'm still deciding and need to talk to Tom before I make up my mind," Ellen replied with a sigh. "Grace has agreed to do her O Levels first, but she wants to do as much modelling work as she can while still at school."

"Mack and I have decided to leave school and move to London," Effy began, "but we've decided we'll perhaps try to go to evening classes to do our A-Levels if we can. What do you think?"

Hester thought about Effy's words for several seconds. "I left school as soon as I could. I had no intention of sitting exams or going to a university. It's done me no harm. It sounds a good idea, knowing what you've told me about both sets of parents. There are some things you might need to think about first. The hours you work may make that hard to do. I sometimes have to work late, until ten at night occasionally, depending on who's doing a shoot. Then there's the travel. Spain and the States will only be the beginning. Paris, Rome, Tokyo, and everywhere else shouldn't prove surprising. The way things are shaping up for everyone here it could be too much to study and cope with working full time. Don't be surprised if you find yourselves jumping on and off aircraft as though you were travelling in taxis."

"What about hiring private tutors?" Mack asked. "We could work on an as-needed basis?"

"You could, I suppose. Do you want me to see if I can find someone?"

"More pressing is somewhere for us to live." Angie joined the conversation. "Can you help us? We understand Alice is moving in with you, now that your flatmate has moved out."

"What they want to know, Hez," Alice joined in, "Can you help them find two decent places to rent. Angie and Effy want to find two flats in the same building."

"What about you, Mack?" Hester looked puzzled. There was an outburst of giggles.

"He's going to commute upstairs and downstairs between them." Teased Ellen.

"And the flats have to be two bedroomed." Insisted Angie. "We'll need somewhere for when Ellen and Grace come down to work."

"Okay, but my flat has a third small single bedroom, so either Ellen or Grace could stopover with me." Hester offered. "Anyway, I know someone who may be able to sort you out. I'll ask Veronica if she'll let me make a transatlantic call. I take it you want to move as soon as we get back? They…"

"Hey! I might still come down," Ellen interrupted, "and I think you'll need somewhere for Bridget to stay. Haven't you heard? Tell her, Eff."

"She's coming to London too. She's accepted Mr MacKinnon's offer of a job in my company. You haven't heard the best of it yet. I've asked my other sister, Aileen, to think about joining the staff. We'll need an office for the company, and the agency and for Mack's photography."

"And I still need a studio," Mack sounded uneasy.

"Leave the studio to me, Mack," Hester answered, her voice filled with confidence. "I know just the place. You'll love it. As for office space, it so happens, I know someone who has a leasehold available slap bang in Soho. It's on Peter Street, around the corner from Wardour Street. I'll have word with Mr MacKinnon, if you'd like me to do that?"

"Is there no end to who you know or what you know, Hester?" Effy's look of amazement was so comical it made everyone in the room burst out laughing."

Their last evening in New York was spent as guests of Eugene Henderson at his favourite restaurant. Opened in 1762, Fraunces Tavern was the oldest surviving restaurant in the city. Located in Lower Manhattan, the tavern stood on the corner of Pearl and Broad Street. Brimming with history, this was where the Sons of Liberty had conspired to trigger the American war of Independence. George Washington was also recorded as having stayed at the tavern.

Henderson had reserved the plush Party room, inviting Mack and the girls to join him. Bridget and her new plus one, Steve Maguire and Robert MacKinnon, were also invited. Greg Williams decided not to attend, pleading feeling unwell. His excuse for not attending was plain. The Silvers were also missing. They had taken an early flight back to England. Problems with legal issues and Joe Silvers looming trial required their presence in London.

When Hester excused herself to go to the restroom, Effy went with her. As soon as the door shut, the words came tumbling out. "Did anything happen between you and Mack when he went missing?"

Effy's words surprised Hester. Looking her straight in the eyes, she responded instantly. "What you want to know is, did I sleep with him? I should have thought that was obvious. No, I didn't. Nothing happened between us, but he did kiss me on the cheek a few times."

Effy let out a visible sigh.

What was the point of telling her she had crept into his bed and slept next to him one night? Nothing had happened. No kisses, no sex, just her spooning with him and talking in whispers when he was at his lowest.

"We spoke a great deal when we stayed at my friend's apartment. I don't think you appreciate and understand how let down and betrayed Mack felt. I don't imagine he's told you about that, has he? After what you did to

244

him, I was amazed he could find it in himself to forgive you and to continue loving you as he does."

"I was tricked…" Effy started to reply, but Hester cut her off.

"Yes, I know all about that. You should have been honest and told him, shouldn't you? It was unfair of you not to have done so. He couldn't understand why you didn't tell him. If I'm honest, Effy Halloran, I'm surprised he didn't end it with you. In his place, I would have. So now you tell me why you didn't tell him?"

Eyes downcast, shoulders dropping, Effy answered, "I was afraid. I was scared of letting everyone else down. I didn't know what to do. Mr Silvers and Greg Williams told me that Silver Fashions stood to lose a great deal of money if the deal didn't go through. They kept saying it would be my fault entirely if that happened. I was told not to say anything to anyone, especially not to Mack. They said he would stop the trip and the deal. Then Mack's father seemed to believe it too. So I said nothing and did as they asked. I hated the dishonesty and the lies. Most of all, I hated myself because I knew I had betrayed him, and I can't forgive myself for what I did."

Hester shook her head, saying nothing. She turned away to check her hair and makeup in the mirror.

"I can't understand why Mack wouldn't tell me what he did or didn't when he went missing. He still won't? What was he doing that he's not willing to talk about?"

"You don't like it when he's keeping a secret, do you?" She saw the tears forming. Hester could not stay annoyed with Effy. Her words had been prompted by a touch of jealousy in her own heart. It wasn't the Yorkshire girl's fault that she had been used and blackmailed. "If you have any doubts, Effy, ask him, be direct. He won't lie to you. You do mean everything to him, perhaps even more than Angie. He must truly love you from the depths of his soul."

Effy tried to stop the tears but couldn't. Hester immediately took out a hanky from her handbag. "Stop it, girl. I don't want you going back looking as if you've sobbed your heart out. I don't want everyone blaming me."

Hester gave her an unexpected, comforting hug. "There are reasons he won't tell you what the two of us were doing. They didn't involve sex but have everything to do with confidentiality and my father. Also, Mack's not one to waste time. He was busy photo shooting some quick assignments. The one thing he wasn't doing was cheating on you. What did he get up to?

You'll find out at the right time. In the meantime, you'll have to remain curious."

"I feel as if he's been punishing me. What can I do to make it right with him?"

Hester sighed and released the hug. "I'm not the best person to give advice on men. My love life is non-existent, and it's miserable. To my shame, I still fall for all the wrong types of men, and I never learn my lesson. Men think all I'm good for is a quick seeing to in bed. I'm just a body they lust after. The worst of it is, I keep falling for their same tired old lines and lies.

The trouble with our line of work is that we seem to attract too many of the wrong sort. There are plenty of them too, as you're finding out. Let me give you this piece of advice, Effy. It's all too easy to take what you have for granted when some new sweet talker surfaces. You can fool yourself into thinking this new guy might be more loving, more passionate, more exciting. A new life with someone else will look dreamier. Their bed will seem softer and sexier, and their romantic allure enticing.

Take it from me, Effy; in our line of work, temptation will be a constant. It's so easy to fall for these handsome lover boys. Look at the lives of most of the top models; their love lives change as fast their undies. To my shame, I'm one of them. For heaven's sake, don't end up like me. Be careful, because you're going to find yourself sucked into their celebrity circus sooner than you think. The pressures on your life as a model and as a designer are going to be immense. Lots of men will want to bed you or control you, or maybe both. Don't allow them to fool you. Much more importantly, *don't fool yourself.*"

Hester paused. A silent Effy seemed absorbed in her words yet somehow at the same time lost in her own thoughts. The girl was in some distress and vulnerable and Hester felt a strange compassion towards her. She needed help, a guardian angel.

"Here's the advice someone gave me, *Treat life like a game, and you'll lose. Live life, and you'll end up a winner.* Don't let other make you a pawn in their games.

Mack is not like most guys and you need to hold on to him. You have to thank your lucky stars that he's yours. All I can say to you is that he must really love you because he's done nothing wrong. Let me be truthful with you, and perhaps I shouldn't be. If he'd tried to make love to me I could not have resisted. I'd rather tell you this because believe it or not I really

246

would like you, and Angie, as my friends. I envy what you and all the other girls have together. I'd like to be a part of your friendships. Going to Spain and getting to know you all was the best thing that's ever happened to me. I'm no competition for you, Effy Halloran, or to Angie, and I never will be. I will be your friend if you'll let me. And if you need my help or advice, I'll be here for you."

Hester studied Effy's face wondering how she was reacting to her words. Effy looked troubled, not reassured. "Maybe you ought to be more like Angie. She never doubts Mack. She knows she loves him no matter what. There are some big questions you perhaps do need to ask yourself, Effy. Give yourself honest answers when you do. *How much do you love him? Really love him, without any doubts or reservations. And how strong is that love for him?*" The answers will tell you what you need to know.

Effy steered the direction of their conversation away from these uncomfortable and provoking questions. She still had her concerns. Although Mack didn't show it and tried to smooth over what had taken place, it still didn't feel right between them. Or was she simply imagining it?

"So how did you just happen to be in New York? At the same time as us?"

"Nate asked me to be here. He knew what was going on. Nate and I had our reasons. I suggest you ask Mack all about the why. We should get back before they start asking why we're taking so long. One thing you should know. Let me warn you. I've known Nate from childhood. He never does anything for nothing. Remain wary of him, but even more so of his brothers. The sisters are lovely, but watch out for the men."

Alice and Hester had seats together towards the rear of the plane. Hester found Alice strange yet so endearing. She was happy that Caroline had left and pleased that Alice was moving in to share her flat. Alice was so adult for an eighteen-year-old. The more she got to know her, the more Hester enjoyed her company. She could talk about a wide range of topics surprising for someone so young. Hester couldn't figure it out. For all her femininity, Alice was also quite masculine in the way she approached problems.

A girl of eighteen, who was on her way to becoming a top model, should have purchased a copy of Vogue or Harper's. Instead, she was reading the New York Times. Alice seemed far more interested in the breaking news of the Detroit riots. There had been escalating violence in some places. The recent riots in nearby Newark had not affected their stay, but the number of riots and disturbances was growing in various parts of the country.

What caught Hester's attention was an item that Alice was studying. Glancing, she saw there was a photo of a barely recognisable Seth Devane. His face was a bloody mess, and both hands were heavily bandaged.

The reporting was brief. An unknown assailant had attacked Devane as he left his studio. The photographer had been severely beaten, the fingers and thumbs on both hands deliberately broken. Devane had also suffered severe facial contusions. This was an understated reference to his broken nose, bust lips, and panda eyes. A police spokesman was quoted as saying; robbery did not appear to have been the motive.

Was Mack the unknown assailant? Nate had told her he could be exceptionally violent. From Alice, she had heard about how he'd dealt with Jack Torrance and the roadie at the party. Then she realized. It could not have been him.

At the time of the assault on Devane, Mack was with her. They were with Angie and Grace on the penthouse terrace doing a night shoot. Effy and Ellen were there too, looking on. The end results had been beautiful, with the New York skyline lit up as a backdrop. Besides, Devane's studio was on 40th West 80th Street on the other side of Central Park. Seeing this news item left Hester with an intense feeling of pleasure. Two years ago, when she was new to modelling, the bastard had taken advantage of her youth and inexperience.

So who could have beaten Devane to a pulp? Whoever had done it, had given him one hell of a beating. She glanced at Alice, who had noticed her reading the item. Now she thought about it, only Alice had been missing. That was ridiculous. Alice?

Alice gave her a mysterious smile, "It couldn't have happened to a nicer bloke, could it? He had it coming."

Robert MacKinnon was relieved when the plane touched down in London. The thought of being away from his wife and new daughter had occupied him constantly. The American trip had almost turned into a disaster. He was thankful that, in the end, it had worked out as well as it had. Now he was faced with getting Effy's company underway. They needed to have an official office quickly. He would need to return to London to check out the premises on Peter Street. If these were suitable, leases on this and the flats would need signing.

Together with Bridget and Ellen, he was heading home to Bradford. On the journey, he would discuss the running of the company with its first employee, Bridget.

Ellen would return in three days to do a shoot for a sports car manufacturer. Bridget was going home long enough to hand in her notice at the solicitors. In the meantime, Bridget would begin taking the assignment booking to relieve Jane and Angie. If Aileen agreed to join her, to work for the new company, they would move to London together. Ellen remained undecided, still worrying about her and Tom. The college place was being deferred for a year. The deferment might prove indefinite.

Mack had photo shoot assignments, so he was staying on in London with Effy and Angie. Nate had arranged for them to use the one-bedroom flat in Grosvenor Street. They could stay there until they found somewhere of their own, as long as Angie kept out of his father's way. Relations between the two were now at their lowest. Appointments to view flats had already been arranged by Hester's acquaintance.

Grace was staying with Hester and Alice for a couple of nights. All three had bookings in the next two days. The one-bedroom flat in Grosvenor Street wasn't big enough for four, which was why Grace was at Hester's.

Silvers Fashions needed Effy to check out some new dresses and fabric prints. She also had numerous planning meetings ahead in the next two weeks as well as new designs to complete. The most important meeting was with representatives from the cosmetic company keen to use her in their advertising campaign. Frantic days were ahead for everyone.

CHAPTER 45

A Bird In The Hand (Is Worth Two In The Bush) – The Velvelettes
(V.I.P. 25030 – 1965)
Tuesday 25 July 1967 – London

Once again, they slept in the same bed together as they had on their first visit to London. It was a poor night's sleep for all three. Trying to readjust to the changes in time difference left them shattered. Angie's chattiness didn't improve matters. For the first time, as she lay silent by Mack's side, Effy experienced a peculiar sensation. She was like an intruder listening to them share fleeting seconds of emotional closeness.

Mack sensed her discomfort and tried to persuade her to join them in, but Effy turned away. They were facing more hectic schedules over the next couple of days. If she pretended to be asleep, Mack and Angie might stop talking. It had the desired effect. Hearing him kiss Angie left Effy feeling a momentary pang of jealousy. As Angie turned away from Mack to sleep, Effy heard her whisper, "Don't forget to give Effy a goodnight kiss. Turn over and cuddle her. I don't want Effy thinking I'm more important to you than to her, because I know I'm not. Somehow, I'll always be second best."

"No, you won't," Mack replied, comforting her, before turning to Effy. A moment later, he placed his free arm around her, his hand cupping her breast. He left a trail of tiny kisses on the back of her neck, whispering, "I love you, Effy, I always have, I always will."

When the alarm clock went off, none of them were too eager to get up. For Effy, it would be an easy day. Unlike Mack and Angie, who were working on shoots, she would enjoy an easy morning. Two short meetings at the boutique and the rest of the day until late afternoon would be hers.

Effy wished she could spend some time with him. They'd had so little time alone in New York. They needed to talk and to be together as a twosome. Effy still couldn't help wondering if he'd completely forgiven her. Hester's words had left a brooding doubt in her mind. *How much do you love him? Really love him, without any doubts?* Did she have doubts? Or was this the effect of exhausting jet lag affecting her thinking and creating these doubts? Was it the mounting pressure of choosing to start a new life? The

250

uncertainty of what lay ahead was stressful, as were the demands and expectations from everyone. Effy knew her American experience had left her emotional life scarred and drained. She loved him and Angie, but had she damaged the relationship between the three of them?

When Angie had learned how she had concealed the truth from her and Mack, she had been so angry. Her words, in the white heat of the moment, had been bitter and distressing. Until Effy had explained her actions, their friendship had teetered on the brink of extinction.

Angie's loyalty and love for Mack were unconditional. Right or wrong, she would stand by him. Even after the truth was out, she wondered if they'd lost their trust in her? How much heartache and lasting damage had she caused? She could not rid herself of thinking their threesome was irreparably marred. Had they put it all behind them? Or were they still harbouring a lingering distrust? Perhaps, today, she would feel better. It was, after all, the beginning of a new chapter in her life.

Mack would be at the studio shooting some female singer in need of promo stills. Later in the day, he had a photo shoot for *Nova* with Angie. After a final fitting this morning, Angie would fetch the two new dresses from the Silvers workshop to the studio. Jane MacKinnon had made the bookings while they were away in America. Mack had hired the studio at Landsdowne Walk with Nate's help.

Since this was not a Silvers Fashion shoot, he was paying the full hire charges. To his relief, the studio had been available, but it wasn't cheap. Something more permanent would need sorting and fast. The cost of setting up would drain his bank balance in no time. He would need to work non-stop to finance his own studio.

They agreed to meet back at Hester's flat in Sloane Square, so Hester could take them to view the rental flats she had located. As they rushed to leave, Angie jogged his memory. "Oi, don't forget." She gave him a knowing look.

"Thanks for reminding me, Angie." Mack pulled out a small, neatly wrapped object from his Harrington jacket pocket. Pulling Effy close to him, he embraced and kissed her passionately. Taking her hand, he pressed the gift into it. "Don't open it now. Open it later this morning, after your meetings. I love you, Effy. Promise me, you won't open it until later?"

She had promised. Then they were gone.

Her meeting with Nate took twenty minutes. They met, on the top floor of Moods Mosaic, in the room reserved for celebrity clients. She was here to see her latest designs in the special fabric prints created by Simon Silvers. The seven dresses looked even better than she had imagined. Nate appeared delighted with the results, but he seemed more preoccupied than usual. He had a busy day ahead. He and his father were meeting with the lawyer representing Joe.

Simon phoned the shop as Nate was leaving. His excuse for not arriving was due to his alarm clock failing to go off. It sounded like a weak excuse. Would Effy like to meet him at Picasso's coffee bar at eleven-thirty instead? It was only a short walk from the boutique along the King's Road. Effy looked forward to seeing him again, experiencing an inexplicable nervous excitement.

Moods Mosaic was busy, so Effy volunteered to help Tina and the new salesgirl until it was time for her to meet Simon. Most of the customers who came in did so only to browse. Like Mary Quant's Bazaar, this was an expensive shop, and it didn't stock her inexpensive catalogue range. The cheapest items on show sold for twenty guineas.

Effy thought she recognised the two debutantes who entered the boutique. Their faces seemed familiar. Then it came to her. They had appeared in a recent issue of Tatler.

Tina, who was attending to them, came over and asked if Effy would mind speaking to them. She couldn't refuse. Her presence as the designer might persuade them to make a purchase. Her willingness to chat did the trick. As she was leaving to meet Simon, she learned from Tina that her brief conversation had resulted in sales. Between them, the two debs had spent nearly two hundred pounds. Oh, to be moneyed and the daughter of some Lord or millionaire tycoon. Well, she would soon be moneyed too. The American deal alone guaranteed her over four thousand pounds a year.

These days, whenever she went walking in London, Effy tried to conceal her identity by going incognito. She was becoming known when out and about. Not that she minded signing the occasional autograph, but she disliked being pestered. It was always the men who did the pestering. Most wanted more than an autograph, and fending them off had become something of an irritation.

Under a broad-brimmed, floppy pale blue sun hat, Effy had attempted to disguise herself. A pair of hex-shaped Polaroid Ray-Bans purchased in New York helped to mask her identity.

As it was a warm sunny summer's day, she had dressed in one of her short sleeve designs. The dress was a narrow A-line mini-dress with a pale blue hexagonal honeycomb print over an indigo background. Seven inches above the knee, the hemline was daring. She wore pale turquoise tights to set off the dress and complement the honeycomb pattern. Given the warmth of the late morning sun, Effy wished she'd settled for white knee socks instead. Dark blue kitten heel shoes with plain gold buckles matched and harmonised the ensemble. The pale blue handbag completed her stunning look. She chose not to notice the attention and head-turning as she walked along the King's Road.

Pretending to be oblivious to the looks she attracted was a deliberate strategy. So she walked with a determined step to prevent being stopped. Not that this prevented men from admiring her. Not only was it the men, but the women too. They would stop to marvel at her striking, chic appearance as she walked past.

She had never been to Picasso's although she recalled passing it in a taxi one night. The place had a garish neon sign advertising its presence at night. She recollected it was near a white building with a curved entrance on a street corner. This, it turned out, belonged to Kendall & Sons the builders. It stood on the junction of King's Road and Shawfield Street. Picasso's was located across this junction, between a record shop and newsagents. A Dolland & Aitcheson's opticians was next to the newsagents.

As she approached, she noticed a plaque high above the newsagent's advertising Woodbine cigarettes. Effy disliked smoking. Sitting in cigarette smoke-filled places was unpleasant. It made her hair and clothes smell. Unfortunately, it was unavoidable. She found it an unpleasant habit and was glad that most of her close friends didn't indulge.

The white letters affixed to wooden slat panels above the frontage announced this was Picasso's. Entry to the coffee bar was through the opening left by a central glass doorway. Along the length of its exterior frontage, there were small tables and chairs under shady parasol covers. Picasso's reminded her of what a pavement café might look like somewhere in Paris.

Next door, a small group had gathered outside the Alex Strickland owned record shop. She would tell Mack about it. He would have to come down to have a rummage through the record racks. Maybe he could find some more of those Soul or Motown records he was always trying to find.

Picasso's was full. It was a popular gathering place for the well-heeled Chelsea set. Effy quickly formed the impression that many of them did not need to work for a living. Sitting outside, on red and white metal-framed chairs around tiny tables, they observed passing street life. On entering, she overheard someone in one of the booths mention wintering in St. Tropez. Every seat inside appeared taken. The distinctive strong smell and smoke of French Gauloise cigarettes hung in the air irritating her throat. Simon had reserved her a seat. Stubbing out a cigarette in the ashtray, on an impulse, he kissed her on the cheek, uncertain how else to greet her. That was unsettling, though not uninvited. It was the kind of greeting she was beginning to accept as normal in fashionable circles.

After ordering a coffee, he started a nervous, uncertain conversation. He talked about the weather and waffled on about a little and nothing. Almost as an afterthought, he asked what did she think about his print designs on her latest dresses. Effy removed her sunglasses. A strange jittery, quivering began to course through her as she studied him. She couldn't avoid noticing his edgy restiveness. He kept talking, sounding incoherent quite a lot of the time, unsure of himself, while staring at her in such a disconcerting way.

Simon was the epitome of the tall, dark, and handsome lover found so often in romantic fiction. Effy smiled, wondering how Barbara Cartland would delight in meeting such a specimen of young manhood? He'd earn a place in the author's next novel for certain. She could not deny she felt some kind of strange yet strong physical attraction. As she listened to him, Effy struggled to understand what was going on inside her head. Peculiar frivolous unwanted thoughts began to appear as if from nowhere along with a surprising, delicious sensation of excited apprehensiveness, of anticipation.

What if she was to decide that she no longer wanted to be Mack's girlfriend? What if she was to fall for this good-looking young man? She'd never had another boyfriend. Would being with Simon be so different? How different? Then it occurred to her, could it be she *was* falling for him? Had all that flirting she'd indulged in on the visit to the RCA affected her? Or was this some sick little fantasy game she was playing out in her head to pass the time? She should feel guilty thinking like this, and she did, but only a little.

Mack had been her only love. She had on rare occasions wondered what it would be like to be with someone else but had never given it serious thought. Now, here at this moment in time, it set her off thinking. Was it right to limit herself to just one person at her age? Was she limiting her experiences of life by only being with Mack? These kinds of thoughts began to slowly form and push her into a curious emotional turmoil as she listened to him. She needed to calm herself and take control of these weird runaway ideas. What was she thinking of playing such silly mind games?

"I can't keep this in any longer," Simon began without warning. Placing his hand on top of hers as it rested on the table, his voice quavered as he spoke, "I fell in love with you the moment I first saw you. Since then, I haven't been able to stop thinking about you. You're on my mind constantly, and the thought of you, Effy Halloran, has driven me crazy."

Effy froze, unable to move her hand. Did she want him to take his hand away? She was unsure. By right, she ought to have done so without hesitation because this was an over-familiarity. It was a bewildering, yet exciting and affecting sensation having another man touch her hand in such an intimate way.

"You're too young to be engaged to him." Simon pushed ahead when she didn't reply, gathering courage from her astonished silence and her failure to remove her hand from his. "You haven't lived or experienced anyone else. How can you tie yourself to him without having experienced what it's like to be with someone else? How can you be sure he's the only one for you? What if I'm the right one, the one you need to be with rather than him?"

Simon's words flooded her thoughts as she found herself unable to take in everything he was saying. His emotional declarations of love were like some insane passionate whirlwind of driven desire.

Engaged? Had Simon said engaged? Effy's heart skipped at those words. She wasn't engaged, not yet, although she had promised Mack they would be one day. Suppose Simon was right? Mack had been her only boyfriend since she was fourteen. Should she experience what other men were like? Did Mack have to be her one and only? Mack had Angie, and Effy knew her friend would never abandon him. If she broke it off with Mack, he would still have Angie. Angie would be happy having him all to herself.

Would he get over her breaking up with him? Could she? Did he still really love her after what she had caused to happen in New York? This internal turmoil was getting worse and scrambling her thoughts. She was trying to make sense of what was happening through the filter of jet-lagged tiredness. Effy Halloran felt vulnerable and not in control of her emotions. She had experienced nothing so disturbing or so frightening in her life. She was listening to Simon, but her mind had shut off his voice, and she was no longer hearing what he was saying.

What would happen to her friendship with Angie? Would Angie feel betrayed if she left the threesome? They'd agreed not to let anyone come between them, not even Mack. So would their friendship survive? Wrestling with these thoughts, Effy wondered what kind of hellish situation she was creating here? It was surreal, unrealistic, exactly like something she might experience while having a bad dream. Except, this was no dream. Did it matter if she never knew or experienced the love of another man? Wasn't Mack good enough for her?

"Why don't you take a chance on me?" Simon continued taking her hand fully in his. Giving it a squeeze, he placed his other hand over the top, trapping her hand between his two. She felt the promise ring dig into her fingers as he squeezed her hand. Effy felt snared and scared. Somehow, this was no longer just a mind game, it was being played out for real.

"Go on, take a chance on me. What do you say? He'd get over it. Guys always do. And anyway, he has someone else to fall back on. You can't possibly be happy having to share him with another girl? If you were mine, I'd never share you with anyone else. I'd keep you all to myself and never let another man near you. So why don't you give me a chance?"

He leaned over, placed his hand on the side of her face, and gave her a long passionate kiss on the lips. Effy recognised his aftershave. It was Old Spice, the same aftershave that Mack wore. What was she doing behaving in this unbelievable way in public? Why was she letting him kiss her? It staggered her, it was so unlike her to behave like this. Had she completely lost her mind? That's when she recollected the words of the two students at the RCA. What had they said? Something like, *he's tried it on with every pretty girl in the department?* Grace thought she hadn't heard them, but she had. That had been more or less the gist of what they'd said. Yes, she had deliberately flirted that day as a bit of fun, not taking it seriously. She had been leading him on with no real intention of it going anywhere. Now the memory was returning, bringing chaos to her mind.

A flood of memories became a torrent streaming through her consciousness. Angie's stories of the way men had fooled and mistreated her returned. Then there was the emptiness of Hester's life? How she flitted from one empty relationship to another in search of that elusive dream called love. Effy was so lucky to have someone like Mack. Did she want to lose what she

256

had only to end up in the same predicament as Hester? The proverb *a bird in the hand is worth more than two in the bush* came to mind.

Mack loved her, and he showed it. Every day he took the time to talk to her and to listen to her. He never laughed at her even if she said something stupid. Mack was passionate, romantic, and *he was her protector*. He was the lover, who never left her sexually disappointed. When they went places, it was he who made other girls jealous of her. What more could she want of him?

"Let's spend the night together. What have you got to lose? I want you, and you know you want me. I want you more than I've ever desired anyone, and I won't apologise for how I feel." Simon was unrelenting as his words disrupted her stream of conscious thought.

She experienced an extraordinary, unfamiliar sensation of almost being willing to give in to this terrible temptation. It was so unnatural and so depraved, and so powerful. The thought of doing so attracted yet repelled her at the same time in equal strength. She could not explain how or why she could feel like this.

Simon knew how to kiss, but he was no better than Mack. What would it be like to have sex with him? Experiencing him fondling her breasts, arousing her and penetrating her body? She tried to imagine it happening. It was bound to be different, but how different? Would she find having sex with him more enjoyable? Would she experience the same tenderness, love, and affection she now had with Mack? Or would Simon simply be satisfying his urges to seduce and use her? The thought of him inside her sent an unnatural erotic thrill through her body. At the same time, the thought of it happening left her disgusted. Even thinking like this was a betrayal of the love she shared with Mack.

Should she take this opportunity? Spend a night with Simon in secret and find out? Should she risk everything she had on someone she hardly knew? Or was she being juvenile, reckless, and stupid thinking like this? Spend the night with Simon? Have sex with him? It would break Mack's heart if she did. And he would find out because her guilt would be obvious. Effy knew she would be incapable of deceiving him. It would all come tumbling out in a confession. That would be the end of everything. It would break them up forever. After New York, there would be no second chances. It would be over. She didn't want to end what was a wonderful love affair in such a cruel, heartless, stupid, and tragic way.

Supposing that she *did* decide to end it with Mack? It would break her heart, knowing she could never be with him again. It would also shatter the dreams they shared as a couple and as a threesome. Could they even work together again, knowing what had happened? Everything would fall apart. Grace might never forgive her, maybe not even Ellen and her other sisters. She could not even begin to imagine a future without Mack. Was a future without him even possible?

Couples broke up, people got divorced. Her friend Chloe had broken up with Tim Smith and started anew with Jersey. So it was possible, but was it desirable in her life? Effy could scarce believe she was allowing herself to even think like this.

What had she come to that she could give serious thoughts to breaking up with Mack? So serious that she was even prepared to act upon them? She was giving serious consideration to the possibility of having sex with Simon. The worst of it was contemplating the actual betrayal of the man she loved. Effy felt sick, the pit of her stomach churning, her heart thudding leaving her faint. This whole situation had gone beyond crazy. Somehow she had trapped her self in this conscious nightmare that was taking place in her head. Here and now, her world of certainties was falling apart. Effy knew she had to end the indecision, one way or another.

The uncertainties had become certain once more.

An incident came to mind as she struggled to cope with these unnatural ideas. They had been in Bradford's central reference library studying. She'd watched Mack staring at some girl during a distracted moment. The memory of it made her smile. Whispering, she had nudged him and quoted from a John Milton passage she was studying. *Seek not temptation then, which to avoid were better*. Is this what she was doing? Was she deliberately seeking temptation and choosing not to avoid it? Was it better avoided? Or was it better to allow your self to be tempted? *Perhaps, even to give in to the temptation?* But then there would be awful consequences, the unavoidable repercussions.

What had Adam and Eve reaped by allowing temptation to enter into their lives? They had lost more than paradise; they had lost the precious trust between a man and a woman and their innocence. This had all the signs of ending as a tragedy. A delusory impulse-driven infatuation was trying to take control. It was willing her to go against all reason and instinct.

In a brief instant, her thoughts shattered and crashed as she found herself plunged back into the unreality of Simon's words.

258

"I love the way you talk, the way you walk, I love everything about you. Go on, let's spend the night together. Deep down, you know you'd like to. Admit it. Don't think I haven't noticed how you look at me. I know you like me. I know you're attracted to me. There's chemistry between us. Let's go back to my place. Let's do it right now, let's not wait, my flat is not too far away. Just say yes and we can there in ten minutes. I just want to make love to you."

What could she say in reply? So far, she had said nothing, not a single word in response. She had sat there speechless, shocked into silence. Effy now understood the terrifying fear a rabbit underwent trapped in a rushing car's headlights. Stay and suffer the consequences, or run for it, and live your life as before? Succumb or survive?

As if believing in his power of persuasion Simon Silvers continued his seductive patter. "Let's face it, if you stay with him, he'll only hurt you and let you down in the long run. His kind always does. Fashion photographers are all the same. They end up sleeping around with their models, and that's a fact. They're notorious for it. How long will it be before he's tumbling into bed with Hester Clayton? She sleeps around with everyone. If you say yes and we go now... "

An interrupting voice made her heart miss a beat as a distressing coldness swamped and paralysed her body.

"Mack's the only one who's proved he loves you."

Effy pulled her hand free from Simon's and turned to find Alice standing close and unnoticed. She had been listening to what he had been saying. How long had she been standing there?

"For a start, he's not slept with anyone else. Nor has he gone looking for anyone else. You know damn well he hasn't. Nor has he had any intention of doing. Not like this joker is suggesting. Mack could have slept with Hester, and Lord knows, you gave him enough cause, but he didn't. *I know that Hester has been open with you.* If she couldn't seduce him when she had the chance, then what does that tell you?"

Taking a pause for breath, Alice glared at her then continued her onslaught on her conscience. "Yes, you do share him with your best friend, but that was *your* choice and *your* decision. Don't try to kid me that you've been miserable with the two of them. You've loved it, being a part of a unique threesome romance. Mack is nothing like loverboy here. This one's only trying to charm you into his bed and out of your undies. No doubt, he'll make you promises of everlasting love too."

"What are you doing here?" Effy asked, regaining some semblance of emotional self-control, seeing and hearing Alice.

"By the look of it, watching you making a right proper idiot of yourself. Tina told me I'd find you here. So I thought I'd see if we could go to lunch together. My shoot finished early. By the look of things, I've arrived in the nick of time. Hester's suggestion that I should check up on how you were doing was a good one. She's been worried about you since leaving New York. By the look of this charmer, with good reason. You have the look of someone about to do something utterly rash and stupid." Alice's unsmiling face said everything to her. "So, this is another wannabe charmer sniffing around you hems? With all that supposed Oxbridge cleverness, can't you see what this one's about? He's another smooth-talking operator. Deep down, you know you'll crash and burn with this one. He's a heartbreaker. Effy, this one's not worth a moment more of your time. Send him slithering on his way."

Simon Silvers looked embarrassed. Irritated and stunned, Alice's unexpected verbal assault left him wondering how to respond. She had placed a foot on the seat next to him in an aggressive, almost masculine manner. Her presence intimidating as she leaned over him. Finally, finding words, he reacted to her intrusion, "I'm sorry! Who the hell do you think you are butting into our private conversation?"

"Alice Liddell, I'm Effy's friend. Right now, I'm here as her Jiminy Cricket to jog her conscience. Wakey, wakey, girl."

Turning to Effy, Alice spoke in a calm, reprimanding voice, "So this is the famous Simon Silvers of print designer fame? I've heard the tale from Angie of how his scumbag brother, Joe, tried to seduce you. Now this one's having a go, and you would give up, Mack, *for him*? This one should come with a health warning: Simonocchio, silver-tongued liar, avoid unless prone to acts of stupidity. He's a regular snake in the grass and no mistake. Effy, for heaven's sake, what the hell are you doing, girl?"

Alice now turned her full attention to Simon Silvers. "Grace has told me all about you. Good thing we girls talk among each other. She overheard some of the female students at your college talking. Their rather unflattering description was of some badly dressed Casanova trying to do the rounds of them all. Well, why am I not surprised? It must run in the family. Slithering in trying to steal another bloke's girl, trying to persuade her to have a taste of your forbidden fruit because you look cute. The trouble is, when sleeping beauty here realises what she'd done, you will have poisoned and destroyed her life for good. Then it wouldn't be so sweet for her anymore. But it wouldn't matter to the likes of you, would it pretty boy? Not as long as you'd got your bell-end away. Yes, you're pretty on the outside, but there's a worm's ugliness eating away inside you."

Simon Silvers didn't know how to react. Open-mouthed, he looked flabbergasted, searching for some sort of response. Alice directed more of her cutting diatribe at him, not giving him the chance to reply. The way she spoke had such swaggering confidence and strength of feeling it left him unsure how to deal with her. Effy's shoulders sagged as her mind began to clear. Simon started to stand, but Alice hadn't finished with him yet.

"Sit down, Mister! Before I lamp you one! I'm not done with you yet..."

"Please excuse me, Simon," Effy cried out, unable to take any more, her face burning red. She rose in a hurry and made for the refuge of the women's toilets. How much had Alice seen and heard? She felt terrible, embarrassed beyond belief, and worst of all, so ridiculous. Everything Alice said made sense. Effy was ready to sob her eyes out.

Locking the toilet cubicle door behind her, she felt the tears welling like waters in a dam about to burst. Why was this happening to her? She hadn't set out this morning expecting any of this. Or maybe deep down she had? What did she think she was doing? She should have stopped him straight away. This was not a stupid game any longer without consequences. Her head was reeling, and she felt as if she was caught and drowning in an emotional whirlpool.

Somewhere between going to America and now she had lost sight of her true self. She was near to losing everyone and everything precious to her. Sheer foolishness and inexperience in dealing with others had caused all this.

Some things were inexplicable. Why was she drawn to Simon like some silly little thirteen-year-old having her first crush? Instinct warned her that he was so wrong, and yet? The thought that it could be some kind of amorous adventure had surfaced with such easy readiness. Had Hester not warned her about the dangers? What was she thinking? That she could have an affair? And that she would have no emotional or physical price to pay? Yes, it would be an adventure of sorts. A short-lived adventure with only one ending and that would definitely not be happy.

Who was this person she had become and now failed to recognise?

Why had it come to this? She had not given him any sign of being interested, at least not consciously. Yes, she had known that he found her attractive. And yes, she had revelled in knowing that he found her desirable, but so did plenty of other men. It was a great feeling realising someone other than Mack adored her. Flirting with him had been such fun. But she had never given Simon cause to believe she would up and leave Mack, let alone jump straight into bed with him in the middle of the day. Her state of mind made no sense. This crisis was of her making. She was playing silly mind games with herself. Her emotions were out of control; her common sense had vanished and was nowhere to be found. It was as if she was being driven by some horrible, self-destructive impulse. Some devilish capriciousness was encouraging her to do the wrong thing for all the wrong reasons. Why?

Opening her handbag, she searched for her hanky. As she did so, her hand alighted on Mack's present. She had forgotten all about it. Mack had told her not to open it until later. This had to be another one of his surprise gifts. Mack always found opportunities to give her surprise gifts, tokens of his love. She unwrapped it and found a small box with the words Tiffany scrolled on the surface. This had to have cost him a great deal of money. She wished he would stop buying her expensive jewellery.

Then it dawned on her. Everything became so clear. *He could only have bought this after he went missing in New York* when they stayed at Henderson's. She recalled how he'd escorted Angie and Alice down to Tiffany's to have a look at the famous jewellers. Both wanted to see the place where Audrey Hepburn, as Holly Golightly, had acted out her role in *Breakfast at Tiffany's*. Effy let out a loud sigh as she examined the contents. At this moment, she felt like a Holly Golightly, her life was in uncontrollable flux.

The gift reawakened more memories as she ran her fingers over it. Effy recalled how she had opened her birthday present on the way to school in the back of his father's car. The solid gold bangle from Mack had brought her such joy. The bangle had been his first birthday gift to her, and she was wearing it on her wrist today. The bangle had cost him a fortune, almost all his wages for the summer. There had been a few other gifts, none of them cheap. The gold necklace with a heart locket he'd bought in Spain. Then there was the promise ring. It had been his idea to buy the promise ring. Oh, how she loved that ring and what it signified. It was his commitment to her. She had insisted on him buying an identical ring for Angie. If they were to live as a threesome, the bond had to be between the three of them. She'd be foolish to give up what they all had together, and for what? For an impulse? For a few fickle words over-riding her instincts and reason?

262

Effy took out the gold charm bracelet with its single gold star charm. The present was so pretty, so beautiful and what she would have chosen for herself. Mack knew her tastes so well. There was a folded note; he always left one with each gift. The words there left her broken-hearted. Tears trickled down her cheeks as she read and made out the words written there in an instant. They were the lyrics of the song *When You Wish Upon A Star*.

The tearfulness slowed, then ceased, and she wiped away her tears. Sighing aloud, Effy made her wish, a desperate plea for her dreams to remain true. Fate had indeed conspired to intervene. It had arrived at the right time like the bolt from the blue mentioned in the song. Would it see her through this crisis? Taking the charm bracelet out of the box, she put it on her wrist, next to the gold bangle. That's where it belonged, that was its rightful place, *but should it stay there?*

To keep these love tokens if they broke up would be so wrong. She would have to return this and all his other gifts. It would be the only right thing to do. Could she do something like that? Erase him from her life, leaving nothing of him as a reminder in hers? That would be the irrevocable consequence of making such a choice.

Gill's words returned to haunt. *What would happen if one of them found someone else?* Effy experienced a terrifying heaviness in her heart, an unbearable sadness. She had brought all this on herself in the space of less than an hour. All because of her lack of faith and trust in Mack and Angie. The temptation to do the wrong thing was so appalling and yet so strong. Opening her compact, another gift from him, she checked her makeup and took a long look at herself in the tiny mirror before snapping it shut.

The room was full of amused onlookers drinking their frothy coffees waiting to overhear the outcome. They must have been listening to whatever words Alice and Simon had exchanged in her absence. There must have been quite a few. The whole affair to them was an entertaining interlude. Something they would joke about and retell to others later. From the outside, they would see nothing more than an inconsequential tiff. An entertaining incident that whiled away some time for them at Picasso's. They would neither see nor understand the crisis tearing a young woman's life apart.

Alice was still stood over Simon, keeping him in check. Her arms folded, her face impassive, she barred his way while he looked up at her in silent teeth-gritting fury, trapped in his seat.

"Well, girlfriend? Have you decided?" Alice demanded as Effy approached. "Which one will it be? *This loser* or Mack?"

Where did *her* destiny lie?

The closing moments of this self-destructive charade played out.

Was Simon the loser?

Or the winner?

Was Mack the winner?

Or the loser?

Treat life like a game, and you'll lose?

Live life, and you'll end up a winner?

Was Hester's advice sound?

Effy glanced at Simon.

Then at the gold star dangling from her wrist.

It was her choice.

It was her move.

Her fate had always been in her own hands.

It always would be.

Sometimes in life, you had to choose common sense.

Sometimes, you just needed to go with your instinct.

Or, she supposed, there was that *other* choice.

You could always go on an impulse and see where that led...

A smile blossomed.

Checkmate.

The End of Book 2 in the Jimmy Mack 1967 trilogy.

The trilogy will conclude in Jimmy Mack 1967 - 'The New Breed'.
More in the series will follow in Jimmy Mack 1968
and related novels.

ACKNOWLEDGEMENTS

I must thank my darling wife Julie for being my Beta reader and long-suffering sounding board. She has provided much needed feedback during the writing of this novel. I don't know what I'd do without her.

My special thanks to my Jimmy Mack super fans, Natalie Finnigan and Graham Wilkinson. They have encouraged me from afar to keep going staying constant in their encouragement to keep writing. I hope you will not be disappointed with this novel. Also, Nikki and Andy Topp-Walker of Mods & More on Facebook. Their kind help in handing out flyers and spreading the word about the books is massively appreciated. Bill Williams, my friend, and neighbour, when I'm in Spain must be included. Thank you so much Bill for being there and for our long chats that have shown me that life can be stranger than we think or imagine. Our long talks sitting on Poniente helped to crystallise so many good ideas for this novel.

Another big thank you must go to Mr Miguel Martorell of the Les Dunes hotel. His father founded the hotel in 1957. The impressive twin towers have long since replaced the original Fifties building. These stand on the original footprint of the first hotel. An extra thank you must go to him for the loan of *Benidorm the truth* by Charles Wilson. This encyclopaedic historical work about the town was extremely helpful in ensuring the accurate detailing of the resort in the sixties

To all the members of my Facebook group, *John Knight @ Jimmy Mack* (No particular order): Kai Ahland, Nigel Deacon, Michael Grogan, Karen Keely & Paul Hooper-Keeley, Jayne Thomas, Vanessa & Tony Beesley, Paul Garner, Mark Aldridge, Paul 'Mod' Wilson, Steven Allen, Jason Brummell, Mickey Danby-Foy, Steve Pilkington, Mark Jones, Phil Thornton, Jayne Hewitt, Richard Newsome, Steve Burke, Tiffany Barton, Ian Nicols, John Barnaby, Denise Tyas, Ray B. Gordon, Jason Disley, Rod Looker, Jayson Sloane, Paul Foster and so many more of you. Please don't feel overlooked if I haven't mentioned you by name.

Finally, at different stages in my youth, all the following young women were instrumental in helping me understand the opposite sex. Some of them were girlfriends and others friends who were girls. If you should come across your name do feel you can get in touch with me again. Gillian Hill, Sharon Povey, Penny Tyrrell, Catherine Wood, Carolyn Sharman, Vera Petrovic, Sally Bradford (nee Pickard), Lorna Poppleton, Carol Inskip, Carol White, Maria Sammarco, Pat Reynolds, Teresa Wlodarczk, Krystyna Tokarewski and last, but not least, Micheline X and Dagmar X.

ABOUT THE AUTHOR

John Knight was born in Halifax, West Yorkshire, in 1949. Although he spent his best teenage years in the town, he lived and was educated in Bradford. Retired, he now lives in Cheshire and divides his time between the UK and Spain. A Mod from the age of sixteen he believes that *once you're a Mod, you're always a Mod.* He is working on a series of novels set in the Sixties following on from *Jimmy Mack (Some Kind of Wonderful).* These will have parallel interweaving storylines.

Jimmy Mack 1967 – Strong Love (Side A) is Part One of the 1967 trilogy and *Let The Good Times Roll (Side B)* is the second. The concluding part of the trilogy will be in *The New Breed.*

He is presently working on *The New Breed* and *Alice* (introduced in *Side A* and featured in *Side B* of the trilogy). Alice's tale can be summed in these words: *Dying is simple. It's coming back when things get interesting.*

John Knight can be followed and contacted via the following:

Website:
johnknightnovelist.wixsite.com/mysite

Facebook:
John Knight @ Jimmy Mack *and* Jimmy Mack's Dedicated Followers of Cool

Twitter: @JKnight_Author
Instagram: johnknightnovelist

THE SOUNDTRACK

The novel's title is taken from Bunny Siglers "Let The Good Times Roll/Feel So Good"
Cameo-Parkway P153 – 1967

01 Talk Of The Grapevine – Donald Height	London HLZ 10062	1966
02 Sharing You – Little Eva	London SHU 8437 LP	1962
03 You've Been Cheating – The Impressions	HMV POP 1498	1965
04 Road Runner – Junior Walker & The All Stars	Tamla Motown TMG 559	1965
05 People Gonna Talk – Lee Dorsey	Top Rank JAR 606 B	1961
06 Ain't There Something That Money Can't Buy – The Young-Holt Trio	Brunswick 55317	1967
07 Yesterday's Papers – Chris Farlowe	Immediate IM 049	1967
08 Watch Your Step – Bobby Parker	Sue Records WI-340	1964
09 Take Some Time Out For Love - The Isley Brothers	Tamla Motown TMG 566	1966
10 The Girl Can't Help It – Little Richard	London 45-HL- 08382	1957
11 With This Ring – The Platters	Stateside SS 2007	1967
12 Happy Together – The Turtles	London HLU 10115	1967
13 You've Got To Pay Price – Al Kent	TRACK 504016	1967
14 It's Growing – The Temptations	Tamla Motown TMG 504	1965
15 You're My Everything – The Temptations	Tamla Motown TMG 620	1967
16 Do Right Woman Do Right Man – Aretha Franklin	Atlantic 584084 B	1967
17 There's Gonna Be Trouble – Sugar Pie DeSanto	Chess CRS 8034	1966
18 Because They're Young – Duane Eddy	London HLW 9162	1960
19 The Kid – Andre Brasseur	CBS 202557	1967
20 Can't Take My Eyes Off You – Vikki Carr	Liberty LBL 83037 LP	1967
21 Peter Gunn Theme – Henry Mancini	RCA 1134	1959
22 Show Me – Joe Tex	Atlantic 584096	1967
23 Groovin' – Book T and The MGs	Stax 601018	1967
24 I'll Never Stop Loving You – Ketty Lester	London HLN 9698 B	1963
25 Sweet Talking Guy – The Chiffons	Stateside SS 512	1966
26 She's Looking Good – Rodger Collins	Galaxy 750 – US	1966
27 I Feel Free – Cream	Reaction 591011	1966
28 The New Breed – Jackie Wilson	Coral 72467 UK B	1963
29 The Cheater – Bob Kuban and The In Men	Stateside SS 448	1966
30 I Fought The Law – Bobby Fuller Four	London HLU 10030	1966
31 Sticks and Stones – Ray Charles	HMV POP	1960
32 Getaway – Georgie Fame and The Blue Flames	Columbia DB7946	1966
33 Walk On The Wild Side (Opening Title & Credits) - Elmer Bernstein	MGM 1164	1962
34 Let Your Conscience Be Your Guide – Marvin Gaye	Tamla Motown TM 21 – LP **	1961
35 I'm A Man of Action – Jimmy Hughes	Atlantic 587068 – LP	1962
36 For What It's Worth – Buffalo Springfield	Atlantic 584077	1966
37 The Day You Take One (You Have To Take The Other) – Marvelettes	Tamla Motown TMG 609 B	1967
38 The Sidewinder - Lee Morgan	Blue Note 45-1911 – US	1964
39 I Put A Spell On You – Nina Simone	Phillips BF1415	1965
40 Just For You – Jerry Butler	Sue WI 4009	1966
41 I Don't Need No Doctor – Ray Charles	HMV POP 1566	1966
42 Pick Up The Pieces – Carla Thomas	Stax UK 601032	1967
43 The Way You Do the Thing You Do – The Temptations	Stateside SS 278	1964
44 Danger Zone – Wilson Picket	Atlantic 584023 B	1966
45 A Bird In The Hand (Is Worth Two In The Bush) – The Velvelettes	V.I.P. 25030	1965

* From the LP 'It Must Be Him' – Vikki Carr Liberty LBL 83037 –1967
** From the LP 'The Soulful Moods of Marvin Gaye' – TM 21 1961
*** From the LP 'Why Not Tonight' – Atlantic 587068 – 1962

JIMMY MACK – SOME KIND OF WONDERFUL

The drug fuelled all-night Mod dance scene of the Sixties is the backdrop to a secret love. Soul music the soundtrack to this intense love affair.

You're never too young to fall in love. Some things are just meant to be. A wink outside church one Sunday brings Fiona "Effy" Halloran into James "Mack" MacKinnon's life. It's 1964 in the West Riding of Yorkshire For the two fifteen year olds the next two years will prove a test of their love and devotion to one another.

Growing up is never easy, nor is being young and in love. When Effy's sister Caitlin becomes pregnant by Mack's brother the lives of their families collide. Dealing with a feuding family, itself divided by religious zeal, becomes a serious obstacle for the young lovers. Separated by circumstances can their love for one another survive?

Over time Mack and Effy learn the truth about their respective families because secrets never stay secret forever.

"Jimmy Mack - Some Kind of Wonderful" is the first of a series of novels set in Bradford and Halifax between 1964 and 1969 involving the twosome and their friends. Parallel interweaving novels in the same time period are in the process of being written.

"...this is a beautiful book. I couldn't wait to finish it and now I'm sad l have as l want more. It is a great journey through teenage life and love that we have all been a part of. I LOVE IT!"

"I absolutely love Jimmy Mack. Nostalgia, rite of passage and fashion and music. You covered it all. I am sad I finished it . I cannot wait for the next one."

AVAILABLE ONLINE FROM:
Feed A Read (feedaread.com) and Amazon (amazon.co.uk)

OR ORDER FROM YOUR LOCAL BOOKSHOP QUOTING:

ISBN-10: 1788760433
ISBN-13: 978-1788760430

JIMMY MACK 1967 – STRONG LOVE (SIDE A)

Mack, Effy and Angie are three smart, sharp and stylish young Mods in
search of a future. Soul music and the all night dance scenes of Halifax, Bradford
and Manchester's famed Twisted Wheel club are the backdrop to their lives.

Mack and Effy's love affair is intense and torrid. Angie is their best friend
but she and Mack share a secret they can never reveal to Effy. As 1967 unfolds their
lives change forever. A fateful encounter at Angie's
eighteenth birthday party will take the three to London.

When a soured drug deal resurfaces Mack's past catches up with him, sparking
revenge and violence.

Their passion for fashion opens a door in Chelsea's King's Road to fledgling
careers. London's Swinging Sixties nightlife will bring them before the full glare
of the press. Are their dreams about to come true? Or will Mack and Angie's secret
destroy everything?

This novel will surprise and challenge reader's understanding of
love and friendship.

**Jimmy Mack 1967 – Strong Love (Side A) is the first part of the 1967 trilogy
and the second in the Jimmy Mack Series. The trilogy follows on from the
opening novel of the forthcoming Jimmy Mack series.**

*What a story. I was intrigued throughout. The twists and turns. Great
writing. I have also written a review on both books on Amazon. Can't wait
for the next book.* **Graham Wilkinson**

*They are amazing. You can't put them down. John Knight has nailed it in
every way. Leaves you thirsting for for more. I'm loving them.* **Natalie Allen**

*Brilliant book, well crafted, great characters and a setting with immaculate
attention to detail.* **Mark Jones**

Wonderful books - I enjoyed them both tremendously. Highly recommended
Paul Hooper-Keeley

AVAILABLE ONLINE FROM:
Feed A Read (feedaread.com) and Amazon (amazon.co.uk)

OR ORDER FROM YOUR LOCAL BOOKSHOP QUOTING:
ISBN: 9781788765534

Hotel Les Dunes (as it was in the 1960s). It has since been rebuilt and remains one of the premier frontline hotels in Benidorm.

COMPARATIVE PRICES

£1967	£2019
1	16.79
5	83.93
10	167.79
20	335.73
25	419.66
50	839.33
100	1678.65
500	8393.26

£ Average Price	1967	2019
House:	£64, 090	£3818
Car:	£960	£16, 115

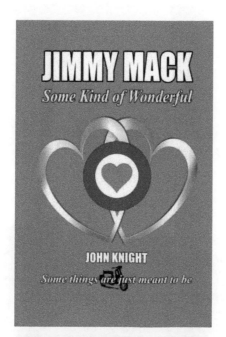

John Knight – The Mod Inside

Lightning Source UK Ltd.
Milton Keynes UK
UKHW011257130520
363213UK00003B/684